D0124096

tHe iVy

VOLUME THREE

RiVaLs

BY LAUREN KUNZE

in collaboration with

RINA ONUR

GREENWILLOW BOOKS

An Imprint of HarperCollins*Publishers*

This book is a work of fiction. References to real people, events, establishments, organizations, or locales are intended only to provide a sense of authenticity, and are used to advance the fictional narrative. All other characters, and all incidents and dialogue, are drawn from the author's imagination and are not to be construed as real.

The Ivy: Rivals
Copyright © 2012 by Lauren Kunze

All rights reserved. No part of this book may be used or reproduced in any manner whatsoever without written permission except in the case of brief quotations embodied in critical articles and reviews. Printed in the United States of America. For information address HarperCollins Children's Books, a division of HarperCollins Publishers, 10 East 53rd Street, New York, NY 10022.
www.epicreads.com

The text of this book was set in Adobe Caslon.
Book design by Christy Hale.

Library of Congress Cataloging-in-Publication Data
Kunze, Lauren.
Rivals / Lauren Kunze with Rina Onur.
p. cm. — (The Ivy ; v. 3)
"Greenwillow Books."
Summary: Callie Andrews has looked forward to this semester but
Lexi is still after her, boyfriend Clint wants her back but Gregory
has decided to fight for her, Vanessa still has not forgiven her,
and working on the *Harvard Crimson* is taking a toll,
causing Callie to yearn for spring break.
ISBN 978-0-06-196049-9 (trade bdg.)
[1. Universities and colleges—Fiction. 2. Roommates—Fiction.
3. Interpersonal relations—Fiction. 4. Dating (Social customs)—Fiction.
5. Journalism—Fiction.] I. Onur, Rina. II. Title.
PZ7.K94966Riv 2012   [Fic]—dc23   2011029169
12 13 14 15 16 LP/RRDH 10 9 8 7 6 5 4 3 2 1
First Edition
 Greenwillow Books

For my friend and
favorite reader,
Corey Reich

Gregory Bolton knelt in front of the love seat in Harvard's Cambridge Queen's Head Pub, staring straight into the green eyes of Callie Andrews and ignoring that his friend and teammate Clint Weber sat beside her, his arm wrapped around her shoulders.

In Gregory's coat pocket was something so small that no one could have ever guessed what an epic misunderstanding it had caused. It was a note: old and faded after months of being forgotten, tucked away among various loose papers in his bedroom. Still, he didn't need to read it to know, almost word for word, what it said.

> What happened at Harvard-Yale was a huge mistake. It was wrong for us to have slept together, and if I could take it back, I would.
>
> I messed up the room dynamic, and I probably blew it with Clint. I may be a terrible person, but if I am, then you are just as bad, if not worse. I cannot believe that I was ever stupid enough to put my trust in someone like you.
>
> There is no hope for us in the future. I don't see how we could even just be friends.
>
> There's nothing I can do about the fact that

we're living in such close quarters—believe
me, if I could, I would—so let's just try to
stay as far away from each other as possible.

Callie

He also knew now what he hadn't known before: that this note
had never been meant for him—as he'd assumed these past few
months—and had instead been a response to a nasty "Manifesto"
written by Callie's roommate Vanessa Von Vorhees and then taped
to Callie's bedroom window. At this point the details of how the
mix-up occurred were irrelevant; all that mattered was that he was
here now, prepared to set the record straight.

And, if it wasn't enough to prove how he felt, he had something
else in his back pocket as well: his cell phone. In the outbox
there were several drafts of unsent messages written and dated in
November after that fateful football game at Harvard-Yale.

To Andrews, Callie: I think
about you every day. It's like
I'm going crazy. Why . . .

To Andrews, Callie: Remember
the balcony when it started to
rain? The way . . .

To Andrews, Callie: I suppose
you want me to leave you alone
until you work th . . .

To Andrews, Callie: As long as
I'm never sending these, I want
you to know that . . .

To Andrews, Callie: I know
you probably think I could
never change, but maybe . . .

To Andrews, Callie: Clint
e-mailed me again, which is why
I'm not sending thes . . .

To Andrews, Callie: Greg,
you're an idiot. You know you'll
never send these.

The messages said what he had been unable to admit out loud before. Soon, however, he might finally be able to bring himself to delete them; for he was resolved, tonight, to tell her everything.

ONE

TOGAS, BOYS,

AND OTHER DANGEROUS THINGS

Dear Second Semester Freshmen,

Or Toddlers, as I prefer to call you, and welcome to your Terrible Twos: otherwise known as second semester. For most of you, surviving your first several months in the Ivy League probably felt like a battle; it's safe to say, however, that the war has only just begun. But before we dive back in to all the drama both in and out of the classroom, what better way to kick off the new year than to take a moment and reflect on what everyone in America knows college is *really* all about. . . .

Parties

(If you guessed "studying the elementary subatomic constituents of matter and radiation," please GO FISH, get a life, and enroll in Leaving the Library 101 this semester.)

Various outsiders might contest that our campus has a better chance of producing prize winners (Nobel, Pulitzer) than parties, but that's only because most Harvard gatherings, including the following, are so exclusive that a rare few ever manage to secure an invite.

Five (In)Famous Harvard Parties (And Your Guide to Getting In)

Delphic Toga: This annual party at one of the eight male Final Clubs risks running a cliché, but we Cantabridgians don our twin-sized sheets from the Target Dorm Collection with a postmodern, ironic spirit—kind of like the way I wear my hot pink Harvard sweatshirt. For the first hour spontaneous speeches that all inevitably begin with "Friends, Romans, Countrymen," ring through the halls, the bagged wine flows like water, and students embody the pinnacle of civilization. . . . Then the DJ shows up, Rome is sacked, and the whole thing degenerates into a drunken, fratty, signature Delphic mess.

Party Grade: A-

Crash-ability Level: Easy; ladies substitute a pillowcase for your sheet and the bouncer will be putty in your hands.

The Social Network: Ever since that wordy Aaron Sorkin tried to capture our antics on film, hopeful partygoers have been storming the Phoenix praying to find the bus full of stripping, drug-doing model-actresses playing state school girls at a "typical" Harvard party from which nerds who aren't half as hot as Jesse Eisenberg will forever be excluded. Apologies for the bubble burst, but those scenes were filmed at the Spee and were the stuff of fiction. Still, give Thursday nights at the PSK a try, and if you don't make it past the front door, go home, crack a beer, write a complex equation on your window, and console yourself by inventing the next Facebook.

Party Grade: C

Crash-ability Level: Medium-Hard (due to all the hype); try calling yourself a "friend of Eduardo's, enemy to Zuck, and hater of all things Winklevoss" at the door and see what happens.

The Great Gatsby: Arguably the best party on campus, this white-tie affair takes place at the Fly Club and truly transports its guests back to the summer of 1922. Based on a strict interpretation of the literary text, no expense is spared, from the live jazz band to the vintage couture and the green light that flashes intermittently that night outside the club's front door.

Party Grade: A+

Crash-ability Level: Impossible; this party is a date event in the strictest of terms—not even Jay Gatsby + Daisy Buchanan could get in if their names weren't on the list.

Spee Eurotrash: Whether you define the word as a "pejorative term for Europeans" or defer to the Urban Dictionary delineation (*Eurotrash*: A human sub-phylum characterized by its apparent affluence, worldliness, social affectation, and addiction to fashion), you will have fun at this shindig celebrating—ironically, of course—our campus's beloved international contingent.

Party Grade: B+

Crash-ability level: Medium; it all depends on your costume and how authentically you can air-kiss, rock tight jeans and greasy hair, and remember that loafers should never be worn with socks.

Boxer, Formerly Known as the "Boxer Rebellion": This outdoor springtime gathering at the Fox Club—where it's difficult to determine which is more awkward: the '80s cover band or the fact that every male present is pants-less—used to derive its name from the proto-nationalist movement in turn-of-the-century China. Until some angsty *Crimson*ites at our beloved school paper started raising hell about political correctness, i.e., the enemy of funny and fun.

Party Grade: A-

Crash-ability Level: Hard; they are extra careful to exclude undercover enemies of fun after the op-ed upset—men, be mindful of your underwear selection and prepare to check your pants at the door.

Work hard/Play hard,
Alexis Thorndike, Advice Columnist
Fifteen Minutes Magazine
Harvard University's Authority on Campus Life since 1873

"Do the two of you ever stop kissing?" OK Zeyna asked, speaking in his BBC British best. "This is a party. You are supposed to socialize; you know, interact with others?"

"You are being *le gross*," Mimi Clément agreed, wrinkling her nose. "All this touching *en public . . . c'est dégoûtant*."

Callie Andrews broke away from her boyfriend—yes, *boyfriend*, which she never tired of saying—and smiled at her neighbor and roommate, aiming for *apologetic* but failing to wipe the gleeful expression from her face. "We're sorry, but—"

"We can't stop," said her boyfriend, pulling Callie back to him. "We're making up for lost time."

Mimi groaned.

"Sorry!" Callie called again, giggling but unable to lean away as he kissed her neck. "Just—give us—"

"That's it! We're going now!" OK cried. "Far, far away—to the bar. Milady?" he added, offering Mimi his arm with a surprisingly dignified look on his face for someone sporting nothing more than a twin-sized sheet with bright, multicolored pink polka dots. He appeared, however, to have fully forgiven Mimi for cajoling him into wearing it earlier that evening.

"You'll be missed!" a muffled voice called, its owner's smirk buried in Callie's short blond hair.

"Mm-hmm," Callie murmured, incapable of saying more as her lips were now otherwise occupied.

"Pfft . . . *Les adolescents de nos jours*," Mimi muttered, shaking her head as she and OK abandoned the new couple standing at the base of the Delphic Club's enormous spiral staircase. After picking their way through the main room where students danced to a DJ, their bodies wrapped in togas and heads wreathed in ivy, she and OK approached the cedar-paneled bar.

Callie watched them order drinks. "Maybe we should . . ."

"Whatever you want," her boyfriend replied.

She smiled impishly, running her fingers along the sides of his navy-colored toga, his hips lingering inches away from her own.

"Do you want a drink?" he asked.

"No," she said, kissing him on the cheek.

"Dance?" He nodded toward the main room.

"No," she said, kissing him on the other cheek.

"We could go upstairs. . . ." His eyes danced wickedly.

"Oh?" She leaned back to look at him.

"They're watching *Animal House* on the big-screen TV."

"No!" she cried, shaking her head and kissing him on the lips.

"Well, there's only one place left. . . ." he said, kissing her in return.

"Hmm?"

"Game room." His head tilted to the right, where there was a large open lounge full of fat leather couches, dark wooden walls, and a pool and a poker table, where the members often played cards.

Turning, Callie spotted Vanessa Von Vorhees, another one of her roommates, sitting on a couch swathed in a Diane Von Furstenberg sheet from the designer's new Home collection. "My own take on the classic wrap dress," Vanessa had called to no one in particular while she safety-pinned the sides of the lavender-colored sheet in the girls' common room in suite C 24 of Wigglesworth Dormitory prior to the party. Such announcements used to be directed at Callie—back when they were still on speaking terms.

These days their interactions were characterized by a cool formality: a volatile politeness that, though uneasy, was still preferable (according to Mimi and Dana Gray, the final of the four roommates) to the shouting matches and slamming doors of the previous semester. The exact reasons for the fight that had escalated from a battle into a full-on war seemed somewhat hazy now. Had Callie *stolen* Vanessa's crush and her Hasty Pudding club membership, or had both simply *chosen* Callie over Vanessa? Had the nasty words Callie wrote after Vanessa trashed her bedroom constituted slander or merely venting, since Callie had never meant for "The Roommate from Hell," a diarylike practice piece for *FM* magazine, to be seen by anyone else's eyes, let alone Vanessa's? Would saving Vanessa from missing their Economics 10a exam—and from possibly flunking out of school—after she had overslept be enough to bridge the divide? Which mattered more: actions or words?

"Actions," Callie accidentally blurted out loud.

"Talking to yourself again?" That smile that she loved so well shined down on her.

"Oops," she said, wrapping her arms around him and resting her chin on his shoulder.

Suddenly Vanessa's face lit up from across the room and she grinned. For a split second Callie's heart stopped. Her hand rose to wave—

But then Tyler Green, whose exact status in relation to Vanessa (Boyfriend? Lover? Consecutive Hookup? Man/Arm Candy?) remained a mystery, sat down next to her, and Vanessa smiled at him—again—with her orthodontia-perfected teeth, tossing her strawberry blonde curls over her shoulder.

"Why the long face?"

"No reason," Callie murmured, tearing her eyes away from Vanessa, who was laughing now and leaning in to Tyler. "Though, actually, I am a little parched. Would you mind—"

"Not at all," he said. With one more parting kiss, he turned and started for the bar.

"Thanks," she said, her gaze flicking back to the game room. Was it weird to feel jealous of Tyler?

While for the time being her fights with Vanessa had ceased, there was also no more giggling about the adventures of the day, lying head to feet on Vanessa's twin bed. There were no more wonky witticisms from the Vanessa Von Vorhees School of Thought on how to dress for class (or mostly how *not* to dress, in Callie's case) and "capture" a potential husband. No more nine-thirty breakfast buddy (Mimi was never conscious before noon, while Dana tended to rise before the ungodly hour of seven); no more spontaneous dance parties or spontaneous "shopping" trips through *Le Closet de Vanessa*; no more GChatting in Lamont Library or in class even though they were sitting right next to each other; and no more safety net in any given 911 social situation.

Yes, she had a boyfriend now—a *perfect* boyfriend, she thought, watching him lean up against the bar while he waited for their drinks—but still no wingman, no Goose to her Maverick, no one with whom she could navigate this new college world of firsts....

At that moment Mimi zoomed past her and into the game room, where she jumped onto the pool table and started shaking a bottle of champagne that she had most likely "borrowed" from the bar. Callie laughed and shook her head. Nobody was more fabulous than Mimi, but Callie had difficulty considering her a *best* friend because she operated on an entirely different wavelength, always seeming to speak her own private language (in addition to the five other foreign tongues she was fluent in, including her native French).

Callie had an even tougher time relating to Dana, though the studious, staunchly moralistic girl was lovable in her own way. But Dana rarely had time for anything other than class, the library, and church with her chaste semi-boyfriend, Adam, and would never last more than five minutes at a party like this. Callie cracked a smile, picturing Dana storming out in a tangled huff of bulky white sheets and disapproving glares. In fact, she and Mimi *had* tried to convince Dana to join them that evening but, even in spite of their well-meaning yet slightly disingenuous references to ancient Rome and "tradition" (reality looked a lot more like cocktails, keg stands, and flashes of colorful undergarments from beneath an even more colorful array of togas), Dana had still refused.

Callie propped herself against the banister at the base of the stairs and sighed. Even though she and her high school BFF, Jessica Stanley, were downright religious about their weekly e-mail updates, something was still lost in translation between the billion miles separating Harvard from Stanford. There was no easy way to convey, for example, how even in the middle of a crowd, Callie still sometimes felt so alone, or how even with invitations to many of the most exclusive events on campus, she still sometimes felt uninvited.

And then there were some things that she felt reluctant to put in writing—like the ginormous mess she had made of last semester, from her botched friendship with Vanessa to her first B *(ever)* to getting cut from *FM* magazine in the final round.

She had only herself to blame for those particular disasters, and even the things that were seemingly beyond her control could not be blamed entirely on others, like:

a) the secret sex tape her diabolical ex-boyfriend, Evan, had made in high school, and
b) the way said tape had fallen into the hands of her arch nemesis and former *FM* COMP director, campus queen bee, Alexis Thorndike, who
c) had then used the tape to coerce Callie into doing her bidding for months.

She, Callie, had put her trust in the wrong person (Evan) for too many years (two). And she, Callie, had been too quick to bend to Lexi's will, doing whatever the older girl asked out of fear that she would expose the tape. Now that Callie had neutralized the threat by coming clean to the entire school in an article for the *Harvard*

Crimson, hindsight was twenty-twenty. What had seemed like the worst that could happen had happened, and the fallout—so far little more than the odd sideways glance or sudden silence when she walked into a room of particularly catty Pudding girls—had been far more manageable than she ever could have imagined.

Callie craned her neck, but she couldn't see Lexi anywhere, not even gossiping at the top of the staircase or on one of the upstairs balconies where she often presided over a party with her entourage of fellow juniors. That had to be the best perk to coming clean: two blissful, Lexi-free weeks and counting.

No, false: the best perk was walking toward her now, two drinks in hand.

"To putting the past in the past," she said, taking a glass and raising it—staring into the set of eyes that made forgetting everything very, very easy.

"To the future," he agreed.

She clinked her cup against his and then took a sip. The future did seem promising. She had learned just as much from her mistakes last year re: friendship, love, and making the right choices as she had inside the classroom from some of the most esteemed professors on Harvard University's payroll. This semester, with new classes, a new COMP director who didn't already hate her guts, renewed friendships or just new ones, and best of all, a new boyfriend, what could possibly go wrong, except—

Whoa—the toga knotted at her back felt loose and started to slip—

Her drink spilled as she reached for the sheet, and she knew, just *knew*, that in one more second she would be standing in front of the entire population of one of Harvard's elite secret societies and their guests in only her bra and underwear—

"Easy there, I got you." His hands were steady, holding the sheet together at the base of her back.

She breathed an enormous sigh. "What would I do without you?"

He laughed. "Go naked in public?"

"Hey!" she cried, swatting him.

"Hold still now, Andrews," he admonished her. "This should only take a minute."

"You're only ten weeks late."

"I know, but I'm here now," he said, taking a step forward, "and I want to talk about what happened."

"What's taking so long back there?" she asked, trying to peer behind her at the knots securing the sheet.

"I changed my mind," he said. In one hand he held her toga together while the other slid around her waist and pulled her into him.

"It's too late." The words nearly choked her.

"But what if I have something that might change your mind?" His hand moved to his pocket again, reaching into the place where he kept his cigarettes.

"Why don't we go home now," he murmured, his lips grazing her ear, "and I can help you take this off instead?"

His resolve appeared unshaken as he pulled not cigarettes but a small white piece of paper from his coat. Worn and folded over several times, the paper rested in the palm of his hand.

"Very tempting . . ." Her fingers traced the lines on the palm of his hand. "But I think I'd prefer to make it out of here without flashing anyone."

"If you say so," he said, chuckling and pulling the corners of the sheet nice and tight. "All set."

"Thank you!" she cried, whirling around and kissing him. Keeping her arms looped behind his neck, she tilted her face and looked at him.

"What?" he said, his easy smile spreading into a grin.

"Nothing," she insisted, standing on her tiptoes to kiss him again. "I'm just so glad . . . that you're *you*!"

He laughed, letting go of her waist. "Well, who else would I be?"

Gregory stared at Callie, still kneeling next to the love seat where she sat with Clint in the Cambridge Queen's Head Pub. "I have to talk to you," he repeated, his eyes never leaving her face.

She shook herself. "Now?"

"Yes," he said.

"Everything all right, man?" Clint asked, glancing between them.

"Yeah," said Gregory. "Yes," he repeated, as if registering his friend and teammate's presence for the first time. "Sorry to interrupt. Just need to borrow . . . It's about . . . class." He gave Callie an imploring look. She said nothing but continued to stare, marveling at how much Gregory, whom she had never known to be without half a dozen sarcastic comments or biting comebacks, seemed to be struggling with his words. Besides, classes hadn't even started yet.

"Would you mind . . . ah, coming outside with me?" he said, tilting his head toward the door.

Outside? It was the end of January in Cambridge, i.e., minus a billion degrees. "Um . . ."

"Need a smoke," he muttered quickly. "Keep me company . . . please?"

"Fine," she said suddenly, grabbing the ugly green poufy jacket that her father had given her. "I'll be right back," she added, leaning in to kiss Clint lightly on the lips.

Gregory turned abruptly, shaking a cigarette out of his pack.

"Take your time," said Clint. "I'll be here."

Outside, the fountain in front of the Science Center had run dry, its edges rimmed with snow and ice. Above them, branches bent spindly and sinister, casting shadows on the pale ground under the cloudy, starless sky. Callie shivered.

"You cold?" Gregory asked, pulling his cigarette from where he'd tucked it behind his ear.

"What do you want?" she retorted.

"I want to talk to you," he said, sparking his lighter.

"Yes, clearly, but what do you *want*?"

"I want . . ." Frowning, he took a long drag and exhaled a cloud of smoke. "I want to talk to you about Harvard-Yale."

A derisive noise escaped her lips. "You're only ten weeks late."

"I know, but I'm here now," he said, taking a step forward, "and I want to talk about what happened. I mean about what happened *after*."

"You mean when I woke up alone in a hotel room and you were gone—or the part where you were completely silent over the break?"

"Callie," said Gregory, tossing his cigarette aside. "I think there was a serious misunderstanding." As he spoke, he reached into his pocket.

"So you didn't have a—ah—*threesome* the second we got back to school?"

His hand froze. "Yes, but that was only after—"

"After you'd already been through everyone else in the greater Boston area?" she interrupted hotly. "Or before the fresh batch of transfer students arrived?"

"Oh, and you're so perfect!" he snapped. "Or at least that's what you're letting Clint think, isn't it? He doesn't have any idea, does he, about what happened between us?"

"We were on a break," Callie said, her voice trembling like the lid on a pot about to boil over.

"Really?" asked Gregory. "Because I'm not so sure he sees it that way, and I think your not telling him makes him look like a—"

"Don't you dare talk to me about him!" Callie exploded. "Don't even speak his name. You could never in a million years be half the boyfriend that he is!"

Gregory recoiled as if she had slapped him.

"I'm sorry," she said, horror-struck. "I don't know where that—I mean—I know it's not relevant. . . ."

"Isn't it, though?" His eyes burned the color of cold blue flames.

"Well, it's not like you ever wanted"—she inhaled sharply, unable to remember when she'd forgotten to breathe—"to be my boyfriend."

White powder was sticking to his dark hair. When did it start to snow? she wondered, noticing suddenly that she was shaking uncontrollably. Her knees knocked together—because it was freezing, and because she was angry, and because no matter what she did her legs would always feel weak when he was around. He breathed in deeply and then exhaled slowly.

"You're right," he said finally.

Am I?

"I'm not good enough. Not like Clint, anyway."

She waited for him to say more, to admit that he *had* wanted to be her boyfriend—or to laugh in her face at the very idea. But he just stood there, looking at her, and suddenly she realized: it was true. He wasn't good enough. At least not based on his past actions: the threesome and all the girls, abandoning her after Harvard-Yale, and even now in his inability to come out and say how he really felt, whether it was all part of a game or because he honestly didn't know what he wanted enough to put it into words.

Callie could remember like it was yesterday when her mother used to constantly quote her therapist during the divorce: *A woman can't change a man; he can only change himself.* Maybe one day Gregory would change, but it would be a colossal mistake to believe that *she* could be the agent of that change. And so Callie sighed and, pained by the dejected look on his face, said:

"You will be one day, for the right girl."

Gregory took another step forward. "What if I'm already looking at her?"

"Then I would say . . ." Callie swallowed, shaking her head. "It's too late." The words nearly choked her. "Clint and I are back together." She was 100 percent confident in her decision, so why did voicing it feel so terrible?

"But what if I have something that might change your mind?" His hand moved to his pocket again, reaching into the place where he kept his cigarettes.

What if . . . Suddenly it felt like every molecule in her body was on fire, aching to know what he had to say. And then, just like that, her blood ran cold and she knew. Nothing could erase his actions, and: "Nothing you could say would change my mind. I chose—I *choose* Clint."

His resolve appeared unshaken as he pulled—not cigarettes— but a small white piece of paper from his coat. Worn and folded over several times, the paper rested in the palm of his hand. She thought that perhaps, whatever it was, he planned to give it to her. But instead he stared straight into her eyes, his expression unreadable.

"You're happy, aren't you," he said after what felt like an eternity had passed.

Not at this precise moment, but . . .

"With him," he clarified. "You're happy with . . . Clint."

Slowly she nodded.

"You should get back inside, then."

She hesitated.

"Go," he said.

And so she went, down the stairs to where it was warm and where Clint was waiting for her, resolved never to look back.

If she had, she would have seen Gregory standing in the snow, lighter in hand, flicking the silver cap back and forth. Once, twice, and then, on the third try, it caught. The flames licked up and consumed the tiny piece of paper in his hand until it was too hot to hold, and he dropped it, watching it flutter to the ground. For a moment it continued to burn until, charred and forgotten, it turned to ash in the snow.

"ROME IS ON FIRE!" OK yelled. "ROME IS ON— Oh, bloody hell," he muttered, realizing that nothing he said could make Callie stop kissing—

"Clint!" Mimi called, separating them. "It is time to go," she continued, spinning Callie around and pushing her toward the door.

"But it's not even midnight!" OK cried.

"Not you, Cinder-poppins," said Mimi, shaking her head. "*Mais elle.* I have promised to make her leave before high noon."

"Right," said Callie, without bothering to correct her. "Crimson COMP starts tomorrow at nine A.M., sharp."

"*Oh, l'humanité,*" Mimi muttered.

"I'll just get my coat," said Clint, starting for the door.

"Bah-bah-bah!" Mimi tutted loudly, grabbing the back of his toga. "She also made me promise to make certain she left *alone.*"

"Oh, the humanity," Clint intoned. "I'm just going to walk her home," he added.

"I have heard that one before," Mimi said, releasing his toga nonetheless. "Just be gone by the time I am home. Wait. Who knows when that will be, least of all *moi-même. . . . Voyons en suite*; in twenty minutes I am calling Dana and I am telling her to get the hose."

Callie laughed. Clint shook his head and then followed her outside.

When they were in front of Wigglesworth, Callie leaned against the entryway. For the hundredth time that night he kissed her but, like every other time that night, it still felt like the first time.

"Thank you," she said when they finally broke apart.

"For what?" he asked. "Walking you home—but *not* coming up?"

"For choosing me," she said, standing on the top step and resting her hands on the lapels of his coat.

"Choosing you?" he repeated, the corners of his eyes crinkling as he smiled. "Over who—all the other applicants?"

"Yes," she said solemnly. "Over anyone else you could have had."

"It was never a choice for me," he answered. "You had me at 'I'm sorry I just spilled coffee all over your sweater.'"

Callie beamed and kissed him one last time before sending him off into the night. Maybe he hadn't fully had her in the beginning, but there was no doubt about it that he had her now.

The next morning Callie lingered in the foyer of the *Harvard Crimson*'s headquarters, staring down the hall that terminated in the stairs leading to the second floor offices, including those for *Fifteen Minutes* magazine. Lexi was probably up there now, putting the fear of God into this semester's round of hopefuls. Taking a deep breath, Callie turned right. Grace Lee, the managing editor who had helped Callie publish her article about the tape, stood at the front of the room with the other staff members, including Callie's closest guy friend, Matt Robinson. Quickly Callie joined the other COMPers, who were arranged among the gray desks and computers.

The second hand of the clock on the wall ticked into the twelve position and the minute hand shivered up to nine. Everyone drew quiet without Grace having to summon their attention. "I'll keep this short and sweet, people." She spoke in a clipped tone. "You do what we ask when we ask you. And now, to introduce you to the people who do the asking, we're going to split into small groups. Business Board," she barked. "You're in the conference room. Graphic design and photography are upstairs at the end of the hall—make a right, not a left, or you'll find yourself interrupting *FM* magazine and at the mercy of their COMP director. Incidentally, all those interested in joining the magazine, leave now and go up to where you belong. Writers and editorial, you stay down here with me."

Nobody moved. Grace exchanged a knowing look with the editors on either side of her. "What do you people think the word *daily* under our byline means? Anyone?" She surveyed the room. "It means that we have to put out a paper every, single day. So move!"

This time they moved. From the front Matt winked at Callie. She chanced a tiny wave in return. "Now," Grace said when everyone had settled, "the newest members of our editorial staff will be coming around to get you set up on the computers. Use your last name followed by your first initial for the log-in, and then pick a password."

Callie smiled and motioned to Matt, who quickly materialized by her side. She sat in front of a computer, and he perched next to her on the edge of the desk.

"In the meantime," Grace continued, "I'm going to tell you about a new feature that we've added to the paper this semester: the FlyBy blog. The FlyBy blog will be an exclusively online source for more-than-daily campus news, oddities, and . . . *gossip*." She grimaced when she said the last word, almost like it had caused a foul taste.

"How is that different from *FM*?" called out a sophomore boy Callie recognized as also having been cut from the magazine last semester.

"It's not that different," said Grace, a tiny spark in her eye. "In fact, it's very similar to the magazine—only better." She grinned wolfishly. "Or it will be soon. That part is up to *you*. Since this division of the paper is new, we've decided for now to allow any staff member to post an article, or even a string of recurring columns, to the blog, to get a feel for what works—including COMPers."

Excited murmurs and glances filled the room. COMPers, as Callie knew all too well from her experience at *FM*, normally weren't allowed to do *anything*. At least not write anything that would ever see the light of day—they were certainly encouraged to do lots of coffee fetching, Red Bull buying, grunt work, and staying until 2 A.M. writing practice articles, and then editing and re-editing until someone came around and yelled at them for doing it wrong, at which point they were expected to edit some more.

And I signed on to do this again? Callie thought. I must be nuts.

"Of course, anything you attempt to post will be subject to my administrative approval," Grace added. "But with that said I do encourage all of you to take this opportunity to publish online and start building a readership. Now I'll leave you in the capable hands of our newest staff members"—Callie grinned at Matt—"who will familiarize you with our basic systems and software. Then we'll reconvene in twenty to discuss your first assignments."

"How cool is Grace?" Callie asked Matt as she turned on her computer.

"She is . . . the coolest," Matt agreed. Leaning over her, he pulled up the home page for the *Crimson*'s internal website.

"Are you going to go for it?" she asked.

"Oh—gee—wow. You know, I don't know because she's, like, my boss, and I don't know if—"

"I meant your own column on FlyBy," Callie said with a small smile.

"Oh, yeah—I knew that," he said, turning away so Callie could key in a password. "And the answer is that I'm not sure—about the *column*, of course," he mused. "My regular workload is going to keep me pretty busy. It'd be a great chance for you to get your stuff out there, though. Maybe you could even reuse some of the pieces that you wrote for *FM*?"

"Interesting idea," Callie murmured, and it was—at least

compared to the alternative, which was burning them, along with everything else that Alexis Thorndike had ever touched. Though technically—she thought as she and Matt pulled up the FlyBy page and started skimming an article about some nerd who had built a tracker back in 1999 that could determine Natalie Portman's exact location on campus for his CS-50 final project—that purging process included Clint.

Blegh. She shivered. She preferred, when possible, to block out the disturbing little factoid that he and Lexi had dated.

"So sorry I'm late," a low alto trilled as its owner breezed into the room. Every single head turned to look. It was like somebody had cued the opening credits to *Baywatch*, and Alessandra Constantine—the frustratingly gorgeous sophomore transfer student and sometimes bedfellow of one Gregory Bolton—bounced in, her tousled dark curls unfurling behind her as if she had her own invisible wind machine. She may as well have been wearing a red bikini instead of a red sweater, the way every man in the room was staring at her now. Grace watched her, too, but her expression appeared scornful rather than stupefied. "Somebody..." Grace said, waving her hands toward Alessandra like she was a spill that needed mopping.

"We'll do it!" Matt cried, his hand rocketing skyward. Callie restrained an eye-roll. Seriously? Was she really *that* good-looking? Gregory certainly seemed to think so, and Matt, even though the Gregory factor of that equation essentially meant that Matt didn't stand a chance—

"Hi, you two," Alessandra said, sitting in front of the free computer next to them and grinning with her full, pouty lips. "We need to create a log-in name and a password, right?" As she spoke, she leaned in toward the monitor, reminding them exactly how apt Callie's private nickname for her was: Perky Boobs.

If cartoon bubbles could materialize in real life, Matt's would currently read, *Durrh....*

Please, spare us the drool, Callie thought, actually rolling her eyes. Reaching over to Alessandra's keyboard, she typed in her new username. Then, she pulled up the *Crimson* home page and clicked on the link to set up a new account, as Matt had done for her five minutes earlier. Alessandra watched closely, hoping perhaps that appearing rapt with attention could atone for her lateness.

"Fast learner." Matt nodded at Callie.

She grinned. "Only with computers," she said wryly. As for the other stuff—friendship, love, and making the right choices —well, we're getting there.

Slowly but surely she was getting there.

TWO

THE VIEW FROM THE INSIDE

flyby *Harvard Life. To go.*

| HOME | HOUSE LIFE | THE SQUARE | HEADLINES | CLUBS |

Feb 3 Behind the Ivy-Covered Walls

6:49 PM By THE IVY INSIDER

Last week *FM* magazine published an article glorifying various "(in)famous" parties on campus. The five events featured are all hosted by one of eight male Final Clubs: institutions that often weather accusations of elitism, sexism, and "just plain dumb." Even though the article purports to be "your guide to getting in," it's no secret that 85 percent of students on this campus will never be allowed through the doors.

So what *really* goes on behind the ivy-covered walls? It's initiation season here at Harvard, and rumors are proliferating while odd events occur across campus. On Tuesday during Shopping Period several female students were spotted wearing mustaches to class. On Wednesday a group of male sophomores performed a synchronized dance in drag to a Katy Perry song on the steps of Memorial Church. But are these arguably lighthearted pranks indicative of what transpires in private away from the public eye?

Not according to a recent blog post on *FM*'s write-in advice page, where an anonymous student from the class of 2013 asks: "Dear Lexi:

One of my roommates came back from a Final Club initiation event with cigarette burns all over his arm. None of the rest of us made it into a club this year, and he refused to tell us what happened. Should we be concerned?" Contrary to the advice proffered by the editors at *FM*, the answer is yes.

Given the recent publicity surrounding an X-rated video created on a high school dare (ref: *"Sex, Lies, and Videotape: The Story of an Initiation Gone Awry"* at www.thecrimson.com), it seems unlikely that clubs will enforce previously documented rituals requiring initiates to snap cell phone photographs of a female in flagrante. However, it's anyone's guess as to what the mob mentality will produce next.

In the meantime, spring punch season is about to begin at the Hasty Pudding social club. Despite an age- and gender-neutral admit policy, this private institution still caters to a predominantly white, trust-fund-wealthy faction of the student body and should be considered anything but progressive. Stay tuned for an insider's look at the rules and values underlying their punch process and what happens at 2 Garden Street, their independently owned building beyond college control. Shocking secrets may soon come to light that could force even the university—officially disaffiliated with the Final Clubs since 1984, when the organizations refused to go coeducational in accordance with Title IX legislation—to stand up and take notice.

"Next up we have Penelope Vandemeer, also from New York, New York," Anne Goldberg, secretary, said as she clicked to a new slide of the PowerPoint presentation she was currently delivering in the living room of the Hasty Pudding social club. "Deerfield alum, like yours truly, and at least half the board," she added, the corners of her mouth curling up—quite demonstrative, given her usual frosty demeanor—like she had just referenced a hilarious inside joke.

"The family has a gorgeous estate in Palm Beach, not to mention the house on the Cape," a girl, one of the Deerfield alums, chimed in. "One week in January she had her father fly half the sophomore class down to Florida for the weekend—in their jet."

Anne nodded. "I think we can all agree that she certainly has a lot to offer?"

"Second!" called Tyler, Clint's roommate and president of the club (in addition to Vanessa's Man-Candy-Consecutive-Whatever), over from where he lay stretched across a chaise lounge.

"Third!" cried OK, which earned him an elevated eyebrow from Mimi, who was perched next to him on the windowsill. "What?" he muttered. "Look at her. Blond and plump: just my type." Mimi smirked and flicked her dark brown hair over her shoulder.

"A show of hands from the board only, please." The speaker, whose sweet, clear voice rang from the front row of folding chairs set up for the occasion, didn't even need to turn her head of flawless chestnut curls in order to command the room.

Alexis Thorndike.

Callie stifled a yawn. She, along with thirty-odd members of the club who were cycling in and out depending on their class schedules, had been cooped up in the living room for hours discussing the list of potential punches for that spring. Everyone had already submitted—anonymously via the secure website HPpunch.com—the names of students whom they thought would be "a good fit, and would uphold the standards and style of our organization." Then Anne had compiled that list and used her résumé-perfect proficiency at Microsoft Office applications, with the aid of photos lifted from Facebook, to create a presentation. Callie couldn't wait to get to class, and not just because it was the first official week of courses now that Shopping Period had drawn to a close.

"It's settled, then," Anne agreed with Lexi, as good sidekicks always do. She made a check on her clipboard. "Next!" she chirped, clicking her way to the subsequent slide. "Chip Scooner Hallisburg the third of Gladwyne, Pennsylvania," she continued, followed by a summary of why he had been overlooked the previous fall.

Callie turned to Clint, who was sitting next to her on a couch in the back by the piano, and gave him a look that clearly read: *When* is this going to be *over*? He squeezed her thigh. "Hang in there, kiddo," he murmured as a heated debate about inbreeding, Quakerism, and unibrows was brewing.

"You said this was supposed to be the 'fun' part," Callie muttered.

"But there's an easy solution here, and we all know what that is," Brittney, a sophomore who made her namesake on *Glee* look like a genius, cried. "MANSCAPING. How else do you think I got rid of the nickname Tarantula Arms back in middle school?"

Clint tilted his head, glancing at Callie from underneath his long, light brown lashes.

"Okay, maybe a little," Callie conceded. "But still—"

"*Ahem.*" someone cleared her throat from the front of the room. Callie dropped her voice to a whisper. "Doesn't the whole thing make you kind of—I don't know—uncomfortable?"

"Which part?" he whispered back. Anne checked *yes* on Chip (inbreeding for the win!) and clicked to the next slide.

"Never seen her before, but she's pretty cute," a guy called from the piano bench.

"Eh," said another senior Callie had never spoken to. "I give her a seven."

"No," countered the other, "at least an eight."

Callie shook her head, then whispered, "The way they're blatantly ranking people based on looks, or money, or what else they can 'bring' to the club—"

Anne glared at her from the front of the room. "Show of hands, please?"

Clint shrugged and whispered back, "How else would you have them do it? GPA? Hours of community service?"

Callie stared at him.

"I'm just saying," he said, shifting in his seat. "I think it's flawed as much as you do, but this is the way it's always been done—

Hey! That guy Dudley," he suddenly called as Anne clicked to the next slide, "is a *sick* squash player. Sophomore walk-on and already starting at third. Definitely gets my vote."

He turned back to Callie. "What's wrong?" he murmured, twining his fingers through hers.

"Nothing . . . I'm just wondering, I guess, um, what they said—about me?" She cringed, bracing herself.

"Cutest freshman on campus, hilarious but usually not because she means to be on purpose, killer smile, awesome eyes, sharp as a whip, and has excellent taste in men."

"No way!" She leaned into him, smiling a little. "Really?"

"Well, no," he said, throwing an arm around her shoulders. "You weren't in the slide show because nobody had any idea who you were before *I* punched you in secret, remember?"

Right. Great. Though perhaps anonymity was preferable to being talked about, if today's discussion was any indication. Good thing she had already made it into the club early first semester, lest her slide read: *Callie Andrews—Boyfriend Stealer; Sex Tape Maker; Failed Candidate for* FM *magazine; Parental Income Tax Bracket: 28%; Current Bank Account Balance: $32.50 . . .*

The sharp sound of a wolf whistle cut across the room. Alessandra Constantine's face filled the giant projector screen.

"Smokin'," said the boy on the piano bench.

"An eleven out of ten," concurred Mr. I-give-her-a-seven.

"What's her phone number, and where can I find her?" another called.

"Careful," Tyler warned. "She's spoken for. Right, Bolton?"

"What?" a distracted-sounding voice from behind Callie asked.

"She's your girlfriend, isn't she?" Tyler prompted, nodding at the slide.

Callie peered over her shoulder. Gregory sat slumped low in an easy chair, a book propped on his knee.

"Sure," he said. "Whatever."

Too cool to pay attention like the rest of us, Callie thought as he resumed reading. Nevertheless, she craned her neck trying to catch the title.... Wait—GIRLFRIEND?!? The one term he had always seemed astronomically incapable of uttering, and now for it to slip out and be confirmed so casually with a mere "sure, whatever" on a random weekday at approximately 1:45 p.m.—

"Ms. Constantine," said Anne, barreling on, "is the daughter of Oliver Constantine, as in Constantine Capital Investments, and Luciana Constantine, neé Garcia, as in the former supermodel. Needless to say, Ms. Constantine is a high-priority punch. Gregory, you'll talk to her"—he nodded—"and ladies, you'll be extra *proactive* about asking her to lunch?"

The lunches started after the first punch event, a cocktail party at the clubhouse, and were supposed to allow members a chance to get to know punches in a more intimate, informal setting. Members were also "unofficially" responsible for footing the bill. Callie tried not to think about how many hamburgers she could afford for $32.50—maybe six, minus the fries? Because nothing says "Elite Secret Society" like a McDonald's McValue Meal.

"All right." Anne summoned their attention. "It's a quarter to two, and I know some of you have class; I think that leaves time for one more: Vanessa Von Vorhees, from New York, New York. As most of you already know, we cut Ms. Von Vorhees in the final round last fall. Normally in these cases, it is club policy not to put the punch through another season, and we cannot overturn a blackball once it has been invoked. However, given that the member who invoked said blackball has graduated—"

"Only took her five and a half years!" the boy on the piano interjected.

"Ah, yes," Anne agreed, "Leanne certainly did take the—er—scenic route. In any event, perhaps we ought to reconsider, given that multiple members submitted her name."

Mimi looked up sharply from the windowsill and stared at Callie. Callie shrugged. It just so happened that she *had* submitted Vanessa after overhearing her remind Mimi every day for a week—not that Callie would ever admit this to anyone, least of all Vanessa.

"No discussion necessary," said Tyler, standing. "I'm the president, and I say that she's in."

"Yeah," someone muttered, "because you want in her pants!"

"That's how all the freshmen girls seem to be doing it these days," Lexi's voice rang out across the room. The juniors sitting next to her broke into giggles. "No offense, Tyler," she continued, turning, her eyes sliding over Callie and Clint as if they weren't even there. "But she doesn't exactly bring anything new to the table."

Clearly Lexi felt no loyalty to the promise she had made Vanessa last semester of a guaranteed membership in the club; probably because Vanessa had failed to deliver her end of the bargain: to provide dirt on Callie. Callie had overheard the entire exchange in the stacks of Lamont Library, where she worked part-time behind the reference desk for roughly two hamburgers an hour. Back then, Vanessa's betrayal had seemed inevitable, but now Callie knew better.

Over by the windowsill, OK was nudging Mimi. She wore the same guilty expression she had every other time someone called on her and she had been only half pretending to pay attention, or was half asleep. Yesterday in the common room Callie had also overheard Vanessa forcing Mimi to rehearse several talking points re: Vanessa's assets for this exact moment.

"Um," Callie mumbled, surprised as the words began to tumble out of her mouth, "as an alum of the Brearley School, Vanessa has multiple connections to this club and beyond. Her mother is on the board of three Manhattan charity organizations, and her father works at Goldman Sachs with, uh, I think—Gregory's dad?"

Mimi beamed, and Clint gave Callie an approving look that seemed to say, *Now you get it: gotta play by the rules to win the game.*

"He doesn't work there anymore," a voice said sharply from over her shoulder. She turned in time to see Gregory snap his book shut.

"Oh, sorry. My bad," she mumbled. "What does he do again?"

"A lot of sailing and scotch drinking, though he does enjoy the occasional cigar."

"He works at a hedge fund," Clint explained. "A really, really famous one, actually. Greg's dad pioneered this specific type of trading—"

Gregory stood suddenly, sticking his book in the back pocket of his jeans. "Cigarette break," he muttered. When he reached the other side of the room, he added, "I'll be outside if anyone needs me."

Was Callie imagining it or had he looked straight at her when he said that?

"I should probably go, too," she murmured to Clint as the people in the front row started discussing whether or not a blackball had a statute of limitations that expired when the blackballer graduated.

"You still have ten minutes to get to class," Clint said, checking his watch.

"Yeah, but it's the first official day, so I don't want to be late."

"All right," Clint said, leaning in to kiss her cheek. "See you later, for dinner? If we're done by then." He laughed.

"Yes," she agreed. "Dinner." Gathering her things, she slipped out of the room.

Gregory, as expected, was sitting on the club's front stoop, midway through a cigarette.

"Hey," she said, hovering near the banister. "Everything okay with you?"

He exhaled a long puff of smoke. "What are you, my friend now?"

"I could be," she said slowly, setting down her book bag and sitting two feet away from him on the stone step.

He took another drag. "Nah," he said, tossing the cigarette away. "I don't have friends who are girls."

"You don't think men and women can be friends?"

"Nope," he said, shaking his head.

Propping her chin in her hands, she watched the cars pass on Garden Street. "Well, I disagree."

"Oh yeah?" he asked, turning to look at her. "Want me to prove it to you?"

His blue eyes honed in on her, and suddenly she felt trapped: torn between the urge to scoot away and to stay exactly where she sat. "How?"

Instead of speaking, he slid over to her, stopping when his knee just barely grazed her jeans. His fingertips were less than a centimeter from hers on the step above. She could see the faint, crescent moon–shaped scar on his chin, only an inch below his lips, as he leaned in, achingly close, until their noses were almost touching. There he remained, unmoving, staring at her with a challenge in his eyes.

Message received.

"I, uh, have to get to class," she stammered, leaping up.

"Me too," he said standing. "Where you headed?"

"The Barker Center."

"Me too," he repeated with mock *well-isn't-this-just-such-a-coincidence* delight.

She narrowed her eyes. "Really."

"Yep."

"Well . . . I . . ."

"Aren't you forgetting something?" he asked.

He had proved his point about being friends, so why was he still standing so close? "Um . . . wha—"

"This," he said, snatching up her book bag.

"Hey!" she cried as he started to walk away.

"Better hurry," he called over his shoulder.

Feeling slightly breathless, she ran to catch up.

"You didn't have to walk me the whole way here—now *you're* going to be late!" She and Gregory were standing in front of the double-glass and wood-paneled doors to the main seminar room in the Barker Center. Cool winter sunlight filtered down through tiny skylights in the impossibly high ceilings, dappling across the pale tiled floors. A green and gold banister rimmed the marble staircase leading upstairs, and a massive wooden archway on their right opened out into a cozy rotunda café.

"Can I have my bag back now?" Callie asked.

"Which class is this?" he retorted instead, peering through the glass at the students who were seating themselves around a huge mahogany table.

"Postwar Fiction and Theory, with that visiting professor Raja?" As she spoke, an elderly gentleman of Indian descent sporting a purple velvet blazer and huge horn-rimmed glasses slipped through the back entrance and assumed his place at the head of the table. "Why?" she asked, rounding on him. "What class do you—"

"Postwar Fiction and Theory, with that visiting professor Raja," he answered with a wicked gleam in his eye, tossing her bag into her arms. Then, without a backward glance, he opened the doors and strode into the room.

She stared after him. He hadn't attended last week's seminar during Shopping Period. What was he trying to pull?

There was nothing to do but follow. Walking in, she took a seat opposite him. He beamed at her and pulled out a notebook and pen from the inside pocket of his coat. She frowned back, but his attention had suddenly shifted elsewhere, to somewhere behind her head. She turned just in time to see Alessandra bounding through the double doors, late as was—apparently—usual. Callie watched her slide into the seat next to Gregory. His eyes flickered ever so briefly at Callie before he leaned in and kissed her near the mouth.

Professor Raja cleared his throat. "My dear friends, thank you for joining our conversation today." His British-Indian accent was so distinguished that anything he said would have sounded brilliant, be it about the central components of de Saussure's structuralist theory of linguistics (signs and signifiers) or what he ate for breakfast (eggs and toast). "Now if you could all be so kind as to retrieve your copies of *Mrs. Dalloway*, which naturally you have all absorbed and digested since our last meeting . . ."

Hmfp—a tiny noise of triumph escaped Callie's lips at the blank look on Gregory's face as she plunked her copy of Virginia Woolf's famous masterpiece on the table. Her smile faded a moment later when he leaned in to share with Alessandra.

"Now," Professor Raja continued, "who wants to provide us with an analysis of the novel's stream of consciousness mechanism insofar as it relates to the underlying issues of mental illness, existentialism, and feminism?"

The room stayed silent.

"Not properly caffeinated this afternoon, I see," he murmured, looking amused. "Well, in that case, let us begin instead with the most deceivingly simple of questions. The novel takes place in a single day. Who can tell me what happens?"

More silence.

"Shy, are we?" Professor Raja commented. "Well, if there are no volunteers, I shall just have to pick one of you," he muttered, shuffling his papers until he identified the class register. Twirling his finger above the page, he stabbed downward and smiled.

Callie swallowed.

"Miss Alessandra Constantine?"

"Uh . . . yes?" Perky Boobs asked in her low alto. Her forehead was creased, her full scarlet lips drawn in a pout. She looked like someone who could flirt her way out of anything—well, almost anything.

Professor Raja smiled tolerantly. "Shall I repeat the question, dear?" She nodded, and he did. Her face remained as blank as before.

Callie knew it was wrong to feel satisfied. Maybe Alessandra had the answer but felt paralyzed due to her proximity to Gregory, who Callie knew better than anyone caused a certain maddening, tongue-tying effect. Still . . .

"Well, Mrs. Dalloway is going to throw, like, a party—or *soiree*, in French—so she's walking around town getting ready and buying flowers and stuff."

Or soiree, *in French*? Clearly this girl needed to repeat Introduction to Bullshit 10a.

Professor Raja's lips were thin and straight like a ruler.

"And honestly not a whole lot else happens, unless you count that Septimus guy who kills himself because he's, like, traumatized. From the war and stuff."

Professor Raja blinked rapidly, his eyes magnified and huge like an owl's through the horn-rimmed spectacles.

"I mean," Alessandra faltered, "that apart from the party with her husband and friends and her ex-boyfriend who also shows up, there isn't too much going on...."

Gregory, who had been fixated on the page in front of him, looked up suddenly. "I believe what Ms. Constantine is trying to say is that there isn't too much, ah, 'going on' in terms of the *action* in the story because the majority of the novel takes place in the *minds* of the characters. The characters' *interior* thoughts ... supersede the *exterior* action, which, ah, renders these seemingly insignificant, ordinary everyday events—a glance, a touch, buying some flowers—significant and ... well, extraordinary. Epic, even."

Ah, and the man with a PhD in Bullshitology weighs in with a phenomenal—no, make that *epic*—rewording of the blurb on the back of the book.

Even Professor Raja seemed to buy it, nodding enthusiastically as he said, "Excellently put. Your name, young man?"

"Gregory Bolton. I'm a last-minute addition," he added as Professor Raja scanned the register and appeared to draw a blank.

"Very good," the professor said, making a note. "Now, Mr. Bolton, perhaps you'd care to elaborate on what you appeared to be suggesting was the paradoxically expansive nature of a seemingly ordinary day ... ?"

Without hesitation Gregory launched into an analysis of the text, which, it soon became clear, he had read on a previous occasion. His words flowed as effortlessly as he could lob a squash ball into a perfect serve or secure a girl's phone number with a single look—in the opposite direction. Callie felt strangely envious: not because of the way Alessandra, and every other girl in the room for that matter, was hanging on his words, but because for him, everything was so easy. He had been born with so much— smarts, looks, athletic ability, and more money than she would see in a lifetime—that he never even had to try. How, she wondered suddenly, could someone with everything be so insufferable 95 percent of the time?

". . . So, as you can see, most of the novel takes place in memory," Gregory concluded. "The central characters are preoccupied by the past, obsessed in particular with the formative decisions that they made—decisions that may have been wrong."

A few students had started taking notes, and Professor Raja's head was in danger of popping off his neck from all the vigorous nodding. "And an example of one of these pivotal decisions might be . . . ?"

"Mrs. Dalloway's—Clarissa's—decision to marry Richard over Peter. In choosing Richard she is choosing practicality over passion: the promise of security and a stable life in exchange for . . . well, true love." His eyes were trained straight ahead. Was it Callie's imagination or had his face grown the slightest shade darker? He shrugged. "She spends the rest of her life regretting it."

"No she doesn't." The words flew out of Callie's mouth before she could stop them. Suddenly all eyes were on her. Professor Raja gave her a small smile. "Do go on, Miss . . . ?"

"Andrews. Callie Andrews. And I was just saying that . . . I disagree. I don't think she regrets her decision. To marry Richard. Instead of Peter, who I'm sure we can all concur is extremely unreliable and incapable of reform, since he never stops chasing other girls and adventures, and is basically kind of a— well . . ." Callie swallowed, unsure if there was a seminar-appropriate synonym for the term *man-slut*. "The point is . . . that she is happy—very happy—with her choice."

"That may be so," Gregory cut in before Professor Raja could respond, "but is she *really* happy in the aftermath? Happy to play the part of the upper-class housewife to her politician? Because she never actually gives Peter an answer when he asks her," he continued, picking up Alessandra's copy of the novel and flipping through it, "on page—"

"It's at the bottom of forty-seven," Callie cut in smoothly. "Right after Peter tells her he's having an affair with a married woman back in India while simultaneously checking out the maid; and right before he falls 'madly in love' with a complete stranger on the street and then follows her all around town!"

"Peter certainly has his flaws," Gregory countered evenly, "but if he's so screwed up, then why, on that same page forty-seven, does she think that, 'If I had married him, this gaiety would have been mine all day'—"

"Fun does not equal stability," Callie interjected. "And even though she *sometimes* has trouble remembering why she didn't choose Peter when he's around because he is quote 'enchanting,' that doesn't mean Richard wasn't the right choice; in fact, as Peter even says himself, compared to Richard he is a 'failure'—"

"—or how about on forty-one," Gregory continued, "when she reflects on how 'impossible it was ever to make up my mind,' and then wonders why she ever did decide 'not to marry' Peter 'that awful summer.'"

"That summer," Callie said through gritted teeth, "the most important relationship on her mind was with her best *female* friend, Sally Seton, with whom she shared the most *quote* 'exquisite moment of her whole life,' which of course Peter could never understand, self-centered egotistical narcissist that he is—"

"Everyone goes a little lesbian in college." Gregory snorted. "Which is beside the point, anyway, because in present day Clarissa and Sally are barely even friends anymore—"

"Perhaps you two ought to reserve the rest of this debate for later," Professor Raja boomed suddenly, "and allow us to hear from some of the other members of this class?"

Oh. Callie blinked. She had completely forgotten that anyone else was in the room. Blushing, she buried her nose in her book and barely glanced over the top of the pages for the remainder of class.

"You guys got a little intense back there," Alessandra said, bridging the gap between Callie and Gregory as they all filed out of the seminar room, drawing them together against their will like an oxygen molecule binds two positively charged and therefore normally repellant atoms of hydrogen. "I'm going to have to step up my game!"

Callie stared at her.

"Harvard is, like, way harder than I ever would have thought," Alessandra continued.

Oh. She means she's going to have to start actually reading before class.

"We're going to grab a late lunch," Alessandra said, stopping in front of the café. "Won't you join us?"

Callie's eyes grew wide. "No—I, uh . . ."

"She has to be at work in Lamont in half an hour," Gregory supplied.

"How did you know that?" Callie blurted.

Alessandra cocked her head.

Gregory shrugged. "Friends know other friends' schedules."

"Is that right?" asked Callie.

"Yep," he said, throwing an arm around Alessandra's shoulders and leading her into the café. "We'll see ya later, *pal.*"

And so the two of them broke away, the bond "smashed to atoms," just as Woolf had written.

THREE

THE WAR OF THE ROSES

To all the gentlemen on campus:

Today is the thirteenth of February, meaning that tomorrow is the day you're going to be in a whole lot of trouble unless—unlike most individuals possessing a Y chromosome—you miraculously remembered that tomorrow is not just Monday but also VALENTINE'S DAY.

Last week a *Crimson* editor published an article on their already flailing upstart, the so-called "more than daily news" FlyBy blog, claiming to be "What Every Harvard Student Needs to Know About Dating: A Guide in Ten Simple Equations." Forgetting, for a moment, that "ten simple equations" is an incredibly moronic oxymoron, let's take a moment to dwell on the disturbing statistic that came to light:

> As a Harvard student, there's a 69 percent chance you were your high school's valedictorian. But there's also a 90 percent chance you're still a virgin.

To remedy these statistical shortcomings (only 69 percent valedictorian: come on, people!), the author launches into a mathematical analysis of dating involving a lot of *if-then* statements that seems guaranteed to fail the 2 percent of people on this planet who can even follow his logic.

More important, this piece proves once and for all—in less than twenty diagrams!—why they at the paper should stick to breaking news and leave the social side to our advice experts at *FM*.

But I digress. And so, without further ado, flow charts, diagrams, or equations:

Appropriate Valentine's Day Gifts:
A Simple Pyramid Based on the Length of Time You've Been Together

A day: A card

A week: Flowers

A month: Chocolates

Six months–1 year: Jewelry

Year+: Really Expensive Jewelry

Not together yet: Tell her how you feel; anything else = creepy

Was that so difficult to parse? If so, then just remember this: whatever you do, don't get her a freaking teddy bear.

Happy V-Day,

(And here's hoping that some of you finally lose those V-Cards!)

Alexis Thorndike, Advice Columnist

Fifteen Minutes Magazine

Harvard University's Authority on Campus Life since 1873

"Caliente, can I use your computer?" Mimi asked from where she was sprawled over the overstuffed chair in their common room.

"What did you just call me?" Callie demanded, looking up sharply from her reading assignment for Postwar Fiction and Theory.

"Caliente. It is Spanish. Gregory is teaching me. I switched to 101 because, after my C *en français*, they told me I would have to repeat the entry level *une autre fois* before advancing."

Callie grimaced. Caliente had been Gregory's special name for her . . . a long, long time ago. "Why do you need my computer?"

"I, er, mine . . . exploded?"

"Exploded?"

"Yes. Bang, bang? It was all the fault of Justin Bieber."

Callie stared.

"She means she downloaded a bunch of music illegally," Vanessa offered from where she sat on the floor, cutting paper hearts out of pink and red construction paper. Apparently—as she had explained earlier to Mimi—if you taped them to the walls, they were like dream catchers but for valentines. *Plus, it's festive!*

"You can get in real trouble with the administration for that!" Dana called, popping her head out of her bedroom. After a moment's hesitation she plopped next to Callie on the couch, unable to resist the opportunity to lecture. "It's in violation of the university code, and against the law. Students have been kicked out for less."

"Well, I learned my lesson," Mimi muttered. "*Un cheval de Troie a mange mon ordinateur.*"

"A . . . horse . . . *ate* your computer?" Dana scrunched up her forehead. "Is that like 'the dog ate my homework'?"

Vanessa laughed. "A *Trojan* horse virus destroyed her operating system."

"*Oui, c'est tragique,*" Mimi agreed. "Caliente? *Se mueva, por favor! Ahora!*"

"Yes, here you go," Callie said, returning from her bedroom with her laptop and handing it to Mimi.

"Password?" asked Mimi, flipping it open.

"Calbear12," Vanessa replied, seemingly automatically, cutting a large, pink heart from construction paper she had just folded in half.

Callie stared at her. "How did y—"

"*Ah oui, c'est vrai,*" Mimi cut her off, her fingers flicking over the keys.

"But—wait—you both know my password?"

"Yes," said Vanessa, grabbing a roll of tape and standing. "Even if you weren't the world's slowest, *loudest* typist," she explained as she stuck the first heart on the wall, "it's not very difficult to guess."

Mimi nodded. "One needs random letters and punctuation and numbers—"

"I have numbers. Twelve. That's a number."

"*Oui,*" said Mimi. "It is also the number on your football sweatshirt—"

"Soccer—"

"And your gym bag, and your seven pairs of *football* shorts—which, by the way, we are glad there are seven because they all look the same and we thought you were very dirty for a while."

"You also sign all of your e-mails 'Calbear,'" Vanessa chimed in. "At least, when you used to . . ." She trailed off, suddenly intent on taping a pink heart inside of a red one.

"And it is your Twitter name," Mimi continued, "and your screen name, and—"

"Okay, okay, I get it!" Callie cried. "It's just that . . . random numbers and letters are hard to remember sometimes."

"C8H5KO4," Dana rattled off instantly. "What? That's easy. It's the molecular formula for potassium hydrogen phthalate." Her eyes grew wide. "Oh no," she muttered, racing into her bedroom. They could hear her fingers clacking frantically at her keyboard.

"Yeah," Vanessa snorted, "because we're *really* going to remember *that*."

There was a knock at the door.

"I'll get it!" Vanessa shrieked, bounding over to the mirror to tug at her curls. "Hello-o . . . Oh. You. Hi. What do you want?"

"Are you going to let me in?" came Matt's voice.

"Are those for *Callie*?" Vanessa shot back.

"Uh, actually, there's one for each of you," Matt explained, walking into the room. His cheeks were nearly the same shade at the four long-stemmed red roses in his hand. In the other he held a giant teddy bear, white with a bright red bow around its neck.

Vanessa's eyes lit up, and she snatched a rose, inhaling its scent like it was the first she had ever received. Maybe it is, Callie suddenly thought, eyeing the paper hearts stuck to the walls. Vanessa frowned suddenly. "Why all of us?" she demanded, suspicious.

"Well, I uh, just thought . . . it'd be nice if . . ." Matt stared at the floor. "My mom made me."

"Your *mom*?" Vanessa repeated. "And who is *that* for?" she added, pointing at the bear.

"No one! I mean, someone, but no one here, okay—not that it's any of your business!"

"Thank you, Matthew. That was extremely thoughtful," Dana said.

"Yes, thank you," said Callie, accepting a rose. "These are beautiful."

"*Merci,*" Mimi echoed, looking up from whatever she was typing.

"So," said Matt, sitting on the couch, "what's everyone up to? Art project?" he added, noticing all the paper hearts strewn across the coffee table and floor.

"Just doing some decorating for my favorite holiday," Vanessa said, unabashed. "Which doesn't make a whole lot of sense, when you think about it, because it's not like I've ever had a *great* Valentine's Day. In fact, I've probably had a lot of bad Valentine's Days. Disastrous, even. But I'm an optimist! Hey"—she broke out of her monologue, surveying Matt—"You're tall-ish. Do you think you could reach above the door?"

"Uh, probably—"

"Great!" she said, thrusting a handful of paper hearts and a spare roll of tape into his hands.

Callie emerged from the bathroom with her Nalgene full of warm water and started arranging the roses on the coffee table. "We have about an hour to kill before this 'Stoplight' party tonight, so—"

"What's a 'Stoplight' party?" Matt interrupted.

"Oh," said Callie. "It's a Pudding thing. Instead of the traditional cocktail party they're—I mean *we're*—doing something a little different for the first event this spring." Two weeks ago she had asked Matt if he wanted her to "punch" him and he had laughed and said, "Only if I ever do something really, really wrong." Dana had similarly declined, despite Mimi's urging that her presence would make the whole thing a "bit less boring," which, coming from Mimi, practically constituted begging. Clearing her throat, Callie lifted Vanessa's invitation off the table, where Vanessa had left it prominently displayed, and read:

THE MEMBERS OF THE HASTY PUDDING SOCIAL CLUB, EST. 1770
Cordially invite you to join us for our first Punch Event of the spring

"STOP! In the name of LOVE!"
Like traffic lights, your attire will send *signals* to the opposite sex

Green means GO:
"I'm totally available (so bring it on)"

Yellow means SLOW DOWN:
"I might be taken—but maybe not (depends who's asking)"

Red means STOP:
"My significant other owns a gun (and is not afraid to use it)"

Monday, February 14th
8:15 P.M.
2 Garden Street
Stoplight Cocktail Attire

"Sounds . . . like a good way to force a lot of conversations that people might not be ready to have?" said Matt, taping another heart over the door.

"What do you mean?" asked Vanessa. "And watch it! Higher. Those look crooked."

"I mean what if you're a dude and you like a girl and you've been on a few dates and you think it's getting pretty serious so you wear red, only then she shows up wearing—"

"Ohmigawd!" Vanessa shrieked. "Oh my god oh my god oh my *god*. What if—what if—" Her sentence cut off abruptly as she dived headfirst into her closet.

A few minutes later she resurfaced. She wore a pale gold top tucked into a red leather miniskirt and a large necklace, its green stones glimmering. "Is it too much?" she asked.

"*C'est parfait,*" said Mimi. "You look exactly like an upside-down traffic light, with hair! What?" she added. "That is what you are going for, no?"

Vanessa groaned, sighed, and then looked at Callie. "What are *you* wearing? Everyone?"

"Purple," said Mimi, back to being absorbed by Callie's computer.

"Red, of course," said Callie. Of course. Right?

Frowning, she pulled out her phone and texted Clint.

WHAT ARE YOU WEARING TONIGHT?

His response came almost instantaneously:

A TIE.

She shook her head.

WHAT COLOR??

RED! :)

Callie glanced at Vanessa, who was now limping around her bedroom on two heels of vastly different heights: one red, one a yellow-green reptile print.

DO YOU KNOW WHAT COLOR
TYLER'S WEARING?

YELLOW? HE'S ON THE FENCE.

Vanessa moaned and kicked off both shoes, then disappeared back into her closet.

WELL, PUSH HIM OVER: TO RED!
VANESSA = SPAZZING.

WILL DO ;)

"I think you should go with the red one that you already laid out," Callie called.

"Of course *you* would suggest the option most likely to humiliate me," Vanessa muttered, flinging dress after dress onto her bed.

Callie shrugged.

All of a sudden Matt yelled and leaped back—just in time to miss the door that had been flung open.

"I came just as soon as I heard!" OK cried, bursting into the room. In his arms he cradled several large heart-shaped candy boxes, each wrapped in ribbons that were also affixed to multiple red balloons.

"Heard what?" asked Dana.

"What you were up to," he said, rounding on Matt. "Very tricky, mate, but I refuse to be outdone by the likes of you!"

"What?" Matt's face was a complete blank.

OK jabbed an accusatory finger at the roses. "*I'm* their favorite neighbor. Ladies?"

"Um, thank you?" said Callie, taking a box of candy. The balloons bobbed in the air.

"Of course you are," Vanessa agreed, coming back into the common room. "Who else would remember to TiVo *The Bachelor* while I was away on vacay?"

"He watches that by himself, too," Matt whispered to Callie.

"What color are *you* wearing tonight, OK?" Vanessa asked, ignoring Matt.

"Green," he said very slowly and deliberately, trying—and failing—not to look at Mimi. "Yes, I will be wearing *green* tonight. . . . Unless someone has a problem—with me wearing *green*? Anyone? No one?"

Mimi still appeared completely engaged by the computer.

"Well, then, here you go, Dana," he said, handing the last of the three boxes to her.

"What about me?" Mimi said, suddenly snapping to attention.

"You said this holiday was a 'stupid fabrication invented by the Hallmark company and that in France St. Valentine is the name of a monster that eats little children's feet!"

"When did I say that?" Mimi asked.

"When I—" OK lowered his voice. "When I asked if you wanted to—"

"He eats their little fingers, too." Mimi nodded vigorously. "And the feet. Now leave me alone; I am needing to finish this."

Everyone suddenly stared at her. "Are you . . ." Callie started. "I mean, you're not . . . *working*—are you?"

"*Oui.*"

"Homework?" asked Dana in disbelief.

Mimi shook her head. "*Pas pour* school."

"What *are* you doing, then?" OK demanded.

"I am building a website that allows friends to connect with one another using a system of social networks."

"No, seriously: what are you doing?" Callie asked. "On *my* computer?"

Mimi exhaled. "I am doing the *Lampoon* COMP."

"What?" Vanessa shrieked from her bedroom. "*Why?*"

Mimi surveyed them as if she were debating whether they were worthy of her trust. Finally she shrugged. "*Il est le seul club à Harvard que je ne suis pas autorisé à entrer.*"

"The only club . . . oh, that you're not authorized to enter? I guess that . . . makes a weird kind of sense," Matt said. "Well, when you make it, we'll be rivals, so you'd better watch out!" He stood. "I should probably get going. OK?"

"Yeah," OK agreed. "Yeah, got to go put on my *green* shirt—"

Callie quickly shook her head at him.

"Oh," he said, staring back at her. "This was in your drop-box." He pulled a small white envelope out of his pocket.

Turning it over in her hands, she saw her name on the front.

"Thanks . . . and thanks for everything, guys!" she called.

"Yes, thank you!"

"*Merci!*"

"What's in the envelope?" Dana asked when they were gone. Her cheeks were slightly flushed as she bit into one of the rich chocolate truffles from her heart-shaped box and then leaned in to inhale the flowers.

"Tickets . . ." Callie said slowly, pulling them out. "Two tickets to hear—oh, wow—Ian McEwan! It looks like he's doing a reading at the Harvard bookstore next month."

"Gandalf?" asked Mimi. "The actor?"

"No, the *author*," Callie answered, rereading the tickets in disbelief.

"Are they from Clint?" Dana ventured.

"Yes, they must be," said Callie, her smile spreading from ear to ear. She had never mentioned that McEwan was one of her favorite authors; Clint must have noticed her reading a copy of *Atonement* at the end of J-term.

There was a knock on the door. Vanessa froze mid-millionth-outfit change. *"No,"* she whispered. "They're not supposed to be here for another fifteen minutes!"

"Come in!" Mimi yelled wickedly.

"Hello," said Adam, walking into the room. "Hi. Happy Valentine's Day."

"I'll kill you!" Vanessa screamed from her bedroom—probably at Mimi, but it was difficult to say for sure.

"Hi," said Dana, beaming shyly.

"I got you something," he said, pulling a small wrapped present from behind his back. His hand froze in midair. "And so did somebody else, apparently." His eyes were flicking from the

Nalgene full of flowers, which was situated right in front of Dana, to the open box of chocolates on her lap.

"Oh, this? It's nothing," Dana said, her voice slightly higher than usual.

"It doesn't look like nothing," Adam replied, drawing himself up to his full five feet, seven inches.

"Really," said Dana, blushing as she stood. "These were just friendly gifts. From your roommates."

This news did not have the desired calming effect. "My *roommates*?" Adam repeated, his voice cracking. "Which one? Gregory? Oh, he's in for a talking to when we get home—"

"Hush, you're being ridiculous," said Dana, shooting an apologetic look at Mimi and Callie. "But if you insist on continuing this conversation, we can do so on the way to dinner. . . ."

"Fine!" Adam snapped.

"We'd better go get dressed," Callie said pointedly to Mimi.

"*Oui, allons-y!*"

Ten minutes later they emerged from their bedrooms: Callie in a little red dress she had ordered online from Forever 21 and Mimi wearing purple as promised.

"Diiing Dong," a muffled voice that sounded like Tyler's called from the hall.

"Ohmygod, they're here," Vanessa shrieked, poking her head out of her room. She was still wearing only her bra and underwear, clutching two dresses—one red and one a pale yellow—tightly in her fists. "Mimi! Mimi, can you let them in while I hide in here and then text me what Tyler's—"

"Red, for crying out loud!" Callie erupted. "He's wearing red. Clint told me. Now hurry up and get dressed and don't come out until you have clothes on!"

"I will get it," Mimi said, intercepting Callie on her way to the door.

"You're leaving?" Callie asked.

Mimi slipped on her coat. "Would not want to be a 'wheel,' as you would say. . . ."

"We come bearing gifts," Tyler said, strolling into the room. He wore maroon under a black blazer, while Clint sported a paler red dress shirt and a dark blue tie, looking amazing as usual.

"I see that," Callie acknowledged. He was carrying a large bouquet of flowers, a box of chocolates, and a card. It seemed he had really taken Lexi's gift advice to heart, only like Vanessa, he had experienced difficulty deciding which level of commitment to signify and so had just decided to buy everything.

Clint swept Callie up in his arms. "Hi, beautiful," he said.

"Hi, you," she said, kissing him.

"I have a little something for you," he started, holding up a small light blue box tied with thick, white ribbon. But before she could take it, Vanessa emerged from her bedroom wearing—

"*Yellow?*" Tyler muttered. He shot Clint a look.

"Your dress is lovely, Vanessa," Clint said, ignoring him.

"Yeah," Tyler echoed, "Lovely and . . . *yellow.*"

"Thanks. Are those all for me?" she asked Tyler, pointing to the gifts, her eyes lit up like a kid's in a candy store. Or just: Vanessa in a candy store.

"Oh, these? These are actually for Callie; Clint just needed an extra set of hands."

Vanessa was not amused. She reached out to snatch the presents, but suddenly she paused, her eyes honing in on the little blue box in Clint's hand. They grew wide, but she said nothing, watching Callie accept the gift.

Callie undid the white ribbon slowly, her pulse thundering as it fell away and revealed TIFFANY & CO. printed across the top. She opened the box.

"It's . . ."

"Here, allow me," Clint said, lifting from the folds of white tissue paper a beautiful heart-shaped pendant with a clear, sparkling stone at its center strung on a silver chain and moving to fasten it around her neck.

"It's . . . it's too much," Callie managed to stammer, nevertheless holding her hair out of the way. She fingered the pendant. It felt cool, a pleasant weight against her chest.

"Do you like it?" Clint grinned apprehensively.

"Like it? I *love* it," she decided, snapping to her senses. "It's just that—well, with the tickets, too, I mean, isn't this too much?"

"Tickets?" asked Clint. "What tickets?"

"*The* tickets," Callie said, lifting the envelope off the table. "You know, the tickets to hear Ian Mc— Oh. These aren't from you?"

"Ian Mc*Who*?" said Clint, squinting at the tickets. "No, definitely not from me." He handed them back to her.

"Oh. Somebody left them in my drop-box and there was no note or anything, so I just assumed it was you."

"Nope." He shook his head.

"Hmm," Callie murmured. Well, then who—

"Time to go!" Tyler cried, offering his arm to Vanessa, who had arranged her own gifts on the coffee table.

"Thank you so much," Callie said to Clint as he helped her into her coat.

"Of course," he said, wrapping his arms around her from behind and kissing her cheek. "I'm just glad you like it."

Her fingers flew to her throat and ran along the chain once more. It was beautiful—and no doubt Vanessa would find a way to make it known exactly how expensive once they were back in the room—but for some reason, during the entire walk to the Pudding, Callie was distracted: wondering who, if not Clint, had left her that envelope.

The inside of the Pudding bore an odd resemblance to their living room: the walls were adorned with huge shiny red hearts and dozens of helium balloons grazed the high ceiling in the main room, their strings dangling—magenta, red, pale pink, and white—fluttering just above the heads of the members and the spring punches.

Callie and Clint stood in front of a table in the foyer filled with rows and rows of nametags. Callie skimmed the names but did not see hers anywhere. She stared down at the table, reading each card one by one, row by row, but still could not find her name. Had they forgotten her? Or did somebody steal it? Maybe Lexi—

"Here you are," said Clint. "Is something wrong?"

"No, nothing," she said, taking deep breaths while he pinned the card to the strap of her dress. It had been there the whole time—on the members' side of the table. She had been scanning the punches.

"Drink?" he asked, nodding toward the main room. There was no bartender tonight; instead, hundreds of flutes of something pink and sparkling lined the tables, a single raspberry bobbing in each glass. "Wait here—I'll be right back," he said, squeezing her hand.

Despite the different decorations and her new status, as denoted by the color of her nametag, the party felt like a déjà vu version of Callie's first punch event. Everyone seemed just as hyperaware of what everyone else was wearing: tonight outfit color simply happened to take precedence over the inside labels. And, while young men in green steered clear of girls in red dresses, punches still flocked to red nametags like moths to a flame. Callie wished she could tell them—especially the ones who were sweating or laughing too loudly while making off-color jokes or longingly eyeing the line for the bathroom—that they didn't have to try so hard: most of the members had already made their decisions during the pre-punch slide show based on factors beyond the punch's control.

But instead she stayed silent, trying to plaster her face with the same unreadable smile worn by the members as they made mental notes of any "character-revealing details" that they would later post anonymously to the punch profiles on HPpunch.com. The supposed purpose of said profiles was to allow members to read up on punches they had missed meeting during the event, but from the way a lot of the older girls were smirking or emitting a tiny cough when a punch turned around, Callie had a bad feeling about the contents of the so-called "punch book."

Suddenly she was surrounded. *Hi, I'm Erica—Nicholas—Reid, so nice to meet you—Pleased to meet you, I'm Beth—Oh, wow, love the dress: Versace, right?—Killer shoes—Who does your hair?—You look familiar, are you in my Ec10 section? There's this great study guide I could pass along—Can I get you anything? A drink?—Your boyfriend's a lucky guy, if you don't mind my saying so—What's your favorite band? Because my dad can get tickets to, like, any show—the* Crimson, *huh? My cousin's a junior editor at the* Wall Street Journal *if you're ever interested in talking about internships—*

Callie turned in a spare second between conversations to locate Clint: she spotted him at the opposite end of the other room, holding two champagne flutes, similarly trapped. Every time he excused himself he made it only two steps closer to her before being intercepted. Seeing Callie, he gave her a *Well, what can you do?* sort of a shrug and set one of the glasses down so he could shake hands.

Give me your cell, we could grab lunch in the d-hall sometime—When do you usually hit the gym?—So I'll just e-mail you about that class, then—Facebook me!

"What a beautiful necklace." It was Lexi. This was the first time she had acknowledged Callie's existence since the article outing the sex tape situation had appeared in the *Crimson*. Callie opened her mouth, but no words came out. "Really, it's stunning," Lexi said. "Enjoy the party." Then she was gone, making her way back to the main room. The punches clustered around Callie quickly said their good-byes and trailed after Lexi, recognizing, perhaps, someone of far superior status.

Her sight-line suddenly clear, Callie saw Gregory stumble out of the coatroom, followed shortly thereafter by Alessandra. She giggled as she watched him redo the top two buttons on his midnight blue shirt—clearly he was too cool for themes—and then adjusted the straps on her fire-engine red dress which, under any other circumstance, would have screamed *GO GO GO* to anyone planning an approach.

"Excuse me," Callie blurted to the sophomore who had just introduced himself, making a beeline for the swinging set of doors that led into the kitchen. When she felt like she could breathe again, she hoisted herself onto a counter, the metal cool where it pressed against the back of her legs.

"Hiding?" a girl's voice came from behind her. "Don't worry, I am, too." Callie turned and saw a girl with long dirty-blond hair and a pageant-worthy smile leaning against the wall near the kitchen sink. She spoke with what sounded like a Texas accent, all chipper and southern. "If I have to kiss one more person's butt tonight," she said, coming over to Callie, "I swear I'm gonna scr—"

Her lips froze in place, her eyes zeroed in on Callie's nametag.

"Oh—oh no, this? No!" Callie cried, throwing her hand over her chest. "I promise I am just as sick of having my butt kissed as you are of, uh, kissing it."

Grinning, the girl hoisted herself onto the counter next to Callie, wiggling to smooth out the wrinkles in her emerald green dress. "Today of all days we should be hunting down boys to kiss, not butts, am I right?"

Callie laughed.

"Though . . . from the looks of it," the girl said, eyeing Callie's dress, "you already have a boyfriend."

"Yep. He's out there."

"And you're in here?"

"He's . . . very . . . popular," Callie said, dissolving into inexplicable giggles.

"I see," said the girl. "I'm Shelby, by the way. Shelby Samuel. No relation to Shell Oil, though, in case you were gonna ask."

"I wasn't."

"Good," said Shelby, lowering her voice in a conspiratorial way. "Because I think the rest of them may have made a terrible mistake."

Callie laughed. "I'm Callie," she said, pointing to her nametag. "Last fall's 'mistake.'"

"*Pssh,*" Shelby snorted with a sassy wave of her hand. "You're the first person I've met tonight who doesn't look like she's trying to balance an invisible book on her head—or how about that one girl who turned up her nose at the very sight of me, as if I'd got dog doo-doo on my shoe?"

"Who—Anne?" Callie blurted gleefully. Swiveling around to make certain they were alone, she whispered, "I wouldn't take it personally. I think that's just the way her face is!"

Shelby threw her head back, her hearty laughter joined with Callie's giggles.

"Ah," Callie finally sighed, wiping her eyes. "But you know," she said, suddenly solemn, "they're not *all* bad."

"Like your boyfriend?"

"Uh-huh." Callie nodded. "And my roommate Mimi—she's amazing—and the guys from across the hall, OK and Gregory—"

"Right," Shelby agreed. "I know who they are."

"Yeah," Callie muttered, remembering that her roommate and neighbors enjoyed something of a celebrity status on campus. "Hey!" she blurted. "Have you ever noticed how it seems like everyone from New York, and all the international students, kind of knew each other beforehand—I mean, like before we even got to school and like they still somehow know . . . I don't know . . . *more* than we do?"

"About what?" Shelby asked in a mock hushed tone, her eyes twinkling—though not unkindly.

"About . . . oh, I don't know, East Coast things: all the unspoken rules and cultural stuff—and, well, don't you ever feel like they're all part of some super-secret members only network or club or something?"

Shelby grinned. "I think you might be right. In fact," she continued in a whisper, "I believe we may have infiltrated their ranks and are trapped inside their headquarters at this very moment!" she said, pointing toward the doors.

"Huh." Callie fiddled with her nametag, remembering the moment of panic she'd experienced earlier while trying to find it, scanning the wrong side of the table. It was the same feeling as when she'd watched Mimi and Vanessa receive those first little white envelopes. Even though she'd had no idea what was inside, she had desperately wanted one, though it was hard to say exactly why. . . .

Why *do* I care? Dana and Matt had no problem saying no when she'd extended the invitation—

"Callie Andrews, may I tell you a secret?" Shelby interrupted her reverie.

"Sure," said Callie.

"When you came in, I wasn't exactly hiding—I was actually looking for a way out."

Callie sighed. "That door in the back leads out to the garden. If you follow the path on your left, it'll take you all the way around the side of the club and out onto Garden Street."

"Hallelujah, amen," Shelby exclaimed dramatically, leaping off the counter and reaching for her coat and purse. "I mean—no offense to y'all or anything—I just thought I'd be stuck here all night!"

"Nope, you're free!" Callie told her with a small smile. "Though—are you sure you don't want to stick around?"

"I'm sure," said Shelby. "But it was nice to meet you, Callie Andrews. Let's do lunch in the dining hall sometime."

"It's a date," Callie called as Shelby pulled the back door shut behind her. A moment later it swung open again, but it wasn't Shelby; it was—

"*You.* Are you following me—*again*?"

Gregory smirked. "Contrary to what you seem to believe, I am not aware of your whereabouts most of the time." Reaching up into one of the cabinets, he pulled out a bottle of Maker's Mark. "I don't do pink," he explained, pouring some into a glass. "Why are you in here anyway?" he asked after he'd taken a sip.

"Just having a minor existential crisis," she muttered.

"Ah. Somebody's been doing her reading for Postwar Fiction and Theory."

"Ugh, the French existentialists are so dense!" she exclaimed. "Personally I can't wait until we get to the later part of the twentieth century and start reading Coetzee, Ishiguro, McEwan—" She stared at him. "It was you."

"Hm?" he asked, arching his eyebrows.

"*You* left those tickets in my drop-box."

"Oh, to hear McEwan?" He swallowed the rest of his whiskey. "Yep, that was me."

So casual. So very, very casual. "Why?"

"I bought them a month ago, before coach gave us our spring schedule. Turns out we have an away game that weekend. I noticed you reading *Atonement* in the library the other day, so I figured you might want them."

But—why—he'd noticed?—*when*—and today, of all days? "There are two tickets," she finally said stupidly.

"Yeah, well . . . you could take Clint," he suggested.

"If you have an away game, won't he be gone that weekend, too?"

Gregory shrugged. His glass made a loud clinking sound as he set it on the counter. "Look, it was either that or the trash, so I figured I'd give the whole *friendly* thing a try—"

"You thought you'd give it a try *today?*" she countered.

"*There* you are," Clint cried, the kitchen doors swinging shut behind him. "We have *got* to get out of here," he said. He had Callie's coat thrown over his arm. Lifting it aside, he revealed a bottle of pink champagne. "We can still salvage the evening if we sneak out now. . . . Oh, hey, man," he added, nodding at Gregory. "It almost seems like someone planned this whole party just to keep people from really celebrating tonight, doesn't it?" he asked his teammate.

Maybe someone did, Callie thought darkly, remembering how genuinely sweet Lexi had sounded earlier when she'd complimented her new necklace.

Gregory nodded.

"Not to mention forcing people to talk about certain things before they're ready," Clint continued. "I think Tyler and Vanessa are about to break up—if they were ever together in the first place. They've been fighting outside the bathroom for the past twenty minutes: she keeps accusing him of flirting with the punches and telling him that they're only interested because he's the president, and no matter what she says, he keeps yelling 'yellow' over and over and over again. We've got to get out of here," he repeated.

Callie laughed.

"Well, I should probably go find *my* girlfriend," Gregory said abruptly, making his way to the door.

Girlfriend? There it was again, this time straight from the horse's mouth.

"Good night," he called.

Callie breathed an enormous sigh as the door *whooshed* shut behind him, and then she beamed at Clint from across the room.

"Ready?" he asked. Coming over to the counter, he looped Callie's coat over her head and used it to pull her toward him, one leg on either side.

"Ah!" she screamed. Then: "Oh . . ." His hands moved from her knees up the length of her thighs, up to the lacy rims of the black stockings Mimi had lent her for the occasion. Wrapping her legs around his waist, she kissed him. His hands on her hips, he pulled her closer, accidentally knocking over the bottle of champagne resting next to her on the counter.

Glancing at it, Callie grinned. "We're in a kitchen," she said.

"I know."

"A *public* kitchen."

"That is correct."

She bit her lip. "Wanna get out of here?"

In response he lifted her off the counter and carried her over to the back door. "I thought you'd never ask."

FOUR

THE LADIES WHO BRUNCH

Feb 19 Behind the Ivy-Covered Walls: Part II

11:13AM By THE IVY INSIDER

On Valentine's Eve, the Hasty Pudding social club hosted a cocktail party called "STOP! In the name of LOVE." The mandatory "stoplight" theme required students to signal their availability for sexual encounters using the color of their clothing. Though perhaps, given the power dynamics that govern the punch process, the term *sexual transactions* is more apt.

This event was the culmination of a grueling thirty-six hours spent poring over a slide show featuring photographs of the club's prospective punches. The top-secret process has sometimes been referred to as "The *Ass*ets Assessment"—pun intended—because the majority of the conversation revolves around the punch's physical appearance and (parental) net worth. This spring's meeting was no exception. Male students ranked female prospects on a scale of 1–10 while female members designated certain underclassmen as "high priority" based on a mysterious value system.

For a further glimpse at the posturing typical of 2 Garden Street, refer to the screenshot below of an anonymously submitted invitation, traditionally slipped under a prospective punch's door in the middle of the night.

It's time for . . .
BRUNCH!
A limousine will await your arrival tomorrow at 11 A.M.
On the corner of Bow and Arrow Streets.
Please come dressed in your Sunday finest
And prepare to postpone any other obligations.
We look forward to seeing you then.

THE HASTY PUDDING SOCIAL CLUB, EST. 1770

Brunches and lunches are a standard means of weeding out people prior to the second event. The school wasn't invited, but perhaps the Insider will be. . . .

"Andrews!" Grace barked at the close of the Sunday morning meeting. The rest of the COMPers stood and started gathering their things. "A word, if you please."

Callie froze, wondering what sort of trouble she might have gotten herself into this time. In the past three weeks since COMP had started, she had completed every assignment on time, never missed a meeting, and had avoided any accidental drunken make-outs with her COMP director's ex-boyfriend. Though if Grace had an ex or even a current boyfriend, Callie doubted she would know, since Grace refused to allow her personal life to interfere with her professional persona—if last week's Teddy Bear Incident was any indication.

(On the Tuesday after Valentine's Day a teddy bear that looked suspiciously like the one Callie had seen Matt carrying in their common room had showed up on Grace's desk. After furiously confronting the staff, who met her with total silence, Grace had used large thumbtacks to secure the bear to the *Crimson*'s main bulletin board with the words *IS THIS YOUR IDEA OF A JOKE?* tacked underneath. Poor Matt—*if* he was responsible.)

"What's your take on these Ivy Insider posts on FlyBy?" Grace asked, coming over and perching on the corner of Callie's desk.

Okay, not what I was expecting. "Um . . . Whoever's writing them seems to strongly dislike social clubs?"

Grace folded her arms, scrutinizing Callie. "So—you don't know *who's* writing it?"

"Don't *you* know?" Callie countered.

"I have my ideas. . . ." Grace was still staring at her in a manner reminiscent of the Terminator or some other robot with X-ray vision. "But I can't say for certain. The person responsible has been posting everything anonymously, subject to my administrative approval—*whoever* that person might be."

Was Grace trying to confide in Callie: to confess that *she* was behind the blog? Callie had known Grace long enough to witness several of her anti-Final Clubs, anti-elitist, anti-hetero-normative, "phallocentricity" of Harvard society rants. But the newspaper itself published frequent op-eds in this vein, so it wouldn't make any sense for Grace to disguise her already highly publicized opinions under a veil of anonymity. Would it?

"Any guesses?" Grace prodded.

"Maybe . . ." said Callie, starting to nod very slowly. "But *whoever* it is must have some kind of inside source, because they seem to know a lot of specific details about certain organizations . . . things that only a member would know."

"Right," Grace agreed, nodding now too. "Maybe a member with a *reason* to hate these institutions but who can still blend in like she—or he—belongs."

"You don't think . . ." Callie stared at Grace, wondering if she could possibly be implying that Callie was the Insider, given the blog's fleeting reference to the sex tape article. "I mean . . . I'm not . . ."

Grace cleared her throat. "While as a journalist first and

foremost I cannot claim to condone the anonymity factor—"

Right, thought Callie.

"—and will continue vetting the content thoroughly to ensure that it does not violate our ethical standards, I certainly sympathize with the motive and general sentiment," Grace finished.

Callie stayed silent. Grace's tone still seemed to signify an implicit double meaning, almost like she had caught Callie red-handed at something but was urging her to continue while she, Grace, looked the other way. "You do know that I'm in the Pudding, and that I COMPed *FM* and that I still read the magazine, right?" Callie finally said.

"Yes," said Grace. "Just like you know that as managing editor of the *Crimson* and head of all its affiliates, I cannot personally disband any of our publications—even the ones that glorify images of certain deplorable institutions that the Insider is working hard to dispel."

"Grace," said Callie. "I'm not the Insider."

"Of course you're not," Grace said, standing. "And I only created FlyBy to offer multiple perspectives on the social side of campus in order to dilute the highly questionable advice and opinions that flow from the corrupt hands of a tiny self-congratulating subset."

"So you're not trying to, like . . ." Callie glanced over her shoulder to where the teddy bear still hung, crucified, on the bulletin board. ". . . *destroy* the magazine or anything, are you?"

Grace stared at her for a full count of three and then erupted into laughter. "Jesus, Andrews, would you look at your face?" she asked. "Remember, I'm not the one with a drawer full of other peoples' secrets locked away in my desk." She laughed again. "Although it is true that there's no telling what will happen to *FM* once FlyBy takes off." She paused, appearing to consider it. "One thing I can say for certain is that from a personal standpoint, I would have no problem seeing a shakedown in the leadership upstairs."

Callie cracked a smile. "That would be something. . . ." she conceded. She pictured Lexi dethroned (from her ergonomic office chair) and forced into exile (i.e., to go live in the quad), allowed to drink only tap water and use only gym-regulation shampoo and obligated to take public transportation to class. A tiny shiver of fear ran through her for entertaining the very thoughts, and she quickly pushed them out of her mind. Her strategy this semester involved lying low and staying as far away from Lexi as possible. So if a showdown was brewing between *FM* and FlyBy, or between Lexi and Grace, Callie refused to be caught in the middle.

"If it's all right with you, I have to run," she said, standing. "I've got a brunch to get to that started ten minutes ago."

"Ah," said Grace with a nod. "For the Pudding, isn't that right?"

"Yep," said Callie.

"Makes sense," Grace replied. "Run along, then. I look forward to reading your next installment."

Callie stopped just before the door. "On the recent renovations to the men's soccer facilities?"

"Right," said Grace, nodding again in that oddly exaggerated way. "On the recent renovations in the men's soccer facilities."

"Good afternoon, and welcome to the Harvard Club of Boston. Please follow me to the main clubhouse dining room," the maitre d' said, leading the way up an enormous staircase carpeted in plush, crimson velvet.

Callie looked at Mimi, her eyes wide. "Mimosas, mimosas," Mimi said by way of encouragement. "Mimosas without bottom—"

"Bottomless," Callie hissed as they made their way up the stairs.

"Watch who you call bottomless; there is not a lot of junk *dans ton* trunk either," Mimi muttered back, smacking Callie on the rear.

Callie shrieked but quickly suppressed her giggles a moment later for they had arrived. With its hanging chandeliers and bay windows draped with thick red curtains to match the Oriental rug and cushiony lining on the ornate wooden chairs, the main dining room was everything that Callie had come to expect from the Harvard Brand. It was also fairly empty for a Sunday, and a little noise went a long way.

Alexis Thorndike, who had been placed by some twisted hand of fate (otherwise known as Tyler) in the same brunch group as Callie, didn't even turn to bother with the *You're-late-and-perpetually-inappropriate* look Anne was giving them now. The two junior girls were seated around a table near the window with four spring punches, including Vanessa, a girl called Penelope whom Callie recognized from the slide show, and another named Sydney whom she'd met at the first event, and, last but certainly not least, Alessandra. The latter sat between Anne and Lexi like she was their favorite little sister. Callie and Mimi, who had missed the limousine due to *Crimson* and *Lampoon* duties respectively, took the empty chairs on either side of Vanessa, completing the punch-member alternating order.

"Quick, you've got a lot of catching up to do," Vanessa muttered. She grabbed a glass pitcher full of orange juice and champagne and filled Mimi's glass. "The limo had an open bar so—"

The rest of her sentence was rendered wholly irrelevant when Anne let forth the most delicate, ladylike burp—but it was still a burp—that Callie had ever heard, followed by quite possibly the oddest thing ever to come out of Alexis Thorndike's mouth, second only to "Callie, you're my best friend": a giggle.

"Mmm! Excuse me," Anne said, slightly mortified. Then, patting the corners of her mouth with a napkin, she drew herself up and, with a look of immense dignity, explained: "In Tokyo the Japanese consider it customary to drink during a business dinner and are reluctant to do dealings with those who abstain. Why? Because they assume that if a person refuses alcohol, it means they have something to hide: some ugly character flaw that would surface if their inhibitions were at bay. And so we must drink during punch brunches, too, to determine if we shall fare well in friendship and in club business. *Kanpai*," she finished, raising her glass.

"Yes," Lexi agreed, "and cheers to Japanese Pop Culture, one of the easier core classes offered at this school and for which we have a study guide on file at the club."

Penelope and Sydney looked suitably impressed, while Vanessa nodded in a very all-knowing, slightly off-putting way and Alessandra gave a tiny shrug as if to say, *Study guides are merely the concern of people who are actually interested in studying.*

Mimi glanced at Callie, her gray eyes wide, and then downed her mimosa in a single gulp. "*Un autre, s'il vous plaît*," she said, waving her hand at Vanessa. The corners of her mouth twitched. "And please do not go forgetting my fellow member and your fellow roommate Caliente, who is also very thirsty."

Vanessa rolled her eyes but filled Callie's glass as well. Leaning back, Callie took a sip, beginning to enjoy herself.

It was short-lived. A waitress arrived and Anne ordered appetizers and entrees for the table, urging their server to "keep the champagne coming." With a sinking sensation, Callie remembered a little tidbit from the pre-punch meeting that she had otherwise conveniently managed to block out of her head: *We expect you—unofficially, of course—to treat the punches to lunch from your personal accounts,* Anne had said. *So it was done for you, and so you shall do for them. . . .*

Callie wondered if she would be able to pick up enough extra shifts at Lamont to cover her portion of the meal. Biting her lip, she exhaled and then downed a giant gulp of her mimosa. Perhaps Anne would consider some kind of an installment plan—if it was even worth the humiliation to ask.

A voice in the back of her head that sounded uncannily like Grace's whispered, "The social clubs offer limited to no financial aid options, making it nearly impossible for students from more disadvantaged socioeconomic backgrounds to join."

Callie took another sip and tried to appear something other than *bored to tears* while Penelope told a harrowing tale from her boarding school days.

". . . and that was the day when my life really changed," Penelope was finishing. "Finally I realized: I don't *like* Gucci—*unless* it's Gucci Premiere haute couture."

"That is just *so* spot on," Anne agreed. "You know, I really wish we had spent more time together when I was still at Deerfield."

"I know exactly what you mean," Vanessa jumped in. "The other day in Armani—"

"Speaking of wishes," Lexi interceded, "Alessandra, I do wish I could persuade you away from the *Crimson* and into joining *FM*. As I'm sure Callie can tell you, we have much more fun."

Callie almost choked on a walnut from her pear and endive salad. Lexi smiled sweetly at her while she took a huge sip of water.

"But Callie's COMPing the *Crimson* with me," Alessandra said slowly. "She helped me get set up on my very first day." Alessandra beamed at her. Callie, still short of breath, could only nod in return.

"Yes, well, most unfortunately Callie was cut from my magazine in the final round—to my great disappointment, as I'm sure you can imagine," Lexi said.

Callie spit the remainder of her mimosa back into her glass; luckily no one seemed to notice, save for Vanessa, who kicked her under the table. Frowning, Callie was about to kick her back when Vanessa shot a *Don't-you-ruin-this-for-me* look in her direction.

"I fancied myself as something of a mentor to her," Lexi breezed on, "but now she's gone over to the dark side, to that dreadful Grace. You'll see soon, dear," she added to Alessandra.

"She is super intense," Alessandra agreed.

"I think she's brilliant," Callie blurted.

"Perhaps," Lexi conceded without missing a beat, "but there is a reason why they call her the femi-nazi. She basically hates everything that any reasonable person would consider 'fun' on this campus. That's why her little FlyBy project will, regrettably, struggle to retain a readership and ultimately fail, because she just doesn't know how to give the readers what they want: glamour, entertainment, and excellent—if I do say so myself—advice."

"A lot of people seem to be talking about that Ivy Insider thing," Vanessa piped up.

Lexi smiled serenely. "A mere fluke on an otherwise uninteresting site," she said, waving her hand. "Honestly I wouldn't be surprised if Grace were writing it herself. It sounds exactly like her: 'Social clubs are the root of all evil; they must be destroyed.' But allow me to let you all in on a little secret."

Everyone at the table leaned forward.

"The beautiful thing about people like Grace is that one day, they always go too far. Even if they appear to be a nuisance or seem to be getting in your way, you don't have to lift a single finger because ultimately, they will always be their own undoing."

A strange hush seemed to have fallen across the room, and Callie felt the same shiver of fear that she'd experienced earlier in the *Crimson*. But then Lexi's expression brightened and she said cheerily, "Enough talk of silly rivalries! Especially when what we really want is to hear more about all of you!"

Sydney and Penelope exchanged a nervous glance.

"Yes," Anne agreed. "We already know where you're from, what subjects you're studying, and what you like to do for fun. . . . Why not tell us something a little juicier—something embarrassing?"

"Or something that you've never told anyone else before," Lexi added, nodding enthusiastically.

Everyone stayed silent. Even the two girls who were undergoing The Lexi Experience for the first time were smart enough not to spill.

Anne's attempt to force—ahem—*facilitate* bonding reminded Callie of the first week of school when her entryway's prefect Charlie Sloane had made them play a game called Two Truths and Lie in an attempt to get everyone better acquainted. She cleared her throat. "We could, uh, play a game?"

"A game?" said Anne.

"Yeah, like, uh . . ." She looked at Mimi and Vanessa.

"Well, there's the classic Fuck-Chuck-Marry," Vanessa dove in, "or Would You Rather, or—ooh—I know, how about we play Never Have I Ever!"

"Never have I ever . . . what?" asked Mimi.

"It's very simple," Vanessa explained. "Everybody holds up five fingers," she said, raising her palm above her half-eaten eggs Benedict, "and then each girl goes around the circle and says something that she's never done before, and if you *have* done the thing she says, you have to put a finger down—and drink!"

"The last girl left standing wins," Anne added.

"Or loses," Alessandra offered with a sultry wink, "depending on how you see it."

"Penelope, why don't you start us off," said Lexi, who, skeptical at first, had warmed to the idea.

"Okay," said Penelope, setting down her fork. "Here's an easy one that ought to knock most, if not all of you, back by a finger. Never have I ever had sex."

Six fingers went down amidst an exchange of smiles and knowing nods. The only two girls left with all five remaining were Penelope and—

"Really, Vanessa?" asked Anne. "You and Tyler haven't . . . ?"

Vanessa, her cheeks slightly pink, shook her head.

Lexi smirked. "Take it from someone older, Vanessa, when I say that you can't expect him to wait forever. He *is* a guy, after all, and this is college, not high school, so the rules—"

"Actually, you *can* expect him to wait forever," Callie interrupted. "Forever or until you're ready, whichever one comes first." And you can always come and talk to me about it if it's bothering you, she added silently, wishing she could say it out loud. Vanessa, however, did not look particularly grateful for the intervention; Callie faltered, staring at the tablecloth.

"Ah, well, in *your* case," Lexi addressed Callie, "caution and taking everything in that arena very, very slowly are certainly advisable." She turned to the others: "I don't know if you had the opportunity to read recently about Callie's little on-screen adventures—"

"Don't worry, *Lex*," Callie blurted before she could stop to think, "Clint and I aren't planning anything with a camera any time soon."

If someone in the downstairs lounge had dropped a cuff link, they all would have been able to hear it.

"NEVER HAVE I EVER," Mimi boomed suddenly. "*Er,*

Jamais je n'ai jamais . . . Oh, je sais: Never have I ever stolen *juste un peu de cocaïne* from *une strip-teaseuse* in Ibiza!"

"What?" said Callie.

"Why are you drinking?" asked Vanessa.

"Because I just remembered," said Mimi, "that I have."

Vanessa shook her head. "My turn! Never have I ever . . ." She shot a sidelong glance at Callie. "Never have I ever hooked up with my best friend's crush."

Thanks a lot, dude, thought Callie, putting down another finger and taking a sip of her drink. Penelope had lowered a finger, too. So had Alessandra.

"In high school," Alessandra volunteered, "when people are petty about that sort of thing. As if I could possibly control the fact that he was never interested in her." She shrugged.

"Women are always complaining about men treating them like objects," Penelope chimed in, "but then we turn around and try to lay claim to ones we barely even know, as if we could call dibs." She laughed.

"I think there's something to be said for loyalty," Lexi said, silencing Penelope's laughter. "Why throw away a friendship for someone who is almost certainly *not* your soul mate? Men," she continued, lifting her glass, "are a dime a dozen, but best friends are forever." She beamed at Anne and they clinked their glasses, the rest of the table soon following suit.

"It's your turn," Vanessa said, nudging Callie.

"Right," said Callie. She glanced down at her nearly empty plate. "Never have I ever dined and dashed." Never have I ever even considered it—until today, she thought miserably. Mimi and Anne both put a finger down. "Also high school," Anne offered apologetically. "On a dare."

Their waitress appeared and began to clear the plates.

Sydney shifted in her chair. "Never have I ever gotten a grade below an A minus," she said.

There was a collective groan, and everyone put a finger down. Callie could practically see Lexi and Anne mentally writing *wet blanket* under Sydney's name on HPpunch.com.

"My turn?" Lexi asked as Anne signaled for the bill. Looking around the table, she took stock of the situation, noting who had the least number of fingers remaining. "Never have I ever hooked up with Gregory Bolton," she said finally with a mischievous glance at Alessandra.

Alessandra inhaled sharply. "What?" she whispered, staring, along with everyone else, at Callie's index finger, which she had unthinkingly lowered.

Crap crap double crap, thought Callie, clenching and unclenching her fist in an attempt to make it appear that random finger spasms were something that happened to her all the time.

Lexi narrowed her eyes at Callie. "When did *that* happen?"

No such luck.

"Freshman week, during le 'camp Harvard,'" Mimi quickly lied. Callie held her breath, waiting for Vanessa to contradict Mimi's story. Vanessa, however, just sipped her water silently.

"It was a silly mistake," Callie said. "The same one that the rest of our dorm and half the school also m— Oh . . . sorry," she said, grimacing at Alessandra. Lexi stared at her hard from across the table.

"I understand he has quite a reputation," Alessandra said, chewing on her lip.

"Pay no attention to them," Lexi said, placing a hand on Alessandra's back, "or to what anyone else has to say about Gregory. I've been friends with his cousin since he was in diapers, and in all that time I've never known him to go out with anyone more than once. Well, maybe twice, but that usually only meant that he forgot about the first time. He's different with you."

"He liiikes you," Anne said, elongating the i in a singsongy voice. Then she handed the waitress her credit card. Callie breathed an enormous sigh. All she had to worry about now was dodging Anne until she had the money to cover her portion of the bill: something that she unfortunately already had experience doing when her club dues had been late last semester. Speaking of which, she still had no idea who had mysteriously paid that hefty price. . . .

"Maybe he *more* than likes you," Lexi suggested, snapping Callie out of her reverie.

"Maybe . . ." Alessandra said slowly. "It's hard to tell. Things were very casual and irregular at first. You know, mostly he called only late at night or—"

"Didn't you read my article about never answering the phone after midnight?" Lexi interrupted with an expression of mock horror on her face.

"I did!" Vanessa cried. "It was totally genius. I also used your five simple steps to trick him out of the bedroom and into the restaurant on Tyler, and they worked like a—"

"Great," Lexi cut her off. "That's really great, Vanessa. Alessandra, you were saying?"

Alessandra smiled. "Something changed right around the time this semester started. He calls at more appropriate hours now. We go on actual dates. Last Sunday he asked if I wanted to get breakfast, and then he asked if I wanted to 'give being exclusive a try'—just like that!"

"Perhaps we can attribute some of the credit to our little Stoplight party," Anne ventured. "And by the way I've been meaning to tell you: I *loved* your dress."

"Ooh, yes, it was to die for," Vanessa agreed. "Did he get you anything special for Valentine's Day? Diamonds? A small island, perhaps? After all, he *is* a Bolton. An island would be, like, only a small chip in the old trust fund."

Alessandra wrinkled her nose. "He got me . . . a book."

Penelope grimaced sympathetically. "Well, you can't let yourself read too much into that, sweetie."

Or . . . you could actually *read* it, thought Callie. "Which book?" she blurted suddenly.

"What?" asked Alessandra.

"Um, you know—what was the title?" Callie asked.

"Honestly," said Alessandra, "I don't even remember. We have so much reading to do for class—it's like he assigned me extra homework."

"I'll have to give him a talking to the next time I see him," Lexi said, her eyes darting to Callie—specifically to her neck. "Although at least a book is a lot more *personal* than some *generic* item of jewelry." Smirking, she pulled a compact out of her purse and checked her lip gloss. Callie's hand flew to the necklace Clint had given her. Jealous much!?

"Actually," Alessandra mused, "I do think it's nice that he doesn't feel the need to flaunt his wealth."

Damn, thought Callie. And just when I was about ready to give myself permission to start calling you Perky Boobs again. Clearly P—*Alessandra*—had yet to meet the Compensation Car: the Porsche 911 Carrera.

"It's your turn," Anne prompted Alessandra. She must have been dying to tell them that never had she ever worn white after Labor Day or something.

"Oh!" said Alessandra. "Let's see. . . . Never have I ever . . . been in love. At least not *yet*," she finished with a smile.

Callie and Lexi watched each other lower a finger like two shooters might while lowering their guns.

"I'm out," Callie said. "I lose."

"*Au contraire*, you win!" Mimi cried. "Is that the limo I see outside?" she added, pointing to the window.

"Yes, it should be here by now," said Anne. "Who's up for swinging by Newbury Street to do a little shopping?"

"I am!" Vanessa cried.

"Me too," said Penelope.

"What time will we get home?" asked Sydney as everyone stood and walked toward the stairs. "Because I have a *lot* of work that I should really get started on. . . ."

"Callie."

Callie stopped walking and turned.

Alessandra had hung back. "Could I talk to you for a second?"

Callie shot Mimi an imploring look, but Mimi just shrugged and bounded down the stairs.

"What's up?" Callie asked when Alessandra had reached her, though she was fairly certain she had an idea.

"We're friends, right?" Alessandra asked.

Callie hesitated.

"What I mean is that I think you're cool and that I would *like* to be friends," Alessandra amended.

"Me too," said Callie slowly. And it was true; at least Callie found disliking Alessandra difficult, even in spite of her growing bond with Lexi . . . and with Gregory.

"Great," said Alessandra. She was quiet for a moment. "Gregory thinks very highly of you," she said eventually.

"What makes you say that?" Callie asked, looking out over the railing at the first floor below.

"Just something he said after class last week," Alessandra answered. "But he didn't need to say anything; I can tell from the way he listens when you talk."

"What did he say?" Callie asked, unable to resist.

"It was kind of nice in a mean way, actually. He said that you'd be a lot less annoying if you weren't so smart. At the time

I thought nothing of it, but now, given that there's a history . . ."

"I wouldn't really call it a *history*," Callie said. Well, at least not if you define *history* by actual events (sum total: ~six hours) rather than amount of time wasted obsessing (sum total: ~way too embarrassing to tally). Or a *history* of pissing me off! "A lot less annoying"—what the hell was that?

"Anyway, we're just friends," Callie finished. "Not even friends, really, just friendly. Maybe even more neighborly than friendly." It all depends on the day of the week, Gregory's mood, and the position of the moon in relation to the earth and sun.

"So . . . that thing at the beginning of the year . . . ?"

"It was just . . ." Callie hesitated. It was one thing to lie by omission but another to do it directly to someone's face, even if she didn't owe Alessandra anything. "One moment, nothing serious," she finished finally. "And it already feels like it happened a million years ago."

Alessandra still watched her, hovering at the top of the stairs.

"I'm really, really happy with my boyfriend, Clint. He's all I want. So I can honestly say that you have nothing to worry about with Gregory—from me at least," Callie said. Can't make any guarantees on behalf of the rest of the female population. "But I think . . . I guess I agree with Lexi that he's capable of reforming and could one day be . . . a really solid guy for someone. And it sounds like, from everything you said, that maybe that person is you."

"You really think so?" Alessandra asked.

"Su—" The rest of the word was lost as Alessandra enveloped her in a boob-crushing hug.

"Isn't Lexi *great*?" Alessandra exclaimed when they finally started down the stairs.

". . . Sure," said Callie, vowing to cut down on the white lies starting tomorrow.

"I'm so glad," Alessandra finished with a huge smile, "that the three of us are all becoming friends."

FIVE

Jackie or Marilyn?

A Brief Q&A with Governor Joseph Hamilton
Brought to you by FM *Magazine*

FM: What type of degree would you recommend for a student who is interested in going into politics (other than the obvious: to make sure that it's from Harvard!)?

Hamilton: Harvard is certainly not a prerequisite; after all, you can get Cs from Yale and still go on to be president of the United States! But in all seriousness, drive and charisma will get you further than whatever you learn in Government or Social Studies, which is what I studied when I was here.

FM: How does it feel to be the first moderate governor elected in a state that has voted Democrat in the last five presidential elections?

Hamilton: It feels great! Frankly I interpret my election as a mandate for change. The people have spoken. That's the beautiful thing about democracy.

FM: What's your favorite thing about your state?

Hamilton: I'd like to be able to say that we have a mighty fine baseball team, but the truth is: I'm a Red Sox fan. Really, though, Maryland is a beautiful state with many local attractions, but it's the people who make us great.

FM: The FDA or NIH?

Hamilton: Both are crucial federal institutes that do very different yet equally important things.

FM: Final question: Jackie or Marilyn?

Hamilton: I'm not really sure what that means, but this seems like a case where I should plead the Fifth.

The Harvard Crimson

Online Edition: Op-Eds

The Word of the Week
By Grace Lee

Nepotism *(noun)*

> (From Italian *nepotismo* < Latin nepos ("nephew"), a reference to the practice of popes appointing relatives (most often nephews) as cardinals during the Middle Ages and Renaissance)
>
> 1. The favoring of relatives or personal friends because of their relationship rather than because of their abilities.
>   *Nepotism can get you very far in the world if you've got the right connections.*

Nepotism runs rampant at Harvard. Of course, students cannot control who—or how famous—their relatives are. What they can control is how they use that favoritism.

Yesterday *FM* was granted an exclusive interview with Governor Hamilton over the *Harvard Crimson*. (His niece happens to be their advice columnist. Coincidence? We think not.)

Of all the things the interviewer could have asked about—his recent tiff with the labor unions, budget cuts to charter schools, teacher layoffs in Baltimore, the declining crime rate—it seems the most important was to learn the Governor's response to the completely asinine question (unfortunately typical of the magazine) "Jackie or Marilyn?" which was, incidentally, no comment.

This *Crimson* editor also has no further comment.

"Thank you all for coming to hear me speak today," Governor Hamilton said from where he was standing behind a podium in the Starr Auditorium at the Harvard Kennedy School of Government. He bore a certain resemblance to the man for whom the center was named, tall and charismatic with boyish good looks and chestnut-colored hair that, save for a sprinkling of gray, was the exact same shade as his niece's. "And remember, no matter what state you hail from, or with which party you vote, I wish you the best of luck wherever your career paths may take you, and in the remainder of the academic year."

"Take enough notes there, Marie Meloney?" Clint asked, watching Callie scribbling in her spiral-bound notebook.

Clint had been poking fun at her with various nicknames ever since he'd caught her Wikipedia-ing "famous female journalists" the other day.

"Marie Meloney started working for the *Washington Post* when she was just sixteen; she interviewed all kinds of famous people, from Mussolini to Marie Curie, and was best friends with Eleanor Roosevelt. I would be extremely lucky to have half the career that she did," Callie retorted, her pen still flitting furiously across the page.

"Okay—jeez," Clint said with a laugh, "by all means go ahead and finish that novel you're working on." It was true that she had, perhaps, been a tad overzealous, trying to write down everything the governor said word-for-word. But Grace had ordered her there on assignment—she loved saying that, "on assignment"—and she was determined to be thorough. "Just don't forget that we have dinner plans," Clint added.

"How could I forget?" she said, finally slamming her notebook shut. "I've been losing sleep over it for days!"

"Relax, they're going to love you," Clint said, rubbing her back.

Callie was not so sure. If Clint had snuck up behind her in the library five minutes earlier while she was surfing the web the other day, he would have found her on the Wiki for "The Webers." Yes, they had their own Wikipedia page. They also had vacation homes in Nantucket (which turned out not to be, as previously believed, the name of an Indian reservation) and the Bahamas, box seats at the DC Opera and FedEx Field (home to the Washington Redskins), a wing named after them in the Smithsonian, and one humble hundred-and-twenty-foot "sailboat." His mom was some sort of famous Washington lobbyist, and his dad worked at a think tank (which turned out not to be, as previously believed, a clear glass enclosure in which you float around and think).

To excuse this Vanessa-ish behavior she could only claim self-defense, and news of Clint's family prestige failed to excite her, unless excitement had the exact same symptoms as dread.

"Eight o'clock at Rialto," Clint reminded her. "Want me to pick you up after you go home to change?"

She raised her eyebrows. "I did this on purpose, you know," she said, pointing to the tomato soup stain on her plain white

T-shirt. Her mom had a rule against white for a reason.

"I know," he said, grabbing her hand and kissing it. "Just like you spilled coffee on me the first time we *officially* met so you'd have an excuse to talk to me."

"Exactly," she said, following him out of the auditorium. "Now tell me one last time: is there anything else I should know about your parents before I meet them? Any pet peeves or—"

"I would avoid mentioning the bill proposing more funding for Virginia school systems that just recently failed to pass—it was one of Emilee's pet projects—and John will only warm up to you if you know something about squash or old Western films or, if all else fails, you ask him about his Princeton days."

That voice, sweet and musical like wind chimes—wind chimes in the middle of a storm, that is—could belong only to one person.

Alexis Thorndike was walking directly behind them, eavesdropping.

"I'm *so* sorry about the mix-up earlier," she said, falling into step beside them. "Callie if I had known you were coming, I would have saved you a seat in the front row as well."

"We were fine in the back, weren't we?" Clint said, smiling at Callie. "But we do appreciate the thought."

We, we, we—the sound of it filled Callie with an unbelievable satisfaction, and not just because it had probably caused Lexi's blood temperature to spike to a whopping 212 degrees Fahrenheit.

"Uncle Joe will be in town through the end of the week if you'd like me to introduce you. Perhaps at the Faculty Club's cocktail party this Thursday evening? I could easily swing you an invitation—both of you."

How very charitable, thought Callie. Will you be able to count that toward your community service hours?

"Thank you," said Clint, picture-perfectly polite, "but unfortunately we have other plans that evening." He took Callie's hand.

"I'll forward you the evite—just in case you change your mind."

"Sounds good," he said, ignoring Callie's frown.

"Well, then," Lexi said, stopping, "I suppose I'll see you later. Do give Emilee and John my fond regards."

When they were just out of hearing range, Callie made a vomiting sound.

Clint closed one eye. "Was that really necessary?"

In response she did it again.

"Real mature," he said, smiling nonetheless.

"I'm sorry, but 'do give Emilee and John my fond regards'?"

"What's wrong with that?" he asked.

"Oh, not much, except for *everything*," she replied.

"I think it's nice," he said mildly.

"Yeah, nice the way the wicked witch fed Hansel and Gretel before she tried to eat them!"

"You certainly have an active imagination, Soupy Meloney."

She was quiet for a moment, watching the uneven bricks exposed beneath patches of sludgy snow on JFK Street disappear beneath her feet. "How'd she know you were coming, anyway?" she blurted suddenly.

"Who?"

"Lexi. She saved you a seat; she must've known you were coming."

"Oh. Right," he said. "We're in the same government class."

Callie scuffed her shoes along the bricks, kicking some dead leaves. They were mushy and far less satisfying than the crisp entrails of autumn or, for that matter, a soccer ball. Or Lexi's stupid face.

"What's wrong?" he asked, managing to sound both tolerant and resigned.

"Nothing," she muttered. "I just didn't realize . . . that you two are friends."

"Is that a problem?" he asked. "Because as much as I hate the idea of making you uncomfortable, *I'm* not comfortable with the idea that my relationship should dictate my choice of friends."

Completely and totally reasonable. Still, she stayed silent.

Stopping, he took both her hands. "But I have only *one* girlfriend," he said, leaning in to kiss her forehead. "And she doesn't have to worry about sharing me with anyone else because she's cute and brilliant and totally adorable."

"Yeah, well, we'll see what your parents have to say about that." They had reached Wigglesworth.

"See you tonight?"

"I can't wait." She forced a smile. For it to be over.

The lounge at Rialto, the four-star restaurant in The Charles Hotel, where Clint's parents were staying, was all cream, black, and beige, lit by pale yellow candles and separated from the main dining room by a set of gauzy curtains. The Webers sat on two stools at the bar, a dapper middle-aged couple whose color scheme was an eerie match for their surroundings. Mrs. Weber, impeccable in black and cream, looked like the love child of Anna Wintour and Coco Chanel, exuding nothing but warmth as she turned, stood, and hugged her son, but then smiling at Callie in a way that seemed more Wintour-ian than Chanel. Mr. Weber wore a black suit, but something in his expression was distinctly—or perhaps indistinctly—beige. His eyes kept flicking back and forth between his wife and their surroundings, tracking her movements almost as a small dog might take cues from its owner. Smiling, he extended his hand toward Callie.

"Mom, Dad," said Clint, who stood next to her and whose face was miraculously calm given how hard she was squeezing his hand, "this is Callie."

"Hi," said Callie, letting go of Clint and shaking hands with Mr. Weber, pressing her knees together to keep them from shaking, too.

"Lovely to meet you, dear," Mrs. Weber said, kissing Callie on the cheek. "We're so pleased that you were able to join us this evening. Clint tells us that you normally keep very busy with class and various extracurriculars."

"Um, I guess—yes," said Callie, following them into the dining room. Was she supposed to sit or remain standing until they did it first—and what was she supposed to do with her coat? At that moment a waiter fell from heaven and offered to take her jacket before pulling out her chair. Relieved, she sank into it. Callie: 1; The Evening: 0.

Looking down, she saw eight different types of cutlery including a weird spoon-shaped utensil looming above her plate. Callie: 1; The Evening: 1.

"She writes for the same magazine as Alexis, isn't that right, sweetheart?" Mrs. Weber asked Clint, smiling at Callie.

"Well, actually," Callie started, wiggling in her chair, "I didn't, well, m—"

"Callie is COMPing the *Harvard Crimson*, which is much more prestigious than the magazine," Clint interceded smoothly, squeezing her hand under the table.

"How *is* Alexis?" Mr. Weber said, blinking rapidly.

"She's doing well," Clint said, opening his menu.

"She sent such a lovely Christmas card this year," Mrs. Weber remarked. "It's too bad we won't get a chance to see her before we leave. Are you *sure* she can't make it to lunch tomorrow with Tyler?"

"She's busy."

"Pity." Mr. Weber grunted, signaling their waiter. "Another Glenlivet on the rocks, please."

"Anything sound good to you?" Clint asked Callie, peering over her shoulder at the menu.

"Er . . ." Mimi had urged Callie to order the most expensive thing on the menu to prove she had *cojones* (Thank you, Spanish lessons with Gregory), but from Vanessa's derisive snort Callie had deduced that this would be ill-advised and had decided ahead of time that she should order something priced in the middle range. The only problem was that there were no prices: just first, second, and third course options, followed by dessert. Not to mention the names of some of the courses:

Raviolini was easy enough to parse—probably some form of miniature ravioli. But *curried skate wing, fontina fonduta,* and *oxtail ragu*? Were they secret words that you learned only in East Coast Society? She wished Vanessa, who was fluent in all dialects of B.S. (Boarding School), P.S. (Prep School), and WASP ("Whatever Are you Speaking of, Penelope?"), were there to guide her through. Vanessa would have remembered to warn her about the possibility of a *prix fixe* menu, and she certainly would have known what to do with the weird spoon-shaped thing above the place settings. All Callie could think was that it looked to be the exact same size as her nose.

"What were you thinking of getting?" she asked Clint.

"Probably the mushroom soup, the gnocchi, and the skate wing. And then maybe the apple-quince crostada for dessert?"

"Nice! Me too," said Callie.

Clint squeezed her hand again three times to signal: *you're doing great*.

Jury's still out, thought Callie.

"Where did you say you were from again, Callie?" Mrs. Weber asked after the waiter had taken their orders.

"Los Angeles," said Callie.

"Oh my, aren't you far from home, then," Mrs. Weber said. "Do you miss it terribly? And how do your poor parents cope?" she continued before Callie could answer. "We discouraged Clint from applying to Stanford for that very reason."

"It was kind of tough to stay in touch at first because of the time difference and what with everything going on. . . . I mean, just that: freshman year is very hectic. My mom used to freak out if I didn't answer her e-mails within twenty-four hours, but now we've scheduled a phone call every Sunday at the same time no matter what; well, my dad was at seven and my mom was eight at first, but now they switch off because my mom said she could tell by my 'lack of enthusiasm' that I was repeating stories for a second time."

"Divorced? I see," Mrs. Weber murmured, arching her perfectly plucked eyebrows. "And what do they do for a living?" she inquired, unfolding her napkin across her lap.

"My parents?" Callie asked, copying her.

"Yes."

"My mom is a lawyer, and my dad is the head of the mathematics department at UCLA." Normally Callie referred to him as an "absent minded professor," or a "professional math geek," but neither of those descriptions seemed to match the lace tablecloth or chandeliers.

"Entertainment law, I presume? She's not *the* Andrews of Andrews, Cuttering, and Donne, is she—"

"Uh, no," said Callie. "She works for the government in the California Department of Public Health."

"Oh," said Mrs. Weber. "Well, the state government certainly needs all the good people it can get," she said charitably. "Your budget's a wreck, and don't even get me started on the state of your school systems!"

Callie nodded, trying to arrange her features in a way that conveyed her sincerest apologies on behalf of her state. Mr. Weber nodded, too, flashing her what she thought just might be a commiserating smile.

"Education is sort of Mom's pet cause," Clint explained.

"Absolutely," said Mrs. Weber. "It's one of the most important things. Where did you say you went to high school again, dear? Was it Harvard-Westlake?"

And just like that, it was Pudding punch all over again.

"No, actually, I went to public school," Callie said.

"Well, that's even more impressive," Mrs. Weber said, sounding sincere. "You must be extremely tenacious." That part sounded less like a compliment.

"She is very impressive," Clint said as what appeared to be the curried skate wing arrived. It looked like some type of fish. Sort of. Bravely, Callie took a bite.

"How's your dinner?" Clint asked, smiling widely at her as if it were all going along swimmingly. Maybe he thought it was. Maybe . . . it was?

"Delicious," Callie lied.

An awkward silence ensued, broken only by the sounds of Mrs. Weber's cutlery as she took miniscule bites of her entrée.

Then again, maybe it wasn't.

"So, Mr. Weber," Callie finally said. "Clint tells me you played squash at Princeton?"

This turned out to be the right thing to say. Like she had unstopped a drain, the fond memories of his Princeton days flowed, from playing squash with wooden rackets in his eating club to working on the *Daily Princetonian*, carrying them all the way through the main course and onto dessert. As much as Callie hated to admit it, Lexi had done her a favor.

"Those were the days," he said after sharing a story about the consecutive all-nighters he had pulled during his tenure at the *Daily Princetonian*. "Tell me, Callie," he said, "are you working on anything interesting right now for the *Crimson*?"

"Yes," she replied. "In fact, just earlier today Clint and I went to hear Governor Hamilton speak at the Kennedy Center so I could take notes for a piece we're doing on his visit to campus this week."

"Oh, did you?" Mrs. Weber said, sounding casual but suddenly seeming far more interested in this line of conversation than anything her husband had uttered in the past half hour.

Clint shifted in his chair and took a big bite of his sorbet. (Mystery of the weird spoon-shaped thing solved!)

"That's *right*," Mrs. Weber continued. "Now that you mention it, I do seem to recall him saying that he would be in town when we had him to dinner last month. No wonder Alexis is too busy to make lunch tomorrow; no doubt she wants to spend as much time as possible with her uncle!"

Eeigah—Callie tried not to flinch at the sound of Alexis's name surfacing in the conversation for the second time. Oddly enough, Clint, whose foot had started jiggling up and down, seemed even more uncomfortable than she felt.

"Tell me, darling: Did you have an opportunity to approach him afterward and raise the possibility of a summer internship like we discussed?"

"No," Clint said shortly.

"Well, when then? Perhaps at the cocktail party this Thursday—"

she said, shattering all pretenses that this turn in the conversation had simply occurred to her out of the blue.

"Callie and I have a previous engagement," Clint said, placing his hand over hers.

Mrs. Weber's eyes flicked after it, and she frowned. "Darling, I'm quite certain that whatever you two have planned isn't more important than your future, wouldn't you agree, Callie?"

"Um—yes?"

"Mom," Clint said softly, setting aside his spoon. "It is my future. *My* future. And I would love the opportunity to intern with Governor Hamilton or anyone else in Washington, which is why I plan to file an application and be considered—just like everyone else."

Mrs. Weber let out a laugh that bore a haunting similarity to Lexi's tinkling giggle—though perhaps the only commonality was that both sounds made Callie's teeth stand on end.

"Another Glenlivet on the rocks, please," Mr. Weber said to the waiter as he cleared their dessert plates.

"Oh, sweetheart," Mrs. Weber said, dabbing the corners of her eyes with her napkin. "We'd all prefer to believe that we live in a meritocratic society, but listen carefully when I tell you that, *especially* when it comes to politics, you have to milk every possible connection that you have while working constantly to forage new ones. That's just how the game goes."

Callie turned sharply to survey Clint. Was that the real reason why he wanted to be friends with Lexi?

Mrs. Weber cleared her throat. "Now, if you would just let me make one phone call—"

"No," said Clint, a little too loudly. "No, thank you. That won't be necessary."

Callie downed a big gulp of water, hoping that the glass would conceal her smile.

"Suit yourself." Mrs. Weber shrugged, signing the bill.

"Well, we both have early classes in the morning so we should probably get going," Clint said. "Mom, Dad: thanks for dinner. I'll see you for lunch tomorrow." Standing, he offered Callie his hand.

"Yes, thank you so much for dinner," Callie echoed. "It was so nice to meet both of you."

"Wonderful to meet you, too, dear," Mrs. Weber said, standing.

"It was our pleasure," Mr. Weber said, smiling at Callie.

"Ready?" asked Clint, taking her coat from the waiter and helping her into the sleeves.

"Yep," she said. "Thanks again," she called over her shoulder, and then followed Clint out of the room.

When they had made it to the brick pavilion outside The Charles Hotel, Callie took what felt like her first breath all evening. "Well," she said, "I guess that wasn't a *total* disaster."

"Are you kidding?" asked Clint, pulling her close. "They loved you!"

"Really?"

Clint laughed. "Well, my dad definitely loved you, and my mom . . . didn't hate you."

Maybe . . . but clearly not as much as she "didn't hate" Lexi. "You sure about that?"

"Yes," Clint affirmed. "And please disregard that whole

'tenacious' comment—she's just overprotective."

"Mm," Callie murmured. Te·na·cious (*adjective*)—as far as she and her old SAT flashcards were concerned—simply meant *persistent*, *determined*, or *not easily dispelled*. In other words, not an insult.

"So . . . my place?" he asked, breaking her reverie.

She gasped in mock horror, whacking him on the arm. "But you just told your mother that we had to be up early for class!"

"Oh, I intend to go straight to bed," he said, grabbing her around the waist and smothering her cheeks with kisses.

"*Ahg!*" she cried until he finally let her up for air. "Okay, okay, you win! Just let me text Mimi to let her know I won't be bringing her dress back until tomorrow."

Breaking away, she pulled out her phone. But, instead of texting Mimi, at the last second she texted Vanessa instead:

> JUST ONE QUESTION: WHAT DOES
> "TENACIOUS" MEAN IN WASP?

A moment later her phone buzzed:

1 New Text Message from Vanessa V

> PROBABLY A SYNONYM FOR GOLD-
> DIGGER. MAYBE GOLD-DIGGING
> WHORE, DEPENDING ON CONTEXT.
> WHY?

Callie looked at Clint, who was smiling and holding open the bright red door to Adams House, before texting back:

> ABSOLUTELY NO REASON.

SIX

A Very Important Date

Dearest Froshies:

It's precisely this time of year when you've survived Valentine's Day and may even be starting to ponder your Spring Break plans that you also begin to wonder: are you and your significant other a good match? Before you book that cozy bed-and-breakfast for two, you might want to complete the following quiz.

Quiz: Is he a Sinner, a Saint, or Simply an Undeniable Douchebag?

1. Saturday is date night and you have a whole evening prepared, but he cancels at the last minute because:

    a. "The Big Game's on TV and it's just us guys, but why don't you drop by after? And oh yeah: wear that thing I like."

    b. "My chemistry class is killing me. Would you mind bringing over some work so we can study together? I promise there's a foot rub in it for you afterward. . . ."

    c. He doesn't bother canceling at all but rather shows up an hour late. You are livid, naturally, but then he makes up for it by surprising you with something bigger and better than you had originally planned.

2. You're in a restaurant and he takes the liberty of ordering for you while you're in the rest room. He:

a. Orders the steak, but there's only one problem: you're a vegetarian. Oh, and he also forgot his wallet in the car.

b. Orders all of your favorite foods, including dessert, and then he pays for it.

c. Orders two options, which you share family style, and then you split the bill, so that you're starting to feel really comfortable: until you get home, and realize that you had food in your teeth the entire night and he said nothing.

3. You ask the fateful question, "Do I look fat in this dress?" Apart from the obvious—what were you thinking?!?—he responds:

a. "'Course not, babe, though your ankles do look a little chubby in those shoes. But that's just 'cause you have chubby ankles. Aw... don't cry.... I *like* your chubby ankles!"

b. "*I* think that you always look terrific in whatever you're wearing, but if *you're* not comfortable, then you should change."

c. "I'm not falling for that one."

4. At a party he:

a. Leaves you on your own for most of the night, but that's all right: you're self-sufficient and doing fine on your own—until you spot him standing a little too close to that cute girl from his Government class.

b. Stays glued to your side all evening until you're starting to wish you had the number for a codependency counselor.

c. Asks you frequently if you're having fun or if he can get you another drink, but he sometimes forgets to introduce you or include you in the actual conversation.

5. When you meet his parents for the first time, they:

a. Laugh, then there's an awkward silence followed by "Girlfriend?"

b. Exchange a knowing smile and say, "So, *this* is the one. . . ."

c. Say it's so lovely to finally meet you, but then one of them accidentally refers to you by the name of his most recent ex.

Mostly (a)s: You are dating a Douchebag. Exit the relationship immediately. He may not even notice that you're gone.

Mostly (b)s: You are dating a Saint. Though almost *too* affectionate at times, this one definitely has marriage on his mind.

Mostly (c)s: You are dating a Sinner, but like Billy Joel said, "I'd rather laugh with the sinners than cry with the saints: the sinners are much more fun." So enjoy it while it lasts, but remember: sometimes even the good relationships die young.

"Ice-skating? That sounds dangerous," Dana said, looking up at Callie from the textbooks she had spread across the coffee table in their common room.

Mimi was also eyeing her skeptically: "You look like a giant poufy white sugar ball—"

"Marshmallow," Callie supplied.

"Marshmallow—even more than usual," Mimi finished.

"I think it's the hat," Dana suggested.

"That is certainly one source of the problem," Mimi murmured. It was a rare occasion when Mimi and Dana agreed, but today the decision seemed unanimous: Callie's outfit for her contentious, potentially future-ruining Thursday night date with Clint was anything but attractive.

"Maybe you need some knee pads," Dana began.

"No, no, the padding is already too much," said Mimi. "*Tu ressembles à un éléphant.*"

"Come on, guys. It's not so bad," Callie said. "This is what you wear when you go ice-skating!" Of course, she didn't really know since she had never actually been ice-skating. In fact, before coming to Harvard, she had never even seen snow: the only kind they had in Los Angeles was a Schedule II controlled substance.

"*I* think that you look perfect just the way you are," Vanessa called, poking her head out of her bedroom. "Positively *tenacious*—"

"Don't make me hurt you!" Callie cried. Half joking, she rushed Vanessa like a linebacker might a quarterback.

Screaming, Vanessa slammed the door to her room, and Callie smacked straight into it. Oddly enough, she bounced.

"Did you guys see that?" She whooped. "I didn't feel a thing! Not a *thing*!" she called, catapulting into the opposite wall and whooping again when she bounced.

"Whoa, what's going on in here?" a male voice called from the doorway, sounding amused.

Callie whirled around. She saw the flowers first, followed by Clint. In a suit.

A suit?

"I didn't realize that ice-skating was a formal event," she cried, cursing herself for getting the dress code wrong—*again*.

Clint chuckled. "Actually . . . there's been a slight change of plans," he explained. "I've been thinking that it might be a good idea for me to swing by that event at the Faculty Club after all."

"The Governor Hamilton thing?" Callie asked, her feet suddenly feeling rooted in place.

"Yes. Do you mind? It started only twenty minutes ago, so if we leave now we won't be too late."

"You couldn't have mentioned this earlier?" she asked, removing her hat. Her hair shot up, wrought with static electricity.

"I'm sorry. I didn't decide until the last minute, and well—I'm just sorry," he said, coming toward her. "I brought flowers?"

Callie stayed where she was. "I thought we were going ice-skating."

"I know," he said, setting the flowers down so he could put his arms around her. "But we can do that anytime, and Governor Hamilton's only in town for one more night. . . ."

"I don't have anything to wear," she muttered. And then, a bit louder: "You didn't leave me time to change!"

"You don't need time—you always look gorgeous, no matter what."

"Now we know he is a liar," Mimi joked from the couch, where she had returned to reviewing her most recent efforts for the *Lampoon*.

"All right." Callie sighed, slinking into her room. Slowly she unwound the scarf she'd picked out especially for ice-skating. Then she began her search for something to wear, opening and closing her dresser drawers with a little more force than necessary.

In two minutes she emerged in her nicest pair of dark jeans and a button-up cardigan.

"Okay, let's get this over with," she said, heading for the door. She paused. Clint hadn't moved. "What?" she demanded.

"Well . . ." he began. "*I* think you look great, but the invitation said "business casual," and I think that means that girls are supposed to wear a dress? I just wouldn't want you to be uncomfortable because you felt underdressed."

Callie stared at him.

"I have an idea," he said. "Why don't you borrow something from Mimi again like you did the other night for dinner?"

"*Bien sûr,*" Mimi said. "Help yourself."

Callie walked into Mimi's room and opened her closet. There

was a wide array of dresses, though only a small subset actually fit Callie, who was something of *un éléphant* to Mimi's size zero. And within this subset Callie only felt comfortable borrowing a precious few with foreign labels that didn't evoke the image of quadruple-digit price tags.

Sighing, she emerged with a simple black dress that would maybe zip with only a little stretching (of both the fabric and the imagination). "Is this okay?" she asked, holding it up.

"It's perfect," said Clint. "It'll look great on you."

"I was asking Mimi," she said.

"Oui, oui," Mimi said, waving her hand.

"Great, just give me a second," she said, heading for her room.

"Take your time," Clint called, sneaking a peek at his watch.

The dress was tight, but it zipped. Quickly Callie smoothed her hair and grabbed a small purse. Then she reentered the common room.

Shoes, she realized with a sinking feeling when Clint glanced down at her bare feet, were going to be a problem. She didn't think she could get away with sporting the flats she had worn to Rialto; Mimi was nowhere near her size, and Vanessa was more likely to throw her Jimmy Choos at Callie's head than to lend them to her. Suddenly her face felt hot; her tear ducts mobilizing as they readied for action. . . .

"Here, try these," Dana offered, pressing a pair of low-heeled, patent leather Mary Janes into her hand—not the trendy, modern variety but the kind Callie had assumed they stopped making back in 1959. The kind that even her grandma was too hip to wear—

and that was saying a lot, since her grandma was dead.

"Thanks," Callie whispered, jamming them onto her feet. "Ready?"

"After you," said Clint, holding the door. As she passed, he leaned down and whispered, "I was right about the dress—it's stunning."

"Mm-hmm, yeah, ah, yes, I see, hmm?" Callie said, smiling and nodding in—what she hoped—were the right places, all the while thinking, Owwww-o-wow, because her feet hurt like hell. Not only that, but Mimi's dress felt like it was cutting into her skin, her stomach was grumbling with hunger, and she wanted to go home; away from the Faculty Club with its semi-creepy portraits of famous professors and university presidents lining the walls, leering at her ominously from between the throngs of faculty and students sucking up to the politico elite.

And it had only been twenty minutes.

Seventeen of which the senior to her left had occupied with an almost uninterrupted monologue, only stopping long enough, it seemed, to let Clint agree with him. Callie, who'd been daydreaming about ice-skating and hot apple cider, tuned back just in time to hear:

". . . everyone knows that global warming is little more than a myth invented by the liberal establishment—"

"Yeah, I heard that we could solve the whole problem and dramatically lower temperatures," Callie began, "if only America would convert to the metric system."

The three boys, including Clint, all paused to stare.

"You know," she floundered, "because Fahrenheit to Celsius would be lower. . . ."

Clint laughed. "That is funny, actually. But going back to what you were saying about campaign strategies in Middle America . . ."

What would January Jones, who played the perfect blond 1960s housewife on *Mad Men*, do? Callie thought, cocking her hand against her hip and doing her best interpretation of standing there and looking pretty. After all, she had the shoes to fit the part, even if the shoes didn't quite fit.

"Can I get you a drink?" she asked Clint during a lull in the conversation.

"That would be wonderful." He grinned, the irony escaping him. "Make it a Jack and Coke, please."

"Coming right up," she said, smiling back when she realized she now had at least a five-minute excuse to escape.

Her feet pinched as she walked away. Then again, Betty Draper was a chain-smoking alcoholic who not-so-secretly hated her children—perhaps a poor choice of fictional character to emulate.

Callie's shoulders relaxed while she waited at the bar for Clint's drink and a diet soda (no *way* was she drinking at an event like this—that'd be almost as stupid as drinking during the first time you met your mother-in-law, or at dinner with the Webers—*not* that those two were related). Take as long as you want, Mr. Bartender, sir, Callie willed him: I could happily stand here all night—

"Hi, Callie!" a low, silky voice said from her left. "How are you?"

Callie turned to find herself facing Perky B—Alessandra, right, because they were "friends" now and it was high time she dropped the nickname—in pearls with less makeup, and cleavage, than usual.

"Hi," Callie said, smiling back. Alessandra + a Cocktail Party could potentially = Gregory: her eyes darted around the room, but she didn't see him anywhere. "How are you?"

"Bored," Alessandra confessed. "I was only invited to this because my dad's a major campaign contributor."

Callie nodded. Big business tycoon + Desire for tax breaks = likely Moderate with Conservative Tendencies, aka closeted Republican with commitment issues in a Democratic-leaning state. "Well, *I* was only invited," she started, "because my boyfriend's mom is a little bit controlling and—"

Alessandra's eyes had suddenly gone wide.

All the blood drained from Callie's face. "He's standing right behind me, isn't he?"

"False," said an unmistakable voice from over Callie's shoulder. "Hiya, neighbor," Gregory continued, swooping in to kiss Callie's cheek before draping an arm over Alessandra's shoulders. "And hello, beautiful."

Without thinking, Callie touched her glass to her cheek, a single square inch of which felt like it was on fire.

"I told you that I don't like it when you call me that," Alessandra said. She rolled her eyes at Callie. "Doesn't it make you feel like he can't even remember who you are, *neighbor*?"

"Okay, wow. Sorry, *Tiffany*."

"It's, like, my *name* is Alessandra," she said, ignoring him and speaking to Callie, "not *Babe*, or *Beautiful*, or—what was it you called me that one time when we were in bed? It was a Spanish word for—"

"TIME for another DRINK," Gregory interrupted loudly.

"Don't bother," Alessandra said, with a perfect execution of her simpering pout. "Ladies' room. If I'm not back in five minutes—"

"You snuck out the window?" Callie supplied.

"Exactly." Alessandra smiled and then excused herself.

Dammit, thought Callie, smiling back. I actually like her. Even if her boobs sometimes seem to divert a significant portion of blood flow away from her brain—and everyone else's brain, if Gregory's face was any indication—she's kind of cool. . . .

"My girlfriend is *hot*," Gregory said. "Possibly the hottest girl at this school. You know she turned down a modeling contract back in LA before she transferred here?"

"I should go," Callie blurted. "Clint's ice is melting," she added, rattling his drink.

"What a lucky guy," said Gregory, "to have someone to fetch his drinks for him."

Callie debated throwing said drink into Gregory's stupid, smirking face. In fact, the only thing that stopped her was the sight of Lexi leading her uncle over to Clint and introducing them. Lexi's hand rested on Clint's upper arm while she laughed at something he'd said, tossing her immaculate curls and exposing her small, even teeth.

"Don't they make the perfect couple?" Gregory remarked, following her gaze.

"Are you actively *trying* to make me hate you," Callie seethed, wheeling around, "or are you really just naturally this detestable?"

This seemed to amuse him to no end, his blue eyes winking in the dim light. Staring at her, he visibly struggled to suppress his laughter. (Apparently the earth-moon-sun position of the evening => Wildly-entertained-at-your-expense.)

"Want to play a game?" he finally asked.

"What?"

"Do you want to play a game?" he repeated, enunciating.

"What kind of game?" she asked, leaning away as he leaned toward her.

"A little game I invented to make tedious social functions like these more bearable. I call it . . . I Bet You Won't Say. I give you a word or phrase that I bet you can't manage to casually insert into a conversation, and if you pull it off, I'll give you . . . a dollar."

"Like what?"

"Like—oh, I don't know—like *platypus*. If you can say *platypus* within the next five minutes without stopping an entire conversation, then I am prepared to make you a very rich lady."

Callie stared at him. "I have to go." Turning, she made her way over to where Clint and Governor Hamilton (though perhaps by now he had asked Clint to call him "Uncle") were yammering away like old fishing buddies while Lexi presided over the exchange.

". . . your article on Reaganomics literally changed my life," Clint was saying. Callie handed him his drink. "Thanks," he said, keeping his eyes on the governor. "I thought I understood the Tax Equity and Fiscal Responsibility Act before," Clint continued, "but I might as well have been a Little League player claiming to understand what it's like to pitch in the World Series. . . ."

"You a Red Sox fan, son?"

"Is the sky blue, Governor?"

"I like him," Governor Hamilton said to Lexi, clapping Clint on the back.

"Oh, excuse me, sorry, sir," Clint said, as if seeing Callie for the first time. "This is my friend Callie."

Friend? Oh, excuse me, sorry, sir, I thought I was your *girlfriend*. My bad!

Lexi beamed. Callie forced a smile and shook hands, hoping she wasn't expected to contribute to the conversation even though baseball and taxes were her two all-time *favorite* topics!

"Now, could you three excuse me for a moment?" Governor Hamilton said. "Professor Madoff's been eyeing me all night—no doubt hoping to talk my ear off about the national debt—and I need to give him five minutes. But don't think I'm letting you off so easy," he said, turning to Clint. "I fully expect you to find me later so we can talk ball—and maybe a little politics, too," he added with a wink.

"Excellent, sir," said Clint, returning the governor's viselike handshake.

"I'll be right back, too," Lexi said, spotting Alessandra, who had just emerged from the rest room (no luck sneaking out the window, it seemed). Callie watched Lexi enfold Alessandra in a hug as if she were her long-lost twin sister—or perhaps just the daughter of her uncle's important campaign donor and the Pudding's most high-priority punch.

Clint turned to Callie. "On a scale of one to ten," he said, his eyebrows knitting together, "how miserable are you?"

Oh, thank god. "Um, eight? And a half," she confessed.

"Well, you're doing great," he said, squeezing her hand.

At what—smiling and nodding? Only speaking when spoken to?

"Is it all right if we stay for just another twenty minutes—a half hour, max? I know I haven't been the most attentive date tonight, and I'm sorry, but getting a little more time alone with the governor could be the deciding factor for a summer internship. You understand, don't you?"

Callie nodded, trying to keep her face from flinching in reaction to her unfortunate shoe situation. Junior summer internships *were* important; everybody knew that. What was her twenty or thirty more minutes of probably-not-going-to-result-in-paralysis foot pain to the future of his career? After all, relationships were supposed to be about compromise. "I'll just go sit over there—by the bar—until you're done."

"Thanks, you're the best," said Clint, leaning to kiss her forehead. Taking a step, she winced, and her ankle twisting, she stumbled.

"Are you okay?" Clint said, catching her. "You didn't have too much to drink, did you?" he asked, his hands on both her arms.

"No!" she said. Suddenly she smiled. "No, it's just my clumsy platypus feet."

Clint laughed. "Platypuses are a graceful aquatic species that would probably be offended by that comparison."

"Hey!" she cried, whacking him but laughing nevertheless.

"I'm sorry," he said, hugging her. "So we're all good?"

"Yep!" she said. "I'll be waiting!" Debating exactly how unacceptable it would be to remove her shoes, she hobbled back over to the bar, where Gregory happened to be sitting on a stool staring into his drink.

"I did it!" she cried, tapping him on the shoulder.

"You did what?" he said, barely turning to look at her. (Uh-oh. The moon-sun-earth position had clearly shifted dramatically in her absence.)

"I said *platypus* in a conversation."

"Good for you," he said, taking a sip of his drink.

"It wasn't even weird or anything," she continued, hopping onto a neighboring stool.

"Have you ever considered that might be because most of what comes out of your mouth is already weird anyway?"

She searched his face for any trace of amusement but found none. "Well . . . you owe me a dollar."

"Shit, not again," he muttered suddenly, pulling his phone out of his pocket. Reading the name on the caller ID, he stood and cursed. "I have to take this," he said. "Here," he added, pulling some bills out of his wallet and flinging them at her.

"But this—"

"Tip the bartender for me," he called over his shoulder. Then he was gone.

Callie stared at the bills in her lap. There were three twenties, a five, and two ones.

What the hell was that about? she wondered, slipping the five to the bartender and pocketing the rest. She would give it back tomorrow, along with a reminder that not everyone could afford to be so damn careless with their funds. Speaking of which—was it possible that Gregory had been playing the role of her Secret Pudding Fairy Godperson?

She knew it wasn't Mimi. . . . There was a chance that it was Clint, but she couldn't bring herself to ask, fearful of how the whole you-have-way-more-money-than-I-do-and-sometimes-I-can't-afford-everything-that-you-can conversation might go. Glancing over her shoulder, she looked for Clint. Quickly she turned back to the bar. He was standing with Lexi again, but his attention seemed focused on the governor, who had his hand on Clint's shoulder like he was offering some fatherly advice.

"I think I'll take that drink now," she said to the bartender, whom she had waved away only moments earlier.

She drank it as slowly as possible, amusing herself with people-watching and silently redubbing their serious conversations based on body language. *Sure, I'll balance your budget if you tell me who did your hair plugs, Professor Platypus!*

Twenty minutes passed, and then thirty, and then forty, at which point she turned again to find Clint. Still cozying up to Lexi on the far end of the room, only this time the governor was nowhere nearby—

Standing, Callie made her way to the back exit of the Faculty Club. Once outside, she slipped off her shoes. On the two-minute walk back to Wigglesworth, the snow stung only slightly more than the tears leaking from her eyes, freezing as they rolled down her cheeks.

"Wake up, Callie . . . wake up!"

Callie groaned into the darkness. "It's the middle of the night."

"I know," Clint whispered. "You really ought to learn to lock your front door."

"What do you want?"

"I'm sorry that the event ran over," he began.

"S'all good," she murmured, burying her face in her pillow in case he could see her expression in the dark.

"No, it's not. I was a jerk, but I'm going to make it up to you."

"Can we talk about this another time?" she asked, rolling over. He stayed where he was, crouched near the head of her tiny twin bed. "We don't have to do any *talking*," he said, "but I am going to have to ask you to come with me."

"Come with you . . . *where*?" she asked.

"That's a secret."

"Are you crazy? It's two o'clock in the morning. I'm not going anywhere with you."

"I think you are," he said, reaching for her coat.

"Clint—seriously? No, what are you doing?"

"Just put this on and come with me. It'll only take a minute, I swear."

She didn't move.

"Please?"

"Only a minute?"

"Yes."

"And then you'll go away and let me sleep?"

"Yes."

"*Fine,*" she murmured, swinging her legs over the side of her bed. "But you literally only get *one* minute. . . ."

Five minutes later they were still walking, though she had lost track of time due to the disorienting effects of the blindfold that, after only a few more minutes of goading, he had somehow convinced her to wear.

"Are we there yet?" she asked, her feet still hurting from earlier as their boots crunched through the snow.

"Almost," he said.

Eventually they came to a stop. The nighttime breeze brushed past her cheek and she shivered. "Can I take the blindfold off now?"

"Just give me one more minute. . . ." he said, guiding her over to something—a bench, maybe—and sitting her down. Then his hands left her shoulders and she could hear him walking away. Maybe the plan was to ditch her not once, but twice in the same evening?

Irritably her fingers worked at the knot in the silk scarf that he had tied around her head.

"All right, you can look now!" he called at the same moment that the blindfold slid off.

She was staring at a tiny ice-skating rink, no more than thirty by thirty feet, around which Clint was hanging the last of four paper lanterns. Jogging back over to where she was sitting, he connected one cable to another. Suddenly, everything lit up, the lanterns hanging from a string of twinkly lights.

"You—you built me an ice-skating rink?" she asked, staring in disbelief.

"No." He laughed. "This was already here. The law school rebuilds it every winter on top of what is otherwise an outdoor volleyball court. But I did set up the lanterns."

Callie looked around. "So this is the law school?"

"Yep," he said. "And hopefully where I'll be in a year and a half from now if I'm lucky. . . . You'll be a junior by then."

She was silent.

"Why the long face?" he asked, chuckling. "You didn't think you could get rid of me *that* easily, did you?"

"Well, this is very pretty," she said after a beat. "But I wanted to *go* ice-skating, not just sit and stare at the place where people do it."

Clint laughed again. "Is that why you think I brought you here—just so we could look at it?"

"But . . . we don't even have any skates."

"Look underneath you," he said.

Standing, she looked. She had not, as she'd imagined, been sitting on a bench after all. Rather, it was a big plastic bin with a lid labeled SKATES.

"Oh."

"Let's see if we can't find something in your size," he said, lifting the lid. Soon he located a pair and then bent in front of her, securing the laces. "How do those feel?" he asked.

"Pretty good," she said, wiggling her toes.

"Well, come on, then," he said holding out his hand after he had put on a pair of his own.

Callie hesitated. "What if I can't do it?"

"It's easy," he said. "You can do it. And if for some reason you can't, there's nobody here to see you but me."

"What if I fall?"

"What *if? You* are definitely going to fall! But it won't hurt if you don't go too fast, and I'll be right there to laugh at you."

"Hey!"

"*And* to pick you up after, too."

"Promise?"

"Promise," he said, taking her hands and pulling her toward the rink. "I've got you," he added as they stepped out onto the ice. He was skating backward, still holding her hands.

"This isn't so b—*ahhh!*" she finished with a cry: after a few successful forward motions she had slipped, catapulting into Clint's arms.

But she didn't fall.

Holding her, Clint laughed. "You really don't believe in doing things halfway, do you? Baby steps now, Andrews."

Still clutching her hands tightly, he began to glide slowly backward. "Move your feet like this," he instructed. Copying him, she started to slide forward.

And just a short while later . . . she was skating!

"I'm doing it! I'm doing it!" she shrieked, picking up the pace.

"You're doing great!" he agreed. "Ready for me to let go—"

"Yes!" she cried, releasing his hands. And then she was really flying: skating around the rink like she'd been doing it for years, her scarf soaring out behind her, faster and faster until—

Her left foot slid out from under her, sending her toward the ice. *"Ahhhhhhhh!"* she cried as she went down.

"Callie! Callie, are you all right?" Clint called, racing over. She wasn't moving: flat on her back across the ice. "Are you hurt—"

"Did you see how fast I went?" she screamed, sitting up suddenly.

A look of relief swept across Clint's face. "You're sure you're not hurt. . . ."

"My butt hurts," she said after a moment. "And it's *cold*," she added, standing and brushing the ice off of her backside.

"Want me to give it a kiss?" Clint asked.

"*Ew*—no!" she cried, skating away.

"Come on, just one little kiss," he pleaded when he caught up. She tried to fight him off for only a moment before she decided that giving in might be even more fun. It was 2 A.M. and there were twinkly lights: how long could you really stay mad inside of your own personal ice rink while the rest of the world lay fast asleep?

Forty-five minutes later, after they'd had their fill of skating, they were sitting back on the bin. Clint had produced a thermos full of hot apple cider, which they were now passing between them. Wrapping an arm around her, he pulled her close. "So . . . am I forgiven?" he asked.

"That depends," she said, sipping the cider. It was sweet and warm and cinnamon-y.

"On . . ."

"On why that *girl* keeps showing up wherever you happen to be."

"Which girl?" Clint asked.

"You *know* which girl," she said, pushing the thermos toward him.

"Oh," he said. "Didn't we already have this conversation a couple of days ago?" he asked, sounding patient nevertheless.

"Yes, but . . ." Callie stopped to think. "But that was before it seemed like she was everywhere! All the time! Even when she's not there, she's still there," she cried, the words tumbling out faster and faster. "Because your mom is talking about her or her uncle is the governor or— I don't know, it's like she has four twin sisters, or that superpower where you can be in two places at once: telekinesis or teleportation or—"

"Stop," he said, laughing a little.

"I'm being serious!" She folded her arms across her chest.

"I know," he said. "But you *seriously* have nothing to worry about. Lex—*Alexis*, is just a friend."

"Oh, great, so she's *Lex* now," Callie muttered.

"Just a friend," he insisted.

"I just . . ." Callie frowned. "I just don't get it. *Why* do you want to be friends with someone who is so . . . well . . . evil?"

Clint sighed. "I know you two have your history; but she and I have a history as well. We dated for over two years. She has a good side and bad side like everyone else: you just happen to have had exposure to the worst side. But that doesn't mean that's all there is to her."

Callie was silent.

"Would it help if I said that part of it had to do with parental pressure about the summer internship?"

"Ugh, no," exclaimed Callie. "That would be worse."

"Look," he started, "I wouldn't fault you if you wanted to be friends with your ex, and he's *clearly* not the greatest—"

"That's totally different," she cut in. "Because Evan is evil and I *don't* talk to him."

Clint sighed. "Well, do you see me getting jealous of any of the other guys chasing after you? Like what about the one from across the hall—"

Callie inhaled sharply.

"What's his name? Matt? The one who's always following you around with the puppy eyes? Or what about when someone at the Pudding or some random party hits on you when I'm not around? Or hey, even with Bolton I sometimes get the sense that I'm interrupting something, even though I know that nothing would ever happen there."

Callie stared at the ground, kicking up some snow.

"The point is that you have a right to be friends with whoever you want," Clint finished. "And while I'm certainly not immune to jealousy, ultimately it doesn't *really* bother me because I trust you. I trust that if you don't want to be with me or if you'd rather be with someone else—that you would tell me."

She stayed silent, watching the snow arc out from her shoe.

Clint sighed. "To be completely honest . . . there is something that I've been keeping from you—"

Callie froze.

"*Only* because I thought it would upset you," he insisted, "but I think telling you now might put these Lexi fears to rest."

She waited.

"When you broke up with me in that e-mail—"

"That Lexi forced me to send," Callie interrupted.

"That you sent of your own free will due to pressure from Alexis," he corrected her. "Anyway, after that, over winter break she tried to get me to take her back. We went skiing with a big group in Vermont, and even though I wasn't with you and thought that you never wanted to speak to me again, I still didn't go for it. Okay?"

"Okay," Callie murmured, feeling more disturbed than comforted. "But I didn't need to know that. I mean, whatever you did those times we were broken up is your business, and it's all in the past now, like we agreed that night at the Harvard Pub when we got back together."

"'Times'?" he asked.

"Hmm?"

"'Times,' as in plural?"

"Yes," she said. "You remember, Harvard-Yale?"

"We weren't broken up then," he said. "We were taking some time to think."

"Yeah," she agreed. "I suppose there's a difference."

"It was a fuzzy gray area," he conceded. "But I still wasn't with Lexi—or anyone else—then either."

Damn. Every time she thought the Gregory incident at

Harvard-Yale was truly best left buried in the past, the universe kept hinting that she should try, once again, to confess. And yet, the more time that went by, the more she had to lose.

"Clint," she finally blurted. "I have to tell you something."

"I have to tell you something, too."

"You first."

"No you."

"No—

"I love you."

What?

"I . . ." she started.

"Wait!" he said. "Don't say it back now just to say it. You should wait until you're ready."

"Okay," she said. "Well, in that case . . . I am ready . . . to do *this*." Pulling him toward her, she kissed him: exceptionally, exceptionally glad that he had gone first.

SEVEN

THE NOT SO GREAT GATSBY

Clint Weber

and

The Gentlemen of the Fly Club Cordially Invite You,

Callie Andrews,

to

THE GREAT GATSBY

on the evening of Saturday, the fifth of March

Let us gather together and celebrate

the colossal vitality of our illusions . . .

Attire: White Tie or 1920s appropriate

By Invitation Only

Tyler Green

and

The Gentleman of the Fly Club Cordially Invite You,

Vanessa Von Vorhees,

to

THE GREAT GATSBY

on the evening of Saturday, the fifth of March

Let us gather together and celebrate

the colossal vitality of our illusions . . .

Attire: White Tie or 1920s appropriate

By Invitation Only

"Tyler, could you please ask Callie to change the radio station? She knows I detest this song," Vanessa said from the backseat of Clint's BMW.

"Clint, could you please tell Tyler to tell Vanessa that I love this song and I'm not changing it?" Callie said from the front.

"What, you're not speaking to *Tyler* now?" Clint asked, sounding amused.

"Oh," said Callie. "Whoops."

"Tyler, could you please tell Callie that she's completely retarde—"

"Enough!" Tyler yelled, throwing his hand over Vanessa's mouth. "This car is *not* big enough for the four of us *and* all of your girlie problems. I don't care who broke whose Britney CD or who told the other one that her butt looked fat—you two are either going to play nice or you're not allowed to talk for the rest of the ride!"

"Fine by me," said Callie. "Though if she can actually stop talking for five minutes, I might die of shock—"

"Is that a promise?" snapped Vanessa. "Because—"

Tyler clamped his hand over her mouth again. "Turn up the radio, man," he said to Clint, while muffled *MMmmmMMMmmmmMM* sounds continued to come from Vanessa. "And change the station, would you? Sorry, Callie, but nobody likes this—*OW!*" Vanessa appeared to have bitten him.

A smooth saxophone filtered from the speakers. "How's this?" Clint asked.

"Nice," said Callie. "Very 1920s jazz age—"

"I don't remember giving you permission to speak," Tyler cut in.

"Fine," Callie muttered, twisting the long string of fake pearls entwined around her neck. In the back Vanessa fiddled with her fishnet stockings.

Tonight they were on their way to, if not the most talked about, then certainly the most exclusive party of the year: The Great Gatsby. Even Mimi had failed to finagle an invitation. With their feather headdresses and flowing silk gowns, Vanessa's a dark red with fringe and Callie's a pearly gray with a skirt that twirled when she spun around, both girls looked like they had stepped out of a Prohibition-era speakeasy. Tyler and Clint wore white tails and white gloves with their tuxedos, because—as Callie had learned in the last five minutes—white tie was a level above black on the continually confusing formal attire scale.

"Why do we have to drive again?" Vanessa asked. "Walking would be faster."

"Because," Tyler said with a sigh, "I didn't think you would want to help us carry eighteen cases of champagne all the way to the Fly. You might break a nail."

"Hey!" Vanessa cried, digging said French-manicured "works of art" into his knee.

"Ours is a very *abusive* relationship," Tyler explained, leaning forward between Clint and Callie. "But I can't help it—she makes me crazy!" he exclaimed, nuzzling her neck in a deliberately annoying way.

"Ow—Tyler—stop—my hair—my *hair*!"

Callie laughed.

"You couldn't have at least warned me that *she* was going to be here?" Vanessa asked when she had finally managed to push Tyler away. Her feather headdress had not survived the skirmish. That would probably earn Tyler a few more bruises and nail scratches later.

"Hey, Clint," said Tyler, cheerful as ever. "Did you know that when women cohabitate, their menstrual cycles often synch? We learned all about it last week in my Women, Gender, and Society seminar. College dorm rooms in particular have been known—"

Vanessa's blow caught him on the back of the head.

"Ow! Woman! That's going to leave a mark," he said, rubbing his head and pretending to look angry. "On second thought, no it's not. You're about as strong as a baby kitten and twice as cute."

"Oh, shut up," said Vanessa. "Are we there yet?"

"Tyler," said Callie, "you deserve a medal."

"I do," he agreed solemnly.

Vanessa snorted and folded her arms.

"Jeez Louise, Clinty," said Tyler, "I hope they're not this bad over spring break."

"What's happening over spring break?" asked Callie.

"Puerto Rico, baby—I booked us a villa. Sleep all day, booze all night, cruise the waves, eat bananas—"

"No way—" Vanessa began.

"Absolutely not," finished Callie.

"What?" asked Tyler. "You don't like bananas? Everybody likes bananas!"

"We are *not* staying in the same villa over spring break," said Vanessa. "I already have to live with her during the year. I shouldn't have to suffer on my vacation, too."

"Hey—easy there," said Clint. "And you can relax because Tyler's only teasing: we booked more than one villa so you two can stay as far away or as close together as you want. Plus," he added, turning the car into the Fly's lot, "as of right now it looks like almost everyone in the Pudding is going, plus half the Phoenix and the Spee." Pulling into a parking space, he killed the engine.

"Finally," said Vanessa, throwing open her door. "Tyler, come on!" she yelled, racing for the staircase at the edge of the parking lot. A faint green light was glimmering above the door at the top: the only entrance through which nonmembers were permitted to enter. Once inside, another set of stairs led straight to the second floor, where guests of members were allowed on special occasions, in contrast to the first floor of the brick mansion, which was strictly off-limits to all but the members.

"Hey," said Tyler as Clint opened the car door for Callie, "do you guys mind if I . . ."

"Go," said Callie. "I can help Clint carry the champagne."

"Thanks, buddy, I owe ya one," he said before Clint could protest.

"Tyler—now!"

"Coming, princess!" he yelled, running to catch up with Vanessa.

"I'm glad you're my girlfriend," said Clint, smiling at Callie as he opened the trunk.

Callie laughed. "I'm glad I'm not Vanessa's boyfriend," she said, reaching for a case of champagne.

"Hey, now—what do you think you're doing?" he asked, putting a hand on her arm.

"Helping you carry the champagne."

"I can't let you do that," he said, shaking his head.

"Seriously?" she asked. "Why not?"

"Need some help over here?" a voice called. Turning, she saw Gregory walking toward them. His bow tie hung loose and untied around his neck, black to Clint's white, and on his arm was . . .

Alexis Thorndike.

Each member got a plus three: one for a date and two for a couple. As Callie had learned last semester when she mistakenly thought Gregory and Lexi were dating, the two of them had a semi-permanent, fully platonic plus-one arrangement. Now the question was which came first: the chicken or the egg? Did Clint ask Gregory and did he invite Lexi—or was it the other way around?

"Hey, man, glad you guys could make it!" said Clint, giving Gregory a handshake-hug. "Lexi," he added, kissing her cheek, "you look lovely as ever."

Before Callie could react, she found herself in Gregory's arms. "Good to see you, *Caliente*," he whispered, pressing his lips against her ear. She could smell the whiskey on his breath.

"Some help would be great," said Clint, grabbing a case of champagne. Gregory followed suit, and then Clint turned to

Callie: "Could you ladies stand guard while we're gone? Normally I wouldn't ask because it's so cold, but the *Lampoon*'s right across the street and they've been known to have sticky fingers."

"Uh . . . sure," said Callie.

"We'll be right back."

Callie eyed the sixteen remaining cases of champagne in the trunk. Sixteen divided by two was eight, times roughly three minutes per case equaled twenty-four minutes alone with Lexi.

"So, uh . . . I like your dress," Callie ventured. And truly the dress was spectacular: black and silver, sequins and fringe and lace.

"Thanks," Lexi muttered.

Silence.

Twenty-three minutes . . .

"Where did you, um, where'd you get it?" Callie asked.

Lexi snorted as if to say, *Oh, just a little store on the corner of Dream-on and You-can't-afford-it.*

Right. Guess I'd better cancel the matching friendship bracelets I just ordered.

Twenty-two minutes . . .

"So where's Alessandra?" Callie asked.

"I believe she has *Crimson* business tonight," Lexi said with a worrisome gleam in her eye. "Which is why I suggested Gregory as a plus one after Clint invited me—though surely he already told you that?"

"Yes," Callie lied, trying to keep her expression blank. "We tell each other everything."

"Somehow I doubt that," Lexi murmured, watching Gregory and Clint reemerge at the top of the stairs.

"What's that supposed to me—"

"I completely forgot," Clint called, coming toward them, "that we have a whole bunch of sophomore initiates just dying to carry things." As he spoke, the back door opened and a group of guys appeared. "Shall we?" he said, offering an arm to Callie.

"Absolutely," she said.

Stepping through the doors to the Fly was like stepping through a time machine back to the summer of 1922. Twinkly lights hung from the ceiling like a canopy of leaves in the forest, casting a soft glow on the couples: guys in white tails with white gloves and girls with white gloves in white dresses. A live jazz band played in the corner of the dance floor. Along the opposite wall an enormous champagne fountain, the golden liquid infused with dashes of red berries, bubbled merrily atop a white tablecloth next to bowls of truffles and chocolate-covered strawberries, platters of gourmet cheeses and fat green grapes. Cigarettes and cigars fanned out in lines on various surfaces, and Callie watched a girl place one in a long old-fashioned cigarette holder, which she extended toward her date for a light.

You were right, Mrs. Jacobsen, Callie mentally conceded to her tenth-grade English teacher, who had given Callie an A- on a paper arguing that the novel—one of Callie's all-time favorites—was beautiful but failed to resonate with the "America of today."

Clearly, the old money "East Egg" contingent was alive and well and Callie, like a "West Egg" party crasher, must strive to blend in as best she could. Harvard, or at least this facet of it, was her green light, her dream, and maybe on Clint's arm she could convince them that she belonged. . . . But maybe, as it had for Gatsby, the dream would soon come crashing down and she would wind up shot in the back of the head, with Lexi or Vanessa standing at the edge of the swimming pool, holding the smoking gun.

"Champagne?" Clint asked.

"Thank you," said Callie, accepting the glass flute.

"Did I tell you that you look beautiful tonight?" he said, pocketing a cigar and leaning in to kiss her on the cheek. "I'm pretty sure I'm the luckiest man in this room."

Callie smiled. The jazz band struck up a faster number.

"Dance?" Clint asked, offering her two white-gloved hands.

"Sure!" she said, setting aside her champagne and placing her palms on his. "Um . . . how . . . ?" She had no idea how to dance to this kind of music.

"I think the fox-trot was popular back then," Clint said, steering her out onto the floor.

"Fox-*what*?"

"Fox . . . oh." He dropped her hands. "Dance wasn't a part of your curriculum back in California?"

"Dance *was* a part of your curriculum in Virginia?" she countered.

"Well—yes." The corners of his eyes crinkled. "There was seventh-grade dance class, when all the girls were a head taller than the boys and the only thing we learned was how to covertly wipe the sweat from our hands and that staring straight ahead *could* get you in a lot of trouble." As he spoke, he took her left hand in his right and wrapped his left arm around her waist. "Now I step forward with my left and you go back with your right," he said, moving his foot in tandem with hers and gripping her tight. "Next there was general cotillion training—that was my freshman year. We were taller, but the girls were just as terrifying. Now you brush your right foot with your left as you step back again," he said, stepping forward as she stepped back. "Good. Now brush your right foot to the left before we step to the side," he explained, and she followed his lead, "and the other foot follows quickly and—rest."

Other couples were twirling around them, but Callie could barely hear the music clipping along, lively and upbeat. She and Clint moved at their own private pace; the rest of the world melted away.

"One more time, slowly," he said, never breaking eye contact. "Back, back, side, together," he directed. "Right, left, right, left . . . Exactly, just like that," he said as they repeated the movements slowly. "Last of all, we had the debutante balls. By then mastering the basic steps was the least of our worries, and we were far more concerned over who would escort whom and everything that came with it. . . . Although the girls were, oddly, still just as terrifying," he finished with a laugh. He stopped suddenly.

"What's wrong?" she asked.

"Why, Ms. Andrews," he said, pulling her close, "I do believe you've mastered the fox-trot!"

"Did I? I did!" she cried. "Ooh, sorry!" she added, leaping off his toes.

He laughed. "Shall we?" he said, holding up his hands again.

"Yes," she agreed, smiling. And then they were dancing. *Back, back, side, together; Right, left, right, left; Slow, slow, quick, quick. Right back slow; left back slow; right side quick; left together quick—*they whirled across the floor as naturally and easily as any other couple under the canopy of lights. Finally, flushed and out of breath, they slowed, the music mellowing into softer, smoother jazz.

Clint's lips brushed against the top of her cheekbone. His breath tickled her ear, his hand firm on the small of her back. She closed her eyes and breathed him in. It was a perfect moment. The perfect moment to say . . .

"Clint," she whispered.

"Yes?"

"I . . ."

Off in the distance, propped against the back of a leather couch, she saw Gregory. He was staring straight at them. He held her gaze for a full two seconds. Then, tossing the stub of his cigarette into an empty glass, he left the room.

"You . . . what?" Clint prompted, leaning back to look at her.

"I—I want to hear more about what it was like to grow up in Virginia," she said quickly.

"Not so fast," he said. "I already told you all about dance class. It's your turn to tell me something about California."

She sighed.

"What?" he asked, twirling her slowly.

"Nothing," she said. "I just miss it."

"What do you miss the most?"

What *didn't* she miss? Back in California everything had always been so easy. Instead of crazy on-again off-again Vanessa she had Jessica, her unwavering best friend since first grade. Parties involved somebody's house, preferably with a pool, and maybe a stolen six-pack—but no themes. The temperature rarely dipped below a cool seventy-two degrees, meaning she could rock shorts seven days a week without giving a second thought to what she was wearing. And she'd barely had time for her boyfriend, let alone boy problems, with soccer practice thirty hours a week— an extracurricular where her talent was so obvious she'd never had anything to prove. Likewise, getting all As was almost an afterthought, with her parents—god, how she *missed* them— always in the background to cheer her on, there to love her no matter what.

"I miss . . . surfing," she finally said.

"Surfing?" he asked.

"Yep," she replied. "Sometimes in the spring Jess and I would roll out of bed at the crack of dawn, head over to the beach, and just ride the waves until the sun came up. It was the only athletic activity we could ever compromise on since she's much more of a Yogalates-because-the-gym-is-right-next-to-Fro-Yo kind of a girl. And even though we'd shower before school, my skin would still smell salty all day. It was the best."

"Sounds amazing," Clint agreed. "I'd love to learn how to surf."

"Maybe if you come to visit one day, I can teach you!" she said. "Plus, Jess has been dying to meet you."

"So you've been talking about me a lot, huh?" he teased.

"Well—yes." She blushed. "But that's only because—I mean not *only* but partly because—Jess and I tell each other *everything*."

"Well, I can't wait to meet her," he said. "The next time we get a vacation, it's a date."

"Speaking of vacations . . ." She frowned slightly. "Well, about spring break."

"Yes?" he prompted. "What about it?"

"It sounds incredible, but won't a trip like that be kind of, well, expensive?"

Clint smiled. "Don't you worry about that," he said, twirling her again.

What was that supposed to mean? Surely he wasn't thinking . . . "Clint I *am* worried, because I'm not sure . . ." Briefly she closed her eyes. "I'm not sure if I can afford it."

"It's already taken care of."

"But—"

"Think of it as an early birthday present."

"But—"

"Excuse me," someone said, tapping Clint on the shoulder. It was Bryan, who had been two years ahead of Callie back at West Hollywood High and was also a member of the Fly. "Sorry to interrupt," he continued, "but Clint, they need you upstairs."

Clint broke away from Callie but did not let go of her hands. "I hate to leave you like this. . . ."

"Go!" she urged, waving him away. "I'll be fine."

"You sure?" he asked.

"Yes."

"Be right back, then," he said, kissing her cheek.

She watched him disappear up a flight of stairs that led to another members only level of the club. Looking around, she spotted Vanessa and Tyler in a darkened corner, making up from whatever pseudo fight had happened most recently. Other than that, she recognized no one; even Lexi and Gregory were nowhere to be found and everyone else was coupled up, older, and totally unapproachable.

Sighing, Callie slipped through a door at the back of the great dance hall into a smaller, quieter room where couples were mingling. The air was hazy with smoke. Her breath caught in her chest and she coughed; Lexi and Anne stood at the end of a long line for the bathroom. Time for Plan B.

Doubling back, she scanned the room once more. Still no Clint. So, glancing over her shoulder, she pushed through another door: this one heavy and made of dark wood that she had only ever seen members passing through.

She was alone on a landing at the top of a staircase leading down. The walls were lined with old photographs (like 1898 old) of former club members. She hesitated, but only for a moment—there was bound to be a bathroom on the first floor, and if someone caught her, she could always play the I-had-to-pee card; after all, what's the worst that could happen?

Treading lightly, she bounded down the stairs and found herself in a large foyer. To her left she saw a dining room with double doors that probably led to a kitchen; on the right, a living room that looked promising. At the far end of the living room a wooden archway opened out into another room: a vast library. Hardcover volumes lined the shelves; lamps with red shades protruding from the walls cast a maroon glow on the wide brown leather couches, also lit dimly by the dull remaining embers in the brick fireplace.

Callie reached out to run her fingers along the spine of a green volume on her right. She was halfway through sliding it off the shelf when she heard a voice, faint at first, but then louder and louder, accompanied by the sound of muffled footsteps coming down the stairs. In another second the speaker would arrive in the living room, effectively trapping her. Shoving the book back into place, she ducked through another arched opening just beyond the shelf.

She stood in a small enclave: the space occupied almost exclusively by a huge mahogany desk with chairs on either side, piled high with winter coats. The walls were lined with more books, including the wall Callie flattened herself against now while she held her breath. Opposite her she noticed a plaque that read, OFFICE OF THE PRESIDENT. Closing her eyes, she prayed that the president, whoever he was, had elected to remain upstairs.

"You can't keep doing this," a male voice said, too muffled to identify. There was a crinkling sound as whoever had spoken sat down on a couch.

Callie listened, straining to hear the answer, but the other person in the room must have spoken very softly or stayed silent.

The first speaker's voice came again in hushed, barely audible fragments: "... I am involved now. . . . You can't just keep covering your tracks and expect to get away with it. . . . A lot of people could get hurt."

Callie held her breath, edging along the wall closer to the opening. She could still hear only snatches of the conversation: ". . . come clean now . . . the fallout will be worse the longer . . ."

Balancing with her left palm on the desk, she leaned forward, inching her right ear as close as possible to the source of the sound—

"IT WASN'T YOURS TO TAKE!" the voice suddenly boomed. Startled, Callie lost her balance and gripped the desk for support. Unfortunately, her fingers closed around a coat. She dragged it with her as she went down, knocking a lamp off the desk in the process. When she hit the floor, several other coats promptly fell on top of her.

For a moment she let herself lie there partially buried, hoping in vain that the coats would conceal her or that the people in the other room hadn't heard the commotion.

"Typical," a voice said, lazy and low. Its owner stood leaning against the archway. "So typical."

"Gregory?"

"Nice underwear," he replied.

Her knees snapped together, and she pushed herself off the floor. Peering around him, she looked out into the library: "Who else is . . . oh," she finished, watching him pocket his cell. "You were on the phone. Who were you talking t—?"

"Shhhh—" he hissed suddenly, grabbing her arm and cocking his head to the right.

"What? Wh—" Her eyes grew wide as he pushed her up against

the books lining the wall, his hand over her mouth, the other raised, a finger to his lips. But in another second she understood, the sounds now audible from the living room.

"We are most certainly *not* crashing this party!" an indignant voice cried. That BBC British accent could belong to only one man on campus and one man alone, but if there was any doubt it was dispelled a moment later.

"Unhand me, you *imbécile pompeux!*" cried the unmistakable voice of Mimi.

"I imagine you thought that by coming in masks, we wouldn't catch you," a third, male speaker said derisively. "Very clever . . ."

"Ah, *merci.*"

"Hey! The masks were *my* idea—"

"Enough!" The male speaker silenced OK.

Gregory, whose hands had fallen to the shelf on either side of Callie, pressed a finger to her lips. His eyes gleamed with the same suppressed laughter he had stopped not a moment too soon.

"Now can you see yourselves to the door," the member continued, "or am I going to have to *literally* kick you out?"

"Spare her!" OK cried theatrically. "And take me instead!"

Callie couldn't help it: she snorted. Her hands flew to her mouth, but fortunately no one—save Gregory—seemed to have heard, the voices dwindling as the member, or so she imagined, dragged Mimi and OK by the scruffs of their necks toward the front door. Gregory, who had instinctively grabbed her wrists, slowly let go as they heard the front door slam, followed by the sound of singular footsteps thudding back upstairs.

"We probably shouldn't be down here," Callie whispered after she finally managed to subdue her elated giggles.

"You're probably right," he agreed, strolling out of the president's office and throwing himself onto a leather couch with irritating bravado. "But 'I've been drunk for about a week now, and I thought it might sober me up to sit in a library.'"

"Gatsby?" she asked, perching on the edge of the couch in spite of herself.

"The one and only."

"It's a favorite of mine, too," she offered.

"I wouldn't exactly call it a *favorite*," he replied.

"Oh, so you just routinely memorize quotes from things that you don't like?"

"You don't have to *like* something to find it interesting or . . . irritatingly persistent."

"'Irritatingly persistent'?" she squawked. "Is that what you'd call one of the greatest American novels of all time!"

Gregory smirked. "Gatsby was a fool. Bending over backward for a chick who wasn't even worth it."

"You don't think it's romantic?" Callie asked, staring him down.

"No, I don't." He shrugged. "Not only does he pick the wrong girl, but he tries to change his whole personality just to fit into her world. What he doesn't realize is that he'll never belong with her, or in East Egg, no matter how many fancy shirts he may buy or parties he may throw."

Callie was quiet, watching the last remaining ember in the fireplace slowly die. "'It is invariably saddening to look through new eyes at things upon which you have expended your own powers of adjustment,'" she murmured finally, speaking almost to herself.

"Who's quoting now?" Gregory asked.

"Who were you on the phone with earlier?" she retorted, her head snapping back to him.

Instead of answering, he stood. "I'm overdue for a smoke," he said, pulling out a pack of cigarettes and walking into the living room.

"You know you can smoke inside tonight," Callie called, following him.

"I know," he said, turning when he reached the club's front door, where their roommates had been cast out only minutes earlier. "But it's no fun when you have permission."

Callie stood for almost a minute after he had gone. Eventually she shook her head and rounded toward the stairs. She was halfway to the top when she nearly collided with a guy on his way down.

"What are you doing here?" he asked, blocking any further passage.

"I was just looking for a bathr—"

"You're not supposed to be down here," he interrupted. "Girls are never allowed in this part of the club until after they graduate or if they are escorted by their husband. You should be upstairs, with your date."

"Okay," said Callie, holding up her hands. "That's where I was headed anyway, so if you could just exc—"

"*If* you even have a date," he finished, narrowing his eyes. "You weren't invited to this party tonight, were you?"

"Yes, I was," she stammered, wondering if he was the same boy who had expelled Mimi and OK.

"By who, then, if you don't mind my asking?" he challenged.

"Clint Weber," she said.

"Clint Weber." The guy snorted. "Nice try, but everyone knows he's got a long-term girlfriend even if she wasn't upstairs looking *pretty* cozy on the couch with him right now."

Callie swayed on the steps; all the feeling had drained out of her legs.

"That's impossible," she finally mustered, "I mean—there must be some kind of a misunderstanding—"

"The only thing I don't understand is how you managed to get in here in the first place. Did you use a fake name at the door?"

"Clint Weber is *my* boyfriend, and I *was* invited to this party!" she cried. "My name is Callie Andrews—you can check the list if you don't believe me!"

"There is no list," he said triumphantly. "The other initiates and I delivered the paper invitations by hand."

"This is ridiculous," said Callie. "Just let me by and Clint will explain the whole thing—"

"Callie Andrews," the guy said slowly, nodding now and surveying her up and down. "I knew I recognized that name somewhere. You're that slutty freshman wannabe porn star who made a sex tape with her high school boyfriend." He laughed. It was an ugly sound.

Turning, she tumbled down the stairs, raced across the foyer, and threw open the front door, determined to keep the tears from flowing until she made it outside. . . .

She could barely see as she bolted down the club's forbidden front steps, smack into—

"Callie? What the—ah!"

"Sorry," Callie mumbled, stooping to help Vanessa to her feet. Her roommate's heels had slipped in the snow.

Vanessa looked livid. "Next time watch where you're going! I could have twisted my ankle or snapped the heel off my Jimmy Choo—" Vanessa's lips froze, pursed in the shape of an "oo." "Are you—you're not . . . crying?"

Callie burst into sobs.

Vanessa stood there, looking stricken. "Do you want me to get Clint?"

"No!" Callie shook her head violently.

"Well, as it just so happens, I was actually on my way home. . . ." Vanessa shifted on her feet. Then she sighed. "I could walk you." Callie nodded, sniffling.

"Well, come on then," said Vanessa. Side by side, they trudged through the snow. Wordlessly Vanessa unwound her silvery beaded shawl from her neck and tossed it to Callie. Grateful, Callie hugged it around her goose-pimply arms.

"Do you wanna like, talk about it?" Vanessa ventured as they made their way past the *Harvard Lampoon*'s castle and onto Linden Street.

"No," Callie managed, staring down at the snow. "It's so stupid."

Fresh tears streamed down her cheeks. "Not worth crying over. It's just—" Her words were swallowed in a sob.

"Hookay, no more talking," Vanessa decided.

They continued on in silence until they reached Mass. Ave.: dark and almost sinister in its unusual emptiness.

"Why did *you* leave?" Callie asked curiously when the tears had eventually ceased.

"Uh . . . I . . ." Vanessa looked away. "Tyler kept making a big deal about how tonight was, like, The Night—you know?" she said with a shrug. "He kept going on and on about how everything was so *special* and *perfect* and wasn't my *first time* at a *real* college party fun and how he couldn't *wait* to get home later. . . . Eventually I got sick of all his oh-so-subtle *hints* and decided to respond with a little *hint* of my own—by sneaking out the back."

Callie nodded.

"Luckily I found you—after you almost killed me—so now *you* can be my excuse. 'Sorry Tyler, but Callie had a crisis. No, worse than the usual wardrobe malfunction.'"

Callie smiled weakly. Suddenly her phone buzzed in her purse. One new text message. It was from Clint: WHERE DID YOU GO?!?

"It's Clint," she said in response to Vanessa's questioning look.

"What are you telling him?" Vanessa asked, watching Callie's fingers fly across her phone's keyboard.

Callie smirked. "So sorry, but Vanessa had a crisis. Nothing worse than the usual wardrobe malfunction."

Vanessa gasped. "How dare you!" she said with mock horror.

"JK, the lies you tell to your boyfriend are none of *my* business."

"That's not what I actually said," Callie muttered. What she had actually said was this:

> SOMETHING WEIRD HAPPENED
> WITH ONE OF THE MEMBERS. IT'S
> NOT A BIG DEAL AND YOU SHOULD
> DEFINITELY STAY AND ENJOY THE
> PARTY. I'M WITH VANESSA AND
> WE'RE HEADED HOME. I'LL TALK TO
> YOU TOMORROW.

A moment later her phone buzzed with an incoming call from *Clint W*. Furrowing her brow, she silenced it—certain that repeating what had happened aloud would only lead to more tears. Plus, just because her night was ruined didn't mean his had to be, too. Her phone buzzed again, this time with a text:

> JUST TRIED TO CALL BUT YOU'RE
> NOT ANSWERING. . . . I HOPE
> WHATEVER HAPPENED WAS NOTHING
> TOO SERIOUS, AND I'M GLAD TO
> HEAR THAT YOU AND VANESSA ARE
> GETTING ALONG! TEXT ME WHEN
> YOU GET HOME SO I KNOW YOU'RE
> SAFE. I'LL SEE YOU TOMORROW.

The bright green door to Wigglesworth loomed ahead. Callie shut her phone. Vanessa paused with her key card poised. "Sooo . . . have you and Clint . . . ?"

"*Mm-hmm*. But not until way after the article came out . . . We waited until we were both completely ready. Now we've been making up for lost time, though," she added with a small smile.

"I know this is probably going to sound totally stupid," said Vanessa, "but I guess I always had this idea in my head about waiting until I was in love . . . or, like, at least five pounds skinnier."

Both good reasons, even the latter, in a weird comfortable-with-your-own-body way.

"And you don't love Tyler?" Callie prompted.

"Sometimes I don't even *like* Tyler," Vanessa said with a laugh. "I don't know; he's great . . . but do you ever feel with Clint that he's just, like, a whole lot older? I mean, I know it's only two years, but still . . . They're worrying about jobs and graduate school and what they're going to do with the rest of their lives, and we're still asking for directions to some of the major buildings on campus and figuring out which foods to avoid in the d-hall." She sighed, scanning her key card against the lock. "He's just not . . . my fish."

Callie smiled. Vanessa had devised Operation Fish Farm back during Shopping Period of their first semester, wherein she advised that they find a "diamond in the rough" freshman with potential, capture him from the wild, raise him, and domesticate him until finally, by senior year, after the culmination of a three-year plan, they would finally have the perfect boyfriend. (Unfortunately their status as fishing buddies had been disrupted when the pond appeared to have only one fish: Gregory—the white whale of the freshman class. No net was big enough.)

"If he's not your fish," Callie said when they were in the hall, "what is he, then?"

"He's . . . a shark. An oversexed shark with big slimy fins!"

Laughing, they opened the door to the common room. Dana sat alone on their couch, the typical array of textbooks surrounding her. Seeing them, she beamed. "Finally!" she called.

"Finally what?" asked Callie.

Dana drew herself up, looking very superior: "Pastor John always said, 'To err is human; to forgive is divine.'"

"I think that was Pope," Callie ventured.

"I'm not Catholic." Dana shook her head. "But I have certainly been praying for you two to make up, and I am happy to see that He has finally answered me!"

"What?" shrieked Vanessa. "We didn't make up!"

"Nuh-uh," Callie echoed, shaking her head.

"That's crazy talk," Vanessa added.

"We're going—I mean, I'm going to bed," Callie said.

"I was going first," Vanessa added.

"So?" asked Callie.

"So . . . get out of my way!" Vanessa cried, pushing past her.

"Fine, just try not to slam the—"

SLAM went the door to Vanessa's room.

". . . door this time," Callie finished. "What?" she added, rounding on Dana. The other girl stared her down until Callie lowered her eyes.

"She started it," Callie mumbled, heading for her room. "Sorry . . . G'night."

"Nonsense," Dana muttered, turning back to her textbook. "Absolute nonsense."

EIGHT

THE FRESHMEN FIFTEEN

The votes are in and now, presented to you by
Fifteen Minutes magazine . . .

The Freshmen Fifteen:
Harvard's Fifteen Hottest Freshmen

(See page 5 for more photos!)

Name: Levi Johnson

From: Philadelphia, PA

Three Words to Describe Yourself: Run, Bike, Swim

Favorite Friday Night Activity: See above

Best Pickup Line: "No, not the guy who impregnated Bristol Palin . . . but how you doin'?"

Name: Okechuwuku Zeyna

From: Nigeria

Three Words to Describe Yourself: Big, Black, and Beautiful

Favorite Friday Night Activity: Grand Theft Auto with my French mistress

Best Pickup Line: "I'm a prince, did you know?"

Name: Lily Hanafee

From: Little Rock, Arkansas

Three Words to Describe Yourself: Southern, Sassy, Adventurous

Favorite Friday Night Activity: Anything that involves dancing

Best Pickup Line: "No thank you."

Name: Marine Aurélie Clément
From: Paris/London/Switzerland
Three Words to Describe Yourself: *Je ne sais quoi*
Favorite Friday Night Activity: Decimating the African Prince in GTA-IV
Best Pickup Line: *"Bonjour."*

Name: Gregory Brentworth Bolton (not pictured)
From: New York, New York
Three Words to Describe Yourself: Are you serious?
Favorite Friday Night Activity: My Jane Austen book club, of course
Best Pickup Line: "Go away, I'm not interested."

Name: Damien "DJ" Zhang
From: Shanghai
Three Words to Describe Yourself: Number One Stunner
Favorite Friday Night Activity: Spinning tables at the clubs
Best Pickup Line: "So, how would you like me to be your first Asian?"

Name: Vanessa Von Vorhees
From: Manhattan
Three Words to Describe Yourself: Classy, Fabulous, and Irreplaceable
Favorite Friday Night Activity: Fighting with my boyfriend
Best Pickup Line: "Oooh, does that come in my size?"

Name: Matt Robinson
From: Ithaca, New York
Three Words to Describe Yourself: Geeky And Proud
Favorite Friday Night Activity: You can usually find me at the *Crimson* with my favorite managing editor ;)
Best Pickup Line: "Oh . . . ah, gee, crap—can I have some more time?"

(profiles continued on page 11)

"Andrews! Robinson!" an unmistakable voice barked. "Does this look like a motel? I thought I told you to stop sleeping here," Grace continued, slamming the door to the offices of the *Crimson* behind her, "and start sleeping in the dormitories that the university has graciously provided you!" She now stood only a few feet away from where Matt lay slumped across the desk next to Callie, but her shouts—even coupled with Callie's frantic nudging—had failed to rouse him.

Grace held up her hand, indicating that Callie should cease, and leaned in toward Matt's ear until she was mere inches away. "Robbbinsonnn . . ." she whispered in a soft, singsong. "Oh, Robinson . . ."

"*Mmm*," he mumbled, smiling in his sleep, a tiny spit bubble forming at his mouth.

Grace blinked. "WAKE YOUR ASS UP RIGHT NOW OR IT'S MINE!"

"HOLYMOTHEROF—*AH!*" Matt screamed, knocking over a coffee cup as he leaped to his feet. "Wha— Grace! Good morning—hello—hi!" His hands flew to his shirt, trying to smooth the wrinkles. Giving up, he went to work on his hair. Callie tried to mime, *You have drool on your face*, with little success.

Sighing, Grace bent over and picked up the mug. "From now

on this building is *not* your crash pad, understood? However, I am glad that the two of you are here. Big day today!"

"What—ah—yes, big day," Callie stammered. She had no idea what Grace was talking about or whether she was supposed to know in the first place. "Big, big day."

"Well, what are you people waiting for? Let's move!" Grace snapped.

Matt suppressed a yawn. "What time is it?" he whispered to Callie as they followed Grace outside.

"Just after ten," she whispered back. "Do you have any idea . . . ?"

"No." Matt grimaced. "There was nothing on my GCal. . . ."

"Pick up the pace back there!" Grace yelled over her shoulder.

"Well, ask!" Callie hissed at Matt.

"You ask," Matt hissed back.

"Fine!" she muttered. "Um, Grace," she called. "Today's the day, isn't it?"

"You can say that again, Andrews."

Callie glared at Matt. "Today . . . is the day," she repeated lamely.

"Exactly," Grace said. Even though her legs were several inches shorter than Callie's, not to mention a full foot shorter than Matt's, they both still had to walk double-time to keep up. "The day we are all going to witness one of *FM*'s oldest and most obscene traditions: 'The Freshmen Fifteen.'"

"'The Freshmen Fifteen'?" Matt echoed.

"Yes, we'll be covering it just in case the Insider doesn't get the scoop," Grace said with a worrisome wink at Callie.

"Grace," Callie started, "you know I'm not—"

"Allowed to publish yet," Grace finished for her. "Yes, of course I know. You'll be assisting Robinson on the FlyBy piece featuring our own version of their perverted popularity pageant. I'm thinking The 'Most Promising Fifteen' or something along those lines, based on academics and extracurriculars, and I'll be following up with an op-ed for the *Crimson* that will hopefully feature some one-on-one interviews with the so-called 'hottest.'" If the speed at which she spoke served as an indicator of her excitement, you'd think she'd just uncovered the next Watergate.

Callie glanced at Matt, grateful that he looked just as confused as she felt.

"Er, Grace," Matt finally said as they tore down Quincy Street, past Lamont Library and the Barker Center. "What exactly is 'The Freshmen Fifteen'?"

Grace whirled around. To their surprise, she smacked herself on the forehead. "Of course you don't know—only freshmen," she muttered. Then she cleared her throat and started walking again. "Every spring *FM* puts out an issue featuring 'The Fifteen Hottest Freshmen.' The editors vote based purely on looks and quote unquote 'personality'. It has historically been one of their highest circulating issues and is, in my opinion, the epitome of everything that is wrong with not only the publication but the mind-set of its editors. We're here," she finished, stopping short.

They were standing outside an enormous brick building flanked by poles with black banners that read THE FOGG MUSEUM. Callie and Matt exchanged nervous glances as they followed Grace up the stone steps. Inside, a curator dressed in black tended the front desk. "We're not open to the public today," she said, smiling apologetically.

"We're here for the photo shoot," Grace explained.

"Oh, excellent," said the curator. "They're upstairs now in the American wing. Shall I phone ahead to inform them of your arrival?"

"That won't be necessary," Grace said shortly. "Andrews, Robinson? It's go time."

She powered up the marble stairs with Callie and Matt trailing closely at her heels. When they reached the third floor, Grace held a finger to her lips. Slowly they crept into the closest room, the white walls lined with paintings by famous American artists from the mid-nineteenth century. Callie paused in front of a work by Winslow Homer, staring at the dark waves tossing a tiny ship at sea.

"Andrews!" Grace hissed, beckoning her. Grace tilted her head in the direction of a neighboring room. As they approached, Callie heard someone speaking.

"Hold still, everyone," a male voice cried. "And please remember to *smise*! That's Tyra talk for *smiling* with your *eyes*."

"Marcus, I thought I told you to hold off on the group picture because we're still missing one of them," a clear, high voice called. Callie didn't need a visual to recognize the speaker: Alexis Thorndike.

"It's been twenty minutes," Marcus—a senior who bartended at the Harvard Pub—replied. "Boyfriend's clearly a no-show."

"Let me try him again on his cell," Lexi said.

Following Grace's lead, Callie stopped just outside the entrance to an enormous room dotted with sculptures fashioned from metal or stone. Inside, an elaborate photo shoot appeared to be taking place. Marcus, overseen by Alexis, stood in front of a camera mounted on a tripod, with bright lights winking on either side. A group of freshmen, including Vanessa, Mimi, and OK, were positioned in awkward poses around several of the sculptures. An upperclassman writer for *FM* named Tom, who had frequently given Callie positive feedback on her pieces, hovered in the background taking notes.

"Just remember," Marcus called as Lexi whipped out her cell, "that the camera is only on reserve till noon so—"

"Just give me a minute!" Lexi snapped.

"As you wish, Your Highness," Marcus said, performing an exaggerated bow.

"Please." Alexis snorted, hanging up her phone. "The only *queen* in this room is y—"

"It's Monday, March seventh, and I'm here in the Fogg Museum at a photo shoot for *FM* magazine's infamous issue featuring 'The Fifteen Hottest Freshmen,'" Grace said loudly, walking into the room. She spoke into the mouthpiece of her iPhone, which ran a voice recording app. Lexi wheeled around. "The day is off to an interesting start," Grace continued, "with a politically incorrect, possibly homophobic slur from the magazine's editor and COMP director, third-year Alexis Th—"

"What do you think you're doing here?" Lexi demanded,

marching up to them. "This isn't *Crimson* business."

Grace smiled and clicked Pause on her phone's voice recorder. "Since you are still affiliated with the paper despite my recent recommendation to the board, everything you do is *Crimson* business—even though little that you do upholds our standards and fundamental commitment to excellence."

"Please," Lexi said, rolling her eyes, "it's a *school* paper, not the *Wall Street Journal*, and you're a college junior, not Carl Bernstein—even if you do have the same seventies-style man's haircut."

"I don't know which I find more insulting," Grace mused, pretending to really consider the question, "your trivializing our *nation*'s oldest continuously published daily university newspaper, which incidentally boasts several alums who are currently staff writers at the *WSJ,* or the fact that you don't like my hair."

"If we are so beneath your standards," Lexi shot back, struggling to keep her cool, "then I repeat: what are you doing here?"

"Well, if you must know," said Grace, "we're doing an opinion piece on your annual popularity contest. I'm quite curious to learn how the rest of the one thousand nine hundred and eighty-five other freshmen at this school feel about not being the quote-unquote 'hottest.'"

Oof, thought Callie, watching Mimi and Vanessa primp and preen for the photograph. When you put it that way . . . Being one of the one thousand nine hundred and eighty-five of the not-worthy-of-an-article and, conversely, *ugliest* freshmen on campus really didn't feel so good.

Lexi exhaled, her lips pressed together in a thin line. "'The Fifteen Hottest Freshmen' is, as you are well aware, one of our oldest traditions—"

"Sometimes it's the oldest traditions that are the most deplorable," Grace interrupted. "Take, for example, slavery, or the disenfranchisement of women—"

"You did *not* just compare some silly magazine article to slavery—"

"So you admit that your articles are *silly*!" Grace retorted, brandishing her iPhone.

Lexi looked murderous. "'The Freshmen Fifteen' is—"

"Fourteen," Matt murmured suddenly.

"What?" Grace and Lexi shouted simultaneously, rounding on him.

"There are only—ah—fourteen people posed for the photo over there," Matt said, seeming to deeply regret his decision to speak. "Not fifteen."

Slowly Grace and Lexi turned to look at the fourteen— indeed there were only fourteen, plus Marcus and Tom— frozen faces, riveted as if they'd scored front row seats to a prize fight. Mimi waved cheerily at Callie. Vanessa flipped her hair. OK struggled to maintain his pose, mimicking the statute of a nude warrior with bow and arrow next to him. Tom coughed uncomfortably. Marcus, a delighted gleam in his eye, snapped several pictures of the two female editors, now inches away from each other's face.

Lexi cleared her throat. "As you can see, I'm afraid that you and your protégées"—she shot a withering death glare at Callie—"are interfering with our shoot, and so I'm sorry, but I'm going to have to ask you to leave."

"And I'm afraid that you don't have the authority to do that," Grace said, infusing her voice with Lexi's signature saccharine quality.

Lexi took a deep breath, but before she could reply, Tom walked over and said, "Actually, it might be to our advantage if they stayed. You're a freshman, right?" he added, turning to Matt.

"Yes," said Matt.

"Well, we're still missing a fifteenth, and it doesn't look like this Bolton character is going to show so . . ." Tom was still looking at Matt. "Perhaps you could stand in?"

"Him?" Lexi asked.

"Me?" Matt echoed. "As one of *the* fifteen—no!—I mean—wait—really?"

"Sure, man," said Tom, clapping him on the shoulder. "You'll be great."

Grace scoffed at the just-won-Miss-America expression on Matt's face. "Never underestimate the power of vanity," she whispered to Callie, nudging her. "It's settled, then," she said so everyone could hear. "Robinson will participate in the shoot—almost as if he was on an undercover assignment," she added pointedly, "and Andrews and I will observe and then shadow the individual interviews."

Lexi was shaking her head. "I don't—"

"We'll be so quiet you won't even know we're here."

"But—"

"Clock's a-tickin', ladies," Marcus called, the flash on his camera flickering as he snapped several more photos of the standoff. "Shall we get this show on the road?"

Callie glanced at Lexi. The older girl had the same about-to-explode air as a grenade. Callie suppressed a smile, watching Lexi take deep, calming breaths. "Fine," Lexi whispered when she could finally talk again. "Carry on."

Matt bounded over to join the group. "And do something about his hair!" she yelled halfheartedly.

Marcus began repositioning his subjects and kept encouraging OK to move to a place of greater prominence. Callie smirked when Vanessa started gesturing frantically from the other side of the room, no doubt insisting that she belonged in the front row and refusing to let OK obscure the brand-new outfit and heels she'd most likely purchased for the occasion. Meanwhile Matt hovered awkwardly in the background, seemingly torn between laughing at and trying to mimic OK's outlandish poses. . . .

"All right, that's a wrap!" Marcus finally called twenty minutes later. "Time for the individual shots: How about we start with you, sugar?" he said, pointing to OK. "Now the first thing we want to know is: single or taken? Gay or straight?"

"Actually, I'll be conducting the interviews, Marcus," Tom interceded, smiling wryly at Callie, whom Grace had assigned to shadow him while she personally covered Lexi, blocking her every move like a basketball player on the court. Callie smiled back and pulled out a pen and paper from her book bag so she could take notes, thankful that she still had several hours until her Economics 10b lecture started. Grace and Lexi had begun bickering again loudly, and from the looks of it, it would be a while before they left the museum....

The next day after their afternoon classes Callie and Matt were, once again, at the Crimson. "I'm starting to feel like we live here," Callie moaned, resting her head on the desk.

"Maybe we should buy a potted plant—decorate or something," Matt offered.

"What I don't get is why *you're* here so much," Callie said, lifting her head. "Aren't you supposed to have way less work now that you've officially made it onto the paper?"

"I, er," Matt stammered, glancing toward the office door that read MANAGING EDITOR. "I'm just trying to make a good impression."

". . . on Grace?" Callie prompted.

"Well, yes, but the other editors, too!" Matt cried, his face going all ripe tomato.

Callie nodded, deciding not to push it. She was glad Matt, who felt more and more like a brother every day, had finally misplaced his misplaced affection elsewhere. (Teddy was still stuck to the bulletin board.)

"Plus, they were all out of issues of *FM* this morning at breakfast and I sort of wanted to snag a paper copy," Matt explained, waving said copy in the air, which featured the results of yesterday's grueling photo shoot on its cover with *The Freshmen Fifteen* written beneath in glossy lettering.

Callie grinned. "We should frame it," she said, grabbing the magazine.

"Stop—"

"No, seriously. You look good!"

Matt stared at his photo for a moment. "I've gotten eighteen new friend requests on Facebook since this morning. Do you suppose it's related?"

"Either way, your stock is through the roof!" she said. And it's about damn time.

"You think?" he muttered, squinting again at his photo.

"Yes I think," she said. "And I also think that maybe you're . . . dare I say . . . enjoying it?"

Matt dropped the magazine, looking guilty. "Well, of course I— well—goes completely against everything we—I mean, me and Grace, or, ah, Grace and I, or yeah, *we* stand for but . . ." Miserable, he frowned.

"It's *okay* to enjoy it," Callie said, placing a hand over his. "You *are* one of the coolest freshmen on this campus, and it's awesome that now everybody else knows it, too!" Matt blushed. Quickly Callie removed her hand. After all, the "we" of "me and Grace, or, ah, Grace and I" only went so far. "I just hope," she added, slightly reproachful, "that maybe now you'll have a bit more sympathy for the fun side of being selected to belong to a supposedly 'exclusive' or 'elite' group on campus."

Matt narrowed his eyes, but then he grinned like he knew that she had him. "Well, I did draw the line at going to that party your Pudding club put on last night in our 'honor.' What was it called? 'The Fortunate Fifteen' or 'Fifteen and Fabulous'—"

"'The Fabulous Fifteen,'" Callie supplied. She had also missed the party thrown for those featured in the article—a high number of whom were already in the Pudding or were punching this spring—due to the volume of her workload, the fact that it was a Monday night, and the small part of her that felt less than "fabulous" after being excluded from the article.

"Besides," Matt was saying, "I wasn't *actually* selected: I was filling in only because Greg decided at the last minute not to show."

"What a flake," Callie exclaimed. "Did you ever find out why he bailed?"

"He said something in the room this morning about 'wanting to keep a low profile.'"

Callie snorted. "Yeah, because that sounds just like him."

Matt shrugged. "I don't know," he said. "I think he might mean it. OK asked if he could borrow his car the other day and Gregory said that it was in the shop but that he might be getting rid of it because he's decided that for a student to have a car on a contained college campus is, and I quote, 'excessive.' Maybe he was lying, though," Matt added, "as I'm not sure OK knows how to drive or that it would be wise to lend him any car—let alone a Porsche—even if he did."

Callie leaned back in her chair, staring at the ceiling. "Weird," she finally said. Maybe Gregory really was undergoing some kind of major personality overhaul, and maybe it had something to do with—well, now, what a coincidence. . . .

"Alessandra! Hi!" Callie called as the girl in question walked into the offices.

"Hey, did you see the issue?" Matt added, sitting up straight and holding the magazine.

"Hi," said Alessandra shortly, setting her purse down by a computer near the back. "I did, and you look *great*," she answered Matt, coming over to where they were sitting. "I'm sorry, but I can't hang around and chat, though—I've got a lot of work to do," she finished, nodding toward the other end of the room.

"No worries," said Callie. "We're, uh, working, too," she added, pulling up a browser, ". . . and checking a few e-mails," she added guiltily, coming face-to-face with her in-box. Whoops.

"See you later then," Alessandra called, walking away to join several other COMPers who were also working quietly in the back of the offices.

"*Whoa,*" said Callie suddenly after turning back to her e-mail. "Look at this!" she cried in a hushed tone, clicking on a message.

From: **Anne Goldberg**

To: **[The Members of the Hasty Pudding social club]**

Subject: Police incident at the club last night

Dear Members,

For those of you who don't already know, the Harvard University police department broke up a party hosted at the club last night, supposedly due to a noise complaint from one of our neighbors. So far our organization has emerged from this incident with only a warning from the HUPD and has yet to be reprimanded by the university, although disciplinary action has been taken against two underage students (a member and a nonmember) who were found in possession of open containers of alcohol outside the club.

However, in light of these events, the board has elected to suspend all gatherings until Leather & Lace, our annual party scheduled for the week after we initiate new members. Until then there are to be no parties and absolutely no alcohol consumption, even by members who are of age, within the club. Thank you in advance for your understanding.

We are looking into the origins of the complaint as this evening was fairly low-key compared to our other events. I will personally keep you posted on any new developments.
Sincerely,
Anne Goldberg, Secretary

"Wow," said Matt, who had been reading over her shoulder. "Good thing neither of us went to that party!"

"Yeah, seriously," said Callie. "I hope nobody we know got in trouble. . . ." Returning to her in-box, she saw another e-mail from Anne, subject heading: *Thank you*. What the . . .

From: **Anne Goldberg**

To: **Callie Andrews**

Subject: Thank you

Callie,

Thank you for your more than generous contribution toward our punch process. However, at the risk of being redundant, I must reiterate that it is ill-advised to leave an envelope full of cash on my desk without, at the very least, notifying me in advance.

Regards,

Anne

What the . . . WHAT?!?

"Huh . . ." said Matt from where he was sitting, staring at his own computer.

"What?" she asked.

"Nothing, just reading Grace's op-ed on the shoot yesterday. . . ."

"Oh, it's up?" said Callie, opening the *Crimson* website.

"Yeah, it's up," Matt murmured, his eyes still trained on his screen. "It's up and it's a little . . . *harsh*."

"A *little* harsh?" Callie repeated incredulously after she had skimmed the article. "It's poisonous," she said in a whisper, looking around to make sure that none of the people working in the back were listening. "Poisonous to the point of being . . . unprofessional."

"Well, I wouldn't go that far."

"Look," Callie said. "I get why she hates the Final Clubs and the Pudding even though it's co-ed—I mean, I get why you do, too—but what I don't fully understand is this rage against *FM*. It just seems so . . . *personal*."

"The magazine does tend to praise certain institutions and practices that . . ." Matt glanced down at the issue that was still open on the page declaring him one of Harvard's hottest freshmen, looking sheepish.

"Even though I have every reason to hate you-know-who," Callie continued, pointing up to the second-floor offices, "I can still admit that I genuinely enjoy the magazine. Yes, sometimes it's trashy, but mostly it's just entertaining, lighthearted, and fun. And you gotta admit that everyone on campus reads her column, whether or not you agree with the advice."

"Sure," Matt said. "There's definitely some value to the lighthearted, entertaining stuff. . . . You know, I really wish they'd given me some more time to come up with my 'best pick-up line.' Like, how about the one where you ask if she has a library card, 'cause 'I wanna check you out'?"

Callie wasn't listening, staring instead at the screen in front of her. "I wonder . . . hmm."

"You wonder what?" asked Matt, setting down the issue and watching her pull up a browser.

"I wonder if Lexi and Grace have some sort of weird history that we don't know about," she explained, starting to type.

A simple Google search revealed nothing. Frowning, she navigated to the page for the *Crimson*'s internal website. "Huh . . . that's strange," she muttered.

"What?" Matt asked.

"Oh, nothing. It just says that it logged me out of our internal server because I was logged in at another location."

Matt shrugged. "Unfortunately that's not unusual; the system gets pretty buggy sometimes. Or your session could have timed out while you were busy reading your *e-mail*—I mean working really hard!" he amended as she socked him on the arm.

"Ooh, look at this!" she said a moment later. "It's a list of everyone who's ever COMPed the *Crimson*. . . . See, there's 'Lee, Grace, in fall 2008,'" she pointed out while Matt leaned in, "And . . . whoa . . . looks like Lexi COMPed the *Crimson* that semester, too! I wonder if she got *cut*," Callie finished excitedly.

Bored, Matt turned back to his own computer. "Frankly I'm not sure why you care."

Callie silenced him with a wave, pulling up the list of everyone who had COMPed *FM*. Frowning as she passed her own name, she continued scrolling down until she found it: *Thorndike, Alexis, spring 2009.*

"Interesting . . ." Callie muttered.

"Oh, I'm sure it is, Nancy Drew," Matt said with a smirk, now busy editing an article.

"Hush!" she admonished him. Then she ran Grace's name through the Harvard College search engine. There were three

Grace Lees but only one who was class of 2012 and currently lived in Dunster (the upperclassman house where Grace resided), after apparently living in Thayer when she was a freshman.

There was only one Alexis Vivienne Thorndike in the system (thank *god*). Class: 2012; Current Residence: Kirkland House; Freshman Dormitory: Weld (*Thayer*).

Thayer in italics and parentheses? The same Thayer where Grace had lived? Now that was intriguing. Quickly Callie pulled up a site that let you search the exact room and residence of every former Harvard freshman (designed to cater to incoming students who liked to brag that Bill Gates or Tommy Lee Jones had once propped his feet up on *their* desk in *their* bedroom, ergo they too would one day invent Windows and win Oscars). Her fingers flew across the keyboard.

Lee, Grace: Thayer 314 (2008-2009)

Thorndike, Alexis: Weld 33 (2008-2009); Thayer 314 (2008)

"Oh my goodness," she said breathlessly. *"Matt!"*

"What?"

"Lexi and Grace were *roommates* during their freshman year!"

"So?" he said, returning to the article he was working on.

"So! Um . . . so . . ." Huh. So what? "Well, Lexi must have transferred out, for one thing, and maybe the reason they hate each other has to do with something that happened back when—"

"Callie?" a voice called from behind them. Turning, she saw Clint strolling into the offices with two lattes in hand. Quickly she shut the browser before standing and throwing her arms around him.

Matt glanced up and gave Clint the usual cursory grunt.

"There's my hottest freshman," Clint said, smiling and handing her a latte.

"Gee, thanks," said Callie, sitting back in her chair. "Glad somebody thinks so."

"It's my word against the school's," Clint said, bending to kiss her cheek.

"Actually, it's your word against the editors'," Callie retorted. "One of whom is your ex-girlfriend. Speaking of which—"

"Oh no," said Clint, shooting Matt a look. "Here we go again." Callie pursed her lips. "I'm just wondering if you know anything about a possible feud between Lexi and Grace."

"Why do you want to know?"

"I'm just curious. From a journalistic perspective."

Sighing, Clint perched on the edge of her desk. "They were roommates for a while, and then something happened—maybe something about stolen shoes?—but Lex and I had only just started dating when she transferred rooms so more than that, I couldn't say."

"Did you know that Lexi COMPed the *Crimson* her first semester freshman year?" Callie asked.

"Yes," said Clint.

"Do you know why she joined *FM* the following semester instead? I mean did she get cut or—"

"I don't really remember," he said shortly.

"Well, then is there anything else you can tell me? Anything that might seem odd or relevant?"

"As much as I love constantly talking about her with you," Clint said without attempting to hide his sarcasm, "it's already ten past four, and I've got to get to squash practice."

"Okay," she said. "Thanks for the coffee. So, I'll see you tonight? I should be done here around seven thirty—"

"Actually, I'm sorry but I can't tonight," said Clint. "Pudding stuff."

"Oh," she said. "Okay. Hey! Is it because of that police thing?"

"Uh—no," he said, "it's something else. . . . Board only, though, so you don't have to worry about it," he finished, kissing the top of her head. "I will see you tomorrow for our weekly Wednesday lunch date."

"Wednesday lunch date it is," she agreed, waving as he left the offices.

A moment later her phone buzzed.

1 NEW TEXT MESSAGE
FROM CLINT WEBER

Smiling, she read:

BTW, I FORGOT TO MENTION: WE HAD A MEETING LAST NIGHT ABOUT THE SOPHOMORE WHO KICKED YOU OUT OF GATSBY AND NOW HE'S BEEN KICKED OUT OF THE CLUB— FOR GOOD. I APOLOGIZE AGAIN THAT THE NIGHT TURNED INTO SUCH A MESS. REALLY, I COULDN'T BE MORE SORRY. . . .

NO WORRIES, she drafted back. Then, after thinking for a few seconds, she added:

P.S. THERE'S SOMETHING I FORGOT

> TO ASK YOU, TOO: TOTALLY RANDOM,
> BUT YOU HAVEN'T BY ANY CHANCE
> BEEN LEAVING ENVELOPES FULL OF
> CASH ON ANNE'S DESK AT THE
> PUDDING WITH MY NAME ON THEM?

Her phone buzzed.

> WEIRD . . . I WONDER WHO IT
> COULD BE—DEFINITELY NOT ME,
> THOUGH!

Callie barely had time to consider his response, since she had been certain that Clint was the only logical explanation left, when her phone buzzed again:

> ALSO . . . I MISS YOU ALREADY!
> CAN'T WAIT FOR WEDNESDAY :)

Staring down at her phone, she beamed.

An odd gagging noise came from the vicinity of Matt's computer.

"What?" she demanded, still unable to stop smiling.

"Nothing," Matt muttered. "There's just something about that guy. . . . He's too shiny."

"Shiny?" Callie repeated with a giggle.

"Yeah," said Matt, sticking to his guns. "Shiny like . . . perfect. Too perfect. Or something."

"Oh, Matt," Callie said, shaking her head and putting her phone away. "There's no such thing as too perfect."

NINE

BUSTED!

flyby

March 8   **Behind the Ivy-Covered Walls: Part III**

4:02PM   By THE IVY INSIDER

An op-ed appeared in the *Harvard Crimson* late this afternoon ("Narcissism and Objectification Run Rampant at Freshmen Fifteen Photo Shoot") decrying one of the magazine's oldest traditional articles, "The Freshmen Fifteen" (also published earlier this morning).

However, it appears the drama over the latest issue of the magazine was not confined to the offices of its editors.

Late last night the Harvard University police busted up a party at the Hasty Pudding social club supposedly intended to honor the so-called "fifteen hottest." Two sophomores whose names have yet to be released were issued MIP citations (Minor in Possession) when discovered with open containers of alcohol on the club's front steps. It is unknown at this point whether further legal action will be taken or if the university will see fit to discipline the individuals.

And yet it seems that their actions are merely a small sampling of what really goes on behind closed doors: the underage drinking, the drugs, and who knows what else. Even an e-mail from the club's secretary sent to members this afternoon notes that the night was "fairly low-key compared to our other events." So why did the police show at all?

What was previously believed to be a noise complaint from a neighboring building has now been confirmed as a whistle-blower from the inside. Perhaps it was an inside job. Maybe even *the* Insider. Stay tuned. . . . After all, actions speak louder than words.

"I'll put two pounds—sorry, dollars—on one fifteen. Over or under?" OK whispered to Adam, who sat next to him in the plush green chairs of the Science Center's D auditorium.

"Under," Adam whispered back, checking his watch and then looking at Mimi, who, after arriving late, had just settled into a seat several rows in front of them.

"What are they doing?" Callie asked Dana, who was frowning and shaking her head while their professor for *Science B-29: The Evolution of Human Nature* fiddled with the overhead projector.

"Gambling," said Dana, her lips a tight, thin line. "He knows I don't approve."

"It's not gambling," Adam said, leaning over to address Callie. "Just a little friendly betting game we like to play to keep class more interesting."

"Class is already interesting," Dana hissed, writing the phrase *The theory of* in front of the word *Evolution* at the top of her page and then underlining *theory* twice.

Callie—who up until recently had been sitting with strangers, having tended to wait for Mimi until she realized doing so was making her late—was intrigued.

"How does it work?" she whispered. Dana harrumphed and bent over her notebook. The professor switched on his microphone and began to speak.

"Well, when we get here I pick a time, say, 1:04, when I think it's likely that Mimi will arrive," Adam began.

"And then I say 'over' or 'under' depending on whether I think she'll show up earlier or later," OK explained.

"When she gets here," Adam continued, "we play double or nothing for the moment when she inevitably falls asleep."

"I get to pick that time, 1:15 in today's case," said OK.

"And then I choose 'over' or 'under,'" Adam finished.

"How is that not gambling?" Dana whispered, tired of pretending she wasn't listening.

"It's not gambling if he never actually pays me," Adam assured her. "You owe me twenty-two dollars, by the way," he murmured to OK under his breath.

"This is Lucy," Professor Hanson—or as he was fondly known around campus, Professor *Handsome*—said. The projector displayed a photograph of what looked like a fossilized Neanderthal. "And this," he continued with a click of his keyboard, "is Lucy's great-great-grandmother."

The screen lit up with the image of an ape scratching its head. Several students giggled.

Callie watched Dana sigh heavily and draw a line down the center of her notes. At the top of the left-hand column she wrote *Learned in Class*, then labeled the other column *Reality*.

"Humans are descended from monkeys," she scribbled on the left-hand side of the page. Then, across from it on the other side, she wrote: *"False: God created the heavens and the universe in six days, and on the seventh day he rested—Genesis."*

"I don't mean to be rude," Callie whispered, "but why are you taking this class?"

"Because it is best to know thine enemy," Dana said. "Why else would I ever watch MSNBC programming?"

"Pay up," said Adam suddenly, extending his hand to OK. It was 1:13 and Mimi was fast asleep.

"Brilliant," said Callie. OK groaned softly. "And does she fall asleep every time?" she asked.

"Every time." Adam nodded. "Except the three times when she never showed. You still owe me for those, too," he added.

"What? No fair! I thought we were calling those a draw!"

Bzzz-bzzz-bzzz, Callie's phone vibrated in her bag. "Sorry," she whispered as Dana sighed again.

> 1 NEW TEXT MESSAGE
> FROM CLINT WEBER
>
> SO IT'S WEDNESDAY . . .

Smiling, she texted back: YEP!
Her phone buzzed again.

> BUT UNFORTUNATELY I CAN'T BRING
> YOUR LUNCH TO LAMONT TODAY
> BECAUSE I HAVE A STUDY GROUP
> FOR MY GOVERNMENT MIDTERM
> TOMORROW MEETING IN WIDENER
> AT 1. SO SORRY. ARE YOU GOING
> TO STARVE?!

It had become a Wednesday tradition for Clint to swing by FlyBy (the to-go food service from which the new more-than-daily-news website derived its name) and bring Callie a bagged lunch at Lamont, where she had to be for her one o'clock shift directly after class.

> NO WORRIES! I CAN RUN BY
> FLYBY; IT'LL ONLY MAKE ME TEN
> MINUTES LATE.

Callie smiled and put her phone back in her book bag, trying to concentrate on Professor Handsome's—ahem—*Hanson*'s words rather than his face. It was a bit difficult with Dana sighing, Adam arguing, OK weaseling his way out of debt, and the sight of Mimi slumped over in her seat where Callie would have bet ten to one that she was snoring.

Plus, a minute later, her phone buzzed again.

> DID YOU REMEMBER TO PICK UP
> YOUR BOOKS FOR FICTION &
> THEORY SO YOU COULD FINISH THE
> READING BY TOMORROW IN TIME FOR
> CLASS?? (THIS IS ME REMINDING
> YOU, AS PROMISED!)

Crap! She could picture the exact location of her books now, sitting on the edge of her bed. Shaking her head, she texted back:

> THANK YOU! I TOTALLY FORGOT,
> AS YOU GUESSED. WILL HAVE TO
> SWING BY WIGG BEFORE WORK.
> BUT DON'T WORRY ABOUT LUNCH,
> I'LL FIGURE SOMETHING OUT!

"Can you *please* put that away?" Dana hissed when Callie's phone buzzed for the third time.

"Sorry," Callie whispered back. Turning the ringer on silent, she stole a covert glance at the screen.

YOU'RE THE BEST. MAYBE WE
CAN GRAB DINNER LATER IF I GET
ENOUGH STUDYING DONE IN TIME.
IF NOT WE'LL DO SOMETHING BIG
SATURDAY NIGHT AFTER WE GET
BACK FROM OUR AWAY GAME.

"Hand it over," said Dana, holding out her hand.

Cringing, Callie passed her the phone. "Sorry!"

"Stop apologizing and start taking notes!" Dana whispered back.

"Okay," said Callie, settling into her chair and jotting dutifully in her notebook for the rest of the hour.

"Someone's in here!" Vanessa called from behind the bathroom door.

"Oh, sorry," said Callie, backing away. "Will you be done soon? Because I kind of have to pee!"

"Go away!" Vanessa yelled.

Oh-kay . . . thought Callie, walking into her room and grabbing her books. Coming back into the common room, she opened the door to the mini-fridge: one four-pack of Red Bull, one banana peel (minus the banana), and a couple of packets of sweet and sour sauce from The Kong. Callie wrinkled her nose. Straightening, she noticed a half-eaten pack of Double Stuf Oreos sitting on the couch. *Bingo*—

Suddenly a weird retching noise came from the bathroom.

Callie paused, looking at the Oreos and then looking back at the bathroom.

"Everything okay in there?" she called, taking a few steps toward the door.

She was met with the whoosh of the toilet flushing.

"It's fine!" Vanessa called, but now Callie could hear something that sounded an awful lot like crying.

Checking the time on her cell phone, she stood for a moment, debating. Then she dialed the front desk at Lamont and told them that she was going to be a little bit late.

"Can I get you anything?" Callie asked. "Water? Red Bull?"

"There's a sink in the bathroom," she heard Vanessa mutter.

"Right," said Callie. "Well, if you want to talk, I'll just stay out here for another minute or so. . . ." She sank onto the floor and rested her back against the bathroom door.

"I don't want to talk about it," Vanessa said in halting tones from where she was also slumped on the floor, her head separated from Callie's by a mere inch and a half of wood.

"Did something happen with Tyler?" Callie ventured.

A sob escaped Vanessa's lips. "I don't want"—sob—"to talk"—sob—"to you!"

"Did he do something?" Callie called. "Pressure you in some way? Because if he did, I'll kill him, or at least have Clint punch him in the—"

"Just—shut up—about—Tyler!"

"Fine," said Callie, hugging her knees to her chest. "I'll talk about something else then. So, OK and Adam have invented this betting game that they play in our Human Nature class, and today . . ."

Vanessa never responded or gave any other sign that she was listening, but midway through the story the crying noises stopped. And, though Callie couldn't be sure, at one point when she had been describing what she could remember of Dana's notes, she thought she heard a giggle.

"You know," Callie said, when she had run out of stories from class, "the day I found out that I tore my ACL—and that my soccer career was basically over—I hid in the bathroom for like six hours. The bathtub, actually, to be specific. But eventually you realize that you have to come out, because it's uncomfortable, or you get hungry . . . maybe for some Double Stuf Oreo—*ah—OW!*"

Callie's head clunked against the tiled floor. Blinking, she stared up at Vanessa, who loomed over her, her hand still on the doorknob from when she had suddenly yanked it open.

"I have to go—to the library," Vanessa said, stepping over Callie and grabbing her bag off the couch. She had washed her face and managed to eradicate all signs of the recent meltdown except for a slight puffy redness around her eyes.

"Great," said Callie, sitting up, "I'm on my way now too so I'll walk you!"

"Actually, I forgot: I have a hair appointment," Vanessa said, heading for the front door.

Sighing and rubbing the back of her head, Callie watched her go.

❧

"I'm *so* sorry I'm late— What . . . what are you doing here?"

Gregory stood in front of the reference desk, holding a bagged lunch in one hand. There was another bag near him on the counter. "Nothing," he said. "I was just leaving."

"Is that—is this for me?" Callie asked, going behind the desk and picking up the bag.

"Uh . . . yes. If you want it," he said.

"Thank you?"

He shrugged. "Clint and I are in the same econ section at noon, and he mentioned that he couldn't do it and how grumpy you get when you're hungry, so I off—I mean he asked me to bring it to you instead . . . since I was already planning to come here to do the reading for class tomorrow anyway. It's no big deal."

"Great minds," said Callie, lifting up her copy of Kazuo Ishiguro's *Never Let Me Go*.

"How are you liking it so far?" Gregory asked, gripping the back of the spare chair next to her desk.

"I'm loving it," she said. "And I would totally be able to finish on time for tomorrow . . . if we didn't also have to get through these," she concluded, pointing to her copies of *Writing and Difference* and *Of Grammatology* by Jacques Derrida, aka her New Least Favorite Unintelligible Postmodern Deconstructionist.

"You know the headline for his obituary in the *New York Times* read, 'Jacques Derrida, Abstruse Philosopher, Dies at Seventy-Four,'" Gregory said with a smile.

"They know what they're talking about over at that *Times*," she said wryly. "Wish I knew what *he* was talking about when he said . . . well, everything. I mean, just listen to this," she said, opening *Writing and Difference* as he sat down.

> *"That philosophy died yesterday, since Hegel or Marx, Nietzsche, or Heidegger—and philosophy should still wander toward the meaning of its death—or that it has always lived knowing itself to be dying . . . that philosophy died one day, within history, or that it has always fed on its own agony, on the violent way it opens history by opposing itself to nonphilosophy, which is its past and its concern, its death and wellspring; that beyond the death, or dying nature, of philosophy, perhaps even because of it, thought still has a future, or even, as is said today, is still entirely to come because of what philosophy has held in store; or, more strangely still, that the future itself has a future—all these are unanswerable questions."*

She looked up. "Seriously, what does that mean?"

"I don't know," said Gregory, laughing a little and unwrapping his sandwich.

"It's all one sentence!" she exclaimed, pulling an orange out of her lunch bag. "Just *one* sentence out of fifty billion others like it! How on earth are we ever supposed to understand this thing?" she cried, letting the book clunk onto the table. Both hands free now, she began to peel her orange.

"I don't know," he repeated, shaking his head.

"I thought that you knew everything," she said, watching him take a bite of his sandwich.

"I do," he said. "With a few very rare exceptions."

"Ha!" she cried before popping a section of the orange into her mouth. Narrowing her eyes, she considered him while she chewed. "Clint said that I get *grumpy* when I'm hungry?"

"More or less," said Gregory. "What he really told me is that you need to be fed every four hours on the dot or else you turn into a gremlin."

Callie gasped. "He did *not*," she cried, throwing part of her orange peel at him.

"Maybe not," he said, catching it, "but I could tell that's what he was thinking."

"You take that back," she said, brandishing the rest of her orange peel, "or I'll—"

"Um, excuse me?" A girl hovered a few feet away, holding a book.

"Don't mind him," Callie said to her, glaring at Gregory and setting down the orange so she could scan and stamp the book.

When the girl had gone, he asked, "So, how do you like working here?"

"Why?" she said. "Are you thinking about applying for a job?"

"Maybe," he said with a look on his face like that would be *just* hilarious.

Oh yes, Gregory, *so* hilarious that some people actually have to work to pay for things! "Why are you here?" she demanded suddenly, angry that she had allowed him yet another opportunity to mock her.

"I already told you," he said. "Clint asked me to drop off your lunch."

"Yes, 'drop off,' exactly," she said. "But why are you *still* here? I mean *here* here, not in the library here."

Gregory frowned, starting to stand. "I'll go."

"That's not what I meant," she said quietly.

He stared at her for a moment. "I guess I thought maybe we could . . . give the whole friends thing a try," he said finally.

She searched his face for the telltale signs that he was making another joke at her expense. But he seemed actually to mean it. "If you're serious . . ." she started, "then I think that I would like that."

"I am serious," he said, sitting back down. "As serious as Tommy is about Ruth," he added, waving his copy of *Never Let Me Go*.

"Tommy is in love with Kathy," Callie cried, "not Ruth!"

Gregory looked equally scandalized. "I hadn't gotten to that part yet!"

"Whoops," she said, clapping a hand over her mouth.

He laughed and then sighed. "I guess that was obvious from the beginning. How many more chapters do I have to go through before he realizes that Ruth is all wrong for him?"

"I'm not saying," she insisted. "Wouldn't want to ruin it!"

They were silent for a moment or two, chewing their food. "So," said Gregory eventually, "things with Clint seem to be going well."

"They are," she said. "Why do you ask?"

"Isn't that what friends do—talk about each other's, ah, relationships?"

"Sure." Callie cracked a smile. "So, how is your 'relationship' going, then?"

"Fine," he said. "Actually," he added, considering her, "I could use a female perspective on something."

"Okay," she said. "Shoot."

"Alessandra and I seem to be having some . . . well, trust issues."

"What is it that makes you feel like you can't trust her?" Callie asked.

"It's more the other way around," he admitted.

"Ah. I see," said Callie, lowering her sandwich. "Well, can you think of anything that you might have done that contributed to her feeling this way?" Other than, you know, the fact that you're you, she added silently. No need to destabilize the new friendship now when they were only five minutes in.

"No," he said "I don't think so." He paused. "Well . . ."

"Yes?" Callie prompted.

"The other day I caught her going through my phone."

"What?" said Callie. "That's totally not cool!"

"I know," he agreed, "but the thing is, she found something. Well, it was nothing really, just some old texts."

"To another girl?" Callie asked, grateful for the hundredth time that she had chosen Clint.

"Kind of. Not exactly. See I forgot to delete some old drafts from a long time ago—stuff I never even actually sent."

"How long ago?" asked Callie. "Before or after you got together?"

"Before," he said. "In November."

"Well, she can't be mad about things that happened before you even met her; that's crazy!" said Callie. "I mean, not *crazy*," she corrected quickly, "just kind of irrational."

"That's what I said," he agreed.

"Unless…" Callie started. "What did these messages say exactly?" Her forehead wrinkled: she tried to picture a sexting situation gone awry. Then she shook her head, trying *not* to picture it. "And who were you planning to send them to?" she added, wondering if that "who" were plural and if Alessandra had uncovered details of the threesome or something even more sordid. *Ew.* "And why didn't you end up sending them?"

"That's not important," he muttered, waving his hand and accidentally knocking over his empty water bottle. "Just tell me," he said, righting it, "as a girl, what you would want me to do to fix it. Please."

"I guess I would start by saying that it's not okay to go through your phone or otherwise violate your privacy but that it's perfectly normal for everyone to feel a little jealous sometimes, and that you would be happy to let her look at your phone or whatever else, if and only *if* she asks your permission first, because you have nothing to hide … if that's the truth."

"It's true now," he said with a mischievous smile, "because I erased everything."

"In the long term," Callie continued, ignoring him, "things could be a bit trickier. Trust is often something that has to be earned, particularly if you—if *one*—has a track record. . . . Or maybe she already has trust issues for reasons that aren't your fault, like an evil ex-boyfriend from high school or, um, whatever." Callie crumpled her napkin. "Either way, having a candid conversation and getting everything—well, ah, *mostly* everything—out in the open can't hurt. And if all else fails, you can always shower her with gifts—that's what Vanessa would probably tell you to do, and who knows, maybe on some girls that type of thing works." She paused to scan several books that a boy had just dropped on the counter.

"I don't suppose you and Clint ever had to deal with anything like this," Gregory mused after the boy had gone.

"Well, you know, we have minor issues every now and then just like any other couple...."

"Yeah," said Gregory, "he did mention that you get jealous of Lexi sometimes."

"Jealous?" Callie repeated incredulously. "He *said* that? I'm not *jealous* of her; I just don't like her! No offense," she added. "I know you two are friends."

"None taken. I can definitely understand why you'd have a problem with her."

Callie's eyebrows knit together. "What's that supposed to mean?"

"Just the whole . . . *saga* of their relationship. From what he's said to me about it—and what she's said—it sounds like the whole thing was pretty intense."

"You mean the constant breaking-up and getting-back-together parts?"

"Sure."

Eugh. Callie cringed, not wanting to think about it anymore. "Hey!" she said suddenly. "How come you didn't ask Lexi about your Alessandra problem?"

"I did ask her a few hours ago on our way to class. She said she'd give me some advice right after I made sure Alessandra planned to join the Pudding."

Callie laughed. "That sounds exactly like her. Wait. She's in your econ class, too?"

"Yeah," said Gregory. "Why?"

"Oh. No reason," Callie said quickly. She had known that Lexi was in Clint's government class, but couldn't remember him mentioning anything about econ, too. "Anyway," she said, "I would never go through Clint's phone, but even if I did, I'm positive that I wouldn't find anything sketchy."

"Of course not," Gregory agreed. "Because he's perfect."

She studied his face, but it seemed devoid of irony. "Yeah, he kind of is," she said with a smile. "So . . ."

"Time to get started?" Gregory finished for her, lifting *Of Grammatology*. Groaning, she nodded.

He settled back in his chair and propped his feet up on the half-open bottom drawer of her desk. Together they read silently, stopping every once in a while to commiserate over a particularly "abstruse" Derrida quote or laugh after reading certain sections out loud. The time flew, and before Callie knew it, the clock read 5:55.

"Hey," said one of her coworkers, wheeling a reshelving cart up behind her desk. "Do you think you could run these over to Widener?" he asked, pointing to a box of books. "They ended up in circulation here by mistake."

"Sure," she said. "I'm off in a few minutes anyway; I can take them on my way home."

"Great," he said, wheeling the now empty cart away. "Thanks."

"So I guess you're headed out, then?" Gregory asked.

"Yep," she said, standing to stretch.

"I'm going to stay and finish this," he said, pointing to *Never Let Me Go.*

"Enjoy," she said, gathering her things. "See you in class tomorrow?"

"Sure. That looks heavy," he added, watching her lift the box of books. "Want me to help you carry it over?"

"That's okay, I've had worse," she said, remembering the days not too long ago when she used to deliver Lexi's premium Norwegian bottled water to her room in Kirkland House, along with her dry cleaning and anything else she happened to want that week.

"Right," he said. "Well, at least if you drop it you'll be spilling books not underwear."

Friendship? Maybe. End of Teasing about the Underwear Incident from Move-in Day? Never.

"You suck!" she called over her shoulder.

"Don't trip," he said, smirking as he returned to his book.

"These were accidentally returned to Lamont," Callie said to the student manning Widener Library's circulation desk, hefting the box of books onto the counter.

"Thanks," said the student.

"Have a good night!" Callie called, turning to leave. Spying a water fountain in the corner of the room, she stopped to take a drink. Straightening, she glanced through the huge glass window that looked down into one of the library's more secluded reading rooms. She took two steps away before doing a double take: Clint sat studying with his head bent over his books at one of the tables below, and directly across from him was—

Wait— *What?*

It couldn't be—

But it was.

Alexis.

Vivienne.

Thorndike.

Pulling out her phone, Callie drafted a text:

HEY, HOW'S THE STUDYING GOING?

Peering back down at the table and confirming that Clint and Lexi were its only occupants, she clicked Send. Then she watched Clint pull out his phone a moment later. Another moment and her phone buzzed in response:

GREAT!

Great? "Great" did not begin to explain what he was doing here, alone, with *her.*

Feeling a bit like a creepy stalker, she looked over her shoulder to make sure no one was watching. Then, she stared back down at the reading room. Lexi had stood suddenly and was making her way to the exit, leaving Clint alone at the table. Callie thought for a few seconds and then texted him again.

IT'S NOT TOO DISTRACTING WHAT
WITH ALL THE OTHER PEOPLE IN
YOUR STUDY GROUP?

Her foot tapped while she waited for his response, feeling a mixture of guilt (for what could quite possibly be considered entrapment), and a strong sense of foreboding. Her phone twitched in her hand. Briefly she closed her eyes. Then, opening them, she read:

> NOPE! IT'S JUST ME AND A COUPLE
> OF GUYS FROM CLASS OVER HERE AT
> WIDENER, AND WE'RE BEING VERY
> PRODUCTIVE :)

Callie sucked in her breath. Her nose almost up against the glass, she willed several students of the male persuasion to materialize miraculously at Clint's table. No matter how hard she prayed, though, there was nothing else down there except Clint, a couple of pencils and pens, and two sets of Government textbooks.

Her feet felt weighted to the floor, her fingers heavy with dread, as she drafted one last text.

> DO YOU THINK YOU'LL HAVE TIME TO
> GRAB DINNER LATER? MY SHIFT AT
> LAMONT JUST ENDED.

Picking up his phone, Clint read the message on the screen, but before he could respond, Lexi returned to the table. She carried two large to-go containers from the Widener Library Café. He set down his phone and said something to her, smiling and shutting his books. Frozen, Callie watched them converse for a full minute and a half until he finally remembered his phone.

Moments later she had her response.

SORRY, BUT I THINK WE'RE JUST
GOING TO TRY TO POWER THROUGH.
I'LL SEE YOU ON SATURDAY NIGHT
AS SOON AS WE GET BACK FROM
PRINCETON, THOUGH, IF I DON'T
GET A CHANCE TO SAY GOOD-BYE
AFTER THE TEST. MISS YOU ALREADY
. . . LOVE YOU!

"Powering through" looked an awful lot like taking a break to eat, talk, flirt and—*seriously?*—ding a pencil at Lexi across the desk. "Miss you already" sounded pretty hollow for someone already excusing himself from saying good-bye, and "Love you" might as well have been the last in what amounted to a string of multiple lies.

"Everything okay over there?" the student behind the circulation desk suddenly called.

"No," Callie muttered, leaping back from the window. Turning, she skidded across the marble floor, flying past the security guard as quickly as possible and bursting out into the cold. Darkness had descended since she'd entered the library, and she almost tripped several times as she tore down the vast stone steps.

"No," she murmured again to no one in particular as she ran home to Wigglesworth. Everything is *not* okay.

TEN

HOW to LOSE a GUY

IN TEN ~~Days~~ MINUTES

Ten Ways to Ruin a Relationship:
A List of High-Risk Relationship Behavior.

1. **Checking a significant other's accounts (and getting caught).** That includes bank accounts, cell phone records, e-mail, Facebook, and any other private venue involving a device and a password. Some couples these days share passwords as a way to foster intimacy. Well, good for them, but unless you are one of those or you have explicit permission from your loved one, resist the urge to snoop! Or, if you can't, at the very least: don't get caught.

2. **Cheating on a significant other (and getting caught).** Duh! This one's kind of a no-brainer, though in today's world it can be hard to know where you stand when it comes to being exclusive, when terms like "dating" or "hooking up" or even "boyfriend" and "girlfriend" are all sliding signifiers. Just remember that if you do decide to cheat, being discovered in the moment isn't the only way to get caught. Once the act is done, it's only a matter of time: the truth will always get out, be it through the grapevine or your infiltrated inbox.

3. **Saying "I love you" either too soon or at the wrong moment.** Sometimes it just slips out. But especially on dates 1–3, lock your lips and hold in that L-bomb unless you want to come off as needy, codependent, or just plain nuts. Note that the wrong moment, like when you're in coitus or the middle of a fight, can prove equally detrimental.

4. **Not saying "I love you" back.** This is the corollary to High-Risk Behavior Number 3 and is equally important to handle properly. Of course, don't say it if you don't mean it, but find a more artful way to do so than with a scream, a "Thank you," or, my personal favorite, "I love me, too."

5. **Too much/too little space.** Do I really have to explain this one? Okay, fine. If you can't stay more than two inches away from each other most of the time in public: you have a problem. If you must stay two inches away from each other at all times in private: you also have a problem. Seek professional help.

6. **Ex-Obsession or Ex-Stalking.** Both afflictions prove fatal to even the strongest relationships. Do not open the Ex file unless absolutely necessary. But, if you have to, do so directly: do not be tempted to take a roundabout way just because you and the ex are at the same school, possibly in some of the same classes. Stalking: bad. Not stalking: good. Simple.

7. **Jealousy, the green-eyed monster.** This is related to High-Risk Behavior Number 6 when said behavior spins out of control to the extent that you become jealous of your boyfriend/girlfriend's friends, extracurriculars, classes, or anything that takes away from "us" time. If you find yourself feeling jealous of inanimate objects (problem sets, footballs, handkerchiefs), seek help immediately. And try to remember Shakespeare's *Othello*: there's a reason why everybody in that play ends up dead by Act V.

8. **Deciding to go abroad.** End it now before you waste a semester on Skype only to break up when he/she returns. If you think he/she is The One, as Beyoncé said: "If you liked it then you shoulda put a ring on it." Well, listen to the diva! Lock it up, down, sideways; put a ring on it, whatever. Just do it before that Italian Stallion from Florence sweeps her onto his moped and she's gone forever . . . *Baci* and *abbracci*.

9. **Upperclassman dating a freshman and vice versa.** Some say Confucius's rule is "half your age plus seven," but even ancient Chinese philosophers sometimes make mistakes. You never should've gone here in the first place: it's High-Risk Territory already. The relationship is doomed! So stick to *my* rule of consecutive grades ($n + 1$), though nothing beats ($n + 0$).

10. **Taking Math 55.** This also turns out to be a deal-breaker. You won't be able to go out. You won't be able to shower. You won't be able to get excited by anything other than numbers. You will, in essence, be dating Math 55. It will be your one true love; there will be no room for anybody else.

If you can't stay together for the kids, then at least stay together for Spring Break,
Alexis Thorndike, Advice Columnist
Fifteen Minutes Magazine
Harvard University's Authority on Campus Life since 1873

"I must admit that, given the title's connotations, I had been hoping for a more religious perspective on *Atonement*," Dana said to Callie as they wandered out of the Harvard bookstore. "But, nevertheless, thank you for bringing me to hear the author speak."

Callie smiled. "He was so awesome, wasn't he?" It was Saturday afternoon and they had just attended Ian McEwan's reading and subsequent book talk, tickets courtesy of Gregory, who was probably on the road back from Princeton with Clint and the rest of the squash team at this very moment.

"Also please thank Clint for the tickets," Dana said, unaware of the tickets' true origins. "That was an extremely thoughtful gift given how much you like the author: especially because he was unable to attend."

"Right," Callie said. "I'll tell him tonight just as soon as he gets home."

In reality, Callie had no idea what she was going to say when she saw Clint. She had been dreading his return since he'd departed on Thursday afternoon following his midterm with no more than a phone call to say good-bye, which she had screened before throwing her phone into her sock drawer and heading to the gym. Nine grueling treadmill miles later, she still didn't know what to do about his Lexi-related lies.

Was this the first time that he'd been dishonest or simply the first time he got caught? What else was he hiding? And what was Lexi's part in all of this? Did she still want him back, or was she plotting something much more—

"WATCH OUT!" Dana screamed, throwing an arm in front of Callie just before she accidentally walked into oncoming traffic.

"Holy crap," Callie said breathlessly, turning white and gripping Dana's arm to stabilize herself. "Thank you."

"You're welcome," Dana said stiffly. "Is everything all right?" she added when the light had turned and they started across the street. "I'm just . . . preoccupied, I guess," Callie muttered.

"Well, snap out of it!" Dana commanded as they walked through Dexter Gate. "Before you get yourself killed and wind up inspiring Mr. McEwan's next novel."

As the author had said himself during the talk, his nickname was "Ian Macabre" for a reason. The narrative in his novels always stemmed from some central disaster, like, for example, a car accident. No argument here that getting smashed to bits on Massachusetts Ave. would be a bad way to go, Callie thought, though the truth was that in a way, when she had seen Clint and Lexi in the library, a part of her felt like it had already been smashed.

A couple of hours later Callie could procrastinate no longer. She had cleaned the entire common room—including that shady-looking spill in the back of their refrigerator that had been there since October—and done several loads of laundry, including one for Mimi and one for Matt, both of whom had given her a funny look when she volunteered. The time had come to confront Clint. He ought to be arriving home at Adams House any minute now.

And so, after dawdling through the streets, Callie found herself outside the door to his suite, mustering the courage to knock. Taking a deep breath, she tapped on the door.

No one answered, but she was pretty sure she could hear movement on the other side.

She knocked louder.

Still no answer, but now she was certain she heard footsteps and what sounded like singing, sort of.

"Hellooo . . ." she called, pushing the door open a crack.

Inside, she spotted Tyler—wearing nothing but boxers—dancing around the common room barefoot with a hot pink feather duster in his hands and headphones in his ears. As he danced and dusted the mantel with his back to her, he sang softly: "I'm too sexy for my oxford . . . too sexy for my polo . . . So sexy, it hurts. And I'm too sexy for The Fly . . . too sexy for The Fly, The Phoenix, and The Spee."

"Uh—Tyler?" Callie called.

Still, he did not hear, leaning forward to use the feather duster as a microphone: "And I'm too sexy for The Pudding . . . too sexy for The Pudding the way I'm disco dancing. I'm the President, you know what I mean. And I do my little turn on the catwalk, yeah, on the catwalk . . ."

"Tyler?"

"I'm too sexy for Harvard—"

"TYLER!"

"Callie!" he cried, wheeling around and yanking off the headphones. Quickly he moved the feather duster in front of his crotch. "How long have you been standing there?"

"I . . . um, thirty seconds? What are you doing?"

"Cleaning," he said, grabbing his T-shirt off the couch and pulling it over his head.

There were only two reasons anyone ever cleaned in college:

1) When you were avoiding confronting your boyfriend about lying about spending time with his ex; and

2) When you were suffering from severe sexual frustration.

In Tyler's case Callie assumed it was the latter.

"Vanessa gave me *this*," he explained, waving the duster. "She told me that she wasn't going to spend the night anymore unless the room is cleaner."

Apparently, though there were only two reasons to clean, there were infinitely creative ways to avoid having sex—an art Vanessa seemed to have mastered.

"I've been meaning to talk to you about Vanessa, actually," said Callie, recalling their non-conversation through the bathroom door. "She seemed pretty upset the other day. Did you two have a fight or something?"

"That's funny," said Tyler, setting down the duster, "because I was going to ask you the same question!"

"So you have no idea what's wrong, then?"

"Not a clue," he confirmed. "I'd been hoping you could tell me or that you two were having one of *your* fights again."

Callie sighed. "And you're *sure* that you didn't . . . *do* anything?"

"Trust me," he said, "I haven't done *anything*. At all. That's why we're about to have the cleanest common room in the greater Boston area," he concluded, tackling the top of the TV with the duster. "Clint's not home yet, but he should be any minute if you want to wait."

"Great," she said, feeling flooded, once again, with dread. "I'll just be in his room, then."

"Cool," said Tyler, grabbing his iPod and lifting the headphones. "Just make sure you shut the door so I can practice ma' moves in private!"

Callie had been sitting at Clint's desk for less than a minute when, bored, she turned on his computer. Pulling up a browser, she punched in the web address for Gmail. Five seconds later the page had auto-redirected: straight into Clint's account.

Leaping out of the chair, she ran to the other side of the room and stared at the wall. The computer still buzzed faintly from atop the desk, beckoning her. Taking a deep breath, she muttered: "Just sit down, and log out." Easy as the click of a button. Just as easy as the click of another button—which would open any message in the account.

Exhaling, she walked back to the desk. Sitting, she averted her eyes from the screen, maneuvering the cursor into the upper corner in the general region of THE RIGHT THING TO DO, aka the log-out button.

That's right, she heard Dana's voice say suddenly in the back of her head. *Just log out and wait for him to come home like you planned.*

Es-tu stupide? a disembodied Mimi chimed in. *He has given you an open invitation by lying!*

Two wrongs don't make a right, Dana warned.

Do it now—before he returns! cried Mimi.

Shut up! she almost said out loud, steeling herself to click the button.

You're such a hypocrite. Vanessa's voice laughed inside her mind. *Or did you already forget everything you said to Gregory in the library?*

Callie shook her head again—violently this time. All these voices could mean only one thing: she was definitely going crazy. Exhaling, she grabbed the lid of the laptop to slam it shut—

Still, the imaginary Vanessa suddenly whispered, *if it were me, I'd want to know the truth.*

Callie scrunched her eyelids closed. Then, slowly, she opened just one eye. I'll only look at the subject headings and the senders, she vowed. After all, "in plain sight" was fair game according to none other than the Constitution of the United States of America.

Better be fast, though: somehow, she didn't think Clint would take too kindly to the argument that she hadn't violated any of his Fourth Amendment rights....

There were an alarmingly high number of e-mails from *Alexis Vivienne Thorndike*, like, one, two, three, four, five, *six*, in just the past few weeks, but most of the subject headings seemed fairly benign. Well, all except for two of them:

INBOX	[Archive]	[Report Spam]	[Delete]	

3/12	athorndike@fas.har ...	**What I told you in the Library** I was only speaking as a ...
3/11	reiley@hls.har ...	**Midterm Grades Available** in 2 Weeks So stop asking!! ...
3/9	athorndike@fas.har ...	**Gov Midterm** Still on for studying today at 1pm?
3/9	facebook@facebo	**Facebook** Hello, Marcus Taylor tagged a photo of you on ...
3/9	gbolton@fas.har ...	**Have you seen my racquet?** Think I left it at the Murr Ce ...
3/8	candrews@fas.har ...	**Re: Lunch Tomorrow?** Yes! See you then!
3/8	coach.bennet@har ...	**Practice Canceled** Hey all, you can take the evening off to ...
3/8	flylists@google.gro ...	**Hilarious youtube video** Check it out, people!
3/8	athorndike@fas.har ...	**RE: We need to talk** I'll swing by your room tonight arou ...
3/7	candrews@fas.har ...	**Dinner tonight** Going to be a little late—stuck at the Crim ...
3/5	tgreen@fas.har ...	**S-Break** Got your check for you + Callie, so you're good t ...
3/2	athorndike@fas.har ...	**Gatsby** So excited! Also, you won't believe what I found i ...
3/1	athorndike@fas.har ...	**Uncle Joe's e-mail** As per your request, here it is! He's us ...
2/28	Emilee_Weber@va ...	**Internship** Darling, Did you follow up with Governor Ha ...
2/27	athorndike@fas.har ...	**Re: Mom says 'hi'** Ha ha how is Emilee anyway? Say hi b ...

What I told you in the Library was highly troubling, as was *RE: We need to talk*. She had to read them both. Immediately.

No! the voice of Dana cried as Callie's hand hovered over the keyboard. *Don't do it.*

Do it but do not get caught, Mimi amended.

Clint's e-mails are none of your business, Vanessa reasoned. *But if he's been lying to you about something—that is your business.*

"Quite right, Imaginary Vanessa," Callie muttered, scrolling back down to *RE: We need to talk*. Click, click.

From: **Alexis Vivienne Thorndike**

To: **Clint Weber**

Subject: RE: We need to talk

I'll come over tonight around 8pm.

xx,

Lex

From: **Clint Weber**

To: **Alexis Vivienne Thorndike**

Subject: We need to talk

Can we meet up when you have a minute?

Let me know,

Clint

That's it? That's all you're going to give me, computer? *What* did they "need" to talk about? And had Lexi come over *here*, to his bedroom, on Tuesday night? Desperation welled within her. Returning to his inbox, she scrolled up to *What I told you in the Library*. Taking a deep breath, she clicked.

From: **Alexis Vivienne Thorndike**
To: **Clint Weber**
Subject: What I told you in the Library

I was only speaking as a friend, and I *was* telling you the truth as far as I know. I would never invent anything to intentionally interfere with your relationship. Well, the old me might have, but the new me is different. I just want you to be happy.

xx,

Lex

For an e-mail titled *What I told you in the Library*, it certainly didn't give much away about what had actually been said. Was Lexi making up lies about her? Of *course* she was trying to "intentionally interfere" with the relationship: that had been her plan since day one when she told Callie to stay away from Clint—or else. Given Lexi's insistence that she was telling the truth, and that she would "never invent anything" (Ha! What *wouldn't* she invent was more like it), it sounded like Clint might have accused her of lying and come to Callie's defense. Did he buy all this "new me" bullshit? What was *really* going on between the exes?

Callie dragged her hands across her face, feeling more confused than ever.

Closing her eyes, she tried to picture the way Clint and Lexi had been looking at each other in the library. Something had passed between them that had been worth lying about; there had to be something here, in this room, to prove what it was one way or another.

Before Callie realized what was happening, she had yanked open the doors to his closet. Jackets, suits, ties, slacks, dress shirts, T-shirts, jeans, and a couple of hangers on one side with several items of women's clothing (all Callie's that she had left there at one sleepover or another)—that's it. On the floor there were several pairs of shoes and one—*jackpot!*—shoe box with the cardboard lid closed tight. Bending over, she opened the box and lifted the folds of tissue paper aside, only to find . . .

More shoes.

"Dammit!" she cursed. Cocking her ear to the common room, she could still hear the faint sounds of Tyler's—er—*interesting* attempts to sing. No sign of Clint's return—yet. Wheeling around, she honed in on his dresser. Sock drawer: that's where everyone hid secrets or, in her case, where she sometimes hid her phone. Pulling it open, she found herself staring down into a sea of socks.

Who knew he was so into argyle? she mused somewhat hysterically as she tossed several pairs over her shoulder and onto the floor. *Aha!* she thought suddenly, unearthing the glossy corner of what appeared to be a photograph of . . . Oh. It was a picture of Callie, and Clint, that someone had snapped at the Delphic Toga party. Her arms were looped around his neck and he was gazing down at her, half smiling, half serious while they stood, unable to keep their hands off each other, at the base of the staircase.

Gingerly she set the photo on top of the dresser.

What am I missing? she wondered, casting around the room. "There has to be something," she murmured, returning to his desk. "There just *has* to be."

Once again she stared at the subject headings of his e-mails. Her fingers hovered above the keyboard. Then, deciding, she opened *Gov Midterm*.

> From: **Alexis Vivienne Thorndike**
> To: **Clint Weber**
> Subject: Gov Midterm
>
> Still on for studying today at 1pm?
> Your <u>friend</u>(!),
> Lex

Your <u>friend</u> underlined, exclamation mark? Shaking her head, Callie clicked on Gatsby.

> From: **Alexis Vivienne Thorndike**
> To: **Clint Weber**
> Subject: Gatsby
> Attachments (1): C:\Users\Thorndike\Photos\Sophomore_Year\Gatsby.jpg
>
> So excited! Also, you won't believe what I found in an old folder on my desktop just now.
> ;) xx Lex

Her pulse thundering, Callie clicked on the attachment. It was a candid photograph of Clint and Lexi taken at the Fly's Gatsby party, presumably during their sophomore year. Even though it probably wasn't more than twelve months old, they both looked younger—happier and more carefree. Lexi wore white: a billowy muslin dress with strands and strands of pearls, and her usually pale cheeks were pink and rosy. Clint stood behind her in a tuxedo, his arms wrapped around her and holding both her hands. His eyes were diverted away from the camera down toward Lexi's collarbone, his smiling lips only inches away from her bare shoulder. Something in his expression seemed to indicate that he had just inhaled, breathing her in.

"Callie?"

Oh god.

She shut the photo; his open e-mail account filled the screen.

"What—what are you *doing*?"

Slowly Callie turned, noting as she did the closet door, still thrown open, the shoe box lid askew, and the socks on the floor near his dresser where the picture lay exposed and the top drawer jutted out.

Clint stood in the doorway, disbelief etched across his face.

"What are you doing?" he repeated, shutting the door behind him.

"I-uh-your, um," she stammered, starting to shake. "I know you were in the library with Lexi, okay!" she finally managed to exclaim.

"You know I was in the library with Lexi doing *what* exactly?" he said, speaking in the same calm tones one might use to coax a wild animal back into its cage.

"Studying!" she cried. "I mean, not just *studying*. It was more than that, and you were alone, and there was no study group, and you were eating, and you LIED to me; you're a *liar*!"

Clint sat down on the edge of his bed and took a deep breath. "And so you decided to hack into my e-mail and see what you could find, is that it?"

"I didn't *hack* into it," she muttered. "I turned on your computer to check *my* e-mail and yours opened by accident."

"Well," he said. "Did you find anything good?"

How the hell could he so *calm* when she had caught him red-handed? Red-handed at what though, exactly? Her mind had gone fuzzy with confusion, doubt, and rage. She couldn't think straight. Gripping the sides of her temples, she breathed in and out, trying to concentrate. Okay, start at the beginning. . . .

"You lied to me last week, on Wednesday before you left for Princeton. You said you had to study, and that there were multiple *guys*, as in men *plural*, in the group, but the only person I could see there with you in Widener was Alexis Thorndike!"

"Were you . . . *spying* on me?"

"I work in the library!" she erupted. "Part of that involves returning books to their proper place, which is what I was doing in Widener when I *happened* to see you."

"Just like you *happened* to see my e-mail?"

"You also told me that you were too busy to get dinner," she continued, ignoring him, "but then you turned around and had dinner with *her*."

"Callie," he said quietly. "I *was* too busy to get dinner; that's why we ate in the library—so we could keep working without wasting any extra time by taking a break."

"But . . ." she sputtered. "But . . . but you still *lied* about the whole study group. There was never any study group." Or was there? She was no longer sure. She had been positive coming into this conversation that she had caught him at something and he would confess; now, with the e-mail still open behind her, argyle all over the floor, the photo on the dresser, and the way he was looking at her, she was starting to feel like it was the other way around.

Clint sighed. "There *is* a study group, actually. It's me, Bryan, a guy named Tom, Alexis, and another girl from class. When I said '*guys*,' I meant it the way you usually mean when you say it, as a gender-neutral term."

Callie shook her head. "Your text said that you *guys* were in the library." She pulled out her phone. "Here it is right here: *It's just me and a couple of guys from class over here at Widener* . . .' Well, I was there, too, Clint, and I know what I saw: Lexi was the only person with you at that table."

She waited for him to explain that away, too, but he was quiet. Finally he said, "You're right. I lied."

I knew it! I . . . knew it. Just like that, the triumph faded and the reality of what might be happening sank in.

"I lied because I thought it would spare you from worrying over nothing more than two friends studying together in the library."

Callie opened her mouth to protest but then stopped, finding it difficult to object to his claim that she would have worried. No matter what he might have said he was doing with Lexi—

studying, saying hi, shopping, skydiving, sitting twenty feet away in the same classroom—knowing that he was with her *did* make Callie anxious to an almost obsessive degree. And he knew it, too, because she had never figured out how to hold her feelings inside when she was upset about something . . . even if the reasons for being upset were unfounded or wrong.

"And, to be honest," Clint continued, "I was tired of having the same conversation over and over and over again. It's tough enough as it is to move on from a past relationship without your current girlfriend bringing it up all the time."

Oh my god, thought Callie, her mind going suddenly crystal clear. *I am wrong.* So he lied. So what? Obviously he only did it because she was crazy—if the state of his room right now was any indication—and he had been trying to keep her from going crazier. If she had called Alessandra "irrational" just for going through Gregory's phone, what did that make her? Certifiable. She was, certifiably, insane.

She stared at him. He seemed far too calm, too cool, too collected. A tiny voice whispered in the back of her head—not Dana's, not Mimi's, not Vanessa's, but her own: Am I really crazy, or is he just making me *think* I'm crazy?

"What about . . ." she started. "There was an, uh, e-mail. . . ."

"Yes?" he prompted. "We both know you went through them; you might as well ask me directly if you're curious about anything."

Fair enough. "Why did you tell Lexi that you 'needed to talk'?" she asked.

"I . . ." he faltered. "When did I say that?"

"On Tuesday morning of last week," she said, glancing at his inbox. "And she wrote back that she would come over at eight. So she was here. In your room. At night. Why?" She unfolded her arms, trying to look less like a lawyer cross-examining a witness. Clint definitely seemed more on edge now, coming over to his computer to read the e-mail thread.

Still, after thinking for a moment, he started to shake his head. "That was a Pudding-related thing. Don't you remember that I told you I had board stuff going on that night when I stopped by the *Crimson* in the afternoon? She and I met up at the club to talk about a punch."

Callie bit her lip, searching for holes in his story and finding none. . . .

"It was about Vanessa, actually," he added, after a beat. "I suspected Lex was planning to have her cut and I thought that maybe I could convince her to drop that little vendetta if I talked to her in private before we hold elections next week."

"She was never in your room?"

"She was never in my room."

Callie sucked in her breath. "You invited her to Gatsby . . ." she started, all the while knowing that an old picture meant nothing and that she was grasping at straws.

"I never said I didn't."

"And she . . ." Callie paused, deciding that referencing the way Lexi had underlined "friend" might seem beyond crazy, even after everything she'd already done. Still, she felt curious about one last thing: her eyes flicked over the subject heading *What I told you in the Library.* Might as well ask—at this point she had nothing left to lose.

"What did Lexi tell you in the library?"

Clint looked at her and sank back onto his bed. "That's actually something that I've been meaning to ask *you* about," he said. "I was waiting until I got back, though, so we could talk in person."

Callie said nothing, staring at him.

"At first, when she told me, I didn't believe her. I thought that after all this time she'd been lying about wanting to be friends and had devised some new form of sabotage—a new strategy to try to break us up."

Exhaling, he continued: "She told me that you hooked up with Gregory. She said that according to you, it happened at the very beginning of the year, during freshman week, but that she had reason to believe that something happened months later, when we were supposedly together—although she wouldn't say who told her or anything more specific than that. Then I said she was a liar and had clearly been manipulating me for months while claiming to be my friend, and I left the library. I guess you were gone by that point," he added ruefully, "and didn't see me storm out."

Callie's eyes were wide. She gripped the sides of her chair, paralyzed and unable to speak.

"I had a chance to think about it over the weekend," he said. "Why believe Lexi—who I know to be capable of doing or saying *anything* in the name of getting what she wants—over you? But then . . . I asked Bolton."

"What did he say?" Callie whispered.

"He said that I should ask you; that it was between the two of us, and then he refused to say anything more."

Callie closed her eyes.

"Is it true?" Clint asked quietly. "Did something happen at the beginning of the year?"

Slowly she shook her head. "Nothing happened at the beginning of the year," she said. "But something did happen in November. At Harvard-Yale."

"So in other words, the day after we agreed to take some time to think," he said.

She swallowed. "It was a fuzzy gray area, like you said."

"Well, what happened? Was it just a kiss?"

She shook her head again.

"More?" he asked.

She nodded.

"And it never occurred to you at any point to tell me this?" For the first time that evening, she detected a significant crack in his calm.

"I—I'm so sorry," she finally managed, silent tears streaming down her cheeks. "I wanted to tell you—I *tried* to tell you so many times. But I thought if we just put the past in the past and moved forward, with 'no more secrets' like we said, that things would be better that way. . . . I'm sorry I didn't tell you."

"What about the fact that you did it in the first place?" he demanded. "Are you sorry about that, too?"

"I—" She certainly regretted it, but that had more to do with the way Gregory had behaved afterward than anything else. "I believed we were on a break. I didn't know what was going to happen next, and you weren't speaking to me, and I had other, bigger problems like the tape crisis hanging over my—"

Clint was shaking his head. "I can't believe Lexi was right."

"She's still trying to break us up," Callie wailed. "Can't you see that?"

"Stop blaming everything on her!" Clint exploded, finally raising his voice. "*You're* the one who slept with someone who I thought was my friend, not her, and *you're* the one who didn't tell me. I'm *lucky* she's in my life so I could hear the truth from someone!"

A full minute of silence passed.

"I should go," Callie said.

"I think that's probably a good idea."

"Are we . . . ?"

Clint shook his head. "I need some time . . . to think about all of this."

Callie chewed on her lip. "So that means . . . ?"

"I suppose you want me to say we're on a 'break' so you can run off and be with Bolton," Clint said with a short, mirthless laugh.

"That is so unfair," Callie said, her face melting, once more, into tears. "I chose you. I *want* you. . . . I love you."

"Yeah, well, I'll keep that in mind while I'm making my decision." Clint stood. "In the meantime, here," he said, reaching into the closet for her clothes. "You should probably take these, and anything else you might have left."

Nodding, she tossed the clothing over one arm and reached for two novels that she had left on his bookshelf. With her free hand she wiped the tears from her eyes and then looked around the room to make sure she hadn't left anything else.

On the nightstand by his bed she spotted a flash of silver— from far away, she could just make out what appeared to be the necklace he had given her on Valentine's Day. She started for it but then stopped.

What if this is really it? she thought. What if we break up and then I have to bring it back because I can't stand the sight of it or because it was too expensive in the first place? Better to leave it there on the bedside table, where she could reclaim it later if— hopefully—things worked out. Right now, however, the outlook was grim.

"I'll call you when I'm ready to talk," Clint said, looking just as upset as she did minus the tears.

With a nod, and a final glance at the necklace, she left the room.

parents weekend, part I:

THE FIRST 24 HOURS

Dear Mommy and Daddy's former little Angels who have, since arriving at college, most likely succumbed to a life of sin:

It's basically common knowledge that there are really only two reasons to clean in college: 1) when procrastinating to avoid an even less desirable activity, and 2) when dealing with unmitigated sexual frustration. There is, however, a third reason: a special circumstance that only surfaces on the Harvard University campus once a year in the early hours of the morning preceding a particular weekend in March, when a massive purging of various contraband takes place within many of the freshman dormitories.

Freshman Parents Weekend: when the adults who gave you the gift of life—and probably also tuition—descend upon Cambridge to witness in person exactly how much their hard-earned wages are going to waste—ahem—*use* by all the partying—ahem—*studying* that their little devil—ahem—*angel* has been up to in the first six months out of the nest.

The weekend itinerary is as follows:

Friday, early afternoon: *The parents arrive in time to attend Friday afternoon classes...*
Meaning you have until early afternoon to take down all the "college humor" posters on your wall (i.e., "CLOTHING OPTIONAL BEYOND THIS

POINT" or "FINISH YOUR BEER, THERE'S SOBER KIDS IN AFRICA"), hide all evidence of sexual activity, including your boyfriend/girlfriend unless you can make he/she presentable by noon, and otherwise parent-proof the premises.

Friday, late afternoon: *Afternoon Tea hosted by the Dean of Harvard College...*

Where you will dress up and drink tea with your pinkie out and pronounce Harvard as "Hahvahd" and say, "Oh yes, Mummy, we take tea and crumpets every Friday afternoon while discussing the state of world affairs" —and other vaguely British-sounding things.

Friday, evening: *Unscheduled...*

An opportunity for your parents to treat you to dinner in Harvard Square, i.e., the only edible meal some of you will enjoy all year, after which you will politely excuse yourself to "get a head start on the reading for class on Monday" and then head straight to the nearest party.

Saturday, morning-afternoon: *Lecture Series (go online for locations/other specifics)...*

You will pretend to care whether your parents choose "Global Economies in a Changing World" with Professor Blah-bitty-blah in Sanders Theatre or "The Physical Properties of Celestial Objects and Other Matters in Astrophysics" in Science Center B with Dr. What's-Her-Name while opening your mouth as little as possible in an effort to conceal your hangover.

Saturday, evening: *Freshman Parents Weekend Dinner in Annenberg Dining Hall...*

Where you will be forced to sit according to where you reside and your parents will meet not only your "loveable" (crazy?) roommates, but their even more "loveable" (crazier?) parents.

Sunday, morning: *Services at Memorial Church...*

When most religious students will try not to let on that this is their first time in a church all year.

Sunday, late morning: *Farewell Brunch...*

If you've made it this far without being disowned or disinherited— CONGRATULATIONS!!! You are now ready for your Masters Degree in Deception.

Alexis Thorndike, Advice Columnist
Fifteen Minutes Magazine
Harvard University's Authority on Campus Life since 1873

Hi sweetie!

I'm sorry to hear you're so "bummed" that I won't be able to make it out there this weekend, but I picked tails and the coin came up heads, fair and square. I know that your dad is very excited even if he hasn't said so out loud. Remember how hard it was to get him to come to your soccer games when you were little but then when he finally started showing up, he had had that T-shirt made with your face on it? Thank goodness it got lost when he moved out. I know I embarrass you from time to time, but I honestly don't think I've ever seen you so mortified!

Anyhow, just remember that we're both proud of you and that I expect updates hourly!

Love,
Mom

No, your father will not be coming, for obvious reasons. I'd say he said to tell you he's sorry, but that would be a lie, and my spiritual guide at the Manhattan Kabbalah Center said I need to stop making excuses for him even if we're not actually Jewish. See you soon, xxx.
Sent via BlackBerry

Dear Adam,
We are very much looking forward to meeting you this weekend. As I am sure Dana told you, we do not have much use for the internet, so if you need to get in touch, please dial our landline at 843-555-9472.

Will your parents be joining us at church on Sunday? Perhaps you might send along their phone number should we need to contact them directly.

Regards,
Mr. and Mrs. Gray

From: **Cecilia Clément**
To: **Marine Aurélie Clément**
Subject: Surprise!

Cher bébé,
Quelle surprise! I know we said we would not be coming, but the dress shop in Paris that we had been planning to use for Renee's wedding did not have le tissu approprié. Can you imagine? We had to fly all the way to New York just for the hem and will have time to stop by for an evening before we return. Your father is, of course, very busy running the country, but Renee et moi sont très, très excité!

Bisous,
Ta mama

P.S. I have been practicing my English: can you notice de cet e-mail?

From: **Marine Aurélie Clément**
To: **Callie Andrews, Dana Gray, Vanessa Von Vorhees**
Subject: RE: EMERGENCY MEETING: Must parent-proof the premises

Be in the common room tomorrow morning at 8 A.M., no excuses.

Hour One (T minus 4 hours until Parental Arrival): In which Mimi arises at a time of the morning previously presumed impossible, and the girls clean their common room.

"That's right: all of it must go!" Dana cried, holding open an extra-large, heavy-duty trash bag, her face radiant with delight while the other three raced to fill it with various items she had declared "contraband."

"This?" asked Mimi, holding up last October's Halloween costume.

"Yes," said Dana.

"This?" asked Mimi, after rushing into her room and returning with a copy of *Hustler*.

"Yes," said Dana.

"Why do you have a copy of *Hustler*?" Callie called from the bathroom, where she was scrubbing the sink.

"These?" asked Mimi, ignoring Callie and coming out of her bedroom with a string of colorful condoms over three feet long.

"Yes!" said Dana.

"*Mais je pouvais encore utiliser—*"

"How useful will they be when you have to explain them to the woman who, by the glory of God, gave you the gift of life?"

"I will just tell her they are yours. . . ." Mimi muttered.

Dana, however, did not take the bait. "Stop dillydallying—into the bag, please!"

This Friday morning marked the beginning of Freshman Parents Weekend, and everyone felt a little nervous—everyone that is, except Dana. She was clearly having the time of her life.

"These?" said Mimi, holding up a box and frowning.

"Are those . . . *latex gloves?*" Callie yelled from the bathroom, looking up from where she was eyeing the toilet, an old toothbrush in hand.

"Oh . . ." Mimi made a face. "Is that what they are called?"

"What have you been using them for?" Callie asked, starting to giggle.

"Never mind, never mind, into the bag!" Dana cried impatiently.

"Wait!" Callie cried, rescuing the box. "Callie, one; the toilet, zero," she murmered, donning a pair of gloves and facing down the bowl. Cleaning the toilet, bathtub, windows, *and* the bathroom floor was probably overkill but—especially since she still hadn't spoken to Clint since their fight the previous Saturday—Callie was finding her Bathroom Task Force duties oddly therapeutic.

"Move," Vanessa muttered, pushing past Callie so she could empty a bottle of rum into the sink. She was on the Common Room Task Force with Dana, special duties including Refrigerator and Freezer De-Booze-ification. Mimi had her own task force, called simply—according to Dana—"I'm not sure there's any hope for you." Vanessa tapped her high-heeled boot impatiently while the rum glugged down the drain. Callie couldn't be sure, but it seemed like Vanessa was in an even worse mood than usual.

"Hurry, please," Dana urged. "I still have to go purify next door!"

"Yes, and Mimi and I have to leave in an hour," said Callie.

"We're already late to Pudding elections as it is!"

"Pffft." Vanessa flounced out of the bathroom with the empty bottle in hand. "If you think that I'm going to clean the boys' room just because I don't have somewhere else to be," she said acidly, "then you are even crazier than I thought."

"It's not cleaning," Dana retorted primly. "It's purifying."

"Whatever," said Vanessa. "I think that's the last of the liquor. Can I go now?"

"Yes, you may," said Dana. "And thank you very much for helping us."

Vanessa rolled her eyes and stalked off into her room.

"What bug is crawling up *her* bum, I wonder," said Mimi.

"What?" Dana and Callie asked at the same time.

"It is a very common expression, no? 'A bug up the bum' . . . meaning she is being very irritable today?"

Dana and Callie stared.

"*Vraiment!*" Mimi exclaimed. "Sometimes I think I am the only one here who is speaking English."

Hour Three (T minus 2 hours until Parental Arrival): In which the Hasty Pudding elections have been derailed by speculation re: the Ivy Insider.

"Order! ORDER!" Anne cried, smacking a hardcover book of the Pudding bylaws on the table in the absence of a gavel.

"It's one of the punches; it has to be," a boy called.

"I don't know why you're so quick to rule out one of our own—"

"It was three stupid articles; what's the big deal?" a girl interrupted.

"Maybe the fact that whoever wrote that last article basically confessed to calling the cops on our Fabulous Fifteen party?" the boy retorted. "Or that this same someone seems to be out to take down our entire organization? Who knows what they'll—"

"Calm down, people, calm down," Lexi said, standing. "We have only twelve hours left to choose our new members: it would be foolish to waste this precious time speculating about the words and possible actions of a singular, bitter individual. Now I'm not saying that this Insider situation hasn't become potentially problematic for our organization, but rather that, at the moment, we have more pressing matters to discuss."

"Thank you," said Anne, exhaling while the rest of the room settled back into their seats.

Callie was sitting next to Mimi on one of the couches. Clint, who sat near the front with Tyler—and Lexi—was still avoiding any interaction with Callie, including eye contact. Suddenly Mimi nudged her.

"Sorry to interrupt," Gregory murmured, walking into the room and taking the longer route to avoid Tyler, Lexi, and Clint. Clearly Callie wasn't the only one in the doghouse. Gregory locked eyes with her and then glanced at the empty spot next to her on the couch. Callie shook her head very deliberately, even though Clint was facing forward and it seemed, as far as he was concerned, that neither of them existed.

Taking the hint, Gregory placed an empty folding chair next to OK.

"Now," said Anne, "to continue our consideration of Mr.

Boyd"—elections had started several hours ago and they were still only on the Bs—"does anyone have any idea why someone posted 'kind of a narc' to his profile on HP punch dot com *other* than to say that he might be the Ivy Insider?" No one said anything. Anne sighed, looking unusually frazzled. "Anyone? I know the member comments are supposed to be anonymous, but if whoever wrote that could just give us some indication as to *why* . . ."

Callie's phone buzzed in her pocket. Her heart soaring, she craned her neck to get a better look at Clint—but both his hands were empty. Frowning, she opened the text:

> 1 NEW TEXT MESSAGE
> FROM GREGORY BOLTON
>
> HEY. WE NEED TO TALK.

NOW IS NOT THE TIME, she texted back. Then she jammed her phone into her pocket.

A second later it buzzed again. WHEN THEN?

Callie thought for a moment, then replied: ARE YOU GOING TO THE DEAN'S TEA LATER?

> NOT SURE YET. MY DAD
> MIGHT NOT BE GETTING IN
> UNTIL SOMETIME TOMORROW.

Callie stared at his answer on the screen. Between the ongoing elections all day today *and* parents all weekend, it would be almost impossible to find time—especially because appearing to have a private conversation with Gregory when Clint was anywhere in the vicinity didn't exactly scream, *I'm so sorry; please forgive me and take me back.*

"CALLIE!" Anne was staring. "If it's not too much to ask, can you kindly put away your phone?"

"Sorry," she called. "It's my *dad*," she added defiantly. Clint shifted in his chair.

"Oh," said Anne. "That reminds me: for the twenty or so of you freshmen who have to leave soon for Parents Weekend–related activities, unfortunately you're going to miss the majority of our discussion—"

"Unfortunately," Mimi muttered.

"—but we will be mass texting you the name of each punch before we vote so you can send us your input remotely by responding with either a yay or a nay. All right. So, back to Mr. Boyd . . ."

"I never thought I would be saying this," Mimi whispered, leaning in toward Callie, "but I am eager for Mama's arrival."

Callie nodded emphatically. "Tell me about it."

Hour Five (T minus 0 Hours until Parental Arrival): In which, after collecting her father, Dr. Thomas Andrews, from Logan Airport, Callie brings him with her to Economics class, followed by Economics discussion section and the Dean's Afternoon Tea.

"Say it just one more time, sir," Matt begged Callie's dad, setting his teacup on its saucer. They were standing in a small group that included Callie and Matt's parents, Mr. and Mrs. Robinson (who, incidentally, could not look anything *less* like Anne Bancroft circa 1967 in *The Graduate*), in the downstairs dining room of the Faculty Club, where the Dean's Tea was currently taking place.

"Please, call me Thomas," her dad said. Callie beamed at him, taking a sip of her tea. She had been actively fighting the urge to hug him every second since he'd landed and had so far managed to pace herself: setting the limit at ten hugs (three at the airport and seven while walking to and from class) but still sneaking in several covert hand squeezes every now and then.

"And it was nothing, really," her father continued, "just a simple error that I'm sure any of you students could have spotted had you the necessary mathematical background."

The incident Matt was referring to had occurred half an hour ago in their Economics 10b section. Their Teaching Fellow—who Matt and Callie referred to as The Ruski, in part because of his thick Russian accent but mostly for the bleak way he referred to anything relating to the economy and the even bleaker way he graded their problem sets—had been trying to explain an economic model by drawing two equations on the board.

$$dx/dt = 2x^2 + 2y^2 - y - 2$$
$$dy/dt = x^2 + y^2 + x - 1$$

Stepping back from the board, The Ruski had then said, "These planar differential equations describe a competitive equilibrium model we are working on in our lab. There are no known solutions to this model, so we must use numerical methods to solve it."

Callie's father had cleared his throat. "Pardon me," he'd said, "but I believe there is one explicit solution."

In a typical move The Ruski had replied rudely, "I'm afraid that's impossible," before turning back to the board.

"On the contrary, it's not impossible," her dad had said. "It's a circle."

And then he had gone on to gently explain, over the TF's bitter protests, why the solution was a limit cycle (i.e., a circle in graphic form) while the rest of the students and their parents looked on, thoroughly impressed, though none more so than Callie—except maybe Matt, who was simply delighted to see The Ruski finally back down, chalk smeared angrily all over his face.

"*It's not impossible. It's a circle!*" Matt repeated, savoring every word. Smiling, he sighed. "It was brilliant. The best thing to happen in Econ all year."

"The, er, 'Ruski' did seem extremely grumpy," Matt's mother chimed in. "You'd expect the teachers to be more accessible what with how much we pay in tuition, wouldn't you?"

"They're just graduate students," Matt said charitably. "They have three times as much work as we do and they have to grade all of our problem sets."

"It's still their job to teach you—and to make sure the information they're teaching is correct," Mr. Robinson said.

"Quite right," Callie's dad agreed. "Although now I do feel a greater sympathy for your grade first semester," he added to Callie. She grimaced.

"It probably would have been even lower if not for Matt's tutoring," she said to his parents. "I think I might have failed without him."

"Is that true, Matty?" his mom exclaimed.

"Greg helped, too," Matt muttered, blushing.

Speaking of . . . Where was Gregory? Callie glanced around the room full of parents and students mixing with members of the faculty and administration but failed to spot him anywhere. Whew.

"Well, Matthew," her father said, "it sounds like you have a fine career in economics ahead of you. . . . Unlike my daughter, who, between you and me, I'm afraid may be planning to become an English major."

"Daddy!" Callie cried, whacking him on the arm.

"My greatest fear realized," he continued, ignoring her, "and the one thing I absolutely forbade her from doing when she came to college!"

"Callie is an excellent writer," Matt volunteered, unfamiliar with her father's humor. "You should be very proud of all the work she's been doing in her English classes and for the *Harvard Crimson*."

"Believe me, I am," her dad said, executing Hug Number Eleven.

Callie grinned. Suddenly her phone vibrated in her pocket. Her face fell. She had been ignoring every text and call since she had left the Pudding to pick up her dad, but she should probably check in at some point to make sure there were no election-related emergencies. . . . Maybe if she snuck into the bathroom she could—

"Go ahead and get that," her dad said, watching her closely. "I think I spy Professor Stanislauss over in the corner there. We were both at Berkeley as graduate students," he explained to Matt's parents. "I'm going to go say hello. I'll be right back, kiddo," he finished, squeezing Callie on the arm.

"Okay," she said. "It was so nice to meet both of you," she added to Matt's parents, who had also excused themselves. Sighing, she whipped out her phone.

It looked like she had missed the opportunity to vote on approximately fifteen prospective members. It was almost six o'clock and they were just getting started on last names beginning with O. No word from Gregory about why he was MIA and no word from Clint about whether he wanted to stay together or never see her again. Sighing once more, she put away her phone.

Her father still stood with Professor Stanislauss, probably talking about some mathematical concept far beyond her grasp. It was wonderful to see him again after these past few months apart, but it also reminded her of how he could no longer solve her problems the way he had when she was eight years old, always ready with a Band-Aid when she scraped her knee or a huge bear hug after a rough day in school, like that one time she'd gotten her hand stuck in the goldfish bowl.

In a weird way the connection to home made her feel more alone than ever. She was on her own, and despite his considerable intellect and general Best-Dad-in-the-World-ness, Dr. Andrews had no solutions for everything going on with Clint, Gregory, or even Vanessa. Unless, of course, she could convince him to kidnap Alexis Thorndike. She almost laughed at the thought of trying to explain Lexi to him. *What is a Thorndike and why is it bothering you so much?* he would probably say, before ruling the entire situation a Mom Problem, just as he had done with periods and her one big fight with Jessica back in high school.

Catching his eye, she smiled at him.

"Ready for dinner, kiddo?" he called, coming over to her.

Smiling, she slipped her arm through his. "You betcha, Daddo!"

A few hours later they were sharing their favorite dessert—an ice cream sundae with extra hot fudge—in the lobby of his hotel.

"Ugh," she groaned, dropping her spoon with a clatter and silencing the never-ending buzz of her phone.

"Seriously, Calbear," said her dad, watching her, "what's the deal with all this phone stuff?"

"I'm sorry," she said. "I should have just turned it off."

"It's okay," he said, taking a huge spoonful of ice cream. "You've been good about it, even though I could see you itching to answer all night. Who keeps calling you, anyway? It's not that boyfriend your mother made me promise to spy on this weekend, is it?"

Callie closed her eyes at the word *boyfriend*, trying not to groan again. "They're not calls; they're texts," she explained. "It's that club I joined last semester," she continued. "Today is the day we're voting on new members and they want to know if I say yay or nay." She paused, picking up her phone. "On . . . *ew* . . . Vandemeer *comma* Penelope."

"Sounds like a nay," said her dad. "I can tell just from the name."

"Very perceptive of you," Callie agreed, spooning some hot fudge covered in crushed walnuts into her mouth. Still, she refrained from responding in the negative, having decided on the way to the airport that the very idea of voting on someone made her uncomfortable. She would make only one exception: to vote yay on Von Vorhees, Vanessa. After what had happened with the Pudding last semester, she owed her that much.

"So, is this club that same Jell-O society that you needed extra money for last semester?"

"It's called the Pudding," she said meekly.

"Well, whatever it's called, your mother and I discussed it and—"

"Wait," said Callie, lowering her spoon. "Since when do you and Mom *discuss* things?"

"What are you talking about? Your mother and I have plenty of amicable discussions."

Callie raised her eyebrows, leveling him with a *look*.

"All right, fine: you got me," he said with a smile, taking another bite of ice cream. "Although you may be surprised to know that your mother and I have become considerably friendlier since you left for college. I think it must be a combination of that empty-nester syndrome and mutual fear that you're going to get yourself in some sort of trouble somehow so far away from home."

Oh, if only he knew. "Trouble" didn't even begin to cover it. She forced a smile. "Hey!" she cried. "First you're *friendlier*, then you're hanging out, and before you know it . . . bam! You're back together."

"Not in this lifetime." He laughed, but it sounded a little sad. "Anyhow, back to the Jell-O. Your mother and I had a few *friendly* conversations about it, and we have no problem with your membership, given your decision to get a job and pay your own way."

Well, not exactly, but close enough. She nodded, shoveling more ice cream into her mouth. She had managed to cover some of her dues with her measly wages from the library, but she had run out of ideas as to who had footed the rest of the outstanding bill.

"But I do worry that you might be losing track of yourself out here, Calbear," he continued. "At home it always seemed like soccer was the thing that kept you focused and grounded, and without it I imagine you may be having a tough time figuring out exactly who you are or how to relieve stress without a ball to kick around the field. And I'm guessing there's plenty of stress to deal with," he finished, looking at her. "And not just schoolwork but other things, too: the kind of stuff that I can't always help you with."

So, so right. Suddenly she found herself blinking rapidly, unsure what to say.

"Fortunately I know I raised you—okay," he admitted, "so your mom helped a little—to be capable of handling anything that comes your way. While it's fine to try new things and even make mistakes, I just want to make sure that you remember who you are and where you come from and that your old man loves you . . . and you're not allowed to marry anyone who isn't willing to move to California."

Callie laughed. "I love you, too, Dad."

"Enough to let me have the last bite?" he asked, pointing to the sundae with his spoon.

"Sure," she said. "Uh-oh, there it goes again," she added while her phone buzzed on the table. The text message notice indicated that it was from Mimi. Opening it, she read:

S.O.S.O.S. WITCH-LADY IS
ALMOST CONVINCING EVERYONE TO
VOTE AGAINST VANESSA. CAN YOU
GET TO LE CLUB???????

"Dad," she said, starting to stand. "I'm so sorry, but—if you don't mind—I really have to go." Fortunately, his hotel, the Sheraton Commander, was on Garden Street less than two blocks away from the Pudding. If she ran, she could make it.

"Is it something for that club?"

"Yes—well, yes and no. I have to do something related to the club, but it's not *for* the club, it's for a friend."

"Well," he said, "go on, then. It was a long flight, and I was planning to hit the hay soon anyway. I'll see you tomorrow," he said, standing and giving her a final hug.

"Thanks, Dad," she said, throwing her arms around him. "Thanks for dinner—and for everything."

He smiled down at her. "You betcha!"

Hour Thirteen (T Minus 40 Hours until Parental Departure): In which Callie sprints to the Pudding and makes a speech of epic proportions.

"Well, it seems like everyone's had their say on Ms. Von Vorhees," said Anne from where she still sat in front of the room. "Time to put it to a vote—"

"WAIT!" Callie cried, exploding into the room, red-faced and panting. "Sorry," she said, bending over and resting her hands on her knees. "Is it all right if I—" she added, taking a sip of Anne's water without waiting for an answer. Looking up, she saw Mimi grinning at her; unfortunately, the double thumbs-up sign didn't inspire any particular words. Everyone stared, including Lexi, Tyler, and Clint, who were all still posted in the front row. Taking a deep breath, Callie decided just to wing it.

"Vanessa *really* wants to join this club. Like, really, *really* wants it."

"So?" said Lexi, smirking. "Since when has that been an aspect of our criteria?"

Callie met her gaze. "Maybe it hasn't been an, er, *aspect* of the criteria in the past, but my point is that it should be. So what if we already have a lot of people like her?" Callie said, naming one of the anonymous complaints she had read on HPpunch.com. "Although I have to say, as someone who lives with her, that there really is no one quite like Vanessa," she added. Mimi nodded in agreement.

"And if it seems like she's 'trying too hard,'" Callie continued, "that's only because of how badly, like I already said, she wants it. And you know what? That's the kind of club that *I* want to be a part of, too. Not the type of place that excludes people just to feel exclusive but somewhere that allows anyone who genuinely wants to be here belong—even if they're a little wacky or annoying from time to time."

Callie took a deep breath, ignoring Anne's horrified expression as she filched another sip of water.

"So," she concluded, "if she goes, I go."

"Fine by me," Lexi muttered.

"*Moi aussi*," Mimi called from the back. "I go, too."

Callie beamed. At least they could all sit alone together in the room on Friday nights with no more clubhouse. . . .

Or maybe not: a couple of the sophomores seemingly on the verge of voting with Lexi previously were glancing anxiously at Mimi who, much like Alessandra, had been one of last semester's high-priority punches.

"Oh, please," said Lexi, rolling her eyes. "This is just ridiculous—"

"I go, too," said another voice, its owner standing.

It was Clint. Callie stared at him, her eyes prickling, and even though his face was carefully devoid of expression, he was, for the first time all week, looking back at her.

"Hell, so do I," said Tyler, leaping to his feet. "I already vowed to beat up everyone who didn't vote for her but now—what the heck—if you don't want her, then I'll resign my presidency."

"Tyler," Lexi said sharply, "you can't just coerce them by threatening—"

"Oh, stop talking," Tyler interrupted, "and let's get on with the vote. Callie, you can sit down now," he added. "Anne?"

"Yes," she said, tearing her eyes away from her now empty water glass. "A show of hands, please."

Hour Fourteen (T Minus 39 Hours until Parental Departure): In which the votes are in and the members of the Pudding summon their new initiates to the John Harvard statue.

Callie and Mimi huddled together at the base of the John Harvard statue, struggling to stay warm. The rest of the members were assembled nearby, preparing to place the calls commanding new members-elect to "*Get to the John Harvard statue, NOW.*" In a matter of minutes they would arrive.

"Hey," said Callie, taking a few steps forward, "is that a . . ."

". . . it is!" she called triumphantly to Mimi a few seconds later. Somebody had left a soccer ball on the grass in the middle of Harvard Yard.

"Weeeeeeeee!" Callie yelled, dribbling full speed while Mimi called after her through chattering teeth and swatted at OK, who had immediately rushed over to offer his services as a personal space heater.

The sounds faded save for the rush of wind through Callie's hair and the soft crunch of the grass beneath her toes. After a long day of sitting and texting and trying not to break teacups, running felt absolutely amazing. At the edge of the Yard, about two hundred feet away from the group now, she doubled back, muttering commentary all the while:

"And Rooney fakes left and then takes it up the side; my god, look how fast—he breaks through the Liverpool fullbacks and then—wait for it—he shoots—he SCOR—*Ahhhhhh!*"

In the darkness, unaware of how fast she'd been moving, she had accidentally kicked the ball as hard as she could straight into the head of an oncoming figure—

THWACK!

The ball smacked against the boy's palms as he caught it—

"And the shot is BLOCKED in a phenomenal save from Liverpool keeper Pepe Reina," Callie heard Gregory cry, her horrified expression melting into a smile as she raced toward him. "But wait," he continued, "Rooney is on the move again, rushing Reina, hoping that he'll make a mistake—but Reina is too quick and—"

"And *oh*, a MASSIVE punt from the Liverpool keeper!" Callie shouted, still in announcer mode, as Gregory kicked the ball. They watched it soar, arc, and then drop, all the way over the fence on the other side of the yard.

"You follow the Premier League football clubs?" Callie asked breathlessly, two bright spots on her cheeks. "I always assumed that was OK who TiVoed all the English games!"

Gregory shook his head. "Never assume that anything of quality was TiVoed by His Highness."

"Seriously!" Callie laughed. "Well, we should totally watch a game together some—"

"I should have known," a voice said suddenly from behind them. The color draining from her face, Callie turned: Clint stood only a few feet away. "I was going to compliment you on the way you stood up for Vanessa," he said, "but I wouldn't want to interrupt."

"No," said Callie, "wait—"

"No, no," Clint reassured them, backing away. "It's fine. I'll leave you two alone."

Dammit!

"Gregory," she said, turning to him, "I'm sorry, but—"

"Go," he said with a nod.

"Sorry," she called again, racing after Clint, who had hurried to rejoin the crowd near the John Harvard statue. The punches had started to arrive, but Callie barely noticed what was happening around her as Tyler began to read from the list of names, calling each new member forward one by one. Her cheeks were still flushed, and her eyes kept darting back to Clint, hoping to catch his gaze: to convey with a look that there was nothing going on with Gregory beyond a random, wild moment of pure—*friendly*—connection, because they were friends now; that's it.

But, as far as Clint seemed to be concerned, she no longer existed.

Nevertheless, she continued hopping anxiously from one foot to the other, her thoughts racing, when suddenly Tyler raised his megaphone and yelled the final name:

"VANESSA VON VORHEES!" he boomed.

Everyone stayed completely silent while Tyler stepped forward to administer the honors personally.

Then, as if in slow motion, everyone started to scream: erupting into a chaotic mass of hugging, shouting, jumping, dancing, and drinking. Squealing and shaking, Vanessa hugged everyone in sight: first Tyler and then Clint, followed by OK, Mimi, and—

"Oh, what the hell?" Vanessa said, smiling at Callie and then embracing her.

"You made it!" Callie cried, holding Vanessa tight. Beaming, they broke away and Vanessa grabbed the bottle out of Tyler's hands, taking a swig and crying "To ME!" before passing it to Callie.

"To you!" Callie agreed, taking a sip and then handing it to Mimi.

Maybe I don't have a boyfriend anymore, she thought as she and Vanessa hugged again, but maybe I have something even better: maybe, just maybe, she had her best friend back.

parents weekend, part II:

The Final 24 Hours

PHILLIP A. BENEDICT, DEAN OF HARVARD COLLEGE,

CORDIALLY INVITES THE CLASS OF 2014

* AND THEIR PARENTS *

TO JOIN HIM FOR DINNER IN ANNENBERG HALL

ON SATURDAY, THE 19TH OF MARCH, AT 6 P.M.

Hour Thirty-six (T Minus 18 Hours until Parental Departure): In which, after a day of attending various lectures and seminars, the students and visiting family members gather for dinner in Annenberg Hall.

Callie had awoken the following morning feeling sleepy, but also cautiously optimistic. As if the weather could read her mood, the sun was shining down on campus for what felt like the first time in months, melting small patches of snow. She and her father had attended several of the special seminars put on for Parents Weekend, including one hosted by her Econ professor, and then spent the rest of the afternoon wandering around Harvard Square. Her dad seemed to be having a great time and had even promised to wear the Harvard sweatshirt she'd purchased for him at the COOP "at least once" back home in California.

Now they were on their way to the Undergraduate Dean's dinner in Annenberg. The dining hall staff had arranged the scuffed brown tables banquet-style: complete with white tablecloths, flowers, and candles. Outfitted in white shirts and black slacks, they stood ready to bring each course to the table (contrary to the usual buffet mode of service). Seating, subject to RSVP, had been assigned according to dormitory and entryway, so the residents of Wigglesworth, entryway C, floor two, plus parents would be sitting together—whether they liked it or not.

"*Whew-whee,*" Callie's dad whistled, locating the place card that read *Callie Andrews + One Guest*. "This school sure is fancy."

"It's not *always* like this," Callie protested as Matt sat down across the table to their left, followed by his parents.

"Yeah," Matt agreed. "They're just trying to impress you: normally they feed us dog food."

"Matty!" said his mom, looking scandalized. "You don't mean it!"

"Of course not, Mom." He chuckled, catching Callie's eye. "Sometimes there's cat food, too." Mrs. Robinson—of sock-label-sewing, care-package-sending fame (contents ranging from strawberry bubble bath to condoms)—actually reminded Callie a lot of her own mom, so she both liked her immediately but understood completely when certain utterances resulted in Matt's total mortification.

Glancing down, she read the place card to her right: *Vanessa Von Vorhees + One Guest*.

Callie, who hadn't had a chance to really talk to Vanessa since last night's festivities, wondered if she were about to meet the man or the missus. Given that Vanessa had often referenced her dad's tendency to work late back when she and Callie were friends, it seemed far more likely that if only one parent were coming, it would be the much-maligned "Housewife who made the cast of the *Real Desperate* look like 'amateurs.'"

Oh no. Callie had been so busy worrying about who would be sitting next to her that she had neglected to read the name card upside-down and opposite her: Gregory pulled out the chair directly across from her and sat down with an empty seat on either side of him, presumably for his parents.

"Hello," said her father, standing. "I don't believe we've met. . . ."

"Gregory Bolton, Professor Andrews, sir," said Gregory, reaching to grip his hand.

"Oh, please, call me Thomas," Callie's dad said, sitting. "Are you a friend of Matthew's?"

"Yes," said Gregory. "We live together, along with that guy," he said, pointing down the table to where Adam was sitting with his parents across from Dana and her parents, "and that tall, ugly one up there," he concluded, gesturing at OK.

OK's head snapped up and he made a fist, pounding it against his palm. Then he turned back to Mimi's mother and continued speaking in abysmal French: "En-Chant-Tay, Mad-eh-moselle. Je vou-drai, er, introduce-ay? Ah vous de mon parents, ici la . . ."

It was a sign of sheer stress that Mimi wasn't laughing hysterically while he blathered on.

"You must be Callie," a voice cooed before a woman—who had to be Vanessa's mother—bent and grabbed her shoulders. "Well, go on: stand up and give me a hug!" she exclaimed. Callie complied, shooting Vanessa a questioning glance while her mother continued, "It's so wonderful to finally meet you—Vee just goes on and on about her 'bestie from California' whenever I can get her on the phone!" Vanessa, her eyes wide, shook her head slowly and held up her hands.

"And you must be Mr. Andrews," Vanessa's mom said, shaking hands with Callie's father after she'd finally released his daughter. "I'm Linda Von Vorhees."

"It's *Dr.* Andrews, Mom," Vanessa muttered, sinking into her seat.

"It's Thomas," Callie's dad insisted.

"And you must call me Linda," she said. "A doctor, did you say?" she added, leaning over Callie as they sat. Vanessa stared straight ahead.

"Er, professional math geek, actually," Thomas Andrews replied, seeming to look more the part when he realized that he had the full attention of an attractive woman. (It didn't happen very often, not because he wasn't handsome in that absentminded, Russell-Crowe-in-*A-Beautiful-Mind*-minus-the-schizophrenia sort of way, but because it was such a rare occasion that he actually left the classroom.) Attractive, though not beautiful (like Mimi's mother, who was currently gabbing to OK's parents about Renee's upcoming nuptials), was the right word for Linda Von Vorhees. She had Vanessa's reddish blond hair (or at least the same highlights and stylist), a similar penchant for colorful designer clothing, and though smaller than Vanessa, she seemed less "anorexic" than her daughter had once described.

"He teaches mathematics at UCLA," Callie supplied in response to Mrs. Von Vorhees's confused expression.

"A college professor: how intriguing!" she cooed. "I didn't finish college myself—ran off with Vee's father when I was twenty-one and never looked back, what a mistake *that* was—but I've always wished . . ." She smiled.

"Well, it's never too late to learn," Thomas said cavalierly. Callie cringed, wondering if this were flirting, how she might go about confirming it as such, and if affirmative, if there was any way that it could be stopped.

From across the table Gregory caught her eye.

". . . Hi," she said.

"Hey."

"Where are your parents?" she asked him while Vanessa turned and introduced herself to OK's father. ("If he's really a prince . . . does that make you a king?")

"Should be here any minute," he replied.

Overhearing, Mrs. Von Vorhees said, "You must be the Boltons' boy, Gregory! I'm on the Committee for the Children with your mother."

"Stepmother," he corrected.

"Yes, of course. So you live right across the hall from the girls?" she asked, eyeing him in a way that proved that even women twice his age weren't entirely immune to his charms.

"That is correct," he affirmed.

"And you two"—she nodded at her daughter—"never?"

"Mom!" Vanessa shrieked.

Gregory smiled graciously. "I think most people eventually find that dating within the dormitory is ill-advised," he said, avoiding Callie's eyes.

Her father smiled. "That seems very wise of you, Gregory. Speaking of dating," he added, turning to Callie. "Your mother phoned again this morning to insist that I 'interrogate' you—yes, that's the word she used—about that Clifford . . . or Clifton. . . ."

"Clint," said Callie, frowning into her lap.

"Yes, that's right," he said. "It's a shame that he was too busy to join us at some point this weekend. Your mother will be extremely disappointed that I didn't figure out how to get a picture for her on the phone camera. Camera phone? It's one of these buttons here she showed me. . . ." he muttered, fiddling with his cell.

"That one there," Callie said with a small smile.

"Vanessa!" her mother exclaimed. "You didn't tell me that Callie has a new boyfriend! Or wait now, Clint, is that the same one from last semester . . . ?" she asked. Then, addressing Callie's father, she added, "I like to stay updated on all the gossip, and since Vanessa and Callie are practically inseparable, I feel like I already know her—almost as if she were one of my own!"

Callie tried to return Mrs. Von Vorhees's affectionate smile, wondering if she had any idea how much of her information was hopelessly out of date.

Her dad nodded politely. "I'm not sure about staying updated on the gossip," he said, "but I do like to know exactly who thinks he can date my daughter and live to tell about it," he finished, clapping a hand on Callie's shoulder.

"Daddy!" she cried.

Gregory smirked.

"I just wanted to meet the guy for five minutes so I could put a healthy amount of fear in his heart," Professor Andrews said with a laugh. "Is that too much to ask?"

"Not at all," Gregory answered, laughing with him.

"So, tell us all about him, then!" Mrs. Von Vorhees pressed Callie, leaning in. "What's he like? Where is he right now? Is it casual or have you two started discussing your future?"

"Well . . ." said Callie, glancing at Gregory, who looked like he wanted to hear about it just as much as she wanted to talk about it. "His name is Clint, he's a junior, he's about *this* tall, he's from Virginia—"

"Yes, but what's he *like*?" Mrs. Von Vorhees asked. "What kind of things does he like to do?"

"Uh . . ." Callie drew a blank. They had been dating for months now—if they were still dating, that is—how could she not know the answer to these questions? "Well, he likes government—"

"He *likes* government? What does that mean?" Vanessa's mom interrupted.

"Oh, ha," said Callie. "I mean, he *studies* government. I'm not sure if he likes government in terms of his political stance—"

"A Republican?" her father demanded.

"I believe his mother prefers the term 'moderate with conservative leanings'?" Callie said, squinting. "And, um, he's on the squash team with Gregory so he definitely likes squash—"

"Really?" said her dad. "Well, then tell me, Gregory: what's your opinion of this Clint character?"

Gregory shrugged. "I guess if I ever had a daughter and she had to date someone, he wouldn't be the worst choice."

Oh, gee, thanks for the ringing endorsement.

"He has been busy lately," Gregory added, "otherwise I'm sure he'd love to meet you."

"So, what do you study, Gregory?" her father asked as the dining hall staff brought out their entrées.

"Economics," he said, "though I'm seriously considering switching to applied mathematics. I'm kind of . . ." He furrowed his brow, as if searching for the right word. "*Disillusioned* with the current state of the financial services industry."

Dr. Andrews nodded. "I can certainly see why. Just today Callie and Matthew's econ professor gave a lecture on white-collar crime and the fine line between ethical business practices and malpractice."

Gregory nodded, pretending—probably—to listen closely in a rare display of politeness.

"A little soft on the complex mathematics side," Dr. Andrews continued, "but still quite relevant as we're continuing to see a proliferation of insider trading, Ponzi schemes, offshore tax evasion, short selling . . . Why, with the lack of regulation when it comes to hedge funds and private equities, it's easy to understand how, even with perfectly legal business practices, some people get in over their heads."

"Mmm," said Gregory, shifting uncomfortably in his seat. Callie tried to send him a telepathic apology for her dad's tendency to lecture both in and out of the classroom. It was part of the reason she'd had such an advantage growing up, but it was also part of the reason that other people sometimes got bored.

Like Mrs. Von Vorhees, for example, who was employing the good old smile and nod tactic of conversation, though she had perked up at the terms *equity* and *hedge funds*. While she most likely couldn't explain the difference between a hedge fund and her garden shrubbery, she did seem to know that the one with *fund* at the end of it involved men in suits and lots of money.

"If I'm not mistaken, didn't your father leave Goldman to start his own, ah, hedge fund?" she asked Gregory politely.

Gregory, who had been midway through a sip of water, began to choke.

"Oh dear," said Mrs. Von Vorhees as he turned red. "Are you all right?"

"Yes," he gasped. "Yes, I'm fine. Water—just went—down—the wrong pipe."

"Your father . . ." Dr. Andrews began thoughtfully, "is he *the* Bolton who cofounded Bolton and Stamford Enterprises?"

Gregory nodded, glancing uncomfortably at his phone. He's probably sick of always hearing about his famous dad, Callie thought suddenly. Where is *the* Mr. Bolton, anyway?

"Oh, that's *right*," Mrs. Von Vorhees said, failing to notice his discomfort. "I remember my husband saying that your father invented some entirely new type of trading algorithm— Algorithm? Is that the right word?"

Gregory shrugged.

"Well, we'll just have to ask him when he gets here! Which will be sometime soon, I hope," she added as a waiter took her dish away. "He's missed almost the entire dinner!"

Frowning, Gregory checked his phone again. "I'm not sure what the holdup is. . . . Work, probably."

Mrs. Von Vorhees nodded. "Oh, certainly. A man like your father must work all the time. Never home, just like Vee's!" she said. "Sweetheart," she added quietly while a waiter set a large slice of chocolate cake in front of Vanessa and she prepared to take an enormous bite, "I thought you said you were skipping desserts these days?"

Vanessa dropped her fork abruptly. "Right," she muttered.

"So, Callie, tell me," Mrs. Von Vorhees said when her father had turned, along with Gregory, to join the Robinsons' conversation. "What's your secret? How *do* you stay so deliciously thin?"

"Er..." Callie said, wondering how Vanessa's mother could fail to notice the way her daughter's shoulders had slumped while she stared miserably at her plate. "Stress?"

Behind her mother's back Vanessa began to eat the cake in huge forkfuls.

"Nonsense, dear, don't be shy," Mrs. Von Vorhees prodded. "Surely you must do some form of exercise to look the way you do."

"Yes," said Callie, thinking of the hours she'd been spending on the treadmill, particularly this past week, until her knee felt like it would explode. "I like to *run*. . . ."

". . . from my problems," she added under her breath. Across the table Gregory smirked, even though he appeared to be fully engaged in a discussion with the Robinsons.

"Maybe one day you could drag Vee with you?" Mrs. Von Vorhees suggested. "I think she would enjoy the exercise if she ever gave it a chance."

Shoving her now empty plate away, Vanessa stood. "I'm going to the bathroom," she announced.

"I'll have to excuse myself, too," Gregory said suddenly, grabbing his phone. "See what's happening with my dad. . . ."

"Send my regards to Trisha!" Mrs. Von Vorhees called after

him—Trisha being, presumably, the stepmother. "She's really very naturally pretty," she added, nodding at Vanessa's retreating back when she and Callie were virtually alone. "If she would only take better care of herself . . . Spend a little less time shopping and a little more at the gym . . ."

Callie was silent.

"I know you think I'm being hard on her," Mrs. Von Vorhees continued, "but I'm only telling her the things that I wish somebody had told me when I was her age. Why, even that Dana girl has a boyfriend, and I worry—"

"Vanessa has a boyfriend," Callie interjected, confused.

"She—she does?" Mrs. Von Vorhees asked.

Whoops. Looks like the fact that she and Callie were no longer "besties" wasn't the only thing *Vee* had been keeping secret.

"She didn't tell you?" Callie asked.

"No," said Mrs. Von Vorhees, her delight seeming to only slightly outweigh her hurt. "What's his name? Is it serious?"

"I'm not sure how serious it is," Callie said, "but his name's Tyler Green, and he's one of Clint's roommates."

"Tyler Green; Tyler Green," Mrs. Von Vorhees repeated, and Callie got the distinct impression that she was memorizing it for the purposes of Googling him later: like mother, like daughter. "The two of you, dating the two of them—well, isn't that lovely!"

Oh yeah, *real* lovely.

"Could you—could you not mention to Vanessa that I told you?" Callie entreated Mrs. Von Vorhees. "She probably, er, wants to surprise you when she's ready."

"Certainly, dear; it'll be our little secret."

Good.

"Though I do sometimes worry about the sort of things that she's been hiding from me . . ." Mrs. Von Vorhees mused.

Sounds like maybe you should be, Callie thought. Suddenly she felt incredibly grateful for her parents. While there were certainly things that she could never in a million years confide in them (i.e., a certain X-rated tape: definitely due in part to the fact that her dad would go to jail for murdering Evan), she still kept them reasonably informed, and knew she could always go to them with a problem and expect them to be supportive instead of tearing her down.

Finding her dad's hand under the table, she squeezed it and he squeezed back.

"It's just been so hard on her these past few months," Mrs. Von Vorhees said with a sigh. "What with her father moving out and now the divorce proceedings underway."

Callie nearly choked on her dessert. "Wh—what?"

"I know that maybe this isn't the proper place, but I just wanted to thank you for being here for her this year. It's nice to know she has a friend she can count on while her father's off doing—things that are inappropriate to say at the dinner table."

Callie's eyes were wide with shock.

"I shouldn't have said that!" Mrs. Von Vorhees muttered, looking around to make sure no one had heard. "I'm sorry. You will look out for her, though, won't you?"

Callie nodded. Her stomach plummeted while she replayed every nasty thing she'd said to Vanessa up until the moment she'd found her crying on the bathroom floor, when Callie had assumed the problem was Tyler-related instead of something much, much bigger.

"I'll do the best I can," she promised Vanessa's mother as both Gregory and Vanessa reentered the dining hall. "My parents are divorced, too, you know," she added in a whisper. "Almost five years now."

"Really?" asked Mrs. Von Vorhees, giving Callie's father another appraising glance.

"They're still completely obsessed with each other," Callie added hastily. It wasn't a total lie: her mom had been known to e-mail, and now to call, her father frequently in matters where their *baby* was concerned.

"Hmm . . ." Mrs. Von Vorhees murmured. "Sweetheart, are you feeling all right?" she added to Vanessa, who had just plopped back into her chair looking pale-faced and sick.

"I'm fine," she replied. "Can we please get out of here now?"

"Well, I was so looking forward to catching up with Trish," Mrs. Von Vorhees said reluctantly, eyeing Gregory. "She's missed the last two Committee meetings. . . ."

"I just spoke with them," Gregory said. "Unfortunately it looks like they won't be able to make it after all."

"Oh, how tragic," Mrs. Von Vorhees replied. "Well, next time you speak with her, would you mind mentioning that we haven't received her checks for the past two months either? I wouldn't ask, but it's for The *Children*," she finished.

"I'll be sure to pass that along," said Gregory, standing although he'd only just sat down. "I should get going, too. So nice to meet you, Mrs. Von Vorhees. And you as well, Dr. Andrews—Thomas," he added, shaking his hand again.

"A real pleasure, Gregory," her father said.

After cappuccinos and more small talk among the roommates' parents, the dinner finally drew to a close.

"That's a great group of friends you've got back there, Calbear," her father said as he and Callie wound their way back to Wigglesworth. "Dana seems like she's got a good head on her shoulders and Matthew . . . and that Gregory!"

"Yeah," said Callie. That Gregory. He'd put on a pretty good show for the grown-ups, but she'd still detected hints of his bad mood at several points during dinner. Maybe when the weekend was over she'd finally have a chance to ask him—as a friend—if something was wrong.

"And the other two—the foreign ones—they're hilarious. Renee, that little one's older sister, seems particularly impressive. . . ."

"Mimi's impressive, too," Callie said defensively.

"They were *all* impressive," her dad agreed. "I had no idea that you and Vanessa were so close!"

You and me both.

"You must be tired," he added, watching her yawn.

"Kind of," she admitted. "But I'm going to try to cram in some work before bedtime."

"On a Saturday night?" he asked.

Welcome to my life. "Yeah, well, you know, there's only one week left until spring break so . . . ." She shrugged.

"Proud of you, kiddo," he said, mussing up her hair.

"Proud of you, too, Dad," she mumbled back, throwing her arms around his waist with such force that he stumbled backward.

"Whoa," he said with a laugh. "If I'd known you missed me so much, I would have visited sooner!"

"'Course I miss you," she mumbled. "Every day. Mom, too."

"Speak of the devil, I think she's calling me right now. . . . Uh-oh, looks like the third time tonight. I'd better take this," he said. "See you tomorrow morning?"

"Yep!"

"Theresa?" he said into his phone, wandering away. "Yes, hi. . . . Fine. . . . How are you? . . . Yes, I remembered to ask about the boyfriend. . . . No, I did not get a picture. . . . Yes, I remembered how to work the button. . . . No, nothing embarrassing . . ."

Callie laughed and shook her head before opening the door to her entryway. "Tell her I love her and that I'll call her tomorrow!" she yelled after him. Turning, her dad waved. Then he disappeared down the stone path that led out onto Massachusetts Avenue.

When Callie reached the common room, Mimi and Dana were already inside. Mimi lay sprawled across the couch with one arm thrown over her forehead like she had just survived a war, and even Dana looked a little shell-shocked from where she sat in the overstuffed armchair.

"*Mon dieu*, what a nightmare," Mimi muttered, letting forth a gigantic sigh.

"You might say it was a bit . . . intense," Dana agreed, whose parents had spent the entire dinner giving Adam the third degree and reminding them of the promise they had "made to God, their parents, and themselves."

"At least I will not be seeing Mama or Renee again until the wedding," Mimi consoled herself. "That is, if *my* wedding does not happen first. . . ."

"What?" asked Callie.

"Didn't you hear?" asked Dana, looking reproachfully at Mimi. "Mimi and OK are engaged."

"It was a *joke*," Mimi insisted, sitting up. "*Elles ne voulaient pas se taire au sujet de mariage de Renee! De plus, si il y avait une chose,*" she cried, holding up one finger, "*que je pensais que je pouvais compter sur de ma mère, c'était son racisme! Mais non,*" she exclaimed, throwing herself back down on the couch. "*Même qui m'a manqué aujourd'hui. J'ai sous-estimé la capacité de ma mère au sens où la royauté est dans la salle. Il s'agit d'un sixième sens avec elle!*"

"What . . ." Callie began.

"We are considering a winter ceremony," Mimi said dolefully, covering her eyes with her hands. "After Renee's in June, *bien sûr!*"

"Well," said Dana. "I should think you learned your lesson: that *lying* can seriously backfire."

"Can I be a bridesmaid?" Callie asked, giggling.

"*Oui,*" said Mimi. "If I do not suicide first."

At that moment the door to the common room opened and Vanessa stepped inside.

"What's so funny?" she demanded, looking from Mimi to Dana.

"Vanessa!" Callie cried. "You're home!" The other two froze. It was the first time in months they had seen one of them issue the other a friendly greeting. "I was hoping that—"

"Don't," Vanessa warned.

Callie frowned. She had no intention of raising the topic of divorce in front of the others, trying merely to suggest that they go somewhere private to chat. After all, she'd made a promise to Vanessa's mother that she planned to keep. "Well, maybe later if you want, we could talk—"

"I *said* DON'T!" Vanessa yelled suddenly, whirling wildly toward Callie. "Whatever you're going to say—DON'T. I don't care. I *hate* you!"

"Vanessa, I—"

"I HATE YOU! I HATE YOU!" Vanessa screamed so loudly that the windows rattled.

Mimi and Dana stayed completely still, looking terrified.

"JUST STAY AWAY FROM ME, OKAY?" Vanessa cried even louder, only inches from Callie's face. "STAY-THE-HELL-AWAY!" And then, she pushed her.

"What the—" Callie exclaimed, stumbling. She didn't fall, but her arms flew to the spot where Vanessa had touched her. "FINE!" Callie erupted. "That's just FINE!"

Mimi and Dana watched both of them run into their respective rooms, followed by two thunderous *SLAMS*. The girls were quiet for a second, and then Dana turned to Mimi.

"Something needs to be done about this," she said.

"*Oui*," Mimi agreed. "It does."

THIRTEEN

Lace, Leather, and Handcuffs

The Hasty Pudding Social Club

invites its members and their friends

for a night of true

DEBAUCHERY

THE ONE · THE ONLY · THE ANNUAL

LEATHER &

LACE

Thursday, March 24th at 10 P.M.

Leather and lace required.

Whips and mesh encouraged.

By Invitation Only

"*C*aaaaalleeeee . . ." Mimi's disembodied voice called from the common room. *"Viens ici, s'il vous plait!"*

"Just a minute!" Callie cried, tucking her white cotton tee into the high-waisted leather skirt she had borrowed from her roommate for the Pudding's infamous S & M–themed party, "Leather & Lace." Then for good measure she donned a chunky necklace (also Mimi's) made of black ribbons and leather beads. Tomorrow afternoon she, Mimi, and—unfortunately—Vanessa would all be flying, along with most of the rest of the Pudding and several of the other Final Clubs, down to a resort on the tiny island of Vieques, just off the coast of Puerto Rico. Tonight, therefore, she was determined to a) find Clint and force a reconciliation; and b) look good while doing it.

He'd had nearly two weeks to think things over. . . . The party would be the perfect place for them to make up, and make out, so that by this time tomorrow they'd be sitting on a beach laughing and drinking mai tais.

At the last second, on sudden inspiration, she traded Mimi's necklace for the silver one with the heart-shaped pendant that Clint had given her. Much to her surprise, she'd found it yesterday while de-cluttering the top of her bureau, and had in fact almost thrown it out, believing the tiny blue box to be empty until it rattled on its way to the trash. She felt a rush of confidence as she secured the chain around her neck: surely, just like the necklace, not all was lost, and maybe tonight it would be the good luck charm she needed to bring Clint back to her.

"Okay, I'm ready!" she announced, strolling into the common room. Mimi stood near the door in skin-tight, red leather pants, a studded belt, and a black mesh T-shirt that showed off her nonexistent tummy. She wore black leather cuffs on both wrists and was holding a whip and a pair of handcuffs (real metal ones, not the pink fuzzy kind). Vanessa hovered in front of their full-length mirror, surveying her figure in a lacy black and white corset dress over fishnet stockings that looked straight out of the Very Sexy section of Victoria's Secret.

She and Callie eyed each other warily.

Just then Dana popped out of her bedroom holding a digital camera. "I have an idea!" she said brightly. "Why don't I take a picture of the three of you before you head out to your night of, um, debauchery?"

Callie stared at her. But before she could fully process the absence of disapproving glares and muttered prayers, Mimi cried, "*C'est une excellente idée!* Everyone together now, squish, squish," she continued, looping her arm through Callie's and grabbing Vanessa by the elbow.

"Great," said Dana, holding up the camera. "Now if you could all three just hold hands—that's it, but a little closer now—"

"What the—" started Vanessa.

"Hey!" Callie cried.

"Say cheese!" Dana yelled.

"*Voilà!*" Mimi screamed as the flash went off, leaping back.

Callie tried to go left and Vanessa moved right but, just as they'd feared—

"HANDCUFFS?" Vanessa looked murderous. "You HANDCUFFED me to *her*!?"

"Okay, ha-ha," said Callie, trying to remain calm. "You got us! Now unlock these, please."

Mimi shook her head.

"*Marine Clément*," Vanessa started, jerking her wrist.

"OW!" Callie yelled. The metal chafed. "Watch it—that hurt!"

"If you don't undo these, right this minute," Vanessa continued, ignoring her, "then I am personally. Going. TO KILL YOU!"

"Actually," said Dana, stepping forward, "it was my idea."

Mimi nodded. "We are tired of living like this. Your stress is becoming our stress, and we have enough of *le stress* without *votre combat stupide*. We will not unlock you until you are friends again."

"Or at least civil," Dana amended.

"Yes, civil," Mimi agreed. "If you cannot learn to be nice and live together . . . *Eh bien*, you will learn the true meaning of living together. *Forever*."

"All right," said Vanessa, "we get the point. We're very sorry, and we'll try not to yell anymore . . . now *please* unlock us."

"Not good enough," said Dana, looking at Mimi.

"*Oui*," said Mimi. "You need to make up and kiss and say you were wrong and then swear *sur le statue de John Harvard* never to be so irritating again."

"This is RIDICULOUS!" Vanessa erupted. "You're making me late to my very first Pudding party as a member!"

"OW!" Callie cried as Vanessa gestured wildly and, once again, tugged her wrist. "Guys, seriously, we understand why you're upset and we are really sorry that we've been difficult to live with these past few months—"

"Thank you for the apology," Dana said graciously, "but what we really want is for you to apologize to each other."

Vanessa groaned.

"And if you do not," Mimi cut in, checking her watch, "by the time we are getting on the plane tomorrow, then I will eat the key and it will be lost. *Forever.*"

Dana shifted. "She's not actually going to—"

"I will eat it," Mimi repeated.

"Okay, then," said Dana. "I'll be right back."

In a moment she returned with a stack of papers in her hand, lugging her desk chair behind her. Then she cleared her throat. "I've been doing some online research on mediation—"

"Of course you have," Vanessa muttered.

"And to start," said Dana, speaking a little louder, "we need to organize ourselves in a circle," she said, motioning Mimi to orient the armchair so that it was facing where Callie and Vanessa were standing in front of the couch.

"Ooh," said Mimi, "this is just like what happened right before I went to the facility in Switzerland! *Maintenant* the first step we need you to take is to admit that you have a problem."

"I think we're past that stage," Dana said, referencing her notes. "Perhaps we should start with this one. . . ."

Mimi shrugged.

"All right," said Dana. "Now I want you each to write down one negative thing and one positive thing about the other, and then we'll put them into a hat—"

"How do you expect us to write when we're handcuffed together?" Callie asked, raising her right arm and dragging Vanessa's left with her.

"Oh. I see your point. Well, it *says* we need to write them down," said Dana. "But I guess we could say them aloud?"

"Unlock me. *Now*," Vanessa demanded from where she had sunk onto the couch. "I'm not kidding. Right now."

"Vanessa, thank you for volunteering," said Dana. "Please say one negative thing and one positive thing about Callie."

Vanessa thought for a moment. "My mother always said that if you don't have something nice to say, then shut your damn mouth!"

"Vanessa . . ." Dana said warningly.

"No," Vanessa interrupted. "This is bullshit. How do you expect me to say something nice about her when she wrote an entire article full of negative crap about me?"

"I told you," Callie interjected, "that I was just venting after *you* completely trashed my bedroom, not to mention falsely accusing me of stealing, and that the article was never meant to be published!"

"It's not just about the stupid article, okay?" Vanessa yelled back. "It's *everything*! Ditching me on my birthday, doing you-know-what with you-know-who at Harvard-Yale, and every other terrible thing you've done!" Vanessa had grown hysterical and suddenly seemed on the verge of tears. "All the bad stuff that's happened this year is *all* your fault . . . because you're a *bad friend*!"

Callie was quiet. "So: Harvard-Yale and the Pudding . . ." she said finally. "Is that what this is really about, Vanessa?"

"Of course that's what this is about!" she snapped, her lower lip trembling.

"And you're sure there's nothing else . . . that's upsetting you?" Callie prompted gently.

"That's it!" Vanessa cried, standing and forcing Callie to stand with her. "I am so out of here. No way am I going to sit through this," she said, addressing Mimi and Dana, "and let *her* take away my first party the way she's taken away everything else!"

"And how exactly do you propose that we—OW!" Callie cried for the third time that night, realizing that Vanessa was dragging her toward the door. "Dammit—stop—or at least slow down—"

"No!" cried Vanessa, grabbing her jacket with her free hand. "*You* keep up!" And with that she flounced out of the room, leaving Callie barely enough time to snatch her own coat before the door banged shut behind them.

Dana and Mimi exchanged a hopeless glance. "I will pray for you," Dana said solemnly, handing her the packet of mediation materials.

Mimi nodded and accepted the papers before reaching for her coat.

"Don't forget the stuff about role-playing on page three," Dana called when she was near the door.

Turning, Mimi raised an eyebrow.

"Oh, you know what I meant!" Dana snapped, flushing.

Mimi grinned and cracked her whip. "*Souhaitez-moi bonne chance!*"

"Good luck," Dana called after her. "You're going to need it."

Strobe lights flashed and techno music pounded out on the darkened dance floor in the dining room of the Pudding. "Will you quit—" Callie cried, stumbling past OK in mesh and short-shorts and Mimi, who were dancing with Marcus: resplendent in ass-less chaps which were not, believe it or not, the most outrageous outfit that evening. *"Ah!"* Callie cried, tripping again as Vanessa dragged her off the dance floor and over to the bar. Vanessa simply rolled her eyes and ordered another drink.

"Triple V!" a voice cried from behind them.

"Penny!" Vanessa yelled back, enveloping Penelope Vandemeer in an enormous hug—as she'd been doing with all the new members since they'd arrived.

Callie sighed and braced herself for another shrieking fest. Whether it was because Vanessa had her dominant right hand free or because Callie felt guilty about her parents' divorce, Vanessa had been running the show so far: forcing Callie to play the part of miserable sidekick.

Callie took a deep, calming breath, waiting for a lull in the conversation. "Can we just go somewhere quiet and talk for a sec—"

"Oh-em-gee, I'm totes bummed that you're not coming to PR!" Vanessa yelped to Penelope, completely ignoring her.

"Oh, I *know*," the girl replied. "Are you going, Callie?" she asked.

"Does it look like we have a choice?" Vanessa chirped ruefully, holding up their hands.

"Taking the theme a little too seriously?" Penelope asked.

"Something like that," Vanessa said with a loud, fake laugh.

"Anyway, if you see Mimi holding a key of any kind, be sure to steal it?"

"Okay!" said Penelope. "You guys are a riot." She shook her head. "I'll see you later."

"Tootles!" Vanessa cried.

"Vanessa," said Callie, "Please, slow down and—"

"Brittney!" Vanessa screamed.

"Hi, girls!" she said, coming over. "Wow," she added, spying the handcuffs. "That really gives new meaning to the term 'best friends *forever*' doesn't it!?"

"HA!" exclaimed Vanessa.

"I should have figured you two would be *literally* attached at the hip"—no, *literally* attached at the wrists, actually, thought Callie, and wow, you literally don't know what *literally* means—"after your speech the other night, Cal," Brittney finished.

"What speech?" said Vanessa, narrowing her eyes.

"Nothing," Callie cut in. "There was no speech!"

"Oh, stop!" said Brittney. "She must have told you how she threatened to quit if we didn't vote you into the club, right? She basically *chained* herself to your membership," she added, seeming pleased with her pun. "Like one of those dirty tree people do with the rain forest."

Vanessa, whose jaw still hung slack, said nothing.

"Brittney, I thought we weren't supposed to talk about anything that happens during election proceedings," said Callie. And with good reason: for nearly no one—including those who were voted in—escaped some form of open criticism or nasty anonymous commentary, which is why in the olden days of paper and ink all the clubs burned their punch books.

"Oh, whatever," said Brittney, waving her hand. "It's not like I published the punch book or anything! Anyway," she continued. "I'm off to the ladies' room, but if I don't run into you again tonight, then I'll see you on spring break!"

"Spring break, *whoo-hoo*!" said Callie, which seemed to be the appropriate response even though her enthusiasm about being trapped on a tiny island with everyone was dwindling by the minute.

Vanessa's lips were pressed together tight. The music swelled around them and the lights flickered nauseatingly. A moment passed, and then two, and then finally she turned to her roommate. "Callie," she started, "what—"

"Callie," someone else said from behind them with a slightly southern lilt.

Clint, of course.

"Hi," said Callie, her left hand flying to her hair.

"Could we talk?" he asked. "Somewhere private."

"Um," she said, raising her right hand. "That's going to be a bit of a problem."

Clint did not look amused. "Maybe you two might consider unlocking those for a minute so we could have a grown-up conversation?"

Callie stared at him. It's not like I *chose* this!

"Mimi did this to us against our will," Vanessa volunteered. "To get us to stop fighting."

"I see," said Clint.

"Mimi!" Vanessa yelled. Seeing the three of them, Mimi stopped dancing and came over.

"We kind of need that key now," Vanessa said in an awkward whisper, tilting her head at Clint.

Mimi's face fell. *Je suis désolé, mais*"—she swallowed—"I left it in the room with Dana."

Clint sighed. "Perhaps we should just go grab coffee early tomorrow morning. . . ."

No! thought Callie. It had already been two weeks and she couldn't stand to wait any longer, especially if the news was bad. Clint's expression wasn't giving anything away, but that seemed like a bad sign. Plus, coffee in the morning meant that they would be leaving separately tonight. . . .

"Maybe we could . . . all . . . go somewhere . . . ?" Callie started. "Vanessa . . . do you . . . ?"

"How about upstairs in Anne's office?" Vanessa volunteered. "I'll be totally quiet," she added. "It'll be like I'm not even there."

"If you're okay with it, then it's fine by me," Clint said with a shrug.

"Let's go," said Callie before anyone could change their mind.

Upstairs in the office Callie (and Vanessa) sat on a cushiony bench while Clint perched on Anne's desk. Callie had never been on this side of the second floor before except once to use the bathroom during her very first punch event. Apart from some framed group photos captioned along the lines of *"Pudding Garden Party: 2010,"* it was pretty much a standard office outfitted in the usual brown leather and wooden furniture.

Clint cleared his throat. Vanessa turned away and stared dutifully at the ceiling, dangling her legs over the side of the bench.

"I'm sorry this is so awkward," Clint said. "But I really do think it's time we talked."

"Yes," Callie agreed. "Before you say anything, I just want you to know again how sorry I am—about Gregory, and going through your room and your e-mails like that, and anything else I might have done wrong. For what it's worth, I swear that what happened at Harvard-Yale was a one-time thing and that you're the only person I want to be with—that I *still* want to be with." Swallowing, she took a deep breath. "As for the rest of it, I have no excuse except to plead temporary insanity induced by jealousy and general insecurity about . . . you know . . ." she finished, acutely aware of Vanessa's presence even though her roommate was doing an excellent job of pretending not to exist.

"I appreciate that," said Clint, "and that you've given me space to think things over."

Callie waited.

"I've decided that I could probably move past the cheating—if you can even call it that," he conceded. "I know it was a fuzzy gray area. And I understand why you kept it from me. I may have even done the same in your shoes. . . ."

She kept waiting. Vanessa continued staring at the ceiling.

"But—"

There it was.

"But I've realized that we have an even bigger problem. With the e-mail, and the jealousy, and maybe one or two other minor things, I'm just not sure if you're ready to be in a mature relationship."

Ouch. It seemed exceptionally unfair since, given the current handcuff situation, this was impossible to argue.

"And also lately I've started to feel like maybe you're not the best . . . *fit* for me. Though of course that goes both ways: I'm sure there's probably somebody out there who's better for you, too— when you're ready."

Double ouch. Now it was Callie's turn to stare at the ceiling, trying to blink back tears.

"So . . . uh . . . I guess that's it," said Clint, straightening.

That's it?

"I'm sorry about . . . everything," he added, though it was unclear if he was referring to something that he had done, or simply that he had broken up with her in front of her ex-best-friend.

"I hope we'll stay friends," he added when he reached the door. Then he left.

Vanessa exhaled slowly, like she'd been holding her breath the entire time.

"Well, that was rough," she said after a moment of silence.

Callie couldn't help it: she started to laugh. The whole thing was just so bizarre, so absurd, that there was nothing else to do. "We're handcuffed together," she said stupidly, doubling over and laughing so hard that tears streamed out of her eyes. "We're handcuffed together—and I just got dumped!"

Vanessa started giggling, too. "You just got dumped—and I was there!" she screeched, leaning into Callie.

"I know, and now you know everything!" Callie cried, positively hooting with laughter. "Like that I'm a psycho stalker and went through Clint's e-mail!"

"I know!" Vanessa cried. "You totally are! *And* you had sex with Gregory!" she shouted gleefully, tears streaming from her eyes now, too. "You slut!"

"You bitch!"

"Whore!"

More laughter.

"Maybe I am kind of a slut," Callie agreed when she could breathe again.

"And I'm *definitely* a bitch," Vanessa said, gasping for breath. "A hot bitch!"

Callie wiped her eyes and sighed. "I guess it's not that funny."

"It is and it isn't," Vanessa offered.

Both of them stared at the wall.

"I'm sorry about your parents," Callie murmured finally.

Vanessa's shoulders sagged. "It's not your fault," she said eventually. "Not unless your name is Trudy and you answer the phones at 'Goldman Sachs Securities, Currency and Commodities division,'" Vanessa said, her voice raised an octave higher. "'How may I direct your call and steal your husband today, ma'am?'"

"No," said Callie. "Really?"

"Really. It's so cliché it's like post-post-post-ironic—or whatever you would say in your fancy literary theory class."

"We would probably say . . . that to leave one's wife for one's secretary is derivative of a classic trope that transcends the traditionally gauche connotations when rendered in a sufficiently postmodern way, though the author still runs the risk of cliché."

"There you go," said Vanessa. "A *plus*."

"Yeah," Callie mumbled, not really sure that her attempt at humor had succeeded. "Well, if you ever want to talk about it with a fellow survivor . . . or just someone to hide in the bathtub with you and eat Oreos . . ."

"Thanks," said Vanessa, sniffling from all the hysteria-induced tears. "I may just take you up on that. Though, if we don't get out of these soon," she added, jingling the cuffs, "there may be some joint bathing in our future whether we like it or not!"

"That Mimi!" said Callie.

"It was Dana's idea," Vanessa reminded her. "Who knew that she could be so . . . *conniving*? I think I'm going to have to reconsider my general dislike of her."

Callie giggled. "In a weird sort of way I think it works. You know: the four of us. We're all really different, but somehow . . ."

"We all complete each other anyway? Yeah, *gag*," said Vanessa, miming the gesture. "Please, spare me from this *Lifetime Original* moment."

Callie turned to give her a half smile, half glare.

"Hey!" Vanessa said suddenly. "What was that speech Brittney was talking about earlier?"

"Oh," said Callie, and then she explained how Lexi had attempted to dissuade people from voting for Vanessa out of spite probably dating back to when Vanessa had refused to give Lexi any dirt on Callie and how Callie had then run in at the eleventh hour and convinced them to vote in Vanessa's favor. "Not that they needed a lot of convincing," Callie amended.

"Aww," said Vanessa. "I can't believe you did all that, even after ... well, how awful I've been these past few months."

Callie shrugged. "It was no big," she said. "To be honest, I mostly did it because I didn't want to *owe* you anything anymore. It was like I had to pay my karmic dues for when we left you alone on your birthday or something."

Vanessa nodded.

"Mimi stood up and threatened to quit for you, too," Callie added, "and Tyler, of course, and ... Clint." She rested her forehead in the palm of her hand.

"You okay?" Vanessa asked.

"Yeah . . ." she muttered. "Yeah. You know, maybe he's right. Maybe he *is* more mature than I am, and maybe that's why he can see that we're not ultimately right for each other. . . ."

"Well, what do you think?" Vanessa prompted. "I mean: were there ever any moments where you felt like *he* wasn't right for *you*?"

"I guess. . . ." Callie closed her eyes, thinking back. "Yeah, I guess there were! Like that night he totally abandoned me at the governor's cocktail party and I just felt horrid and awful and out of place, even though he made it up to me later. And then I suppose there were other times, too: like at dinner with his parents—I think his mom might have been worried that I was, like, after their money or something!"

"People with money are usually the ones who are most worried about it," Vanessa supplied. "How to keep it and get more. I guess people with money are just funny about money!"

"Who said that?" asked Callie.

"Me, of course!"

Yes! Callie laughed. The wonky witticisms were back!

"Well, the money thing was kind of an issue on its own, too," she said after a beat. "He just paid for spring break without discussing it with me first, and then refused to talk about it later! And stuff like that all contributed to my feeling like I never *really* belonged; that I was only somewhere like Gatsby as *his* guest, at *his* pleasure or on *his* terms or something. Even with the Pudding!" she exclaimed. "Somebody's been paying my dues since the end of last semester, and I'm almost positive that it was Clint, but when I confronted him, he insisted that it wasn't!"

"Actually," Vanessa started, "that person paying your dues . . . is me."

"YOU!" Callie cried. "Why?"

"Well," said Vanessa, "you know how you said that part of the reason you made that speech is because you didn't want to owe me? After the Ec exam—when you essentially saved me from flunking out of school and risked flunking out yourself—I was having a hard time hating you even with the things you'd written in that article. So . . . I decided to buy the right to hate you."

"Wow," said Callie. "Money really does solve everything!"

"I'm serious!" Vanessa insisted. "Anyhow, it was trivial to sneak up here and leave some cash in an envelope on Anne's desk."

"I can't believe you did that," Callie said, shaking her head.

Vanessa shrugged. "It's not like it's my money anyway," she said. "In a weird way you were probably helping me drain what was otherwise my dad's Mistress Gift Fund."

"Gross," said Callie.

"Yeah," Vanessa agreed. "But going back to this Clint thing—it's so nice that we can *finally* talk about it, though I suppose double dates are probably out of the question at this point. Come to think of it, now that I'm in the Pudding I don't know how much longer I'll be keeping Tyler around—"

"Vanessa!"

"Kidding! Anyway, you were saying—about how you never really felt like you belonged . . . ?"

"Oh yeah," said Callie. "There were just so many social situations that I had to struggle through where it seemed like someone more like Lexi would have no trouble at all . . . or maybe not just someone *like* Lexi but the Devil-woman herself. After all, he *did* date her for two years."

Vanessa's eyes were wide. "You don't think . . ."

"I don't know," said Callie, and then she launched into an account of how she'd believed she'd "caught" Clint in the library and how it had led her to ransack his room and e-mail in-box.

"You know," said Vanessa, fiddling with the ends of her hair, "from everything you've told me about how he justified those e-mails, it *seems* like there's a perfectly logical explanation for each and every one of them."

Callie nodded. It was her worst fear realized: the same thought that had struck her when Clint walked into his room and she spotted the socks on the floor and the closet torn asunder—that she had gone totally crazy and invented the whole thing. That she deserved to be dumped—and not the other way around.

"But the thing is," Vanessa went on, "I *don't* think it's all in your head. It can't be! The bottom line isn't whether or not he has a rational explanation for all his shady behavior—it's that something was bothering you in the first place! At the end of the day you've got to trust your instincts, and do what's right for you."

Callie turned to her. "Are we having another *Lifetime Original* moment?"

"Oh, just shut up and give me a hug," Vanessa cried, embracing her.

Breaking away a second later, they grinned.

"Back to the party?" asked Callie.

"Eh," said Vanessa. "It's not all it's cracked up to be. What'd'ya say we head home for some bathtub and Oreos time?"

"And force Dana to give us the key!" Callie added.

"And start plotting our revenge!" Vanessa finished.

"Deal," said Callie.

"Mimi, we're leaving," Callie informed her when they were back downstairs.

"Together?" Mimi asked. "Together!" she confirmed, taking in Callie's expression. "Do not fear," she added, "for you can thank me later!"

"You're lucky that we're going to let you live," Vanessa muttered.

"*Oh là là, maintenant on peut enfin se sentir excité vacances de printemps!*"

"What?" asked Callie and Vanessa.

"SPRING BREAK!" Mimi cried. *"Whoo-hoo!"*

"Oh!" said Vanessa. "Yes, it's very exciting."

"I could definitely use a vacation," Callie agreed. "Although . . ." she added, casting around until she spotted Clint sitting on a couch in the living room.

"Don't worry," Vanessa reassured her. "We'll figure out how to deal with the sleeping arrangements when we're in the air!"

"What is this 'sleeping' that the two of you speak of? There is no sleeping *pendant les vacances de printemps!*"

"Okay, Meems," Vanessa said. Then she muttered in Callie's ear: "We'll see what she has to say about that when we have to drag her out of bed and onto the plane tomorrow."

Callie laughed. "Bye, Mimi!" she called. "Don't stay out too late!" Then, handcuff-in-handcuff, they made their way to the club's front door.

There was just one problem.

Alexis Thorndike stood at the end of the foyer, blocking their exit.

"Leaving so soon?" she asked with mock disappointment.

"We're . . ." Suddenly Callie found herself momentarily blinded by a flash of silver from Lexi's chest.

It was a necklace. Callie's necklace. Except that Callie's necklace was still exactly where it should be: safe and secure around her neck.

Then it was as if everything was happening in flashes.

FLASH: "What a beautiful necklace," Lexi had said on Valentine's Day right here at the Pudding, with an odd look in her eye, like she had a secret. "Really, it's stunning."

FLASH: At brunch when Lexi had said, again with that *I-know-a-secret* expression, "At least a book is a lot more *personal* than some *generic* item of jewelry."

FLASH: The same spark of silver on Clint's bedside table that Callie had assumed, from far away, must be her necklace, only to find that . . .

FLASH: Yesterday afternoon it had been in its Tiffany box on her bureau all along. . . .

Generic item of jewelry . . . What a beautiful necklace . . . The bedside table . . . I'll come over tonight around 8 p.m. . . . The bedside table . . . Lexi, staring into her eyes wearing the same necklace now, triumphant . . .

"Oh. My. God."

SPRING BREAK

Town

Main Road

Spring Break ^UP
Sleeping Arrangements

Villa Whale
OK + Matt
Mimi

Villa Seashell
(Callie) +Clint
Vanessa +Tyler
(Gregory + Alessandra)

Villa Sandcastle
Lexi
Anne + Bryan

FOURTEEN

SPRING BREAKUP

Spring Break To-DON'T Pack Checklist
Brought to you by the editors at FM *Magazine*

- **SUNSCREEN**: You've been borderline albino all year long, and this is your one chance to rectify it. . . . Plus, we think the only *protection* you'll need on whatever desert island is of a slightly different nature (wink-wink, nudge-nudge).
- **CLOTHING**: Pack only your skimpiest fare, as tropical temperatures will be spiking over 80 degrees daily, while the nights have potential to get even steamier.
- **DIGNITY**: What happens on the island, stays on the island (but possibly also ends up on Facebook—so maybe don't go *too* crazy).
- **YOUR RELATIONSHIP**: Spring break is the prime time for a transient one-night (if not one-hour) fling, so leave all that drama (and possibly the person, too!) on the mainland.
- **HOMEWORK**: Seriously, people, do we even need to put this one on here?
- **ANY READING MATERIAL THAT IS NOT A WEEKLY GOSSIP MAG**: Because you can finish the last 4,299 pages of Marcel Proust's *À la recherche du temps perdu* when we return to campus and thus avoid exorbitant airline heavy-baggage fees.
- **YOUR SMARTPHONE**: No, Twitter will not break nor will the planets collide if you miss a few days of telling us, in 140 characters or less, what you had for breakfast.
- **EXTRA BAGGAGE/STRESS OF ANY KIND . . .**

. . . because it's time to sit back, relax, and **HAVE FUN!!! HAPPY SPRING BREAK!!!**

"That was the most awkward plane ride of my entire life, and I have traveled on *beaucoup, beaucoup d'avions et jets privés*," Mimi announced, letting her bags slump off her shoulders.

"Even *I* can't remember exactly who is mad at whom," Vanessa exclaimed, "and I could tell you the entire plot for every season of *Days of Our Lives* in what my mother calls 'excruciating detail.'"

"Let's just get unpacked and get to the pool," Callie muttered from underneath the large hat and even larger oversized sunglasses that her roommates had lent her. Then she wheeled her luggage over to where Mimi's and Vanessa's were piled on the stone floor of what had to be the most adorable accommodations on the entire island of Vieques: Villa Whale.

Granted, the island was barely four miles wide, but still, with its nautical-themed white and blue furnishings and decorative wooden whales adorning the walls, the villa was completely picturesque: remote from the towering main resort building that loomed behind it. The living room's entire far wall consisted of nothing more than two huge sliding glass doors, which looked out on an enormous pool—more like a small lake, actually—and beyond that, the beach, where pale blue waves lapped gently on untouched white sands.

Callie inhaled a deep, fresh, and slightly salty-smelling breath, feeling more relaxed already. Never mind the other villas also dotted around the pool, separated from them by only a few sparse palm trees and the hammocks here and there suspended between the trunks. Never mind, in particular, Villa Seashell, where she had originally planned to stay with Clint. And never mind that, according to OK, Gregory and Alessandra also had transferred out to Villa Sandcastle at the last minute, while Lexi had transferred in.

"Oi!" OK cried, bursting into the living room with Matt at his heels. Callie grinned at Matt, who had buckled to his mother's pressure over Parents Weekend when, after learning that both OK and Gregory were going to Puerto Rico, she insisted that spring break was "a pivotal aspect of the college experience" and that she and his father would treat. "Which one's our room, love?" OK continued, coming over to Mimi and squeezing her sides.

"*Your* room *est là*," she said, wiggling away and pointing to the smallest of the three bedrooms, which contained two twin beds. "*Avec lui,*" she added, gesturing at Matt. "*Je suis très désolé, mais* you are the last to arrive and so you must eat the smelly egg, as one might say in America." Then, turning, she lugged her bags into the largest bedroom—the one with a single enormous, king-size bed—and pulled the door shut behind her.

Callie and Vanessa glanced at each other, and then across the living room at Matt and OK. Everyone froze for a single moment before Vanessa and Callie screamed and made a mad dash with their luggage for the next largest bedroom (the one with two double beds), beating out the boys by a fraction of a second.

"No fair. Can't you see how big and tall and strong we are—"

OK's cries of outrage were silenced when Vanessa slammed

the door. Giggling and copying Callie, she flung herself backward onto the bed. Staring up at the ceiling, they sighed.

"Hey," Callie said a minute later, rolling onto her side and propping her chin up on one elbow. "If you don't mind my asking . . . why exactly did you decide to break up with Tyler?"

"Solidarity, babe," Vanessa said shortly, leaping up and flinging open her suitcase.

"*No*," Callie remarked, watching her toss several colorful bikinis onto the bed. "Really?"

Vanessa laughed. "Not exactly . . . although the reason we started fighting on the way to the airport was because he refused to answer when I asked if he knew anything about the . . . ah . . . you-know-what situation involving you-know-who and, uh, yeah . . ." She wrinkled her nose, flinching at the expression on Callie's face. "Sorry," Vanessa muttered. "Here, hold this for a sec," she added, tossing a gold lamé bathing-suit-like contraption onto Callie's lap.

"What . . . is this?" Callie inquired, holding it up. "A . . . bathing suit?"

"Of course," Vanessa snapped, "You just can't get it wet is all."

"Oh," said Callie, setting it aside and walking over to her own suitcase to retrieve her single black bikini. (Yes, she owned more than one, but her mother had laughed almost to the point of tears when she had tried to pack all seven for college—insisting that Callie stick her hand inside the freezer before pulling up the Cambridge weather forecast.)

Vanessa slipped into one of her many suits and sighed. "If you really wanna know," she said, "the reason I broke up with Tyler is because I ran out of feather dusters." Pausing, she frowned. "Meaning—"

"Actually, I think I already know," said Callie, pulling on a pair of shorts over her bikini. "Hot pink, about *yay* long, and a very clever excuse not to spend the night because the room was too filthy, am I right?"

"Yep," said Vanessa. "That about sums it up!"

Callie came over and sat next to her on the bed. "He wasn't the one?"

Vanessa shrugged.

"He couldn't stop hinting at how big the king-size beds are over in Villa Seashell?"

"Exactly!" said Vanessa, clapping a hand on Callie's knee. "Besides, spring break isn't the time for a boyfriend! It's a time for romance, and adventure, and random encounters with the non-English-speaking cabana boys. . . . Though, a word to the wise: if you are going to end it with someone at the airport, do it on the *arriving*, rather than the *departing* side, i.e., before you embark on a multi-hour plane ride."

"I will keep that in mind," Callie said, slapping her disguise—*ahem*, hat and sunglasses—back on. "Now let's get our newly single butts to the pool!"

"That's the spirit," Vanessa chirped, pleased that Callie appeared to have internalized her lecture on changing their mind sets from Depressed and Dumped to Single and Fabulous. "Oh, Mimi!" she cried as she and Callie strolled out into the living room.

"To the pool?" Mimi asked, lifting an enormous stack of trashy magazines.

"To the pool!" Vanessa cried. And then, arm in arm, they slipped through the sliding glass doors, making their way to some lounge chairs near the ocean and (what a coincidence!) far, far away from Villa Seashell, in search of scandals (Mimi), sexy cabana boys (Vanessa), and solitude (Callie).

After several hours of sunning followed by a light, late dinner at one of the resort's three restaurants (so late in fact that the restaurant had been nearly empty—imagine that!), the girls, along with Matt and OK, were making their way to the one bar within walking distance of the resort: "Vick's Beach Bar & Nightclub." Apparently Vick's compensated for being the only nightlife option available by rotating through various themes: Sports Night, Karaoke, Trivia, Dance Club, Discotheque, and so forth.

Tonight happened to be—much to Callie's chagrin as they trudged through the sand and then up the rickety wooden staircase to where the bar stood on a stone outcropping jutting over the beach and suspended high above the water—Tiki night. The Caribbean theme evoked memories of Calypso: the first big party she had attended at Harvard, which also happened to be the first night she had met Clint.

"Now, remember," said Vanessa as they stood outside the building's front doors, flanked by palm trees and two flaming tiki torches, "single and fabulous. Repeat it with me now: *single* . . . and *fabulous*."

"Single and fabulous," Callie muttered, wondering if Vanessa had considered a career as a motivational speaker.

Mimi rolled her eyes. "More like *sober* and *frustrated*," she amended, grabbing Matt and OK and pushing through the doors. Callie glanced behind her down the staircase from whence they'd come, but before she could open her mouth to explain how she was *really very jet-lagged* and *not in a party mood*, Vanessa grabbed her and cried: "Oh, no you don't!" before yanking her into the bar.

Callie recognized the faces of many of her fellow classmates clustered among the locals and other vacationers on the crowded dance floor lined with sand. Outside, more people stood on a large wraparound deck overlooking the water, the huge yellow moon looming low above the waves.

"See?" Vanessa cried over the sound of reggaeton, a popular form of Latin dance music. "Not so bad, right?"

Callie shrugged, her eyes flicking over the couples dancing closely or laughing in larger groups, tropical drinks in hand. OK and Matt had already latched on to a gaggle of young girls who looked like locals and who seemed to be greatly impressed by their considerable heights. One extremely fresh-faced girl appeared to have taken a particular liking to Matt, hanging on his every word.

"Let's go grab some drinks and then hit the dance flo— Oh." Vanessa stopped suddenly, wheeling Callie in the opposite direction. "Changed my mind!" she cried hurriedly.

"Wha—"

"Piña coladas have so many calories," Vanessa interrupted her.

"Why don't we just go outside instead?" Now her roommate was practically pushing Callie toward the back balcony.

"Vanessa," she started, "what is going—"

Oh. One of the couples who had looked particularly intimate over in a dark corner on the other side of the room, and who some, in fact, might describe as *glued* together—particularly at the lips and hips—suddenly grew recognizable as Callie's eyes adjusted to the dim light.

Alexis Thorndike. Soon to be rechristened Thorndike-*Weber*, from the way Clint was kissing her, pressed up against the wall like there was no tomorrow. Actually, make that: no five minutes from now.

Callie barely felt Vanessa's hand on her shoulder while her roommate murmured something about stepping outside. It was one thing to know—to realize as she left the Pudding the night of Leather & Lace—that Clint had lied to her: that Lexi *had* been in his room, and had left her necklace behind. But it was quite another to have the hitherto unconfirmed suspicions shoved suddenly in front of her face—in front of nearly everyone she knew from school, no less.

Callie . . . Callie . . . Vanessa's cries seemed to echo from some faraway place. Absentmindedly Callie swatted away the hand beckoning her to move and continued to stare: as if the longer she stared, the more what was unfolding in front of her might start to make sense.

Yet, no matter how hard she squinted or tilted her head, nothing made sense anymore. Clint insisting he was over Lexi. Lexi behaving with such reckless abandon in public. Was it the tropical climate? Or had their reunion always been bound to happen, written in the cards dealt their freshman year: predestined, unavoidable, fated? Maybe Lexi had known all along and merely acted to expedite the inevitable: forcing Callie to stay away from Clint and then break up with him, promising that their relationship was no more than a "fling," that Clint was completely wrong for her, and that Lexi was sparing her the pain of finding that out the "hard way."

Was he ever really mine? Callie wondered. Did she even know him at all—this person pressed up against her mortal enemy?

All of sudden she could no longer breathe. Doubled over at the waist, she let Vanessa lead her outside. Then, rushing to the railing, Callie leaned over the wood, hyperventilating. A breeze billowed off the ocean and dark waves tossed against the sand, but Callie failed to notice, her vision now completely blurred.

"Is she okay?" a male voice called, coming closer, followed by footsteps and the smell of tobacco.

"Gregory, I really think we should mind our own business—"

That had to be Alessandra, trailing at his heels, but Callie didn't bother to look: leaning over the railing and dry heaving despite being stone-cold sober.

"What's wrong?" the voice—Gregory's—repeated. Quiet, insistent.

"It's that jerk-faced a-hole," Vanessa muttered in reply. "He's inside . . . with Lexi," she added, patting Callie on the back.

"With Lexi *what*?" Gregory demanded.

"Gregory!" Alessandra's voice was higher now and louder. "This isn't any of our—"

"Procreating." Vanessa snorted ruefully. "Or practically, anyway. Oh—jeez—I'm sorry, I'm an idiot," she murmured, realizing she'd sent Callie collapsing into a fresh gale of sobs. "Look, I'm not really sure your being here is help—"

"Where?" Gregory's voice had gone low and dangerous. "Inside? Now? *In front of her?*"

"Gregory, what are you—"

"Wait!" Vanessa interrupted Alessandra, whose hands Gregory had just thrown off his retreating back. "They're not together anymore; they br— Shit. Shit!" she yelled. Clearly he hadn't heard a word, already inside and halfway across the dance floor.

Pulling herself together, Callie turned just in time to see Alessandra running after him, cursing under her breath. "What—"

Vanessa spread one hand over her eyes and groaned. "I think we may be in for Mad Hatter's: Spring Break edition."

"What!" Callie cried, wiping her cheeks.

"Come on," Vanessa said warily, grabbing Callie's hand and pulling her back inside.

Total chaos appeared to have broken loose:

The music had stopped.

A large circle had formed around the dance floor.

Gregory stood in one corner, struggling against the restraining grips of Matt, OK, and another freshman guy. Blood gushed from his lip, but he appeared not to notice, fighting for his freedom so he could presumably take another crack at Clint.

Tyler stood in front of Clint in the opposite corner, one palm planted firmly against his chest, the other gripping his shoulder. He was whispering fiercely at Clint, who had one hand clapped over his left eye and kept shaking his head and pointing at Gregory.

Both boys were shouting, but it was difficult to decipher the words over the sounds of Alessandra's and Alexis's screams, rising above a chorus of other taunts and cries:

"Hit him again!"

"Should we call the cops?"

"Somebody get the hose!"

"GET HIM OUT OF HERE!" a man who looked like the manager—or was perhaps Vick himself—ordered Matt and OK. Quickly they hustled Gregory to the door.

"Wait!" Callie and Vanessa heard Alessandra scream as she rushed past them to intercept Gregory. They could no longer hear her by the time she caught up with him just outside the door, but they could see her continuing to gesticulate wildly, tilting her head toward Clint—and then Callie, her full lips moving rapidly all the while.

Guiltily Callie turned away.

Clint had sat in a chair at one of the small tables, his hand still clutching his face while Tyler hovered over him. Slowly, from across the room, his unobstructed eye locked on Callie. It was impossible to tell what he was thinking—if he blamed her for what had just happened, or felt remorseful, or guilty, or none of the above. Personally, she felt torn between the urge to ask if he was okay, or to march over and inform him that he had gotten what he deserved, to turn on her heel and leave, or demand an explanation about what exactly was going on—and *had been* going on—between him and Lexi . . .

Speak of the devil, there she was: materializing by his side with a cloth full of ice, which she pressed against his eye, kneeling next to him. The expression on her face registered more *calm* than *concerned*, like a person who knew herself to be in complete control of a situation.

Clint broke away from Callie's gaze and smiled down at Lexi, his hand wrapped around her pale wrist as she continued nursing his eye.

A white hot surge of rage rippled through Callie, following shortly by a sweeping sadness. Confused, she stood rooted to the spot, unresponsive to whatever Vanessa had been saying.

Suddenly Tyler stood in front of them. "Callie," he started. "I'm so sorry, but I don't think now is the best time—"

"To what?" Vanessa interjected. "We're just standing here! It's a free country, you know."

"I was simply going to suggest that we all give this some space to blow over," Tyler protested, shifting uncomfortably. "And that maybe—"

"Who's 'we'?" Vanessa demanded. "*We*," she said, gesturing between she and Callie, "didn't do anything wrong. *They*, on the other hand," she continued, pointing at Lexi and Clint, "are a different story."

"Vanessa," Callie murmured quietly, "I'm gonna . . ." she gestured toward the door.

"Hang on just a sec, I'll leave with you," Vanessa said before turning back to Tyler. "Now, exactly whose side are you on?"

"I'm not on any side here except Clint's!" Tyler said. "And I'm going to support him with whatever he decides to do!"

"Oh!" Vanessa retorted, her voice rising, "Sure, pick your scumbag friend over your *girlfriend*, that's just great—typical! So. Typical!"

Completely forgotten, Callie slipped away unnoticed as Tyler moved within inches of Vanessa's face. "I don't know what girlfriend you're talking about since mine broke up with me on the way to the airport!"

"Well, I suppose you'd rather be off making out with the first person you happen to see just like your roommate over there—"

Callie almost laughed as the crowd closed around the former (?) couple and their voices faded abruptly. Almost.

In a few short minutes she had made it down the stairs, across the beach, up the stone path winding around the pool, and back to Villa Whale. Without bothering to turn on the light or remove her cotton dress, she stepped out of her shoes and crawled between the cool white sheets of the bed in the room she shared with Vanessa. Pulling the covers all the way over her head, she closed her eyes and prayed that somehow, miraculously, by the time she awoke the break would be over and the nightmare finally at an end.

⌘

"Bluuughhhhh . . ." Callie moaned, rolling over in bed. The room was still pitch-black; the clock on the wicker nightstand read 4:04 A.M. Bleary-eyed, she glanced at Vanessa's bed: empty. Hmm . . . That's odd. . . .

Suddenly she shot straight up.

A light rapping had just sounded from the other end of the room, near the sliding glass doors that led, like the pair in the living room, outside to the swimming pool.

Rap, rap, rap—the noise came again, louder this time.

Was Vanessa locked out?

Or had Gregory come to explain why he'd gone all Chuck Norris on Clint's face?

Jumping out from under the covers, she tiptoed over to the doors and threw back the light blue curtains.

Clint stood outside. His hands were jammed in his pockets, his black eye now in full bloom.

"Could we talk?" he mouthed through the glass.

Callie glared at him, her lips pressed together.

He held up five fingers and mouthed, *"Five minutes? Please?"*

Shaking her head, Callie unlatched the door and pushed it open.

"What do you want?" she whispered.

"Can we talk?" he repeated.

"It's four in the morning." She folded her arms.

"I wanted to explain and, uh . . ." He looked at the ground. "To apologize."

She stared at him for a moment, deciding.

"All right," she said finally, stepping outside. This ought to be good.

They walked in silence, stopping at the edge of the pool. The moon had long since departed, but yellow lights shone from under the water, and in little lanterns dotting the paths, walkways, and small footbridges over the narrower sections of the swimming pool. The air felt warm, and Callie plopped onto the ground without invitation, dangling her still bare feet in the water. Clint followed her lead, sitting down beside her and sliding off his loafers.

Under different circumstances it might have been terribly romantic.

As it was, Callie sat silently, skimming her toes on the surface of the water and waiting.

Clint eventually sighed. "I'm sorry . . . about what you saw tonight."

Callie said nothing.

"I know it's only technically been about twenty-four hours since we broke up, though the problems really started several weeks ago. But still . . . I know you must be feeling that after everything that's been said I've acted somewhat hypocritically. . . ."

Callie waited until his rambling petered off and he gave up walking the fine, infuriating line between justification and apology. Staring off into the distance at the dark mass that was the ocean, she said, "I may be young, and I may be naive, and maybe you were even right when you said I lack the maturity necessary for a serious relationship. . . . But one thing I'm *not* is stupid." She turned to face him. "I know."

"You know what?" he said, feigning innocent confusion.

"I know that you and Lexi didn't rekindle things starting tonight. I know it goes back a lot longer. Maybe even to your freshman year—maybe it was never really over." She knew that now *she* was rambling. Frowning, she curled her feet, causing a small splash in the water below.

"I really did think it was over," Clint said, tugging a hand through his hair. "I truly, sincerely believed that it would never . . . that we would never . . ."

"The funny thing is," Callie continued disjointedly as if she hadn't heard him, "that if you had been more creative in your choice of gifts, I never would have known that you lied to me. That she *was* in your room that night. That she was there long enough, and with reason enough, to take off her necklace— and who knows what else—and leave it on your bedside table where I later thought that maybe it was mine . . . until I realized mine had been in my room the entire time." All this she said matter-of-factly and devoid of emotion, as if she were merely relaying the steps to solving a particularly uninteresting equation in economics section.

"You're right," Clint murmured. "And I'm sorry. She did come over to my room that night—to talk. . . ."

"Not about Vanessa," Callie remarked flatly.

"Not about Vanessa," he echoed. "About what happened . . ." He sighed again, dragging his feet through the water. "About what happened at Gatsby."

Callie nodded slowly, gazing vacantly over the edge of the pool.

"The thing you should know first of all is that during our—*my*— sophomore year, Gatsby was a real high point in the relationship with Lexi. We both have really fond memories of that night, and it was one of the first times that— Well, never mind, the point is that when you suddenly left, the memories sort of overtook me and we—she and I—well, we got sort of swept up in the moment. Now, I could sit here and tell you that I'd had too much to drink and that I felt responsible for keeping her company because Bolton had mysteriously vanished, too. . . ." He shook himself, as if to expel the sudden bitterness that had crept into his tone. "And none of that would be a lie, but the real truth is that when we were alone, I remembered how it used to be back when things were really good, before all the games and manipulation and constant fighting . . . back when I used to believe that we belonged together and that we would be together for . . . well, I guess, forever. And so . . . we kissed."

Callie continued staring straight ahead, forcing her face to stay slack.

"I felt terrible the next day, and confused, but I knew the first thing I needed to do was talk to her and tell her that we—that *I* had made a huge mistake. And that if I *was* confused about my feelings that I needed to, at the very least, sort through them and figure out where we—I mean *you and I*—stood before anything else happened."

Callie nodded again.

"When she came over, I told her that I still wanted to be with you, and that furthermore I wanted someone like you where things didn't always feel so complicated and like I was constantly searching for a hidden agenda because the other person might not have my best interests at heart. I expected her to argue and to tell me that I didn't know what I wanted, and that I was only kidding myself—like she'd done before, when we were in Vermont—but instead . . . she agreed with me. She said she finally understood and that in our time apart she had really thought about everything that had happened and knew what she'd done wrong. She claimed that she had changed now and that she wanted only what was best for me. . . .

"And then, I don't know: it's like one minute we were on the verge of fighting and then the next minute . . ."

Stopping for a second, he sighed.

"In the morning I felt horrible. Honestly, worse than I've ever felt. She could tell and we immediately agreed that it was a mistake and that we should go back to being friends and pretend that nothing had ever happened."

Callie closed her eyes, thinking of the flash of silver on the bedside table and trying not to picture what had happened the night before. Lexi had probably left the necklace behind on purpose and had probably also planned the entire interaction ahead of time down to the minute, executing it flawlessly. Callie almost felt sorry for Clint, who clearly still failed to see, even after two years, how manipulative Lexi really was.

"The next day we decided to keep our study date and proceed as we otherwise would have when everything was normal. But I kept it from you because I felt so guilty. And then in the library when she told me about you and Gregory, I snapped—I was sure she'd made it up and that everything she'd said about changing was also bullshit . . . so I left, certain she'd been trying to sabotage our relationship the entire time."

A derisive snort escaped Callie's lips.

"It was true about Gregory, though, wasn't it?" he said quietly.

Callie leaned back, propped up on her arms. "So you're back together."

"I don't know what we are. I do know that staying apart was harder than I thought it would be. But I'm still not sure if I believe people can really change. . . . Although maybe they can, if Bolton is any indication." He chuckled ruefully. "All it took was the right girl—though granted she's a total sweetheart and basically looks like a supermodel—and now he's essentially whipped. A full one-eighty . . ."

Callie was barely listening.

Instead her thoughts kept returning to the necklace. How she might never have known who Clint really was if she hadn't noticed Lexi wearing the same one. How he had clearly never known who she, Callie, really was, or else he might have chosen a different gift; rather than something fancy and expensive— i.e., perfect for Lexi—he might have picked something more thoughtful and personal, like tickets to hear one of her favorite authors do a reading. . . .

Quickly she shoved the thought from her mind. Clint was still saying something, but after yawning pointedly, she interrupted.

"So: were you really just going to let me walk away from this thinking it was mostly my fault for going crazy on you?" she asked. "Although I wasn't *really* crazy, was I?" she added before he could answer. "I was right to be suspicious. There *was* something going on."

"You were right," he agreed. "Though maybe also a little crazy." He turned to her with the faintest hint of a smile, but seeing that she was not amused, he continued: "Once I knew that it was over between us anyway, I figured there was no point to hurting you any more than necessary. I suppose I just figured that what you didn't know couldn't hurt you."

Oh yes. She'd heard that one before. That's exactly what Evan had said about secretly filming them while having sex. No need to draw the comparison out loud. Instead she said, "So you figured that it would hurt less to see you publicly making out in front of all of my friends?"

"I said I was sorry," Clint repeated. He did look sorry. But he also seemed to be tiring of saying it, on the brink of snapping that she wasn't exactly innocent either—or maybe that was just the black eye reminding her who had given it to him and why. Although why *exactly* still remained unclear . . . Gregory had obviously thought she and Clint were still together and that he was defending her honor. Maybe that's just what he did: randomly punching people like James Hoffmeyer for groping Vanessa and now Clint for cheating—or so he thought—in public.

"Why did you lie?" she asked finally. "When I read your e-mails, I mean. Why not just explain everything then?"

"At that point I wasn't sure. I thought perhaps there was a chance that we could still work things out. And I figured that if I told you the truth, it would destroy that chance. It was selfish but . . ." He shrugged.

"I understand," she said shortly. And she did. After all, she too had kept secrets for similar reasons.

"Thanks," he said as she stood. "And thanks for listening."

Wordlessly, they began to walk back to her villa. When they were almost there, Clint added, "Maybe now we can . . . well, you know, one day . . ."

Callie rounded on him. "I understand why you lied," she repeated, "and maybe even why you did what you did. But that doesn't mean I forgive you or that I'm interested in being friends."

Grimly Clint nodded. "I'll do my best to stay out of your way then for the rest . . . of the trip."

"Likewise," she said civilly, her hand poised above the handle on the sliding door. "Oh, and Clint?" she called as he turned to walk away.

"Yes?"

"I just wanted to say that . . . I wish you—*both* of you—the best."

Before he could respond, she stepped inside, pulling the glass and then the curtain shut behind her. With a tiny smile on her face she crept back to her bed, careful not to wake Vanessa, who had returned at some point in her absence. Wishing Clint and Lexi well had been rather mature, Callie decided. Especially because she had meant every word: for if they successfully reunited, she could imagine no greater punishment for Clint than having Lexi as a girlfriend.

And thus utterly exhausted, Callie crawled back into bed, where she sank, almost immediately, into a mercifully dreamless sleep.

> From: **Callie Andrews**
> To: **Jessica Marie Stanley**
> Subject: Spring Nightmare: DAY TWO

Dear my beloved and bestest long-lost friend,

So I know I promised to call the second we landed on the island, but nobody has cell service *anywhere*. (Trust me, if it was possible, Vanessa would have figured it out by now—this morning I caught her with her iPhone literally trying to climb a palm tree!). Anyway, the resort is so isolated except for over a hundred Harvard people and a few random vacationers that it's feeling a bit like *Lost*, only instead of crashing on a deserted island I actually *chose* to be here. (What was I thinking!? I should have taken Dana up on her offer to go build a church in South America with Habitat for Humanity. Local guerilla warfare probably would have been safer than this.)

Why so miserable in "paradise," you ask?

Well, I have now not only been dumped but also humiliated—and in a very public manner. (Wait: are you noticing a trend here?!?) Last night Mimi and Vanessa dragged me to the one bar on the island (yes, you read that right, there is only *one*), where I saw Clint making out with The Bitch from Hell (i.e., Alexis Thorndike). Long story short: my previous suspicions involving the necklace/cheating incident have been confirmed, and Gregory, who I guess thought Clint and I were still together, punched Clint in the face because of what can only be described as a damsel-in-distress complex and is not, I repeat *not* specific to me, as you'll recall the night he also saved Vanessa by punching some dude in the face—though maybe it's just the punching, and not the saving part, that he likes. But I digress . . .

WAIT! Before you write back saying "OMG, HE LOVES YOU!!!" or threatening to make T-shirts that say TEAM GREGORY (which, please, you've got to stop doing, because there are no "teams"—this is my *life*!), first let me tell you what happened next.

In the morning after I talked to Clint (who shall henceforth be referred to as That Lying, Cheating Bastard—doesn't that sound nice and dramatic and very nineteenth-century?) and he apologized/confessed(/*whatever*, moving on), I wanted to avoid the pool, and the beach, and pretty much every other human being on the island, so I grabbed a book and climbed into the hammock between our villa and the one next door. I must have been there for less than twenty minutes when Gregory came—*holding the same book* (I mean, duh, we're in the same class, not really a coincidence)—and almost leaped into the hammock on top of me before he realized I was there. I will try to write what happened next like a scene so you get a sense.

GREGORY: Oh, hey, sorry. Didn't realize someone was in there.
CALLIE: No worries. Oh, wow, your lip . . . Are you okay?
GREGORY (*gruffly, swatting away the hand that yours truly hadn't even realized* she'd *been reaching out as if to touch his face*): I'm fine.
CALLIE: Fine, okay. Um . . . Thanks?
GREGORY: For what?
CALLIE: For last night.

GREGORY (*looking uncharacteristically embarrassed*): I didn't realize that you two had broken up. . . . Otherwise I wouldn't have . . . (*Runs hands through luscious, luscious dark brown hair, which, if I may digress again for a moment, is basically— Oh, wait. Okay, sorry. So he runs hands through hair, looking all tormented*) I really shouldn't have . . .

CALLIE (*quietly, trying—and probably failing miserably— to strike an attractive angle while lying awkwardly in the hammock*): Well, I'm glad you did. I mean, not that I wanted you to get hurt—either of you . . . well, maybe Clint a little. He *did* cheat on me. Not last night but before . . .

GREGORY: I wish I could say that surprises me, but from everything I know about their relationship . . . It seemed like one of those "can't live with you, can't live without you" type of things. She's addicted to torturing him, and he's addicted to the pain. They both feed on the drama and the crazy, even though they sometimes pretend otherwise. . . . (*Shrugs. Looks embarrassed again: perhaps for speaking at such great length about relationships; perhaps just for speaking at such great length about anything.*)

CALLIE: Maybe you're right. Anyway (*picking up book, very smooth, very cool*), I'm glad that it's over. He wasn't right for me. He *seemed* right, but in the end it was all wrong. Isn't that funny? How wrong you can be about what you think is right for you and how wrong can sometimes be—(*About to pull off very suave commentary full of subconscious—okay, maybe slightly conscious—meaning when loses balance in hammock. Hammock twists. Occupant does not fall—but book is not so lucky.*)

GREGORY (*picking up book*): I should go. (*Does not move. Very contrary—very typical.*)

CALLIE: Oh?

GREGORY: Alessandra . . . wouldn't like it if she knew I was talking to you. Alone. Like this.

CALLIE: Well, it's not up to her to control who your friends are, is it?! (*cries indignantly, yet secretly aware is "pulling a Clint," i.e., using foolproof logic to justify complete sketchiness.*) *Long pause while GREGORY thinks and CALLIE wishes she could read minds.*

GREGORY (*slowly shakes head*): I meant what I said in the library, about wanting to be your friend . . . But I guess maybe I always knew that it was never . . . that we could never *really* be just . . .

CALLIE *sits on hands in hammock to avoid shaking the ends of his sentences out of him. Hands start to incur funny hammock-string-shaped prints. Suspects funny prints are probably unattractive, thus, continues to sit on hands.*

GREGORY (*continuing*): Anyway, Alessandra has been jealous ever since she found out about Harvard-Yale—

CALLIE (*almost toppling out of hammock again—mortification, total*): Wait—she knows, too?!

GREGORY: Yes. Ever since she went through my phone.

CALLIE: Your phone?

GREGORY: Yes. Like I said, she found some text messages that I . . . Oh. It's not important. She got over it when I promised there was nothing going on and that there was zero chance of anything happening in the future. Except that now, after last night, she thinks . . .

CALLIE: That you're all obsessed with me again?

GREGORY: Again? (*Laughs—very loud, very obnoxious. Granted, word choice with "obsessed" may have been a bit bold. Whatevs.*)

CALLIE: You know what I meant!

GREGORY: Yeah. (*Devastating smile. Heroine manages to stay in hammock, just barely.*) I really should go.

CALLIE: So that's it, then? Not even friends?

GREGORY: (*shaking his head*) I was kidding myself to think I ever could be. Your friend.

Exit: stage pool-side. Director's note: whoever shall play GREGORY must play him shirtless for authenticity. (Did I mention the part where he is shirtless the entire time?)

So! I should probably stick to journalism rather than play writing for the future, eh? But anyway, you get the gist. So now, as you can see, I've gone from what you kept insisting was a "love triangle" (it wasn't, because I *chose* Clint, and Gregory was never even a real option!) to a big love ZERO. I can't even claim either of them as friends. Oh well. Maybe it's what I deserve.

Okay, now you are fully updated, and it is time for me to stop obsessing and hiding in the villa and go back to hiding in the hammock! I will keep you posted on any further developments, though there shouldn't be any, since I plan to stay on villa-hammock rotation for the remainder of the week.

Miss you miss you MISS YOU SO MUCH, love you, and I wish our breaks were at the same time!

Cal (Not Ripken Jr.)

From: **Callie Andrews**
To: **Jessica Marie Stanley**
Subject: Spring Nightmare: DAY FOUR

Jess!

Things are definitely looking up! 1) My skin is less translucent than when we arrived (can't actually see the veins anymore—a miracle!); 2) No one has punched anyone else that I know of; 3) In my efforts to avoid the majority of my classmates I have talked the other occupants of Villa Whale into doing some pretty amazing* cultural things!

Overall, I am starting to feel *much* more relaxed: almost like this is an actual vacation and not some form of self-inflicted torture! Or severance package—for getting dumped.

I can picture the exact look on your face right now as you shake your head and shout "Culture shmulture—let's get to the good stuff!" And so, before you reply to this e-mail insisting that I "stop holding back" and fill you in on "all the *drama*," I'll see what I can do here. . . .

There has definitely been a lot of tension between the upper- and underclassmen. It is tough to keep track of who is avoiding who. Clint, as promised, is staying away from me, and I have yet to witness any further disturbing PDA between him and Alexis Thorndike (you were right in your last e-mail, BTW: she does not need any more nicknames, as Thorndike just sounds inherently evil!). But Clint also seems to be avoiding Gregory, or maybe it's the other way around, and by extension, Alessandra is avoiding all the juniors, too, and the freshmen, or me at least, and Vanessa and Tyler seem to be going out of their way to run into each other so they can yell at each other about avoiding each other and accuse each other of orchestrating the interaction on purpose. It's all very confusing.

Last night, for example, the juniors and seniors had a barbecue at Villa Seashell, so we (most of the freshmen and some of the sophomores) went to Vick's for what turned out to be Karaoke night. I actually sang a song with Vanessa (I guess that answers your question about whether or not we've been "hitting the bottle"), but luckily we only embarrassed ourselves in front of a small subset of fellow freshmen and several unfortunate locals who happened to be at the bar that night.

Speaking of locals, Matt and OK have made some new friends. Matt seems especially popular with some of the young female inhabitants of the island, though one in particular—we think her name is Carolina? But we're not sure because her English is almost as poor as Matt's Spanish—is smitten and follows him everywhere when we go out. I think he's actually beginning to enjoy the attention, and he hasn't even mentioned Grace—who he insists he admires in a "purely professional capacity"—in the past forty-eight hours. (Now you can officially stop insisting that the Love-ZERO-formerly-known-as-the-Love-Triangle was actually a square because I promise you that is/was never going to happen.)

I suspect OK (who I know is your "favorite") would be faring better in the week-long romance department with a Puerto Rican girl or even some of the sophomores or juniors who seem interested but—heaven help him—he is still so in love with Mimi that it's positively *painful* to watch at this point. I seriously just wish she'd put him out of his misery—and put us all out of *our* misery—already. But . . . who am I to say that they'd be perfect together, or give any kind of relationship advice to anyone?

As for me, I am hard at work on the most important relationship I will ever have (to quote you—or was that you quoting someone else?). The relationship I have with myself! Plus, it's impossible to mope when the beach is so beautiful and the hardest decision you have to make all day is between the pool versus the ocean!

*The night before last we went swimming in the island's bioluminescent bay, which is full of this special algae and other microorganisms that flash neon blue and green whenever the water is disturbed—so cool! And during the day we visited the tomb of the town founder, a Spanish fort turned museum built by colonialists in the 19th-century, and a tree that's over 300 years old (I was the only one who thought that was cool). Then we spent most of this morning and afternoon jet-skiing, which I know is not exactly "cultural" but was still super fun and also happened to be on the side of the island farthest from the resort.

Love you, wish you were here!

Cal

From: **Callie Andrews**
To: **Jessica Marie Stanley**
Subject: Spring Nightmare: DAY SIX

Hello, hello, hello!

That's right: I HAVE SURVIVED THE WEEK! Yay! And now all that's left to do is get through tonight: the very last night before we leave early tomorrow morning for Vieques airport, where we will take another tiny plane back to the Puerto Rican mainland, and then several hours later, a much larger plane back to Boston, which I'm sure will still be freezing cold despite the fact that it's April. Why, why didn't I choose Stanford?

I am happy to report that my mission to lay low has been a success. Others, unfortunately, have not been so lucky. Like Matt, for example—oh dear . . . So, last night we were at Vick's again because the seniors were having another big villa party (I swear, it's like the grades divorced and now we have this weird unspoken joint custody of the bar and other areas of the island—and actually of Mimi, too, who they kidnapped last night and the night before, much to our annoyance.) Anyway, Matt and his local girl were outside on the deck having this big romantic moment and I think they were about to kiss when this angry middle-aged man stormed in screaming (we later learned he was her father) and get this: she is only FIFTEEN YEARS OLD! No wonder she looked so young! She'd been sneaking out every night to come hang with us. Poor, poor Matt. I've never seen him look so terrified in his life while he tried to explain—in terrible, terrible Spanish—that he had no idea she was underage.

Perhaps Matt, OK, and I will all start a club for spurned lovers. Vanessa will be barred from joining until she confesses why she hasn't come home until 5 or 6 A.M. on two occasions. (Tyler . . . or a cabana boy??? The mystery continues.) Anyway, I hope that doesn't come off as self-pitying as it probably sounds—all in all I'd say the week has been fun and I couldn't have picked anyone better to spend it with than the occupants of Villa Whale. (Oh, Villa Whale—I will be so sad to leave our little bungalow of paradise for the smelly old dorms. Sigh.)

And last of all, no: no matter how many times you asked in your last e-mail, there is NOTHING HAPPENING WITH GREGORY. In fact, I've barely seen him since the hammock incident at the beginning of the week and I repeat, once again, that HE DOES NOT LOVE ME. I think you're right, though—about him not loving Alessandra either. But it's hard to tell. On the one hand, he has definitely proven that monogamy and a real relationship are not outside the realm of possibility, and from everything I gather (though no, I'm not spying/stalking/totally-hopelessly-obsessed), he's even turning out to be a halfway decent boyfriend. But on the other hand, he's been so moody lately about who knows what, that it's hard to tell if he's happy. I hope he is, even if we're not really friends and even if he sort of secretly hates me—though again, I don't really know because it's impossible to know what he's thinking. Immmpoosssssssibbble!

OH CRAP! Gotta go—Mimi and Vanessa are yelling at me that the sun's about to set! Tonight we're skipping the big farewell bash at Vick's (since *everyone* is going to be there) and heading down to the beach with a bottle of tequila Mimi "found" (don't ask how)—just us girls. OKAY really gotta go now talk to you when I get back love you miss you bye! Cal

FIFTEEN

WHat Happens on tHe Island...

... STAYS ON THE ISLAND

From: **Jessica Marie Stanley**

To: **Callie Andrews**

Subject: RE: Spring Nightmare: DAY SIX

Callie, let me preface this by saying that I love you with all my heart . . . but: NEVER IN MY LIFE HAVE I BEEN MORE OVERCOME BY THE DESIRE TO SLAP YOU—HARD!

Why? I think deep down you already know even if you weren't quite smart enough to get into the Harvard of the West Coast. ;)

You are CLEARLY in love with Gregory. And what's more, he is CLEARLY in love with you back. SLAP! SLAP! SLAP! WAKE UP AND SMELL THE SUNSCREEN!

He would not go punching and brooding and lunch-bringing and long-walk-taking all over school and then all over the island for anything less than love. I do not care what anyone else—even he—has to say about it. I'm right—as usual—and the sooner you accept that, the better. Now I don't know how, or what, or where, or why, your wires got crossed, or why he's still with that Boob girl who is overly Perky (or whatever you call her), or why you wasted so much time with, as OK might say (yes, I do love him, and Mimi is also an idiot), *Sweater Vest* to begin with.

NONE OF THAT MATTERS. Tonight I command you to find him and do the (*gasp*) unthinkable and actually *tell him how you feel*. (Whether or not you admit it to yourself first!)

I know! So crazy, right? It can't possibly work. No one in her right mind has ever tried *that* looney-tunes idea before!

WRONG. You'd better do it and do it tonight, or I am never speaking to you again until at least mid-April. Consider this an intervention. And from this point forth I am cutting you off: you may not write or say anything else concerning your thoughts on Gregory's thoughts on you and Gregory and his luscious, luscious anything (though I admit some light Facebook stalking has led me to conclude that in this area, you are not exaggerating).

You may, of course, detail any *action* you decide to take. Starting with what happens after you tell him. Tonight. Or at 4 A.M. this morning when you get back from your Sapphic romp on the beach and eagerly open my latest correspondence in order to soak up the wisdom it contains.

Hate that I love you even when I hate you,

FACE-SLAP,

Jess

The bonfire that would have made Callie's former leader of Girl Scout Troop #47, Westwood, California, Chapter proud blazed against the orange sky, casting flickering shadows over the pale sand as the sea grew a darker and darker shade of blue in the wake of the setting sun. Callie, Mimi, and Vanessa sat side-by-side facing the flames atop some blankets Mimi had also "borrowed" from the hotel.

"If I ever am stuck on a desert island I am bringing you, *ma petite* Girl Scout!" Mimi cried, gesturing at the fire and patting Callie jovially on the back. "And let us not forget *vous, Monsieur Bouteille, aussi!*" she finished, brandishing the bottle of tequila.

"Hey!" Vanessa screamed, whacking. "What about *me*?"

"What skills do you have?" Mimi turned to her, pretending to look serious. "Your iPhone *applications ne sont pas utiles ici* . . . in the wild."

Pouting, Vanessa grabbed the bottle and took a swig. "No matter where I am, I can always find food." She sniffed indignantly.

"*Mais oui, c'est vrai! Et si tu ne pouves pas trouver de la nourriture, nous pouvons toujours tu mangez! D'accord,* you may accompany me to my island."

"Did you just threaten to eat me?" Vanessa demanded.

"Uh-oh," Callie interrupted, frowning and turning the now-empty bottle upside down. "No more . . ."

"*C'est fini!*" Mimi cried, throwing herself back on the blanket. "All of it is over. Tomorrow we must return...."

Callie and Vanessa groaned.

"*Mais ce soir nous sommes come des dieux!*" she finished, leaping to her feet.

"English, please?" Callie requested.

"Tonight we must live like gods," Mimi said, suddenly grave. "*Et alors ... prends ça!*" she yelped, slipping off her tank top and tossing it onto the sand.

"Mimi." Vanessa giggled. "Did you forget that our bathing suits are back at the villa?"

"*Alors quoi?*" Mimi challenged her. "This is how we do it at home in France." Then, to their surprise, she slipped off her skirt as well and started running toward the water's edge. "Are you duckies coming or no?" she cried over her shoulder.

"It's 'chickens'!" Callie shouted after her automatically. She turned to Vanessa.

Vanessa shrugged and stood up, pulling her sundress over her head. "Everyone else is at Vick's and it's too dark to see anything now anyway," she said giddily. "Come on, hurry up!"

Quickly Callie obeyed, and soon they were sprinting down the final stretch of beach to join Mimi in the ocean.

An hour later they were lying flat on their backs in the sand by the fire, wrapped in blankets and staring at the cloudless nighttime sky.

"This is the best," Callie said with a happy sigh. "I don't know why anyone would ever want a boyfriend if she had you guys."

"Awww!" said Vanessa, cuddling closer under the blankets.

Mimi giggled. "*Que tu vas devenir une lesbienne?*"

Callie gazed thoughtfully up at the stars. "If sexuality *were* a choice, then maybe I *would* become a lesbian, given my fabulous track record with men . . . though I don't suppose being gay is any easier. Let's see now," she continued, rolling over woozily and still feeling the effects of the tequila. "Lemme just get this straight. My first boyfriend, who I thought I loved, made a secret sex tape of us and showed it to the whole soccer team, followed by his fraternity. My second boyfriend, who I also thought I loved, cheated on me with his ex-girlfriend, who used that same sex tape to blackmail me and otherwise ruin my life. Am I stupid?"

"You forgot the part where you had sex with the biggest man-whore at Harvard!" Vanessa exclaimed gleefully.

"I am stupid!" Callie cried, smacking herself. "Only a stupid . . . head would manage to get herself dumped in an e-mail and *then* get herself dumped while handcuffed to you!" she finished, collapsing into giggles on top of Vanessa's shoulder.

"That's right, I was there," Vanessa said, patting Callie's hair. "And it was *ugly*," she added, addressing Mimi.

"Who needs boys!" Callie erupted, sitting up suddenly. Raising an imaginary glass, she said solemnly, "I hereby swear to renounce henceforth from now to the ends of eternity all members of the male persuasion—"

"Including Matt," Mimi interjected.

"Including Matt, who is also a boy, despite the fact that he is nice and has very soft hands, very soft . . . and yes, so henceforth until the sands of time, we swear—"

"Yes, *we*!" Mimi echoed, raising a second imaginary glass.

"Forever and ever and ever and—"

"I MISS TYLER!" Vanessa wailed suddenly.

"Oh jeez," Callie muttered, throwing herself back on the blanket. "You just had to go there, didn't you . . ."

"Sorry!" Vanessa moaned. "But it's true!"

"I miss Dana," Mimi said thoughtfully after a moment.

"Really?" Callie and Vanessa asked in unison.

"*Oui,*" said Mimi. "We have done the bonding while I was sick of being the Berlin Wall and then also the third wheel of the tricycle."

"Tricycles *need* three wheels to function," Callie pointed out.

Mimi waved her hand dismissively. "Well, *que diriez-tu?*"

"Yes," Vanessa agreed. "Callie: who do you miss? Cl—I mean The Lying, Cheating Bastard? It's okay if you do a little. We won't judge—even though I still can't believe that you allowed him to speak to you. . . ."

"I don't think I really do—miss him," Callie mused. "I did at first—back when I went through his e-mails and wanted to stay together more than anything when I thought I was crazy and he was perfect, but now . . ." She shrugged. "I miss my mom, mostly, and my dad, and my best friend from home, Jessica, and . . ."

"And?" Vanessa prompted.

"And . . . Gregory, I guess," Callie blurted. "Though I know that doesn't make any sense because I never even had him in the first place."

"Well, now, whose fault is that?" Vanessa chastised her.

"Um . . . mine?"

"Exactly," Vanessa agreed. "By the way, there's something that I've been *dying* to ask you about for months but couldn't because I was too busy hating your guts: whatever happened after Gregory told you about that whole note mix-up?"

"What note mix-up?"

"You know, like, the note," Vanessa said. "The one you wrote to me in response to what I wrote to you that Gregory somehow found and thought was meant for *him* . . ."

"Whoa, whoa, whoa," said Callie. "Slow down. What are you talking about?"

"Yes," Mimi echoed. "This is very confusing."

"The note!" Vanessa repeated, growing frustrated. "You know, 'Sorry for Harvard-Yale, it was all a huge mistake, you're a terrible person, blah blah blah . . .'"

"Oh!" said Callie. "That note. You saw that? I thought I threw it away. Whoops. Sorry," she added sheepishly. "I was only responding to your, ah, 'Manifesto.'"

"No, no, *no*," said Vanessa, shaking her head. "The point is that I *didn't* see it—well, not until much later at the end of J-term, anyway—and that Gregory found it and thought it was addressed to *him* instead."

"Huh?" said Callie, her brows knitting together.

"I think she is quite drunk," Mimi muttered to Callie.

"I'm not drunk!" Vanessa hiccupped. "I am drunk! But I know what I'm talking about. Okay. *You* wrote a note to me saying all this stuff about Harvard-Yale and our fight and whatever, but that same note got accidentally delivered to *Gregory*, who I'm pretty sure thought that all that stuff applied to him."

"What?" Callie asked dumbly. "What stuff? This isn't making any sense—"

"Ugh!" Vanessa cried. "You *know*, stuff about screwing things up with the room dynamic and with Clint, and how you didn't want to be friends, and . . . oh yeah, I think at the end there was something like, 'Let's just stay as far away from each other as possible'—or something."

Suddenly Callie sat straight up. "Oh . . . my . . . god . . ."

"What?" Mimi demanded, her eyes darting between Callie and Vanessa.

"So . . . so when he said we should stay away . . . and he said *I said* it first . . . only I didn't say . . . and the threesome . . . the threesome that was *after*," Callie muttered, staring vacantly ahead of her into the now pitch-black night, save for the dull glow of the dying fire.

"After *what*?" Mimi cried.

"The paper!" Callie exclaimed. "That worn-out piece of paper he was holding the night he found me in the pub . . . said he needed to talk to me . . . Oh my god. Vanessa!" she snapped suddenly. "You said you saw this, this *note* during J-term?"

"Yes," Vanessa said, nodding. "I was over in the boys' room and I found it, and then Gregory and I had a very similar conversation to the one we're having now—"

"Oh my god," Callie said for a third time. "And then he came to me with it but before . . . asked if I was happy . . . I *was* happy. . . . I thought I was happy. . . . I have to go!" Callie cried, leaping up and showering the other two with sand.

"WHAT is going ON here?" Mimi erupted. "You are making me be the tricycle again!"

"Wait!" Vanessa called after her. "Where are you—"

"I have to find Gregory!" Callie yelled. "I have to find him and tell him—OW!" she screeched suddenly, tripping over something in the darkness.

"Are you okay?" Mimi shouted.

". . . yes . . ."

"For heaven's sake, come back!" Vanessa ordered.

Limping, Callie returned to the blanket and sat down between her roommates.

"Mais qu'est-ce qui se passe?" Mimi implored once more.

"Callie likes Gregory, and Gregory likes—or maybe *liked*, sorry—Callie, only they were both too stupid to tell each other directly and then everything got needlessly complicated," Vanessa explained for Mimi's benefit.

"Oh," said Mimi. "That is all? But I already knew that!"

"Yes," Vanessa agreed. "You and everyone else who lives on our floor."

"*Ow*," Callie whimpered, cradling her injured toe. "I have to tell him," she repeated meekly, less sure of herself now.

"Maybe you should wait until the morning," Vanessa suggested, "when you're sober."

"*Oui,*" Mimi agreed, "and when he is not in bed with somebody else."

Ah, right. Alessandra. Callie's face fell.

"At least give yourself some time to think it over first," Vanessa offered gently. "I mean, would knowing what you know now *really* have changed your mind back then? Not that we were on speaking terms or anything, but you seemed pretty happy with Clint."

"I was . . ." Callie admitted. Vanessa had an excellent point. *Would* knowing about the miscommunication with the note have been enough to change her mind? Probably not, she finally decided. She had made her decision because she believed, based on everything Gregory had done—regardless of what had been said, accidentally or on purpose—that he needed to change.

And maybe he finally had . . . except that maybe now it was too late. . . . But maybe not . . .

Lying back on the blanket, Callie yawned. "I'm sleepy," she said.

"Moi aussi," Mimi concurred, pulling the blankets up close under her chin.

"Me"—yawn—"too," Vanessa chimed in, curling up next to Callie in the fetal position. "Positive . . . ly . . . ex . . . hausted . . ." she managed through more yawns. The last flames of the fire had finally snuffed out.

"Should we . . ." Callie started, but before she could finish the thought, they were all fast asleep.

"There they are: I see them! Look—over there!"

Callie's eyelids fluttered. In her dream she could hear Matt yelling from somewhere far away. Yawning, she rolled over. Her body collided with another large mass, soft and warm—

"Ge-roff me." Vanessa groaned, shoving her.

"Callie! Vanessa! Wake up! Wake up!"

"Mimi!" The voice of OK had now entered her dream. *"Get up—we're late!"*

"WAKE UP!" dream-Matt suddenly boomed.

Callie's eyes flew open.

Real-Matt was standing over them, a look of panic on his face.

"Oh, shit," Callie muttered.

"We—oh my god—we overslept—we—did we miss the plane?" Vanessa screamed, leaping upright.

"Not yet," said OK, who had just arrived at a run. "But we need to go—now."

"Mimi," Callie started, gathering the blankets. "Mimi, wake up!"

"Merde," they heard her mutter finally. OK pulled her to her feet.

No one said a word while they raced back to the villa, where Matt and OK did their best to aid the girls with any final packing necessities. Drawers slammed; doors opened and closed; heads popped under the beds and behind the shower curtains to check for any lingering bikini tops or toiletries until at last the last zipper zipped and they found themselves at the front door, luggage assembled and ready to go.

"Good-bye, Villa Whale," Callie murmured as they flew up the stone pathway back to the main resort. And: hello . . . reality.

Reality was, unfortunately, one solitary taxi van pulling out of the rounded driveway in front of the main resort.

"WAAAIT!" Matt cried, chasing after it.

Miraculously the van stopped. A moment later the sliding door opened and Gregory popped out.

"Need a lift?" he called, a huge grin on his face.

"Oh, thank god," Vanessa screamed, rushing over and practically throwing herself into his arms. Callie and the others quickly followed. "I was worried that we were going to have to take the ferry," Vanessa exclaimed, "but I simply can't because I get so seasick and what if it was too slow and we missed our other flight and—"

"Relax," said Gregory, hefting her enormous Louis Vuitton luggage into the trunk.

Callie stole a glance at the backseat and spotted Alessandra wearing an oversized pair of sunglasses not unlike the pair Callie had borrowed from Mimi. "Looks like you made it just in time," she remarked, giving Callie a tight-lipped smile and folding her arms across her chest.

Callie smiled awkwardly in return and then turned to help the boys with the suitcases. In the meantime Vanessa and Mimi dived into the backseat. Matt and OK clambered in next, with OK graciously offering Matt the front seat while he squished into the back.

Now only Gregory and Callie were left standing outside the van.

There was just one problem.

With all the luggage now inside there were no more empty seats.

"Shit," Gregory muttered.

"Maybe we could . . ." Callie started, eyeing the front seat.

"No," the driver called, reading her mind. "Is already too crowded!"

"Gregory . . ." Alessandra started, barely audible from where she was squeezed between Vanessa and the side of the van.

Just then another taxi pulled into the driveway.

Gregory exhaled with relief, motioning it forward.

"Go ahead," Callie urged them. "We'll be right behind you."

"Okay," Vanessa called. "We'll see you at the airport th—"

The side door slammed, and the van pulled away from the hotel, making room for the cab to roll up in its place. Callie and Gregory hopped inside.

"Aeropuerto, por favor," Gregory said. Then he began speaking rapid-fire Spanish.

Eventually the driver nodded. *"Sí, señor, yo entiendo,"* he said, and then he hit the gas.

"What did you tell him?" Callie asked, buckling her seat belt.

"Essentially, the faster we get there, the bigger his tip," Gregory explained. "I hope you have cash," he added. "I only have a card."

Callie nodded, praying that the few remaining bills in her wallet would suffice.

They made it to the airport in record time, and Callie handed the driver the entire contents of her wallet while thanking him profusely. Then she and Gregory disembarked and ran into the tiny airport. Panting and out of breath, they arrived at the ticketing counter.

"Just in time," a pretty lady with a red suit said, smiling at them and motioning at the lone security guard to undo the rope he had just fastened between the two poles that led the way to the aircraft. "Names, please?" she asked, stepping behind the counter.

"Callie Andrews," Callie said. "My ticket should be on hold."

"Hmm . . ." said the lady, scrolling through the entries on her computer. "We don't seem to have an entry on file for you."

Callie's eyes grew wide, but then the lady said, "Oh, wait. No, here it is under Clint Weber for two. It looks like Mr. Weber already picked up your tickets and boarded the plane."

"So do I just go back there and get my ticket from him—" Callie began, making her way toward the poles.

"Please do not step over the line," the security guard said, blocking her passage.

"I'm afraid we cannot let you onto the aircraft without a ticket," the lady explained politely.

"But if my ticket's on the plane . . ."

"Actually," said the lady, checking the computer, "it appears that both tickets have already been used."

"*What?*" asked Callie.

"Mr. Weber picked up two tickets and appears to have used them both. Ah yes, here it is. He changed the secondary passenger's name from 'Callie Andrews' to 'Alexis Thorndike' about twenty minutes ago."

"Can they—they can do that?"

She nodded. "Next, please," she said, looking at Gregory.

"But—but—isn't this supposed to be part of the United States of America? What about terrorism and code orange and bomb threats and—"

"Ma'am, I'm going to have to ask you not to say 'bomb' here in

335

the airport or you will be escorted from the premises," said the lady, arching her eyebrows at the guard. "Next, please."

Gregory placed a hand on Callie's wrist. "Do you have any extra seats left on the plane?" he asked.

"Yes," said the lady, flashing him a smile that made it seem like she wanted Callie out of the picture for reasons other than *bombs.* "There are still three available seats."

"Great," said Gregory, turning on the charm. "I have a ticket reserved for purchase under Bolton, and I'll take another seat, for her, right now."

The woman's smile faded a fraction, but she nodded, typing into her computer. "Very good, sir. Now will you be paying for both tickets debit or credit?"

"Credit," he said, reaching into his wallet and pulling out his black Amex.

"Gregory," Callie began, "I can't let you—"

"Don't be ridiculous," he murmured.

Taking his card, the woman behind the counter scanned it. Frowning, she scanned it again. Then she looked up. "I'm sorry, sir, but there seems to be a problem with your card."

Gregory froze.

"Do you have another one we could try?" she asked.

For a full three seconds he said nothing. Then, shaking himself, he reached into his wallet and pulled out a Visa.

"Amex doesn't always work with our computer," she said, taking the new card.

Gregory and Callie both stared, watching her scan it.

Once ...

Twice ...

"I'm sorry, sir," she said. "This one is also declined. Do you have another one we could tr—"

"*Shit!*" Gregory erupted suddenly, throwing his wallet on the counter. Several other credit cards spilled out. "Shit, shit, shit," he continued under his breath, wheeling around and stumbling away.

Callie and the lady in the red suit both stared.

The lady recovered first: "Sir, is everything ..."

Gregory appeared not to hear her, still cursing and running his hands through his hair.

"Er ... sir, it seems you've left your wallet," she tried again, raising her voice.

"Um, we're sorry," said Callie, reaching down to collect the wallet. "We, um, seem to have made a mistake. We'll, uh, try to catch the next flight. ... Come on," she ordered, grabbing Gregory by the arm. He had gone completely silent now but seemed to be in some sort of trance, numbly letting her drag him out of the waiting area, and then out of the airport, where she hoped the fresh air might calm him down.

Gently she pushed him onto a stone bench and then sat beside him.

From here she could see the tiny plane. Silently she watched it taxi and then race along the runway until it lifted off, above the harbor and into the sky. With it went their luggage, their friends, and any hope of getting home.

Stranded.

Next to her Gregory sat motionless, doubled over with his face pressed into his hands.

"Uh . . . Gregory?" she tried tentatively.

"Just give me a minute," he said through his fingers.

After what felt more like five minutes, he finally lifted his head. "You gave all your cash to the cab driver?" he asked.

"Yes."

"And you don't have a credit card, do you?"

"No."

They were quiet again.

"Gregory," she finally said softly, "why aren't any of yours working—your credit cards, I mean?"

For a second she thought he was going to explode at her, but eventually he just sighed, massaging his temples. "It's my dad. . . ." he started. Callie waited for him to go on, but he just shook his head angrily.

"Is that . . . Is that who you've been fighting with—on the, ah, phone?" she inquired.

Grimly he nodded.

Callie thought for a moment. "So he's upset about something and because of that . . . he cut you off?" she guessed.

"Something like that," Gregory muttered darkly.

"Wow," said Callie. "That seems pretty extreme."

Gregory inhaled deeply but offered nothing more.

Maybe having money could cause almost as many problems as not having money, she marveled, feeling that her funding issues regarding spring break and the Pudding seemed somewhat small in comparison to what Gregory appeared to be going through with his father.

Then again, having money right now—at least enough to afford two plane tickets back to the mainland—would certainly be preferable to the present circumstances.

However, a tiny voice piped up in the back of her head. If you *had* to be stranded on a desert island with only one other person—

"We could take the ferry back to the mainland." He interrupted her thoughts. "We still have almost six hours to catch our other flight."

"Doesn't the ferry cost money, too?" she asked quietly.

"Yeah," he admitted. "Yeah, but not nearly as much as a plane.... Right," he said finally. "Okay." He stood. "I have an idea."

"Which is . . . ?"

"Can you walk in those shoes?" he asked.

"Of course," Callie said, looking at her flip-flops.

"Good," he said, holding out a hand to help her up. "Let's go, then. This way," he added, gesturing toward the road that led to one of the local towns situated on the harbor side of the island.

She stayed silent while they walked, sensing his stress and uneager to add to it with questions about the so-called "plan" or even mindless, void-filling chatter. Now also seemed like a bad time to bring up last night's revelation or finally admit her feelings, which she had yet to finish sorting through. Plus, what if something went wrong? If he *does* love Alessandra, or doesn't feel the same way about me? Then she'd be trapped—literally stuck on a desert island—with nowhere left to run....

After nearly half an hour they finally arrived in town. They passed a couple of local shops before Gregory came to a halt outside a restaurant.

Callie's stomach grumbled; she realized that she hadn't eaten all day. However, stopping for food seemed impossible under the circumstances, especially because: how on earth were they supposed to pay for it?

"Uh . . . Gregory?"

"Wait here," he said, opening the door. "I'll be right back."

In a few minutes he returned.

"Gregory, what are you—"

"Come on," he said, shaking his head. "There's another place right up there where Alessandra and I had lunch the other day."

Aha! So this is where you've been hiding all week.

"Okay?" he prompted. "Let's go."

Instead of a traditional door the next restaurant had two saloon-style slats of wood that opened and closed when patrons pushed through them. The place was small but clean and crowded with customers. A waiter hurried past them and the scent of fried plantains wafted under Callie's nostrils, making her stomach growl once more.

Gregory headed straight for the open kitchen in back, currently manned by a single chef. He greeted Gregory like an old friend, and they began conversing in Spanish. Gregory pointed to the kitchen as he asked a question and the man nodded rapidly. Finally he broke into English and smiled at Callie.

"*Si, si,* you picked a good day to stop by, *amigo.* Pedro called in sick and the sink is starting to back up *con todos los platos sin lavar.*"

Before Callie could ask what was going on, Gregory turned to her and smiled. "Roll up your sleeves, *Caliente.* I'll wash if you dry."

Two hours later Callie found herself wiping down the last of the lunch rush dishes. Strangely, it felt as if barely twenty minutes had passed: the time racing by while she and Gregory attempted to imagine out loud what it would be like to be stuck in a similar situation with various other occupants of C 23 and C 24—some of whom they both agreed had probably never done a dish in their lives. And even though her hair was soaked and her clothes—the same she had slept in and worn the day before—were covered in soap and grime, she couldn't remember having laughed so hard in weeks, doubling over in hysterics at several points during the conversation.

When they were done, the chef, whose name was Jose, came over and put a hand on each of their shoulders. "Good thing you don't live around here," he said, surveying their work, "or Pedro would be out of a job."

"Thank you for giving us the opportunity," Gregory said. "You really saved *el culo,*" he added, causing Jose to chuckle as he slid a twenty dollar bill into Gregory's hand: exactly enough for two ferry tickets off the island.

"You must stay for lunch," Jose urged them.

At the word *lunch* Callie suddenly felt almost faint with hunger, but she shook her head, "We'd love to, but we can't afford ..."

"Nonsense," said Jose. "There are plenty of leftovers—if you don't eat them, they will go to waste."

Callie looked at Gregory. "Unfortunately, we don't have time," he said after checking his watch. "The ferry leaves every hour on the hour, right?"

"*Si, amigo.* Can you at least spare a minute, though? I could pack something for you to go."

Callie's stomach growled loudly in reply.

Gregory laughed. "I think we'd better take you up on that."

"Yes, and thank you so much!" Callie called.

Fifteen minutes later they were boarding the ferry carrying a to-go bag filled with fried plantains, *arroz con habichuelas* (rice and beans), and *canoas*, ripe plantains shaped like canoes and stuffed with ground meat and melted cheese. For drink, there was fresh coconut water in little cardboard cartons. Soon they were sitting on the ship's upper deck with the food spread out across their laps, facing toward the mainland, where their airplane would be waiting to take them back to Boston.

A horn tooted and the ferry's engines chugged to life. Silently they continued to eat what was quite possibly the most delicious food Callie had ever tasted while the boat glided through the water. "I still can't believe we pulled it off," Callie murmured when her hunger finally began to subside. A light breeze started to blow as the boat picked up speed, providing cool relief from the hot afternoon sun.

"We make a good team," Gregory remarked mildly, handing her a carton of coconut water. "You done with that?" he added, pointing at the remains of her meal. She nodded, and he swept the used napkins and paper plates back into the bag.

"I don't know that I actually contributed much," she insisted. "You were the one who thought of the restaurant and knew where to go to find it, and you're the one who can speak Spanish. I mean, what if I'd *actually* gotten stranded with someone else or, even worse, on my own? I'm not—"

"I'm sure you would have figured something out," Gregory said. "You're a very resourceful girl."

Callie narrowed her eyes. *"Tenacious."*

"Yes," he replied. "You have an ample vocabulary as well."

She laughed, leaning into him a little. He draped his arm over the metal frame of her chair, his fingers grazing her shoulder.

"Um . . ." she started, her mind drawing a complete blank as she looked into his eyes: bluer, even, than the water.

He met her gaze and—maybe she was imagining it—he seemed to be leaning in. . . . And now he was definitely reaching out to brush an errant strand of hair—wild with grime and soap and sand—out of her no-doubt dirty and sunburned face. . . .

Suddenly he frowned and quickly retracted his arm, turning away from her and staring out over the railing.

"Gregory—"

"Sorry," he muttered.

"No, Gregory, I—"

"I *said* sorry. I didn't—"

"I KNOW ABOUT THE NOTE!" she blurted.

Horrified, she froze. Why, why, *why* do I always have to open my big fat mouth without at least thinking a *little* bit first?

Slowly he turned back to look at her.

"So . . . what?" he finally said.

Her stomach plummeted.

"So . . ."

"Would knowing that earlier have changed anything?" he demanded.

"I . . . Maybe not," she admitted.

He was silent.

This was it: do or die.

She picked *do*.

"Maybe knowing then wouldn't have changed my mind, but what matters is that right now . . . well . . . it seems like *you've* changed, and I know that it's probably because you're with someone else, and oh god, you're with someone else, and maybe I should be asking you if you're happy before I say this, and if you are, then maybe I should leave you alone because that's what you did for me when . . ." Deliberately ignoring his facial expressions she spoke faster and faster.

Her monologue had already spiraled totally out of control and yet she knew: "If I don't say it now, then maybe I never will and maybe I should also—stop saying maybe and just—well, it seems like everything has changed: *you* changed, Clint changed, or maybe— *ugh*, there it is again, sorry—but really Clint was probably always this way and I'm just finally seeing things clearly and well . . . one thing that hasn't changed are my feelings. . . ."

Oh god. She closed her eyes.

"My feelings . . . I still have . . . for you . . . I mean, I always . . . and I do—"

"Callie."

Cool. Calm. Worst of all . . . amused.

Flinching, she opened her eyes.

He was less than two inches from her face.

He took her hands in his. "Stop. Talking," he whispered.

And then he kissed her.

Wait—no he didn't. He came within an inch and then stopped, which she realized when she opened her eyes again, mortified for the second time. Or the 327,834th time, depending on when you'd started counting.

"Callie," he repeated slowly, still holding her hands. "I feel . . . the same way."

You do???

You do!

Wait.

But then why?

Oh no. He was mocking her again—he had been the whole time. He—

"But—"

Here it comes: the part where he laughs in my face.

"Before anything can happen, I have to talk to Alessandra first."

Oh. Oh! She exhaled. How maddeningly-terribly-wonderfully-un-Clintlike-yet-frustratingly-torturous at the same time!

"Okay," she finally managed, trying and failing to lean away.

"I know neither of us is perfect," he started.

Good: because the guy she previously believed defined that term, *perfect*, didn't really work out so well.

"And that we've both made mistakes . . ."

Right now the only mistake she could think of was why she hadn't spent every possible waking moment kissing him—

"And I'm sure I'm probably going to make a few more."

"Uh-huh . . ." How about starting with forgetting to wait to tell Alessandra? Would it really be *so* bad?

"But I want to start this the right way."

"Right," she agreed. "Right."

Still, neither of them moved.

"OH MY GOD—I SEE THEM—I SEE THEM!" Vanessa's voice cut shrilly across the water.

"Callie!"

"Gregory!"

"Oh, we were so worried—"

"—we thought—"

"Knew you would find a way!"

"Why are you still up there?"

At some point during their conversation the boat had docked, and most of its passengers had disembarked. Neither of them had noticed.

"Get off quick, before the ferry goes back to the island!"

Callie and Gregory looked at each other and started to laugh.

"What do you think?" he asked. "We could give up our lives on the mainland and just live here from now on. . . . Maybe open a restaurant—*maybe*—if that maybe seems like a good idea to you?"

"Gee, I don't know," she said, pretending to think about it. "School is kind of important."

"You're right," he agreed, standing. "And there are several pressing matters I need to attend to just as soon as we return."

She smiled. "Well, in that case," she said, jumping up, "the sooner we leave, the better!"

OK, Matt, Mimi, and Vanessa enveloped them as soon as they reached the dock, smothering them with hugs and reassurances and demanding to know what had happened. At one point Callie met Gregory's eyes and he smiled. In the grand scheme of things the present interruption—and even the added complication of someone else, who was probably waiting for him back at the airport now with the rest of the upperclassmen—barely mattered. From this moment on they had all the time in the world. And, for the first time since school had started, Callie couldn't wait to get back to Cambridge.

SIXTEEN

INSIDER OUTED

Apr 4 **Behind the Ivy-Covered Walls: Part IV**

6:32AM By THE IVY INSIDER

The "Punch Book" is a traditionally written paper document or booklet used by Final or other social clubs during the punch process to record and share anonymous commentary on prospective members. Often considered one of the most confidential parts of the process, the punches (and all nonmembers) are supposed to remain ignorant of said punch book's existence. In the service of maintaining secrecy many Final Clubs literally burn the paper book before inaugurating a new class of punches: a purging ritual deemed to be in the best interests of members new and old.

Recently, several clubs, including the Hasty Pudding, have recreated the aspects of the punch book online for convenience sake; however, with modernity comes a new set of problems on how to eradicate the primarily anonymous remarks—which one can infer might have the potential to be damaging to both the punches and the members.

Although elections for this spring's class have long since drawn to a close, it seems the Hasty Pudding social club has neglected to erase the electronic record containing their private thoughts on each of their new members and those less fortunate who did not make the cut. The comments compiled on the password-protected site HPpunch.com appear to illuminate the true membership criteria for the Pudding, the inner workings of the society, and the values espoused by the members of the club.

Some particularly telling examples include the following:

Of Shelby Samuel, Class of 2014, one member writes,

"ABORT! ABORT! She is NOT, as previously believed, THE Samuel of Shell Oil."

Of Sydney Hauser, Class of 2013, another writes,

"If she talks about how much homework she has or anything else school-related one more time, I'm going to stick a fork in my friggin' eye. Headed on the fast track to Cutsville: let's kick this nerd to the curb before I lose a perfectly good eye over it."

Of Penelope Vandemeer, Class of 2014, someone notes,

"Grating. So grating. Is the private jet really worth a monologue on the merits of Prada over Gucci?"

Another member disagrees, and finds Ms. Vandemeer, *"charming, classy,"* and in possession of an *"excellent taste in fashion."*

Of Vanessa Von Vorhees, Class of 2014,

"What a leech! Give me some room to breathe, woman! Though you can tell she really wants it, if personal space invasion is any indicator."

Of Aaron Thomas, Class of 2014,

"Enough with these recruited athletes! I sure hope he can throw a football better than he can carry on a conversation."

Of Chip Hallisburg, Class of 2013,

"One word: unibrow."

Of Hugh Herbertson, Class of 2012,

"So, so gay. And I mean that in the best possible way. ;)"

Of Alessandra Constantine, Class of 2013,

"Yeah, yeah, I can see that everyone else loves her, but what good is she to me if she already has a boyfriend?"

Women, or so it seems according to the remarks above, are only valuable in terms of their personal or parental assets (be it a jet or lack of oil shares) and sexual availability, while derided for other commitments, most notably to academics.

Members appear to go easier on their male punches, noting that athletic skill may not compensate for a lack of social grace, though clearly not all male prospective members were immune to comments regarding their physical appearance or sexual orientation.*

*While the site is no longer live, readers can view the full contents of the punch book online here:
<u>Behind the Ivy-Covered Walls: Part V – Pudding Punch Book Revealed</u>

allie raced back to Wigglesworth and took the stairs two at a time, determined to find Gregory—despite her previous resolution to give him some space so he could gracefully end things with Alessandra—and discover why he had missed that morning's emergency meeting at the Pudding.

Highlights from the meeting—or lowlights, depending on how you looked at it—kept echoing through Callie's head as she flew down the second-floor hallway:

Anne urging that they settle down to keep this from "turning into a witch hunt."

Tyler reprimanding several male upperclassmen members for almost violently accusing various new admits of being the Insider, and then saying, with a very grave look on his face, that the article was "indisputably an inside job."

Lexi agreeing and pointing out that only a member could have accessed the password-protected site.

Members blindly accusing other members of being too "bitchy" or "superficial" or "downright deplorable" in their commentary, which was met with cries about speaking "under the condition of anonymity," or "can't you take a joke?" or "personally I wouldn't take back a single thing I said."

People glancing around the room suspiciously, noting that only half the club had even showed up for the meeting, though obviously it was Monday morning and people had class or simply had yet to check their e-mail.

Penelope marching in to say that while she wasn't "deactivating—*yet*," she hoped they all knew that the jet was not available for club use.

Someone wailing that "technology will be the end of us!" and insisting they should have stuck to tradition and a paper book because paper, unlike computers, can still burn. The member and computer science major who had set up HPpunch.com shaking his head in disbelief and then concurring with Lexi and Tyler that only a person in possession of the password could have breached the site's security.

Tyler finally kicking everyone out except the board but warning members that they could expect to set aside a fair amount of time for further discussion and possible questioning in the following week.

No doubt about it, the meeting had been bad. Very bad. Callie was still having a hard time wrapping her mind around having, as Tyler had so dramatically cried, "a traitor in our midst." Who would do such a thing?

Without knocking, Callie burst into the common room of C 23.

"*Gregor*—oh. Ah, hi . . ."

Alessandra sat slumped on the couch while OK gingerly patted her back. She looked as if she'd been crying. Apparently Gregory, who did not appear to be on the premises, had failed to end things as "gracefully" as he had hoped. What's more, he seemed to have left the task of comforting his now ex-girlfriend in the questionably capable hands of OK.

Alessandra glanced at Callie, distraught written all over her face. "I just can't believe it. . . ."

"I . . ." Callie grimaced. "I'm so sorry," she apologized uncomfortably, staying by the door.

"Did you know about all of this before I did?" Alessandra demanded.

"I—well—no—I mean, I suppose I had an idea . . . what was coming. . . ."

"Really?" Alessandra screeched. "Because I didn't have a clue!" Then, to what looked like OK's extreme discomfort, she threw her head onto his chest. "How could he not say something earlier!" she wailed. "How could he *leave* me just like that: all of a sudden and with no warning?"

Callie stood there stricken. OK appeared equally unsure what to say. "There, there, chin up," he eventually started, lightly stroking Alessandra's hair. "None of us could have seen this coming . . . He didn't say anything to us either, and we're his roommates."

Callie arched her eyebrows at OK, trying to communicate that he was overdoing it just a bit. After all, from what Vanessa and Mimi had said on the beach, everyone on their floor had suspected that Callie and Gregory might end up together sometime soon, even if neither of them had expressly said anything since their return late Saturday night.

". . . just gone when we woke up this morning," OK was continuing. "Must have left in the middle of the night."

Wait—what?

"Left . . . as in left *Cambridge*?" Callie said slowly. Not Alessandra?

"I thought you said you knew!" Alessandra cried from the crook of OK's chest.

"Knew what exactly?" Callie asked, her eyes darting from OK to Alessandra.

"About what happened to Bolton," OK said. "Why he left school without saying anything to anyone."

"Left *school*?" Callie repeated in alarm. Without thinking, she darted into his bedroom, the door to which had been left wide open. Drawers jutted out from his dresser, practically empty except for the odd T-shirt or sock. Most of the hangers in the closet stood bare as well, save for several jackets, slacks, and dress shirts. His squash racket and gym bag rested on the floor, but other than that, there were no suitcases anywhere, including the one he'd used over spring break.

"He's really gone," Callie murmured numbly, wandering back into the common room.

Alessandra moaned.

"But . . ." Callie started. "What . . . Why . . ."

"Here," said OK, lifting his iPad off the coffee table.

"What . . ."

"Just read it," he instructed, gesturing pointedly at Alessandra.

Taking the tablet, Callie spotted the familiar format of the *New York Times* online edition. Frowning, she sank onto the couch opposite OK and Alessandra and started to read.

http://www.nytimes.com/pages/business/index.html

The New York Times

Monday, April 4, 2011

Business

**Famed Hedge Fund Founder Files for Personal Bankruptcy
Investors Panic as the SEC Steps in to Investigate Potential
Illegalities within the Firm**

By ROB DUNBARTON

MANHATTAN – On Wall Street, the brand of "Bolton and Stamford"
was once widely believed to be the makings of a financial legend. Today
doubts have arisen around that brand and the men behind the fund.

On April 3, 2011, founding partner Pierce Bolton, a former CFO at
Goldman Sachs, filed for personal bankruptcy. Widespread rumors
within the Manhattan financial community speculate that Mr.
Bolton had been using his personal wealth (estimated at $9 billion at
the end of the 2009 fiscal year) to pay off investors with holdings at
Bolton and Stamford Enterprises after a series of toxic investments.
According to 2010 filings, Bolton and Stamford Enterprises, founded
in 1990, oversees roughly $23 billion in assets.

Mr. Bolton allegedly failed to inform investors regarding the
perilous state of their assets and has been taken in for questioning
by the State of New York in conjunction with the U.S. Securities and
Exchange Commission. As of this morning, no warrant has been
issued for Mr. Bolton's arrest, and a criminal complaint has yet to be
filed in the Manhattan federal courts.

Regulators are working to determine the scope of the crisis.
Says Eliza Chapham, director of the hedge funds division at the

Securities and Exchange Commission, "We are doing everything we can to protect the investors' remaining assets. Bolton and Stamford Enterprises was a highly respected and widely used firm, and this clearly has the potential to be devastating for its investors."

A spokesperson at the firm urged investors to "remain patient" while they liquidated assets in order to meet the large number of withdrawals requested this morning by their clientele. Mr. Stamford, as well as several other associates at the firm, could not be reached for comment. Both Bolton and Stamford were known to be very generous with charities over the years.

Mr. Bolton's legal counsel issued the following statement this morning: "Pierce Bolton has been a pillar of the financial services industry for over thirty years. We are just as eager as the authorities to affirm publicly that Mr. Bolton's personal bankruptcy is unrelated to the fiscal health of Bolton and Stamford enterprises and that no failure to disclose properly the state of investors' assets has occurred."

Mr. Bolton's second wife, Trisha Bolton, and his son, Gregory, a freshman at Harvard University, declined to comment on the developing situation.

"We have people working round the clock to discover if Mr. Bolton's personal financial crisis is in any way connected to the current predicament facing the rest of the firm," says Chapham of the SEC. "The most important thing right now is to ensure that the state of one man's personal affairs does not cause a widespread panic among investors at his hedge fund or other hedge funds located in the state of New York."

"We can't believe this is happening after all the other hedge-fund-related fraud this year," said another SEC official, who wished to remain anonymous. "The lesson is if the trading algorithm seems too good to be true, it *is* too good to be true."

Only time will tell if Mr. Bolton and his family will be the singular casualties of his bankruptcy filings.

"This can't be happening," Callie murmured, barely understanding what she had read. "I mean, it has to be a joke or something—"

"Some joke," OK muttered.

"He did mention problems with his dad," she continued vaguely, "but I thought . . . had no idea . . . So, he really didn't say anything to you, Alessandra?" she asked, raising her voice. "About this or—um—anything else before he left?"

Alessandra shook her head.

"I have to call him," Callie said, standing. "Make sure that he's okay. . . ."

"You don't think that we already thought of that?" Alessandra said acidly, glaring at her.

OK nodded grimly. "I've already dialed his cell about a billion times."

Crap, thought Callie. Worry was quickly evolving into panic. Forcing a deep breath, she pulled out her phone. "It can't hurt just to try," she murmured. Maybe, for her, he would answer.

Fingers shaking, she dialed his number. Her romantic concerns felt petty and irrelevant now—all she cared about was whether he was all right and that he knew she would be there for him through whatever happened next, in whatever capacity—friend, girlfriend—that he needed.

The line rang and rang.

Nobody picked up. Then the automated recording started instructing her to leave a voice mail, but suddenly, halfway through, she heard the familiar beep of Call Waiting.

Oh, thank god.

"Gregory? Gregory," she exclaimed. "We were all so worr—"

"Callie. It's Grace." The newspaper editor's voice crackled over the line.

"Grace? What—"

"Where are you?" Grace demanded.

"In Wigglesworth . . ." Callie said slowly. From Grace's tone something sounded severely wrong. Well, something *was* severely wrong, but even if Grace knew about Gregory, why would she contact Callie? She didn't even know Gregory or that he and Callie were semi-involved—

"Wigglesworth!" Grace exclaimed. "You were supposed to be here ten minutes ago!"

Oh, crap. Between unpacking from spring break and everything else that had happened in the past few hours, Callie must have completely forgotten some important *Crimson* business.

"Grace, I'm so sorry," she started, motioning apologetically to OK and Alessandra that she had to leave. "I'll come back as soon as I can," she whispered to them, covering the mouthpiece of her phone. Alessandra looked like *never* would also be perfectly acceptable, but OK gave her a grateful wave before she walked out the door. "Just give me two minutes," she continued speaking to Grace, "and I'll meet you over there at the *Crimson.*"

"The *Crimson*?" Grace screeched. "No, just come straight to University Hall. I'm already here—like I said, the meeting was supposed to start ten minutes ago!"

"What meeting?" Callie asked, stopping in her tracks. "What about University Hall?"

There was a pause on the other end of the line. "You didn't see the e-mail, did you?" Grace said quietly.

"No," said Callie, opening the door to C 24. "I was at an emergency meeting for the Pudding all morning because of the latest Insider article. . . ." Quickly Callie walked into her bedroom and clicked on her laptop.

"Yeah, well, your Pudding *friends* weren't the only ones who decided that the latest installment from the Insider caused a bit of an emergency," Grace snapped. "The administrative board also noticed, and they summoned both of us to appear before them in a meeting at noon. Which was now . . . twelve minutes ago."

Her eyes wide, Callie skimmed the e-mail at the top of her in-box that was indeed from the administrative board, summoning her to a mandatory meeting in University Hall at noon.

"But . . . why *me*?" Callie cried, wondering if everything that had happened in the last half hour was all just part of some crazy nightmare. In a daze she pinched her arm. No luck: she still stood in front of her computer, her bed neatly made.

"Just get over here," Grace said. "We'll be waiting."

Then the line went dead.

"Ms. Andrews, thank you for joining us today," Dean of Harvard College, Phillip A. Benedict, boomed from the head of a rectangular table in a conference room in University Hall. Callie had never met him in person, but she recognized him from his photograph in the brochure for Freshman Parents Weekend. A man and a woman sat on either side of him, wearing suits and looking stone-faced and severe, while Grace was at the other end of the table closest to the door. Obeying Dean Benedict's gesture that she should sit, Callie took the chair next to her managing editor.

"I was just explaining to Ms. Lee," the dean continued, "what a grave situation we have on our hands here with this most recent column from the person who calls herself the, ah, 'Ivy Insider,'" he said, waving a printout of the article. "The author of this article has, to my mind, clearly crossed an ethical line—would you agree, Ms. Lee?"

Grace shifted in her chair. "Free speech protection ought to allow any member of this campus to express an opinion—or fact—about social clubs or any other aspect of Harvard life. . . ." Grace shifted again. "But in cases similar to this one where an article has reported harsh remarks aimed at an individual student, the *Crimson* has generally adhered to a precedent of redacting names for the sake of protecting student privacy."

Dean Benedict nodded thoughtfully. "And yet you, as managing editor, who had to approve this article before it was published to your new online section of the school paper, the FlyBy Blog, did not see fit to redact the names of specific students in these circumstances. Why?"

Grace swallowed. "I admit I made a very serious error in judgment by allowing the article to be published unedited."

The woman sitting next to Dean Benedict cleared her throat. "I'll say. We're lucky no one has filed harassment charges—*yet*. This is a gross and egregious violation of student privacy. What's worse is that it seems clear to me that you could have easily removed those names without interfering with the nature and spirit of the article."

Grace nodded, staring down at the table. "I agree. The inclusion of the names was unacceptable, and I mistakenly allowed a personal bias to interfere with the professional duty with which I have been entrusted. . . . And yet, I would like to note that it is still my firm belief that the student body and the administration have a right to know what goes on inside these private institutions and to form a judgment about what I think we can all agree are questionable practices, from gender discrimination to elitism to hazing to—"

The man on the other side of the dean was shaking his head. "These institutions that you are referring to are all private organizations unaffiliated with the university, in contrast to our charter organizations like the *Crimson*, which we have a duty to regulate and, in cases such as these when a potentially harmful incident has occurred, discipline as we see fit."

Callie hadn't dared to move during the entire exchange, wondering what on earth was going on but, above all, *why* she was here. From what she gathered, Grace was in a lot of trouble for approving the Insider article because of the nasty comments about specific individuals in the Pudding. If that was the case, Callie couldn't help but agree with the administrators: there was absolutely no need for the Insider to publish such malicious remarks for the entire school to see even though the members of the Pudding *had* written them in the first place. The article could have achieved the exact same effect without sending Penelope into tears or Vanessa running around the common room demanding to know who had called her a "leech."

However, while Grace may be partially responsible, wasn't the Insider the true culprit?

And again, if the Insider is to blame, then why am *I* here?

"Um, I'm sorry to . . . uh, change the subject," Callie piped up suddenly. "But I'm not exactly sure . . . um . . . well, why am I here—exactly?"

She was met with three blank faces from across the table, but Grace turned to her as if Callie had just thrown her under the bus.

Callie stared back at Grace. "You didn't . . . Did you tell them—that *I* had something to do with this?"

"Callie . . ." Grace started.

"But I have nothing to do with this!" she repeated, addressing the board.

"Callie," Grace said again. "I'm sorry, but they already know. . . ."

"How—how could you *say* that?" Callie demanded, rounding on her. "I already told you when you asked me months ago that it wasn't me! I'm *not* the Insider!"

"Ms. Andrews," Dean Benedict interceded smoothly, "in situations like these it is within our rights as a disciplinary committee to requisition all log-in records from any university-owned computer. Your log-in name is a match for the date and time of every article posted by the Insider."

"That's . . . but that's . . . impossible. . . ."

"I'm afraid this case may go beyond a simple violation of student privacy," Dean Benedict continued. "While we might not have charges of libel or defamation on our hands, legal action could be brought for violating what is known as the tort of 'False Light,' which is intended to protect a person's mental or emotional well-being after another person enacts a public disclosure of private facts or information that is not of public concern and would prove damaging or offensive to a reasonable individual. Though, with all that said, defamation charges are still not outside the realm of possibility . . . and, as my colleague mentioned, while as of right now no student has lodged a formal complaint, many of the comments published may constitute harassment under our codes of conduct in the Harvard University Student Handbook. . . .

"Ms. Andrews? Ms. Andrews, are you listening? Do you have anything to say regarding these allegations? Ms. Andrews!"

Callie blinked. "I . . . I don't have anything to say . . . because I didn't *do* it. I am not the author of those articles, despite what any log-in records may have led you to believe."

Dean Benedict sighed and peered at her over the rims of his glasses. "Ms. Andrews, I have to say that based on the present facts, you may be hard-pressed to prove your innocence. However, given that there is no precedent for interpreting and applying the rules and standards of conduct of the college in this circumstance, we are turning the matter of your discipline over to the Student-Faculty Judicial Board, which will hear your case sometime in the coming months. You will have the opportunity to defend yourself at that time and otherwise present your case. As of right now, however, you are on academic probation and suspended from COMP indefinitely."

Callie gaped at him. How was this happening?

"And Ms. Lee," he continued, "you will be removed as managing editor and will remain on the paper in an exclusively advisory capacity pending a further ruling from the board."

Callie turned to Grace, who was staring vacantly straight ahead.

"Your replacement for the interim should be here any minute...." said the dean. "Ah, there she is right now."

"Sorry I'm late," a voice said suddenly from over their shoulders.

Slowly Callie turned to look. By the time she rotated fully in her chair she was white as a sheet despite her recent tan.

"Dean Benedict, so nice to see you again," Alexis Thorndike said sweetly, taking a seat. "So, what'd I miss?"

ACKNOWLEDGMENTS

Many thanks again to all the usual suspects: the staff at Greenwillow Books, the Stimola Literary Studio, friends and family, and, above all, my mom, Susan Adler, who has supported me in countless ways, from listening to three-hour monologues about subplots to reminding me to eat. Third installments can be tricky, but your edits and encouragement made it possible. Lastly, a huge thanks to you, reader, for coming this far with Callie—your enthusiasm for the series means the world to me.

JOIN
THE COMMUNITY AT

Epic Reads
Your World. Your Books.

DISCUSS
what's on
your reading
wish list

FIND
the latest
books

CREATE
your own book
news and
activities to share
with friends

ACCESS
exclusive
contests and
videos

**Don't miss out on any upcoming
EPIC READS!**

**Visit the site and browse the
categories to find out more.**

www.epicreads.com

HARPER TEEN
An Imprint of HarperCollinsPublishers